WEB GAMES

Also by Lior Samson

Bashert

The Dome

Available from www.liorsamson.com
and from Amazon.com and other retailers.

WEB GAMES

a novel by Lior Samson

Gesher Press is an imprint of Ampersand Press
Rowley, MA 01969

Gesher Press | Ampersand Press
58 Kathleen Circle
Rowley, MA 01969
Author site: www.liorsamson.com

Gesher Press and the bridge logo are trademarks of Ampersand Press.

Printed in the United States of America.
5 4 3 2 1

ISBN 978-0-9843772-2-0

Cover photo: Lukas Kurtz (LuxTonnerre on Flickr.com), used with permission.

Cover and book design: Larry Constantine.
Text set in Calisto MT with title and headings in Exotic 350 Bold and DemiBold BT.

*To Tovah, my bright math and music girl
and one of the enduring lights in my life.*

Acknowledgements

As is most always the case with constructed reality, the edifice invariably reflects the contributions of a rather large and diverse backstage construction crew. Early creative credit must go to my many colleagues involved in automation programming and power systems management and control who, over countless lunches in company cafeterias, helped me to understand the ins and outs of SCADA systems and PLC programming. It was these unrecorded and unacknowledged discussions that first got me to thinking about the vulnerability of the electric power grid and power generation plants to exploits by terrorist elements and that planted the seeds for the story in this book.

The finer points of the narrative were sharpened and the surfaces smoothed with the aid of very knowledgeable and generous reviewers who helped save me from any over-enthusiastic ignorance. I am grateful to both David Taylor and Werner Hoefler for vetting the manuscript from their expertise and experience in Internet security and power generation and distribution. My friend and frequent workmate, Helmut Windl, who has given every novel I have written the benefit of his intelligence and insight, once more pitched in with his perspective. And Dave Tutelman, old friend and erstwhile MIT companion, gave me the gift of unvarnished and invaluable early feedback as well as perceptive proofreading. For the final and critical polish that distinguishes professional work from its amateur imitators, I am immensely grateful to my copyeditor, Janet Lemnah, whose attentive efficiency and enthusiastic intelligence makes her a pleasure to work with.

And finally, to my always-committed collaborator, my partner in planning and execution who approves every plot twist, who challenges every inept turn of phrase, who pushes me to write better female characters than I could ever manage on my own, and whose tolerance extends even to my not infrequent disappearances into the distant worlds of my writing, to Lucy—my editor, my publisher, my wife, and my friend—to Lucy goes, once again, my humblest and most heartfelt thanks for all the help and handholding.

Prologue

FROM HIS OFFICE WINDOW, Gaijin could look down over the East Gardens of the Imperial Palace and see the Sapia Tower at the JR Central Railroad Station in the distance, but tonight the blinds were drawn to the dazzling lights of Tokyo, and the tiny office was lit only by the glow of the twin LCD computer monitors on his desk. Two bags of organic blue corn tortilla chips brought by a cousin from America rested atop a bird's nest of business cards in Japanese, English, Hebrew, and Ukrainian; an empty can of Coke stood squeezed in among assorted joysticks and game controllers; and a red iPod Nano, its white ear-bud cord dangling over the edge of the desk, perched atop a stack of magazines and unopened envelopes that nearly crowded out an outsized keyboard packed with extra color-coded keys.

Gaijin stuffed another handful of corn chips into his mouth, wiped his hands on his tee-shirt, then returned them to the keyboard. He frowned in concentration. He was deep down into the kernel, the very heart of the software, trying to slip the last little fragment of his methodically planned modification into it before the production team burned the master DVD for manufacturing.

The theme from Battlestar Galactica announced an incoming call on his cell phone. He retrieved it from beneath the detritus on his desk, flipped it open, and said, "Yo!!" in a quiet but assertive tone.

"It's me, you know, except you told us we aren't supposed to use names, so I just say it's me." The high, breathy voice on the line was slightly choppy and rang with a buzzy metallic echo, symptoms of a VOIP call from a computer with a low-bandwidth connection rather than one made on a land line.

"I know, asshole. I said don't call. I've got," he glanced at his on-screen clock, "just sixteen minutes before they lock down the binary and transmit it to Taiwan. Go away."

"No, don't hang up, we have trouble. Elliot's not ready with the communications link for Nagasaki. He..."

"I warned you that the kike was a loser. Screw it. We go ahead anyway. Look, you write the damned communication protocols. Suck the specs off Elliot's machine and get it coded. Now! Absolutely correct! We can test against my package after the go-live."

"But, what if..."

"No ifs. My code is spot on. It's always spot on. We'll be right. Just you get your routines right. Test-driven development, remember, and regression test on integration into the software suite. Best practices, methodical, all the way. I don't want anything else to break because of some bonehead little mistake by you—or anybody. And lose that Jew before he pulls the whole thing apart."

"He'll want to be paid. And he's been asking who the client is."

"Tell him the client is an Australian. That's all he needs to know, all anyone needs to know." Gaijin thumbed the off button and held it until the phone powered down. He slipped it into his jacket pocket while continuing one-finger typing with his free hand. He slowly and methodically scanned the meticulously crafted program patch displayed on his screen. He had typed it in from memory rather than risking accidental discovery of a file sitting on his machine or on the server. He would have preferred to load it from a thumb drive, but security was so tight that management had disabled all the USB ports on every computer in the place. No worries, he thought. He knew there was always more than one way to mine a harbor, as eco-terrorists had taught the Kiwis when a fishing boat loaded with orange roughy had been scuttled by remote control off the coast of New Zealand.

The short block of code displayed on his screen was, of course, only the last small bit that linked and completed scattered pieces of code in the patchwork quilt that he had surreptitiously stitched together over the past year. It had been his second-shift job, a secret job with no employer of record. Even Gaijin was not sure exactly who his off-hours client was, although he knew well the organization that was his immediate contact. In any case, the generous payments were regularly wired to his account, which was part, but only part, of the payoff of his work.

He was proud of what he had accomplished, both for his Japanese employer and for his other client. It was, as he unabashedly told his covert and nameless colleagues, a work of art, although only he knew how deep the artistry went. This final piece was the keystone of a bridge, a bridge between two technologies that, once linked, would be unbreakable. He congratulated himself now on his foresight on a previous contract when he had installed a backdoor into software that would soon become the other anchor point in the span he was building. It distinguished his style from that of the lesser beings who surrounded him. He did not see each programming job as an end in itself or as merely a means to pay for food and fun, but as one stone in a larger edifice, a structure he had been carefully crafting for years.

He had learned his craft from the best: his weird cousin from the States who brought him corn chips; the skinny Bulgarian electrical engineer, Konstantinov; the Ukrainian hackers who boasted about their criminal connections; Paulo, the Brazilian student with whom he had swapped tools and coding tricks but never met; and now the Japanese programmers. He had learned from the best and was now ready to best them all. If he succeeded, no one would ever see his code. That was the whole idea. No one would ever know.

Gaijin was not his name, but it had become his handle, his code name, since he had started as one of the small coterie of *gaijin*, foreigners, brought in as contract programmers to help the Japanese electronic games giant, Aniromoto, produce its next-generation video game system. The programmers were working on-site instead of through remote access because the company was absolutely paranoid about leaks and terrified of the competition. In their presence, the contract employees were referred to by the less dismissive term *gaikokujin*, foreign nationals, but everyone knew what they were called in their absence and how they were viewed by the fiercely tribal in-group of the company's own local game developers. It was precisely for this reason that Gaijin had embraced the moniker.

Gaijin was not logged in on his own account, and he was exploiting a bug in the version-control software that managed updates and revisions to the complex game programs. He entered the authorization sequence that would allow him to overwrite the binary image, the actual ready-to-run computer code, by copying the doctored image from his computer to the code safe, the server where the production-ready program and other resources were stored.

A quiet ding and a message box flanked by exclamation points told him that the substitution had been rejected because of an invalid checksum. The checksum was just a number, a number computed from all the numbers comprising the computer program, but a number that made it possible to catch transmission errors—or tampering.

Now what? he thought. He had double-checked everything. He had verified that his patches wouldn't change the checksum. That was the cleverest part of the carefully calculated dummy code that he had left in his routines, creating space in which to overwrite with his patches without changing the checksum. He cursed mentally. Some idiot must have done an unauthorized and unlogged change after the release candidate of the software had been frozen. He wondered how he would now force the patch through without it being detected. He glanced at the time—not enough time to write a routine with which to search for values that could fill in some empty table and force the correct checksum. "Shit!" he said to the screen. "What the fuck am I going to do? Gotta think."

He would need to make an actual revision as a cover, but one that could be explained away without raising too much suspicion. He stared at his own reflection, just faintly visible on the glossy monitor screen. His pitch dark eyes were two voids in his pale round face. You've been away from the sun too long, mate, he said to himself. And look at you, with your hair pulled back in a ponytail. Where do you belong now, *gaijin*? In a flash of inspiration he started typing, his index fingers dancing over the keyboard.

"What in blazes are you doing?"

Gaijin jumped at the voice but kept typing, completing the coding and then the command that would force the system to accept his changes and, in the process, compute a new checksum.

"Just a last-minute flourish, nothing consequential," he said as he retyped the authorization code to confirm and complete the operation. He turned to look up into the battered face of Markus Wildemann, German ex-pat and lead software architect for the team of contract programmers that he had assembled for the project. Wildemann was respected by his team, not for his modest coding skills but for his negotiating prowess.

"You know that's the final release image," Wildemann said with a sweep of his hand. "No one touches that code. No one. We burn masters in the morning. How the hell did you even make a change at this point? It's supposed to be frozen. And, wait a minute," he added, leaning closer to the screen. "Why are you logged in under Martine's account?"

Gaijin held up his hands as if surrendering to the police. "Look, no worries, mate. Martine just borrowed my machine late this afternoon and forgot to log out. Don't be hard on her; she's probably anxious about the baby, you know. Anyway, I went to log out for her and just got this flash of perverse inspiration. You know how I am. Anyway, everything is cool, Markus. I didn't really change anything."

"What did you do, then? Why is the code safe showing a new version flag? If we have to delay rollout in order to run the entire series of regression tests again just to prove out the system, I'll have you fired. I'll have you blacklisted! Hell, I'll castrate you myself with my own bare hands."

"It's nothing. I'll show you." Gaijin launched a hardware emulator that would make his computer function as if it were the new model of the company's game console, then checked out a copy of the newly tweaked program file from the version control system and dragged it to the emulator. The company's inimitable animated splash screen started its visual pyrotechnics on the second monitor.

"It's in the Easter egg," he said, referring to a hidden bonus feature that game developers sometimes embed in their work. Carefully positioning his hands above the keyboard, he pressed five keys at once. Suddenly, the splash screen disappeared to be replaced by a series of disembodied heads careering across the display. As each reached center screen, it paused briefly while the name of one of the project team members appeared beneath it before name and face both faded out. Some of the faces were photos, some sketches, some big-eyed animé caricatures, but one was a blank white silhouette, a fat, pony-tailed profile with a black question mark over it. When it paused in the center, instead of a name, two Japanese characters appeared below it, *kanji* for "outside" and "person": *gaijin*.

Part One

1

THE PHONE WAS RINGING. Des knew that the answering machine would pick up, but it irritated her irrationally to be only feet from the phone and unable to answer in person. It violated some unstated law of symmetry in human-machine relations. Des Allen preferred technology to keep to its place, assisting without intruding, responding like a good waiter: as—and only as—needed. To her, answering machines and voicemail were in that ambiguous borderland between help and hindrance, a technological no-man's land of ever-growing proportions.

She was just unlocking the deadbolt on the apartment door as her recorded greeting ended and the caller started talking. She quickly entered, struggled with her wet boots, got one off, then hopped on one stocking foot down the short hallway.

"Listen," a man's voice said, "I posted and posted but you never seem to reply, which is why I am calling again. The team needs you. If you're not going to play, then opt out. Pick up if you're there so we can strategize."

She reached the phone and picked up the handset. "Who is this? What are you talking about? Why do you keep calling me?" Too late. The caller had already hung up. She looked at the caller ID on the base station: Out of area—caller ID unavailable. She had no idea who the caller was but recognized the man's voice from earlier, equally assertive and mysterious messages. They had started just after her birthday, two weeks earlier. Although she assumed they were just wrong numbers from a caller who still hadn't caught on, they had begun to creep her out.

There were three other messages: two from Harry—"just checking in"—and one from her best friend. "It's me, Dina. Thanks for forwarding me the confirmation from your boss. I'm so glad he said yes, even thinks it's a good idea for you to go to the conference with me to broaden your background, shake up your creative juices, as he put it. Course, he would say that, since it doesn't cost him anything. Sid sure is a sweetie, though. Lucky you. My boss is a prick. Anyway, I got us a room at the new Meredith, the official conference hotel—better to soak up the ambiance—so we're roomies again, like old times. Text me when you get this. Or no, you better give me a call. I got lots to talk about, as in 'LG,' and I don't mean the Korean high-tech company."

Edina Gustafson, who called herself Dina ("Dina as in Shore, Gustafson as in Swede") had been her college roommate at George Washington University. The agnostic Minnesota Lutheran and the secular Los Angeles Jew had quickly discovered they had many things in common, starting with a guilt complex as wide as a soccer field coupled with a deep sense of social responsibility that had been hammered home by their once-radical parents. The aggregate in the cement of their relationship included chunks of mild mutual envy—each thought the other to be the "pretty one" of the pair—and a few grains of well-sublimated sibling rivalry, a late addition to the interpersonal repertoires of the two young women, both of them only children.

Both had become international relations majors, brimming with unwarranted idealism and unrealistic career fantasies, but Dina had stumbled into a job in DC as a journalist the day after graduating from GW, having barged into the offices of the Business News Network to protest what she regarded as a garbled news story on small businesses engaged in inter-national trade. Des, more cautious and methodical, had waited anxious months for the State Department to respond to her résumé. State and every other agency on her short list rejected her in turn. She had always suspected her parents were to blame.

Celise Greenberg, her mother, was not merely a well-known economist; she had a well earned reputation as a radical, a perennial pest, critical of administration economic policy regardless of which administration was setting it. Her area of interest in recent years was energy economics, and she had become a major force in the peak oil perspective, which maintained that the world was at or very near the half-way point in using up the planet's fossil fuel. No one likes a doomsayer, least of all a doomsayer who was beginning to look more and more like she might be absolutely right.

Des's father, Josh Allen, with his years in the front ranks of protest marches of every ilk and his drop-out lifestyle, was completely beyond the pale. Des was quite sure that the FBI had thick dossiers on both of them. So, to pay the rent, she had punted, parlaying a computer graphics elective in college and a summer job at Razorfish into a career in web design that ultimately landed her at Scenaria, in Reston, Virginia. The network security firm paid her what she thought was a bit too much for work that was a bit too easy, but she was not one to argue with fortune. The price of the deal was an occasional spasm of self-doubt about selling out to the corporate world, a spasm usually soon quieted by the rationalization that, if not on the front lines of the fight for a better world, she was at least working on the right side of the good-and-evil divide.

"Destiny Allen is an artist. Like her father," her dad would say. "It's in her blood. Creativity courses in her veins." It was a dig at his wife, who, by her own and everyone's assessment, did not have so much as a creative corpuscle in her. To the dig, Celise typically responded with a jab of her own, yet another reminder that, as a tenured full professor of economics, she earned twice what her husband did from his part-time job as a welder and the sporadic sales of his gonzo sculptures. But she was also the one who had lobbied for IR as a job ticket for their daughter, and neither Josh nor Des would ever let her live it down.

Des had tried on many occasions to set her father straight. "I do web graphics, Dad, mostly on the intranet, the internal corporate site, so basically nobody even sees my work anyway. I'm as much an artist as the poor schlemiel who stencils names on the doors." But nothing she said or did would dampen his fatherly pride. "My daughter, Destiny, the graphic artist," was how he would introduce her.

Beside her telephone, Des had some of her father's art: a weird miniature he had given her as a birthday gift when she turned sixteen. She once confessed to him that she thought it looked like a rust-hued, skeletal horse being mounted by a misshapen frog. He had just smiled and said, "Whatever floats your boat, honey." He never explained any of his work to anyone. "The art speaks for itself. It is what it is," he always insisted. Appropriately, all his major works had been named simply with question marks. His latest sculpture, titled "???????????????????????????" and 28th in the series, stood in the entrance hall to the Orange County Museum of Contemporary Art. It was his first major commission and earned him a grand total of $5,000 for four months of welding, cutting, sanding, and grinding. The check, never cashed, was still push-pinned to the wall of the garage where he worked. He matched his wife's professional and personal passion for all things economic with a complete disdain for monetary matters. "Art is not about function or finances," he would say. His wife would say it was an altogether convenient conviction, given that so few of his works ever sold.

Des put down the rusty sculpture that she had been holding absent-mindedly. She picked up her phone and called Edina but got her voicemail. She hated telephone tag, so she said only that she'd email. Then she dialed Harry Krebber's cell phone.

"Hey you," she said sweetly.

"Not a good time," he answered, with an impatient tone. "If it's about the meeting next week, catch me first thing at the office Monday."

"Ah, I get it. Dottie's there. But we're still on for lunch, aren't we? A long lunch?"

"Yes, I think that will work. I'll have the draft of the specifications ready."

"Great! I'll make the res as usual."

"I concur. Good action plan," he said, still speaking in code. There was a tinkling crash and a squeal of toddler laughter in the background. "Gotta go, duty calls."

"I love you."

"Right," he said and hung up.

Des put the handset back in its cradle, hopped back to the door, and tugged off her other boot. As she headed back down the short hallway, she paused at the mirror, where she could not resist smiling at what she saw: wisps of ginger hair draping her forehead, light gray eyes smiling above cheeks still pink from the chill. In temperament she was her father's daughter, but she had inherited her mother's slim build and sweet, inviting face. She smiled again.

"Don't be smug, you slut," she reproached herself. "This is going nowhere. He's got kids, for God sake. But you are looking good, girl. A bit of office intrigue does do wonders for the complexion, to say nothing of how romance helps with your seasonal affective disorder." She unwound the cashmere scarf from around her neck and hung it on a peg beside the mirror. A present from Harry, it had arrived with a note saying that jewelry would be a better expression of his true feelings but too conspicuous at the office. Jewelry might have been cheaper, too, as she had learned after checking out the price of the designer-label scarf on the Nieman Marcus web-site.

It's all out there on the Web, she thought, everything stacked and stored in cyberspace. There are no secrets anymore, no lapses of memory. Nothing is ever forgotten; our every step leaves a digital footprint. The Internet has become God, all-knowing, everywhere, incapable of forgetting. If you did it or said it, somewhere there was a record, etched in magnetic domains or scribed in microscopic charges, and someday someone would find it. And use it.

She thought about Harry, the calls, the trysts. They were leaving a trail, she knew, though they both were savvy and had been cautious from the beginning. They paid cash at restaurants and hotels. Their frequent calls on company cell phones were like tracks in the snow, but would be easy to explain because their work required collaboration. The big risk would be someone from Scenaria seeing them together, a risk that haunted them both. Well, we'll burn that bridge when we cross it, she thought. Is it worth it, girl? Don't know yet, but God, it is good while it lasts. And it does last, doesn't it. She grinned at the thought of slow, unhurried lovemaking.

She undressed to her slip on the way to the kitchen, tossing her clothes into a hamper as she passed her bedroom door. A quick survey of the refrigerator turned up nothing promising. She thought of calling for takeout from the Thai place down the block, but settled on a frozen entrée. She stabbed the plastic cover several times with a kitchen knife, slid the tray into the microwave, and impatiently speed-dialed 444 on the touchpad before pressing start and heading back to the living room, where she opened the roll-top desk in the corner and booted up her laptop. Des was not one to sit quietly waiting—ever.

There was email from Dina with a link to the conference details. She clicked through, and the website for GAME IX, the ninth annual Game Arts and Media Expo, opened with an animated splash page of strange metallic creatures carrying bright neon bull's-eyes as they scurried in and out of a graphic landscape littered with deformed trees and rainbow-tinged rocks. A voiceover that sounded like a sex-starved female buzz saw invited visitors to "Hit the target for GAME IX, *the* place for electronic game designers and developers!" Finding no link to skip the intro, Des hit the escape key and was rewarded by a spinning visual vortex that brought the conference homepage into view.

By comparison to the over-the-top splash page, the main site of GAME IX was tame, with a straightforward layout and simple navigation. Des mentally rated it an acceptable but uninspiring B-minus. She quickly downloaded details of the presentation schedule and special events, then called Dina again only to have to leave another message: "I'm good. I'll take the train into the city and meet you at the conference registration at nine Monday morning. I still don't know why I'm going to a conference for game developers. I do dull graphics for corporate. But I'll be there."

She was about to say more when she jumped at a sound. Her heart was pounding as she said a quick goodbye and set the phone down. She could hear someone in her kitchen.

2

HARRY KREBBER, JAW SET and forehead furrowed beneath his receding hairline, hunched over in the posture chair, studying the monitor screen as if ready to pounce on anything suspect. His index finger flicked rhythmically on the wheel of his mouse as he scrolled slowly through the logs for the third time. There was nothing there, and yet, he had seen the activity with his own eyes. On special request from the big boss, Richard Talpa, the Scenaria network was being shut down over the weekend for system maintenance. He hated having to come into the office on a weekend and knew he would be hassled by his wife, Dottie, for the absence from home, but Scenaria had a new project starting for the Department of Defense, and he needed to be sure that everything was shipshape and up to date for the unannounced but not unexpected site visit coming up.

Two telescoping LED task lights cast pools of ghostly brightness over the keyboard and a couple of open service manuals. Harry, convinced it helped focus his attention, kept the overhead fluorescents turned off whenever he was working on a tough problem. There was little of interest to see around the room. Despite Harry's pivotal position in the firm, the crowded office was the epitome of grungy pragmatism, its walls lined with dun-colored filing cabinets and dull gray metal utility shelving, every shelf filled with manuals and books and binders. A second desk that Harry used as a work table was spread with papers and manila folders. Save for the soft ticka-ticking of a disk drive, the ratcheting of the scroll wheel on his mouse, and the muted hiss of cooling fans, the office was quiet. The only other person in the entire building was DB, an overweight database administrator and resident übergeek at Scenaria. DB, thinking that nobody knew, was contentedly playing computer games. Harry knew, and Talpa knew, but neither of them cared, because Douglass Botteneau, known as DB to everyone except his mother, worked 16-hour days, delivered his assignments on time, and never asked for overtime pay or extra leave. Besides, he was the best database man in the business.

Harry knew it wasn't DB. DB's computer was connected to a subnet that had been completely isolated. Nothing could go in or out. And yet there it was. The little flashes on a display panel that said something in the server bank was trying to talk to the outside world when nothing should have been. A few packets, that was all, and then it was gone. But Harry just happened to be looking at the right moment, and now he couldn't stop looking.

Had he worked any place else in the world, Harry Krebber would have written the glitches off as gremlins in the machine, an irreproducible fluke, and then gotten on with other work. But Scenaria was not any place else. Scenaria was, by the slimmest of margins, the leading security software vendor in the country and arguably among the best in the world. Many thousands of companies and dozens of countries depended on Scenaria to protect them against malware, the endless and growing varieties of malicious software swimming like sharks through cyberspace. Scenaria was the arch enemy of software Trojans, viruses, worms, spyware, browser exploits, spam email, phishing scams, and drive-by downloads. Scenaria's products were the frontline troops and the last lines of defense against digital dreck and electronic evil. They kept hackers from altering websites and from turning PCs into zombies vomiting millions of unwanted email messages under remote command. They kept modern-day mafias and contemporary computing cabals from creating networks of bots that could batter the computer barricades and bring down a company—or a country. The attack on Estonia a few years earlier had been a crude warning shot across the bow that proved the concept, and the capability had grown exponentially in the years since. That capability, the capacity for malicious action, was the soil within which Scenaria's seeds took root and flourished. They thrived on the spreading paranoia and were nourished by virtual threats.

And now it looked to Harry that Scenaria's own systems might have been compromised. This was serious enough to take all the way to the top. And Richard Talpa, who was not given to speechmaking when not on camera, would say two words: "Fix it!" First, Harry had to isolate it, reproduce it, figure out what it was and what it was doing. Then he could think about fixing it.

He had disconnected the Scenaria system completely from the Internet. The company's web servers in Herndon, Virginia, were still online, telling the world that all was well and everyone could sleep secure, but Scenaria itself was no longer part of that world. Harry next plugged in a specialized instrument and turned it on. It was a hardware packet sniffer, a small metal box that did nothing but sit and watch every chunk of information—every packet—that passed between Scenaria's computer systems and the outside world. Software packet sniffers were more sophisticated and more flexible, but the crude capability of hardwired equipment was all that Harry would trust at the moment, since his job had taught him well that software, however carefully conceived, however thoroughly protected, could never be made absolutely inviolable. On the other hand, the wires and gates of hardware were what they were and did what they did. Period. No patch or email attachment or web script could make them do or become anything else.

Harry knew that the safety of hardware was, of course, only relative, because almost everything in the world of any sophistication was now computer controlled, and the computers were controlled in turn by software programs. DVD players, clock radios, copiers, TV sets, electrical meters, aircraft, and even power plants and substations, all were controlled by computer programs. His mini-van in the company parking lot not only had a main computer that monitored and controlled the engine and most vital electronic functions but also dozens of smaller, simpler, more specialized computers of more limited capability. And every single one of them, like almost everything digital on the planet, had a program in it—software.

Everything, that is, except for his shoe-box sized packet sniffer: a custom-engineered, handcrafted instrument that Harry, an engineer by training and a lifelong electronics hobbyist, had wired himself. It was as big as it was because it was built out of hundreds of separate logic gates and components. It was Harry's obsession as Network Manager to have at least one tool that could not, even in theory, be compromised. It could not be programmed to do anything else but what it was wired to do. There was no program embedded in it. For this reason it was also obsolescent. There was no way to update it to deal with changing technology other than to take it apart and rewire it. Mostly it sat on a shelf in Harry's office, where it served as a conversation starter with job applicants but otherwise gathered dust.

Now, its power-on light was glowing again, and Harry was staring at the front panel. After twenty minutes without activity, Harry gave up. Under other circumstances, he might have headed for the company workout room to push his frustration into a vigorous round of weight training, but instead, he paced the halls aimlessly, obsessing, mentally chasing chimera, until he passed the only occupied cubicle in the building. Reflexively, DB shifted his display to show a complex entity-relationship diagram the moment he heard someone approaching. The diagram was a picture, an abstract and obscure one, of a proposed new scheme for storing information coming back from Scenaria customers.

Harry made small talk with DB, feigning interest in the data modeling problem on the display and pretending not to know that DB had been playing games. As long as the talk was technical, DB could be garrulous, quick to offer an opinion or suggestion, always eager to help, but Harry knew that the moment conversation became personal, even in the most casual way, DB could become awkward, retreating into monosyllables and shrugs. The whole office was curious about the photo of a young woman that had recently appeared taped to DB's computer monitor, but everyone knew better than to ask. Rumor had it that she was somebody he had met online.

"When are the servers going to be back online?" DB asked, after a few minutes of chitchat about database normalization and the high art of configuring stored data for speed and reliability of access and update. "I need to stash a backup copy of this model before too long. We are not supposed to have the only current copy on our desktop machines. The Mole doesn't like it." He had used the nickname by which most of the techie types in the firm referred to their CEO. Some of the newer hires conjectured that he had once been a spy, a mole, for the CIA, and some stories even said that it was his work as a spy that had landed him in a wheelchair, but Harry knew that Talpa had lost his legs in the last days of the war in Vietnam and that the nickname had followed him since childhood, after a school chum had discovered that *talpa* was the Italian word for mole.

"I'm working on a puzzle," Harry said, without offering further explanation. "We should have the servers up and all of us back online to the world pretty soon. An hour, maybe two. I promise." He turned and departed for his office.

Harry's magic box was still winking silently, but a strip of paper was sticking out like a mocking white tongue from the built-in logging printer. On it were a few printed lines of network activity, including some asterisks for packets of types the box had not been wired to recognize. Harry checked several displays to verify that nothing was running except the bare core of the operating system, yet something was trying to talk with the outside world. What if I actually reconnect and let the packets out, he wondered. Who or what might respond? He threw a switch on a hardware firewall and waited and watched, checking displays for twenty minutes before the printer once more spat out a few lines. Nothing came back, but when he returned a half hour later with a grande latte from the Starbucks down the block, the printout showed a single packet, flagged with an error code. Harry stared at the undeciphered message from the outside world before ripping off the strip of paper and wadding it into a tiny ball that he snapped with precision into the wastebasket beside his desk.

Despite his promise to DB, he kept the servers offline over the entire weekend. Nothing more appeared on the printer of his magic box. Maybe it was gremlins. Harry, however, did not believe in gremlins. And neither did his boss. There was going to be hell to pay on Monday unless he found something, an explanation, or at least devised a plausible story. But he knew that only actually figuring it out and fixing it would be fully acceptable to Talpa—or to himself. He took another sip of coffee before setting out on the tedious task of rebuilding the system software from scratch. It would take him all night.

He was still at it when he heard a soft whine as Richard Talpa came rolling down the hall just after seven in the morning. Talpa pivoted his computerized wheelchair smartly and precisely into Harry's office. Always at the leading edge of any technology, Talpa had signed up for the $26,000 "mobility system" when the iBOT was first announced and then bought four more just before the product had been discontinued in 2009. Talpa and his wheelchair were the face of Scenaria. Photos of the broad-chested billionaire with his buzz-cut gray hair and bushy eyebrows—always dressed in his trademark black blazer and gray MIT tee shirt combo and seated like Internet royalty in his high-tech mobile throne— were almost as ubiquitous in the trade press as the company logo was.

Talpa would be among the first to acknowledge that he was not the only genius at Scenaria—he prided himself in attracting and retaining the brainiest in the business—but he was the one who had started the company and steered it on the road to success. His patented algorithms for recognizing the telltale signatures of malicious software and detecting suspicious program activity were the engines that powered their products, and his knack for astute business moves just ahead of the competition had steered them steadily toward market domination. They were on their way to becoming the Google and the Microsoft of security software largely because of his brains and his determination. He was an aggressive manager who would do whatever it took to build the company—his company—and he was not above bending rules if it advanced his agenda. Employees and suppliers said he acted like he owned the place; as majority stockholder, he did.

"What's up?" he said, as he pulled up beside Harry, a hint of impatience impressed on the casual question. "The network is still down?" His dark Mediterranean eyes narrowed as he cocked his head.

Harry put his head in his hands for a moment before answering. "We got malware in one of the servers, I think. Can't see how, but it was there. Doesn't seem to do anything as far as I can tell. All the files seem fine, and none of the computers I checked has been turned into a zombie, but there was something in there that was trying to call home. Now it just seems to be waiting for Godot.

"The thing only seems to be on one box, and it was pure luck that I found it. I've done a byte-by-byte check of the operating system files and turned up nothing. Then I wiped and scrubbed the disk and rebuilt the system from scratch and got the same signal that shouldn't be there. I finally just powered down the box. I don't know what else to do at this point."

"That doesn't make sense, Harry. There's just no way our systems could get infected. And surely you had the box isolated when you worked on it." Harry nodded. "All right. Do what you have to. Just make sure we are clean. Absolutely clean. Understood?"

"Yeah. I've got a hardwired packet sniffer that I'll use to check each box before it goes back online. Don't worry, I'll give you a clean system. I promise."

But it turned out to be a promise he couldn't keep.

3

KARL LUSTIG SAT, TURTLE-LIKE, his shoulders hunched, his white-bearded chin tucked into the front of his down jacket as he fussed over the final paragraphs of his regular blog for iTech Weekly Online. He had already turned down the heat in the apartment in preparation for once again abandoning his Beacon Hill pied-à-terre and returning to Israel. The business trip had been a sweet-sour success, a messy multi-way negotiation of property swaps and purchase-and-sales agreements the net result of which had been to dump an apartment building that had become the victim of both the real-estate slump and shifting demographics. It was not a good time to be selling property in Boston, but the complicated deal Karl had managed would help to minimize his losses. Karl did not enjoy managing Benjamin and Hamm LLC, the business he had, in effect, inherited, when he had married Shira, the widow of an old college chum. He would have preferred to cash out completely, but it was also not a good economic climate in which to be thinking of unloading the business. On the plus side, the corporation did give him regular excuses to fly back to Boston and see friends. On the minus side, it took him away from his family and the work he really loved, which was not the work that showed on his business card, the one that read: Consultant and Technical Writer. Someday he wanted to be able to strike the first three words.

Karl finally gave up trying to find just the right wording for the closing paragraph of his blog and simply posted it as it was. He knew that few other bloggers and even fewer of his nerdy readers would care that much about his choice of words or his phrasing, but he had a perfectionist streak a yard wide and held himself to high standards. It was, he knew, one of the things that kept him from progressing toward the one-word business card of his dreams.

He was about to close his laptop and finish packing for the trip home when he noticed an icon in the system tray winking at him from the lower corner of the screen. There was a text message from Anat Dorfman in Israel that asked him to call her on her private office line before leaving Boston. The number was intentionally not in his contact list nor his phone book, and it had been some time since there had been any need of calling her, so he had to open an encrypted folder to retrieve the phone number.

She answered in Hebrew but then switched to English when she realized who was calling. "I am so glad I caught you before you left the U.S. I could have gotten your new cell number from Shira, but, well, I have a small favor to ask, and I didn't want to bother her."

Karl hesitated, but said, "Sure. How can I help?" In his experience with Anat and her cohorts, small favors had a way of ballooning into bigger favors and even bigger trouble. Anat worked for *HaMossad l'Modiin u'l'Tafkidim Meyuhadim*, the

Institute for Intelligence and Special Operations, the elite Israeli intelligence group known colloquially as simply *HaMossad*, the Institute.

"Your itinerary shows you are flying back through IAD," she said.

His impulse was to ask her how she knew his flights, but, of course, knowing things was her job, and as Chief of Technical Services, she had the technology to find out pretty much whatever she wanted. Karl just grunted noncommittally into the phone.

"Look," she said, "we need to rebook your return with a stopover in DC so you can attend a conference next week and check out some people for us. The usual arrangement."

This time Karl groaned in response. The "usual arrangement" made Karl a temporary *Mossad* asset but would leave him swinging alone in the wind if anything went wrong. He was neither a trained agent nor a mere *sayan*, one of the thousands of unpaid volunteer sympathizers who provided selective support and occasional services for the *katsas*, the field operatives of *HaMossad*. Karl had, in a sense, married into the business after becoming involved with the widow of one of the Institute's star players. His was a life of liminality, poised on a threshold, neither inside nor outside, his roles as fluid and shifting as the sands on the Cape Cod shoreline.

"Karl, I wouldn't ask, but we just recalled our permanent senior DC *katsa*. We would much rather use professional resources and, if we had the right person in place with a plausible cover story ready we would, but we need some information quickly, it's technology deep, and you just happened to be there now, ready-equipped with a real cover story. We just need some preliminary intelligence to give us a leg up while we assemble the right resources. Nothing really high risk for you, not at this point. You still carry, don't you?"

"No real risk, eh? Yes, I still carry. But I haven't had any need for a handgun since that target practice with the robots."

Anat laughed at the allusion to his last work on behalf of *HaMossad*, when he had ended up being drawn into fending off an assault on *Har HaBayit*, the Temple Mount. "Well, you shouldn't need it," she said. "It's just video games this time."

"Now I'll admit you have my interest," he said. "Fill me in."

"Not now. We'll courier a package to you through the Embassy in DC."

"Okay, I had better get on the phone and try to postpone my flight back to Tel Aviv."

There was a muffled conversation in the background, a quick exchange in Hebrew. "No need to do anything, Karl. My people just took care of that for you. And we already arranged with your publisher for you to be on a new assignment, which your editor will explain. We have you booked into the brand new Meredith Hotel. Pretty posh digs. The conference is in the convention facility practically across the street. But all the details are in the package. Look, it's late here, and I still have some things to sort out on this end. Good luck."

"You seem to be way ahead of me on this, Anat. You do know, don't you, that I might have said no."

"No, you could not have said no. We know you, Karl Lustig. We know you. So, have fun in DC. Work fast, be careful. Shalom."

Karl wanted to ask another question but just said, "Shalom." Anat had already hung up.

He checked his watch and started ticking off items on his mental to-do list. He would need to let Shira know. The details would have to wait until after he picked up his package in DC, but in the meantime he needed to work on his own "plausible cover story" for his wife. He quickly drafted an email saying that he had gotten a bonus assignment from InterMetroGroup and would be staying over a few extra days in Washington. If she learned he was working with Anat again, she would not be happy, particularly since he had promised after the baby had arrived not to get involved anymore. So much for promises, he thought. Karl winced. He prided himself in being loyal and trustworthy, and he hated even the smallest deception when it came to Shira. But he also knew that saying more now would only make her needlessly anxious. She had enough on her plate with taking care of the kids alone and keeping up with her business. A successful silversmith, she had recently accepted a request to design a complete line of jewelry for an upscale American chain. It was a new direction for her, and she was working long hours against an approaching deadline. Karl did not want to give her yet another reason to be stressed.

He finished his email to her with an apology for the change of plans, his hopes that the work on her new contract was going well, and a promise to call her from DC after he was settled in there.

Working his way down his revised list of things to take care of, he started to pull apart the telescoping handle of his well-traveled rolling duffle bag. From inside the thick extrusion, he retrieved the parts of a one-of-a-kind Glock that was on long-term loan from Ulrich Bremer, an industrial designer and old friend in Germany. No ordinary weapon, the

9mm automatic had been designed and custom built by hand to break down and fit discreetly into the luggage handle. With its exotic materials and its few metal parts designed to cast ambiguous shadows in x-ray images, the handgun and the bag had already made it through airport security in seven countries without detection.

Karl reassembled the Glock, checked the action, and pantomimed a few practice shots before breaking it down again and restoring it into the storage space inside the handle. Karl, whose shooting skills had first been honed on the target range in college competitions when he was still a student at MIT, had never particularly liked the Glock, but it had proved useful on more than one occasion ever since Ulrich had tricked him into taking it with him on his very first trip to Israel, the trip when he had met Shira and started on the path that had led him to a new home and a new life. It was a life that had proved to have a perverse way of entangling him in intrigue.

He wondered what Anat was getting him into that would prompt her to ask if he was carrying. He would find out soon enough, he surmised.

— —

In a small office in a non-descript high-rise building in Tel Aviv, Anat Dorfman finished an on-screen form and turned to her assistant. "I know what you are thinking, but it's right up his alley, and he'll be on-site in the morning. It's about computer programming, just programming and technology, stuff he is good at." She arched her thick eyebrows and opened her broad mouth as if posing an unasked question or looking for approval from Rahel. Technically, Rahel Hassan was her assistant, but, ever since Anat had taken over as Chief of Technical Services, they had developed a close working relationship that was more like a partnership than boss and subordinate.

Rahel, who in her typical rush-around fashion had already started to leave for her own desk across the hall, swiveled quickly with a toss of her short ponytail. The worried look that was her everyday face deepened with disapproval. "Lev set a bad precedent," she said, referring to Lev Novikov, Anat's husband and predecessor in the post Anat now held. "Karl is a nice guy, not one of us."

Anat took a deep breath. "You're right, of course. And he's an amateur. But he consistently comes through. He is calm in a crisis and can, when needed, be deadly. If he were younger, I would be recruiting him. As it turns out, his age is to his and our advantage. Who would suspect a quiet, gentleman geek with white hair? He's American, a journalist, of sorts, and has deep loyalties to Israel. He knows how our game is played, and he plays it with dogged precision. Need I go on?" She flipped open a folder on her desk. "Anything new from the analysts who have been going over the disk from that laptop?"

"Not yet. That's what we have: one missing hacker, presumed dead, and a hard drive full of incriminating emails and cryptic code. We do know that Elliot Feldersmann was registered for this conference in DC and had booked a flight but never got on the plane. He left behind his laptop, his MP3 player, a video game console, and all his clothes. We presume we got to his apartment before *Shabak* or anyone else did because we had him under surveillance since he was released from custody and knew the very instant he was a no-show for his flight. There could be hell to pay if it ever comes out that we were operating inside Israel and stepping on *Shabak's* shoes, but Feldersmann did contact us first from Japan before he was deported." The territorial disputes between *Shabak*, Israel's domestic intelligence unit, also known as *Shin Bet*, and *HaMossad*, it's elite international agency, were a long standing tradition in the intelligence community, much as were the occasional skirmishes between the FBI and the CIA in the United States. In both countries there was both cooperation and competition—the cooperation sometimes somewhat short of full and the competition not always of the friendliest variety.

"Well, I hope Karl can get something for us quickly. Of course, not all our eggs are in that basket. Stay close to Shimon and his computer cowboys, and let me know the minute they decipher anything more." Shimon Weiszkopf was in charge of the computers that were, to the consternation of some of the old-timers, increasingly becoming the eyes and ears and memory of *HaMossad*. Weiszkopf also honchoed some of the brightest computer hackers in Israel, an elite group of gifted mental misfits he had personally recruited and nurtured into a vital resource in the current era of cybercrime and Internet terrorism. It was *HaMossad's* unofficial and unacknowledged answer to Unit 8200, the military intelligence group known for its cyber-warfare exploits. Relationships between the Institute and *Aman*, which oversaw military intelligence, were often as muddy as those with *Shabak*.

"This is decidedly weird business," Anat added, after a pause. "Why computer games? Why security software? We depend on that software for the integrity of our own computer systems. We need to figure out what is the link between Feldersmann and this Destiny Allen, who works in software security but is attending a computer game conference. What is the connection here?"

Rahel chewed on her lip, but said nothing.

4

THE RECEPTION AREA for GAME IX was semi-coordinated chaos, pulsing with a rhythmic randomness like some media-player visualization. Developers, in scruffy jeans and tee-shirts emblazoned with mottos ranging from cute or clever to the obscure or simply tasteless, crisscrossed the lobby, jockeyed for position in the registration lines, and jostled with a scattering of corporate types in ties and jackets. Young women dressed in little more than swimsuits and sashes emblazoned with "GAME IX: PLAY NOW, PLAY HARD" handed out tchochkes and discount coupons and fended off passes from the dweebs trying to hit on them. A bearded man in his forties munched on a donut as he paraded back and forth wearing a sandwich board inscribed with "Will Code for Cash. C#, C++ or Assembly. Games, Embedded Apps, Hacks."

Scanning the crowd for Dina, Des noticed a man in desert-camouflage combat fatigues elbowing people aside as he strode in her direction. He looked as if he might have just stepped off a military transport plane returning from Iraq.

Suddenly, he pulled a machine pistol and a hand grenade from underneath his jacket, shouted, "Let the games begin!" and started firing into the air. In an instant, people were running, screaming, diving behind the registration booths. Some just stood where they were, looking bewildered or amused. A few started to laugh.

The man marched purposefully through the scattering crowd. Suddenly, Des became aware that she had frozen and was standing right in his path.

"You're in my way, lady," he said, under his breath. She cringed and took a quick step to the side just as he lowered his gun and started firing toward the entrance. She turned to look in that direction, where a shimmering apparition was emerging from a misty cloud that roiled across the room. The figure started advancing toward the crowd—a dancing, laser-like image of another man in combat fatigues armed with a heavy machine gun. The man near Des dropped to one knee and started spraying gunfire at his opponent, who kept approaching, unfazed, with a grim smile. Without stopping his firing, the kneeling man pulled the pin on the grenade with his teeth, spat it out toward Des, and swung side-arm to send the grenade rolling across the lobby. It clattered toward the opponent. Suddenly, with an enormous flash, an eardrum-busting boom shook the room. Pieces of metal and body parts flew in every direction. Debris fell from the ceiling and dust filled the air.

Then it was all gone: grenade, debris, body parts. Only a light mist hung in the air. For a moment, no one moved or spoke. The silence was broken when the man beside Des leapt up and shouted with a fist in the air, "iShoot rules! See us and the new iShoot 212 projection game system at booth 126."

The crowd exploded into applause with shouts of "All right!" "Sick, mega sick!" and "Yeehah!"

Behind Des, someone muttered, "Lame! And way over-priced is what I say. A fifty-inch plasma screen is cheaper and a shitload more realistic."

Des turned toward the voice. "Say what?" she said.

"I said it's a fucking stunt. The system sucks big time. You have to have this stupid fog machine in your living room or you can't see the projection. I mean, what planet did these designers come from? Give me a break." He scowled at Des expectantly. He looked to be barely out of his teens, and his tee-shirt declared in brick-red block letters, "I Cut Code, Not Corners. Right-Angle Rendering Engines, Inc." When Des didn't reply, he turned and walked away, muttering, "Whatever."

As the crowd settled down again, Des queued up once more to register. She had already retrieved both badges and conference bags when Dina finally showed up—late, as usual—her soft, corn-silk blonde hair bouncing as she rushed through the crowd and planted herself beside Des.

"Sorry, Des, I had to finish a story. I know, I know. You think I'm always late, but it's not true. There was that dinner, once, back in 2002, where I was actually early and waited for you. Remember?" She grinned, bringing smile wrinkles to her cobalt-blue eyes. "How are you, girl?"

"Fine. I'm good. My hearing is almost back to normal after the opening stunt. Did you hear it on your way in? No? Smart of you to miss the show. I tell you, I am more than ever wondering whether I really want to spend the next three days surrounded by gamer geeks and little boys with their high-tech toys."

"What gives? I thought you were twenty-first century right down to your electric underwear."

"I may be a woman of the twenty-first century, but that doesn't mean I am never ambivalent about technology. Apart from my ears ringing from today's goofball advertising stunt, I had a start last night. I thought I heard somebody in the apartment, so I grabbed an umbrella and tiptoed into the kitchen. What a genius!. As if I could fend off an intruder with an umbrella. As I reached for the light switch, something skittered past my feet, whirring softly away across the room. I almost bumped my head on the ceiling, I jumped so high."

"What was it? Don't tell me you have rats."

"No. It was the fucking Roomba, which was not supposed to be running at all while I was home, but there it was, scootering around the kitchen on some mission. Picking up stray crumbs and ferreting out dust bunnies, I suppose. It's had a mind of it's own ever since DB, this geek from work, read an article in *Make Magazine* about hacking the Roomba. He convinced me to let him 'customize' it for me. DB is forever offering to help or to 'fix' something for me." Des had entertained the notion that DB might have a kind of adolescent crush on her, but she always found him hard to read.

"Anyway," Des continued, "my squat little cleaning companion now has its own wi-fi so it can be programmed remotely from my notebook computer. How convenient. That electric Frisbee also has its own overly complicated user interface, meaning one more thing that I have to master merely to get on with my life. So, anyway, I was up until the wee hours trying to re-program the little bugger. It's still not right. If I didn't know better, I'd say it had a virus. And if I keep pulling these late-nighters I'm going to be the one to catch a virus. I'm wiped. Plus, I was just finally falling asleep when I got another one of those weird calls from that guy whose been leaving messages on my machine. I yelled into the phone, but once again, he had hung up by the time I answered."

"Poor baby. I was up late, too, with LG. But I'm not complaining. He had to duck into the office early this morning, and then he was suppose to meet me here. He is never late, not for this sort of thing." She stood on tiptoes and looked around the crowd. "My bet is we will probably find him already at the exhibits."

They flashed their conference name badges to the security guard at the entrance to the exhibit hall and started strolling up and down the aisles. The exhibitors were an odd mix of development companies with demos of their latest games and vendors hawking highly technical programming tools aimed at the game developers themselves. In the center of the hall the towering booths of Microsoft and Sony competed for attention with the new darling of the gaming world, the Japanese startup, Aniromoto, that had come from nowhere but now had the bigger rivals looking anxiously over their corporate shoulders. Industry pundits expected Aniromoto to make a major announcement about their new game system during the conference.

Ahead a few booths, Des noticed a small but enthusiastic crowd gathered before a semi-circle of overhead screens displaying a bloody urban war in progress. It was the latest incarnation of a classic first-person shooter game, in which the on-screen point of view was the player's perspective and an endless escalation of attackers jumped, leapt, dropped, or simply appeared in front of the player. It was kill or be killed, requiring accurate shooting, quick reflexes, and deft decision making.

The hallmark of this particular game was its extraordinarily graphic violence, with the human opponents gushing blood and screaming in agony as they were shot to pieces. The player of the moment, whose face was being picked up by a webcam and displayed on the center screen overhead, was clearly enjoying the game, and the audience whooped approvingly whenever another arm was shot off or a head exploded in a shower of blood, brains, and skull fragments.

Des almost felt like retching. To Dina she said, "What is it with these guys? I don't get it. How can anyone who isn't a certifiable psychopath enjoy killing like that?" She had to almost shout to be heard above the gunfire, laser zaps, screeches, and explosions coming from every direction in the packed exhibit hall.

In front of her, a squat young man with straight, greasy, shoulder-length hair turned around and said, "Sister, it's just a fucking game. It's not real. Chill out." He turned back to the action. The shooter had run out of ammunition and had just thrown a tactical knife at the olive-skinned "enemy combatant" who had risen from behind a barricade. When the knife lodged almost to the hilt in the guy's eye, he screamed and sprayed bullets wildly as he spun around and fell to the ground. A pool of dark blood spread rapidly in a halo around his head. Some of the stray bullets must have hit the player's character, because a game-over message flashed on the screen. The gathering around the booth cheered when "New High Score: 246,500 points" appeared. "Taps" started playing through the loudspeakers as the image zoomed back and a flag-draped coffin was slowly carried across the screen by a military honor guard.

Des was shaking her head slowly from side to side when the defeated but still triumphant player pushed his way back through the knot of admiring fans to stand in front of Dina and her.

"This is my friend, LG Cole," Dina said, taking his arm and leaning her head on it in a way that said it all to Des.

LG grinned. He was wearing dark-green jungle combat fatigues and a corporate-style golf shirt with "VirtexGo LLC" embroidered above the pocket. His conference badge had a "PRESENTER" ribbon dangling from it. The tiny blonde wisp of a goatee sprouting from his narrow chin wiggled as he puckered and blew a thin-lipped kiss down at the top of Dina's head. He was tall and slim, more bony than athletic, hardly the sort of solid fitness freak Dina usually picked.

"And this is Des Allen," Dina said. "My best friend on the planet."

"Well, hello to you, best friend on the planet," he cracked, taking Des's left hand in both of his. "You don't look like a gamer."

"I'm not. I do web graphics. Dina dragged me along—as a witness, I guess—for the piece she's writing on the game culture."

"Game culture? Now there's an oxymoron. Bunch of uncultured coders who wipe their boogers on the table napkins."

Dina nudged him. "LG, please."

"Seriously. And I'm exhibit one for the prosecution," he said, doing a slow pirouette. "You do play games, though, don't you? I mean, everyone's a player," he added provocatively.

Des chose to ignore his weak attempt at word play but decided to quickly squash what almost sounded like it might be flirtation. "My boyfriend has been trying to get me interested, but, no, I don't really do games. I prefer real reality to virtual reality. And you? Do you just like playing violent games or do you also create this stuff."

"Both. First-person shooter. On both. Those are the real games. And I'm with you. The more real the better, I say. I have been trying to persuade my design director at VirtexGo that we should shift to slo-mo the moment the bullet hits home so you can see the blood spurting and trickling down and the pieces of flesh being torn out, and..."

"Ew, please," Dina said, pushing him away. "Not before lunch. And not after either. I don't think either of us are into that kind of stuff. It's a guy thing, I guess."

She sent LG off to pick up copies of the pocket program guide, while she and Des made their way out to the nearest scrolling "Today's Events" display to figure out where to go. Dina announced that a panel on "Flying Fractals and Cultured Crashes" in the Lafayette Suite sounded promising. Des groaned but didn't argue. Looking for signage, she craned her neck to see over the crowd of people now streaming out of the exhibits hall. Suddenly one of them split off from the flow and stopped, planting himself in front of her. He was short, with wild, nearly black hair, and intense, coal-dark eyes. Des didn't recognize him and started to back away.

"Hi. I thought it was you," he said closing the distance to less than a foot in front of her. "WebGraph '06. We talked. You're Destiny. I mean that's your name. I thought that was funny, but it was on your badge. That was just before I went to China and Japan, so I probably didn't look too good. I'm a lot better now. They have really great ways of treating CFS in China. Beijing, anyway. CFS, that's chronic fatigue syndrome." His voice was breathy and high as he spoke, and he twitched his nose at intervals as if repositioning his glasses.

"I've been working on WoW lately," he continued, hardly stopping for breath. "That's World of Warcraft, you know. And doing some plug-ins for Life 2.0. The Klingon Klothes Kloset is my work. Mostly. I'm sure you've seen some of the avatars looking like they teleported in from Star Trek. I think that Life 2.0 is way better than Second Life, even though some call it a rip-off clone. Really, it has much better graphics, and the rules are even looser. I also like their API—more flexible and so much easier to program to. The Klingon Klothes Kloset—that's all Ks—sells pretty well. I did $26,430 last year on that. Before taxes. I don't really have a license from the Star Trek people. My buds in Second Life say it was disloyal to jump ship, but I say code is code and Life 2.0 is going to leave them in the dust. And I still don't have a regular job. Well, not one I can talk about, anyway. But I can't say more about that. It's, you know, secret. Actually top secret. But I shouldn't even say that."

He paused and stared up into her face. "I think your face is looking a little pudgy; you put on weight since we first met. You don't want to do that. Body mass index correlates with CFS, you know. You don't suffer from chronic fatigue syndrome, do you?"

"No, I..." She wasn't sure what to say. The guy looked vaguely familiar, but she couldn't place him and had no idea what was prompting him to prattle on as if they were old friends. "I was at WebGraph in '06," she said, nodding, "but..."

LG, arriving with the programs, interrupted. "So was I. Who are you?" he asked, turning.

"Marky. I'm Marky Collier-Adams. Who are you?"

LG laughed. "If you don't know who I am, check out your conference program. My name and headshot are all over it. And we're trying to make it to a session."

"What session are you going to? Maybe I'm going to the same one."

LG took Dina's arm and started herding her down the hall. "I doubt it. But nice talking to you. See you later." Under his breath he muttered, "Loser!"

"Hey, LG, make nice, just because he's a little socially awkward doesn't mean you can be rude." She leaned over and half-whispered to Des, "Who was that?"

"Just one of those geeky guys who's a little far out on the autistic spectrum. Sometimes I think I'm a magnet for them. But he's harmless. I think. I've seen him a couple times at conferences, now that I recall. He's just like that."

LG smirked. "Creepy little bugger. I bet he lives with his mother."

"Hey, you live with your mother," Dina said, elbowing him. "So what are you talking about."

"That's different, only temporary, until VirtexGo can start paying salaries." To Des he said, "We're a startup, see. We have some proprietary technology that can do hyper-real graphics even on underpowered computers. We've got these Ukrainians working for us—awesome programmers but scary characters—who can code circles around anyone I have ever seen before. And they work cheap. We pay them less than half of what I make."

Dina scowled. "What do you mean, LG, you don't get paid anything."

"Yet. But when we make it big with 'Vengeance is Mine'—that's the working title—I'll be sitting pretty and those guys will still be doing online contract work through Rent-a-Coder.

"Look, I'm off to a session on multi-threaded programming for quad-core processors. What are you girls doing?"

When Dina told him, he whooped with laughter. "I don't think it's what you think it is, but you'll find out. Have fun. I'll see you for lunch and introduce you to some of the crowd from Hunted Arts. You think I'm bad? Those dudes are seriously warped. Seriously. But you'll see. Then again, some women like the rough stuff, right?" He looked right at Des.

Dina gave him a disapproving look. "You'll have to do lunch just with your buddies. Remember, I'm on assignment. My boss has suddenly decided to team me with some tech writer from Israel, and I have to coordinate with him over lunch."

"And I've got an appointment for lunch," Des added. "Sorry."

LG shrugged, then turned without a word and headed down the corridor.

Des shook her head. "Your new boy friend is," she searched for words, "an interesting guy."

Before she could say more, Dina put a hand on her shoulder. "And who's the one who's sleeping with a married man, a coworker to boot? An appointment for lunch, you say? I can just bet what's on the menu. Look, LG may be a little abrupt at times, and he may have a somewhat warped sense of fun, but he is very smart, very attentive, and single. I like him."

"Yeah, I'm sorry. I just met LG. I guess I get a little queasy around all the blood and guts and the people who like gore and violence, even if it's virtual violence. So many of the guys at work—and it's almost entirely guys—are into that. Even Harry, except he plays role-playing mystery games, you know, figuring out who did it with what in the whatever room."

Dina nodded. "I haven't made up my mind yet about all this, either. That's part of why I took the assignment: to understand the culture and the mindset of the players and the people who create and sell the games. But it seems to me that the case can be made that they are just games, however violent or realistic they may seem to us."

Des raised an eyebrow. "Really? I just wonder what is happening to the people who play the games, I mean games like Grand Theft Auto. What about the middle-school kid who shoves a prostitute into a car, does the simulated nasty, then scores extra points for killing her in cold blood? Don't tell me this is making him a better future citizen."

"I don't know, Des, really. From what I could find in my research on the Web, there is not a lot that we really do know, one way or the other. It seems true that kids who are troubled spend more time playing video games, but what is cause and what is the effect? We do know that kids who play more have faster reflexes and do better with quick decision making. Seems to be good training for future soldiers or pilots or..."

"My point exactly," Des interrupted.

"Or surgeons," Dina finished. "They found that. Really."

"I'm a skeptic. Seems to me that the more realistic they make video games, the more the boundary between the game and the real world blurs."

Someone standing to one side cleared his throat. "Excuse me for interrupting. I couldn't help overhearing. And I noticed your press badges." The man, wearing a blue blazer, open dress shirt, and khakis, did not fit the stereotype of either the scruffy developers or the spiffy corporate types. "Let me put it all in context for you. Both my son and I are serious gamers, heavy players of first-person shooter games, and believe me, we don't ever get confused about the difference between real life and what dances across the monitor screen. Neither of us thinks that what we are doing when we are playing a game is real."

Des took a deep breath. "Look, I am sure you and your son are very much in touch with reality, and I don't really want to get into a debate on this with someone I don't know, but do you condone the kind of malicious and gratuitous violence encouraged by games like GTA?"

"Don't get me wrong. I'm a God-fearing, church-going man, and I am raising my son to be the same way. I just don't think the world needs all the squeamish, bleeding heart liberals to tell us not to play harmless games. Frankly, I think it's the same Bambi-lovers who try to stop us from hunting because they think its cruel or violates animal rights. Heck, they don't even want us to go off-road with our ATVs because they think it pollutes some damned mud puddle or damages precious weeds."

Des took another breath. "That's a lot of territory to smear with suppositions. I..."

Dina held out a hand between them. "Uh, I'm a journalist with BNN. Can I just ask a simple question? Are you part of the computer game industry?"

"Yes, I am. I own QVB, the company that produces DistUrbia 3000. You can see our games at booth A81, just inside the hall and to the left. My name is Dalton Amundson. Do I need to spell that for you? All my business cards are at the booth at the moment. Anyway, the company is based in Salt Lake. You can get corporate details off our website. I can give you the URL or you can just Google us."

Des fumed, but Dina just nodded as she flipped open her notepad and started writing. "Well, then, leaving aside the other questions, as somewhat of an expert and an insider, what do you think of the argument that violent games, particularly first-person shooter games, desensitize players to real-world violence?"

"You know, that could be," he said thoughtfully. "It's possible. But maybe that's not really such a bad thing. Maybe we need to desensitize our sons a bit so they don't grow up to be weak-kneed wimps. We should be preparing them to man up, to hang tough and cope with a world that *is* violent. That's just the way things are, and I don't think they are going to get a whole lot better anytime soon. We need to be readying our kids to relate with that reality."

"Yeah, right," Des interrupted, her brow deeply creased with a critical scowl. "So, I once saw a boy, maybe eight or ten, in an airport overseas. He was playing a martial arts game where you get to pick the appearance of your computer opponent. He picked a figure of a slim blonde girl in a ponytail, then took great relish in punching her in the face and kicking her in the stomach. You can't tell me that this was laying the ground for healthy future relationships with women.

"And—just let me finish—it seems to me that knowing that it's just a game might be beside the point. The airlines and the military train their pilots in simulators. I am sure the pilots know they are, in a sense, playing a game inside the simulator, a particularly realistic game, perhaps. Still, they are learning how to do something in the real world. They are learning to fly. So when you play a realistic game of killing people—and they do keep getting more realistic all the time—what are you being trained to do?"

"It's not the same," the man said, shaking his head and sighing. "But I'm not sure I can explain it to you."

Des, like a terrier in hot pursuit of a chipmunk, pressed on. "You also have to wonder about the way video games are helping to create a generation of house-bound couch potatoes. Clearly, kids would be better off competing out on the soccer field than sitting in front of a plasma screen exercising their thumbs."

Dalton shook his head sadly. "You call what passes for youth sports today competition? Do you know that the league my son used to play in would not let a team win by more than six points? What kind of a life lesson is that? They would even fine any coach who overshot the limit. Incredible! If a team was really good, they'd spend the second half of a match trying to avoid scoring or desperately trying to give away goals to the other team. Pathetic. I would rather have my son shooting terrorists in an honest video game than trying to shoot goals in a rigged soccer game. Life doesn't reward losers or give everyone who starts a business a little ribbon just for trying."

He shrugged. "Maybe you have to get into it first, experience them for yourself, play some *real* games before you can understand. Anyway, I do hope you enjoy the conference. And check us out. That's QVB, booth A81." He turned away and melted back into the crowd.

Dina looked at Des. "You really like stirring the pot, don't you. I have never liked arguing. My parents did way too much of it. My heart starts pounding and my knees go rubbery when I try to argue with anyone, especially people I don't know. Which is part of why I like hiding behind a reporter's notebook and do most of my research online."

Des put her hand on Dina's shoulder. "That guy? He's just a stranger. Makes it easy. We'll never see him again."

"I wouldn't bet on it. But let's head for our session."

5

THE PANEL HAD TURNED OUT to be a verbal bout of ad hominem jabs and techno-babble punches that mostly went over both their heads. The second session, on color and mood in virtual worlds, was on the other end of the spectrum. Des finally whispered, "This is trivia. There's nothing new or interesting here. Unless you want to stay, I say let's go for coffee."

"Sure. We can stop off in the Press Room where the coffee and donuts are gratis. I want to pick up some press packets from vendors and see who else might be covering here."

In the Press Room, over coffee and Danish pastries like soggy plastic, Dina grumbled about the assignment and wondered how she was going to get a series out of it for her boss, while Des complained that she was hard put to see how anything she learned might help her design internal websites for Scenaria. She was proposing that she call it a day and head back to the hotel to get some work done when a well-tanned, white-haired man entered the room, did a quick one-eighty scan, and then headed straight toward them.

"Sorry, I hope I am not interrupting anything. You can see from my badge," he said, addressing Dina, "that we work for the same company, or at least we help to pack the pockets of the same corporate crowd headquartered who knows where on the planet."

Dina looked at him warily, but held out her hand anyway. "I'm Edina Gustafson," she said. "Do we...do we know each other?"

"I'm Karl Lustig with iTech Weekly Online, another part of the vast InterMetroGroup empire that bought out your Business News Network last year. I was told that you and I are supposed to collaborate on a series about the future of the video games industry. You were going to do the business and culture angles, and I was to tackle the technology stuff. I thought you knew."

"Hang on. You said iTech Weekly? You're from Haifa, right? I, oh, I thought, I mean, I expected someone..."

"Someone taller, maybe? Or with longer hair? Or..."

"Now you're teasing me. I mean, I just wasn't expecting..."

"Someone quite so, so mature?" he said with a big grin.

Clearly embarrassed, Dina tried to explain. "Well, technology blogging is mostly, well, I think of younger people. I suppose that when I was Googling you, I should have checked your birth date on Wikipedia."

"It wouldn't have helped; the Wikipedia article on me is just a stub and mostly wrong."

"Really?" She gave him a skeptical look. "I would think there would be more. You do have a somewhat dashing reputation, from what I could learn. Maybe that's why I pictured someone, well, you know. Didn't you have something to do with the CIA or something like that awhile back? Something about nuclear terrorism? Yes, now I remember. I came across your name when I was researching a piece on so-called 'Material Unaccounted For,' collaborating with an old friend from the Boston Globe. You went to MIT, didn't you?"

"I admit to that last bit but categorically deny everything else," he said, covering his discomfort with a laugh. He had always thought that there were no traces that could connect him back to the MIT affair. "What I really do is pretty mundane. I write news and analysis bits for iTech, mostly on the Israeli high-tech scene. I'm here because Israel's got some up-and-comers in the computer games business who are doing their dog-and-pony show here at the conference, and my editor somehow made contact with yours." It was the truth, though hardly the whole truth. The collaboration was a setup, of course, although he still did not have the whole picture of what they were being set up for.

Dina took a step back and said, "This is my friend, Des Allen."

Karl tilted his head and smiled. "Nice to meet you. You're also a reporter?"

"No, it just says that on my badge so I can tag along with Dina. I'm not sure how much help I'm going to be."

"And what do you do, then, when you are not passing yourself off as a journalist," he said, teasing.

"I do web graphics for Scenaria, a local software security firm."

Karl nodded and turned back to face Dina. "Well, here we are, like Woodward and Bernstein, teamed to expose the ugly underbelly of computer games today." He grinned. "So, do you want to compare notes and strategize?" He pulled out a slick, leather-bound journal and a very fat pen. "Just wait a minute while I boot up my pen." He laughed. "I tell you, I never won anything in my life, and I walk in this morning to the sound of my name being called over the PA system as a winner in the first drawing. It's a LiveScribe Pulse SmartPen. It records everything you draw or write along with a synchronized audio recording if you want it. I've been trying it out. I think it could be a reporter's best friend. Pretty cool, huh?" He grinned like a schoolboy just being let out for recess. "I'm ready."

Des looked on as Dina deftly shifted into her professional persona and the two of them got into a lively discussion of what they already knew and what they needed to learn. It was a treat to see her friend at work, to get a glimpse into another side of her. And Karl Lustig was a delight to watch—confident and charming, with a disarming sense of humor. He was the sort of man that Des's mother would have described as "a well-preserved older gentleman," the sort that her mother would comment on in the occasional attempt to raise a twinge of jealousy in her husband, who, being either sublimely confident of his own place in her heart or clueless about the intent of her remarks, never rose to the bait. Des knew her father loved her mother, but expressions of jealousy were just not in his social vocabulary.

"Okay," Dina said, closing her notebook. "That divvies up the responsibilities. Let's split up and meet back at the end of the day. How about doing dinner? Des, can you join us?"

"Can't. I have plans. My lunch appointment got postponed until the end of the day. It's likely to go long. You know how it is."

"Oh, right, of course," she said, raising her voice ever so slightly and sending a glance Des's way. Karl, pretending not to notice, said nothing. "I'll see you back at the room after," Dina continued. "If you are coming back to the room." She gave Des a raised-eyebrows look.

"Yes, I'll be back. Hey, we're roomies again. I wouldn't want to miss jabbering into the night with you."

"Good. Right now, why don't you come with us back to the exhibit hall. Karl says that Aniromoto is about to do a mega demo and introduce their new game system."

They all grabbed their stuff and hurried back toward the exhibit area, Karl trailing just behind Des and Dina. Des slowed her pace just enough to come abreast of him.

"So, you're from Israel. Haifa, right?" she asked. "But you don't have an accent."

"Not yet, anyway. I've only lived there a few years. People do tell me I speak Hebrew with a terrible American accent. My fault for not getting the proper upbringing and going to Hebrew school." He smiled at her warmly. "You're probably wondering how I ended up in Israel." Des nodded.

"I'm your basic American mongrel. German on my father's side if you go back far enough, and English on my mother's, at least we think. She was adopted during the War and the records were lost in the Blitz. So, I'm just a kid from Upper Peninsula Michigan who ended up marrying a wonderful Jewish girl in Haifa, although she'd object to the 'girl' part but probably not quarrel with the 'wonderful' bit. It's a long story—she's actually American, too, but grew up in England, and.... I won't bore you. Suffice to say that life sometimes has a script for us that is different from the one we first read. And you?"

"California girl who came East to school. My mom's an academic and my dad's an artist, so money was never our strong suit, but I got a scholarship to Phillips Andover. And I really loved Israel when I went there on Youth-to-Israel, a subsidized program from the Lappin Foundation, but I haven't been back since. I moved down here when I started college and ended up working here, too."

"Hey, and here we are!" Karl announced, interrupting as they turned the corner. "Along with everybody else in the game world it would seem."

The entrance to the exhibit hall was jammed as people pushed and shoved to get in before the show started. Karl said, "Follow me!" and steered the two of them off to the side. "I know it doesn't seem to make sense, but it's systems dynamics: the flow at the side, along the wall, is fastest because of fewer collisions among particles. That's us: people particles. So, never head straight in." They quickly reached the harried security guard on their side, who was scrambling to check everyone's badges as the crowd pressed forward. Karl approached from behind, held out his badge at arms length, leaned into the guy's ear, and said, "Press. You got your hands full. Can we just slip in behind you?"

The guard said, "Ah, sure, I suppose." And just like that they were in and clear of the crowds.

"Wow, pretty slick," Dina said. "You sure know your stuff."

"Just a geek who's been at it for a long time. Look, Aniromoto is booth C212, not far from Sony," he said, checking the map in his pocket guide. "If we want to get there the fastest, we go all the way around and approach from the rear on aisle D. Quick, just stay close so we don't get split up." He headed off, with Des and Dina scrambling to keep up.

"Not bad for a 'mature gentleman,' as my mother might say," Des remarked over her shoulder. "This guy is smart. And fast." They clung as close to him as possible as he pushed through the crowds, then suddenly found themselves in the front, at the ropes and stanchions that ringed the Aniromoto booth.

The demo was flashy and loud and punctuated by frequent whoops from the crowd, but it left both Des and Dina wondering what all the hoopla was about. As the crush of onlookers gave way to smaller pockets of dedicated nerds who wanted to quiz the company reps about technical details, Karl led the way back to the coffee and snack area where he gestured toward a table. "I'll buy. What are you having?"

Both Dina and Des shook their heads. "Nothing, thanks. I'm about to float," said Des.

"Me, too," Karl said, grinning, "but caffeine is my drug of choice and I need another fix. A jetlagged java junky can be an ugly sight." He returned quickly with coffee in a tall paper cup.

"I don't get it," Dina said as Karl seated himself across from the two of them. "What is the excitement about. All I saw was basically the same stuff their competitors have, just in a different colored case, with slightly different graphics on the display. Maybe better graphics, but it was all the same games."

"It's not on the screen or the outside of the box, it's under the hood," Karl explained. "It's all about connectivity, or ConNEXTivity, to use their branding. There are two parts of it. Part one is the networking. Their new system has built-in wi-fi—802.11b, g, and n—plus Bluetooth and their own proprietary medium range wireless—although that is supposed to be disabled on the units sold in Europe—all seamlessly and automatically integrated. The customer doesn't have to do a thing or know anything. Just be within reach of any other unit and automatically you can be doing multiplayer games, swap data, even share resources. It's scalable, too. You buy three Aniromoto boxes, put them in the same room, and they start talking with each other to automatically link up into a distributed supercomputer—no wires, no configuring. Great graphics become stunning graphics. If there is a PC nearby, it can see the Aniromotos on the network and chat with them. And they can access any fast Internet connection. Every Aniromoto in the world is, in practice, part of a vast, ad hoc, peer-to-peer network. In effect, it's a single system.

"Wasn't something about that already out at CES in Vegas last week," Dina asked.

"Yes, Aniromoto announced at the Consumer Electronic Show, which is why they have sold nearly one-and-a-half million units overnight. That and their very aggressive pricing. But the second part of what they are doing is what has the developers here going gonzo, because Aniromoto has proprietary technology that enables games developed for any competing platform to be almost effortlessly ported to theirs. And the same software allows automatic links to smartphones and netbooks and what have you, all part of a totally connected gaming universe.

"It has the competition going nuts, giving hordes of lawyers more money they don't really need or deserve. At least a dozen lawsuits are already in motion, but it looks like these Japanese cats know their stuff. They've been accumulating a string of obscure patents—their own and ones they acquired in a binge of buy-outs over the last couple of years. It's like a vast legal moat around the thick castle walls of the secret software that is at the heart of their system. And they claim to be clean, without any violations of any other intellectual property. We'll see. In a sense, it's all been done before, but never so slickly or comprehensively. One of my colleagues said it could be as big as the World Wide Web."

"Now that's scary," Des declared. "Just what we need, a web of unreality, a vast virtual empire, separate and distinct, totally connected in real time and totally disconnected from real things."

Karl was thinking that he agreed, in part, but let that slide. "Well, not completely disconnected from real things," he said. "You'd be surprised to know what is online today. Even some cars are now connected in real time to the Internet with systems like Continental's AutoLinQ." He shook his head in mock despair. "The Web on wheels. It would be amusing if it weren't so misguided. Just what we need: hackers planting software Trojans in cars. Imagine zipping along the Beltway in traffic when somebody remotely cuts off your engine. Law enforcement actually wants that particular capability to be built into cars, but if it's there, you know some joker will find a way to hack into it."

Des gave him a squinty smile. "You're beginning to sound more like a glum Luddite than a technology tout."

"Not so. I love gadgets and gizmos and believe in bright prospects for a high-tech future. However, I am a realist when it comes to human nature. Given half a chance, we will soon turn any new technology into a weapon or a stunt or both.

That's what people do." He locked eyes with Des as if his position somehow applied particularly to her.

"Well," she said, pushing back her chair, "let's go learn what we can about what people do with technology, at least what they do when they are using it for playing games."

6

THE REST OF THE DAY was a blur of conversations and demos. Des had decided to tag along with Karl and Dina as they made their rounds of the booths and chatted with attendees in the halls. Karl mostly let Dina take the lead, but would pop in now and then with a question, usually quite technical, that would take the conversation down a completely new path. Late in the afternoon he excused himself, saying that he needed to hit the Aniromoto booth again with some more questions about their communications platform.

Mid-afternoon, Des got another call from Harry saying he was still sorting out the mess at the office and needed to cancel their dinner plans. Des was disappointed and annoyed but felt guilty for feeling that way. Tired and a little depressed, she went back across the street to the hotel room alone and ordered in from room service. She was just finishing her soggy portabella mushroom club sandwich when the phone in the room rang. She picked it up eagerly, expecting it to be Dina.

"Look, are you going to play or not?" It was the voice again. "The group needs you, but we voted that we would rather play one member short than waste more time chasing after you. The hunt has already begun. In or out?"

"Who is this?" Des demanded.

"Blue Leader. Who do you think?"

"Who Lieter? I don't know anyone named Lieter. What the hell are you talking about? And how did you get this number? Any more of this harassment and I will have to report you to the telephone company. No, to the police. I work in security, and I know people."

"Okay, play dumb, if that's your tactic, lady. You're the one who signed on. Just remember, the game started today at nine. Just because you're not cooperating doesn't mean you're not part of it." Click.

"Goddamn it. What is going on?" Only the dial tone answered. She immediately dialed Harry's cell number. It rang and rang, and she was about to give up when he finally answered.

"What's up?" he said with a note of impatience.

"Are you home?"

"No, I'm still at the office, trying to puzzle out that problem and get the system ready for the upcoming site visit. DB is here with me. Do you want to talk?" He covered the mouthpiece but she could still make out what he was saying to DB: "It's the wife. Do you mind?" She couldn't hear DB's reply, but Harry uncovered the phone. "Go ahead. We can talk now."

She told him about the string of calls.

"Oh, my sweet Destiny," he said. "I am sorry. Those stupid screw-ups. I put a special request on the order form, but they must have missed it. I told them not to start until Friday.

It was supposed to be a surprise, for our 'hemiversary,' you know."

"No, I don't know. Now I'm even more confused. What are you saying, that you're behind all these weirdo calls I've been getting?"

"Sweetheart, it's a game. It was supposed to be a surprise. I bought you a subscription to TNG. It was not supposed to start until after I had a chance to tell you. I thought it would be a fun surprise for you."

Des was becoming impatient. "I still don't get it. TNG? Something to do with 'Star Trek: The Next Generation?'"

"No. TNG, The New Game. You must have heard about it. It's a mystery game, a digital age Clue if you will. Everybody is playing it. Everybody who can afford to, anyway. It's run by the same people who do Life 2.0, the Horvaths. Subscribers get assigned to teams. The idea is to be the first team to solve a complicated mystery. The teams meet and strategize in Life 2.0. You start out knowing nothing and get clues that you have to track down either on the Internet or in, well, the real world. It's really fun, with real prizes. You'll love it."

"You think so, do you? Well, it is not looking like a lot of fun right now. What made you think of that as a present for me?"

"Well, Des, you like puzzles, you're smart, and I thought maybe it was time you took the leap into multiplayer online games. And I wanted to give you something but was worried about tangible gifts. So…" His voice trailed off.

"I suppose it's the thought that counts," she said without much conviction. "Still, thanks, but no thanks. If you knew me well enough, you would know I would not get into this.

Please, just cancel the subscription. Get your money back. Take me out of the game."

"I am not sure how to do that? I think one of the rules is that once you are in, you're in. But I suppose you don't have to play. If you don't help, though, it could piss off your team-mates."

"I think it already has. But maybe if you at least try to cancel, this guy will stop calling at all hours."

"Look, I am sorry. I'll see what I can do to get you off the hook once I am done here. I gotta go now. I have my own mysteries to solve and DB will be back any second."

"DB makes me anxious. He always seems to be around, checking on me, wanting to do stuff for me."

"He's okay, darling, just another geek. Look, I'll see you on Thursday, as planned. Okay?"

"Okay. I love you."

"Yeah. Right. Bye."

— —

DB, carrying two mugs of coffee in one hand and one of the just-released models of the Aniromoto all-in-one, hand-held game system in the other, kicked the door open. It banged against the waste basket, shattering the quiet in the office. He stood with the feet-splayed stance of the high-BMI male and wore an expression somewhere between envy and annoyance. "It must be nice," he said.

"What must be?" Harry asked.

"Having, well, someone."

Harry looked up into DB's pudgy, acne-scarred face. He wanted to be able to reassure DB that he, too, would find someone, but he couldn't say it with any conviction. Instead, he just grunted and turned back to his keyboard. "Let's try that other database of rootkit signatures. I am still convinced that something malicious has installed itself deep down someplace where we can't ferret it out now. The Internet activity is still there when it shouldn't be, yet when we look, we don't see anything. Even when we start from clean copies of the software and reinstall everything, we still we get these blips on the radar, so to speak."

DB was already off in his own world, thumbs twitching away on the matte-black game console in his lap, a Bluetooth headset blinking in his left ear.

"You listening, DB?"

"Yeah," he said without looking up for a moment. "We've done everything and done everything right. So if there really is something there, then it's either in what we think are the clean copies or it reinstalls itself again every time we rebuild the system."

"But the system is completely isolated—no wires in or out except for the power cord. How the hell is anything going to install itself? Over thin air?"

"Well, yeah," DB said as he got up and left the room, still playing his game and listening to the sound of another world.

— —

In the end, Harry lied. More correctly, he told the truth rather than answer the question he was asked.

When Richard Talpa, showed up, dressed as always in his blazer-and-tee-shirt uniform, the legs of his like-new blue jeans folded under him, he looked up at Harry from his wheelchair and asked, "So, you finally found the culprit? The system is absolutely clean?"

"We rebuilt the system from scratch with clean copies of everything and scanned it not only with all our software, but with all of our competitors' suites as well. It passed every test: everything says it's absolutely clean. Everything is running again like clockwork." All this was the truth and nothing but the truth. But the whole truth would have been that they still had these sporadic packet exchanges over the Internet that neither he nor DB could account for or explain.

Talpa spun his chair around full-circle and pumped the air with his fist. "All right! We'll show those smartasses at Morton Security who can run circles around whom. And the Defense people can let loose their dogs of war at us. We're ready.

"Great work, Harry, absolutely great work. I know you killed yourself over this one, so as soon as the 'surprise' DoD visit is over, take a long weekend off. My treat. I'll give you the keys to my place in the mountains. Just kick back and relax with your lady."

Harry noted the choice of words and wondered whether Richard knew about his affair. But, of course, he didn't ask.

7

DES AND DINA ENDED UP sprawled on their beds, talking through most of the night. Life and Life 2.0, underwear and outerwear, politics, people you hate and people you love— they covered the gamut.

"So how did you meet this guy, Dina? And what does LG stand for?"

"L. Graham Cole. The L is for Lyle, which he never uses, and it was like pulling teeth to get him to tell me. We met online, through a discussion thread about age-play in Life 2.0."

"Age-play?"

"Boy are you out of it. Age-play is where you act out seduction online, pretending to be a different age than you are. It started way back with Second Life, but they eventually banned it, and now Life 2.0 is the epicenter with the fewest restrictions, which means there are a fair number of virtual couplings where she is pretending to be a sweet sixteen with a sexy, slim avatar to match, and he is a lecherous forty-something, although not always with the corresponding avatar. It's a little controversial in some circles, but I just figure to each his own jollies. Virtual reality ought to be one place you can be unreal, indulge in fantasy, nibble on forbidden fruit."

Des raised her eyebrows in disbelief. "You're kidding," she said. "No, you're serious. You mean even pedophilia is okay, as long as you're just playing 'let's pretend.' Doesn't sound very wholesome to me."

"Look, this is not, technically, pedophilia, and I would never be defending pedophilia or child abuse in any case. I am just talking about fantasy. Remember that old Pete Seeger political folk song, *Die Gedanken Sind Frei,*? Well, the thoughts are free. No one can rule over what you think. You are free to imagine, to fantasize whatever you want. It's only when you start actually doing something that the limits and laws apply and the consequences kick in. Besides, even in Life 2.0, puberty is the cutoff. Age-play under thirteen is strictly off limits. They catch you, and you get booted off the system, plus your details get turned over to the authorities, just in case you might have stuff on your hard drive that you shouldn't ought to have."

Des bit at her lip. "So, do I dare ask, do you and LG, I mean, are you into this, this age-play stuff? If it's not too personal, I mean."

"Des, Des, look at me. You can ask me anything, absolutely anything. We're like the sisters we never had, right? So, no. LG is more into other stuff, but we ended up on the same side of the argument in the discussion forum and kind of hit it off. We took our dialogue offline, and the rest is history."

"Teenagers and middle-aged guys, huh." Des grimaced. "Tell me, is there a lot of that in Life 2.0?"

"Remember, no one under 21 or without a credit card even gets to join Life 2.0. Second, it's just role playing. And third, how much older than you is Harry? Is it okay in your book if there's a real age difference but not if you fake it? Wouldn't you find it fun to go back and be in junior high again, whether or not you let yourself get picked up and 'educated' by some handsome older guy?"

"Hell no, I hated junior high. And I had no interest in older guys, handsome or not. At Phillips Academy, I did have the hots for Jimmy Goldberg for awhile, but he was a few years behind me, so I didn't dare let on to anyone. Just too embarrassing."

"So, now the truth comes out, a fantasy cradle robber. Maybe you should find yourself a boy toy at the conference. There are a lot of cute young geeks hanging around with their tongues out. Or join Life 2.0 and do some age-play of your own."

Des looked thoughtful, then opened her mouth to speak, only to close it again.

"What? Tell me," Dina prodded.

"Well, I just don't think of it that way. I don't think about Harry as older. I fell for him because he's Harry, not because he's losing his hair. I have never had a 'type' that I went for. You know, short, tall, blonde, muscular, slim, whatever."

"You are weird. You know that, don't you? Besides, you do have preferences, at least there must be types you wouldn't go for. I've never seen you with a fatty, for instance. And like that dweeb today, Marky what's-his-face. You can't tell me you could go for someone like that."

"No, but not because he's short or has a pug nose. He's not my type because of the way he is, the way he thinks and talks and the things he does."

"Oh, so now you know this guy? You've only seen him for, like, four minutes at a time at a couple of conferences, and you even know how he thinks?"

"No, you know what I mean. You can tell. I can relate to guys who are a bit self-absorbed, a bit inept socially, kind of out there on the autistic spectrum. I mean, that could describe most of the men I've dated. It could describe me. But there are limits."

Dina shook a finger at Des. "You know what else could describe the men you've dated? Well-heeled and well-established. It's a pattern, Des. You may not think of yourself as interested in older men, but you're not interested in anyone just starting out or without a substantial 401K. No starving artists or magnates-to-be for you. You want someone who already has it made, which is why, I figure, all the guys you have ever dated seriously have been quite a bit older."

Des exhaled sharply. "That's not true."

"Oh? Name one."

"Well," she grimaced in concentration, "what about Hernando. He was younger, from Puerto Rico, and he grew up poor."

"You had what, maybe two dates with him? Three? No, Des, most of us girls are looking for a revised edition of our dads. I think you are looking for your mom in pants: someone steady, established, caretaking, responsible."

"Okay, enough psychoanalysis for tonight. I'm going to log into this online game thing that Harry has signed me up for."

"You? Online games? I never thought I'd live to see the day."

"Look, I'm just going to see if I can squelch the whole thing. I'm tired of annoying phone calls at odd hours. Just turn over, ignore me, and go to sleep. You've still got a couple of hours before the sun comes up."

There was a message waiting for Des after she completed the login process at Life 2.0. It was from Blue Leader: "In the morning, see the man at the newspaper stand around the corner from your hotel. Tell him you are Blue Point. The passphrase is 'About Horvath and Company.' He'll understand. You'll understand."

What Des didn't understand was how a player in The New Game could know her whereabouts and the proximity of the newsstand. The game was becoming unsettlingly real.

8

DES FELT LIKE A FOOL, but she rounded the windy corner and walked briskly up to the man in scruffy bib overalls pacing in front of the newsstand. "Er, I was told to tell you that I was, uh, Blue Point. I have no idea what that means, but that was what I was told." The man stuck his hands in his overalls and looked at her with a blank stare. "Oh, yes, it's, uh, about Horvath and Company," she added.

Without a word, the man reached over and pulled a magazine from behind a stack on the rack, slipped it into a thin white paper bag, folded the top over, creased it, and handed the package to her. "That'll be $3.95, lady," he said holding out his hand.

"Oh, right, yes, of course, silly of me." She pulled a five from her purse. "Here, keep the change."

"You don't gotta tip me, lady. I'm no cabby," he said, as he pocketed the money and turned away.

While Des walked back into the hotel to get breakfast, curiosity got the best of her. She opened the bag and slipped the magazine partway out. It was a copy of *'NetWeek*, with a picture of Donna and Erno Horvath on the cover and the headline "Advancing Avatars." It was a recent issue, not the latest, but Des couldn't remember seeing it. She slipped it back into the bag as she pushed through the revolving doors into the hotel.

Dina was waiting in the café. "What's in the bag?" she asked.

"Just some stupid magazine," Des said, laying it on the table. "Thanks for ordering for me." She picked up the grapefruit-size cranberry muffin at her place and started to tear off small bits.

Dina reached across and slipped the magazine out of the bag. "How odd. This is another InterMetroGroup rag, and keeping up with Internet news is part of my job, but I don't recognize the issue. She flipped it open. "Wait a darned minute. There are no ads in this thing, and half the pages are blank."

"Hey, give me that. Let me see it."

"Don't grab!" Dina said, pulling it closer. "This is real interesting. The masthead is right, and the contents page, but the rest is some kind of whitepaper followed by blank pages." She held the magazine up and studied it as she turned it in the light. "This isn't real. The cover isn't offset printing, it's inkjet. Like POD."

"You're saying this is a print-on-demand mockup, like someone dummied up the thing to make it look like a regular magazine?"

"Yup. And listen to this report. 'Confidential inquiry into the whereabouts of Erno and Donna Horvath.' Definitely weird stuff, Des. Any chance this is part of your virtual detective game."

Des nodded and swallowed the bite of muffin. "Yeah, but I don't get it. This is hardly virtual, and the news dealer I got it from was as solid as you and me. If it's a game, it's one really mixed-up game. Hey, are you listening to me?"

Dina was skimming through the dummy magazine. "This is pretty interesting stuff, Des. You ought to read it."

"I'd like to, if I could get my hands on it."

"Oh, sorry," Dina said, passing it back. "Look, we better get over to the conference. First sessions will be starting in a few minutes."

"No, you go ahead. I'll catch up later. If I miss you, we can meet up at noon by the registration desk, okay?"

Dina nodded, grabbed her purse, and headed for the door, leaving Des with the report, two half-eaten muffins, and the check. Des looked at the first page of the report where a faint pink watermark of "CONFIDENTIAL" repeated like wallpaper in the background. The opening paragraph declared that the entire contents were for use solely by members of the TNG Blue Team and were not to be shown to any other persons or reproduced or transmitted in any form or media, digital or otherwise.

Des looked around anxiously, unsure whether she was getting nervous over the game or simply embarrassed about being involved in it. Deciding on impulse to go back to the room instead of over to the conference, she turned over the check, noted the over-the-top total, and laughed. Fishing a twenty out of her purse, she tucked it and the check under the edge of her plate, tore off another bit of muffin and popped it in her mouth, then got up and strode to the bank of elevators. Just as she arrived, one of the doors slid open and Marky Collier-Adams stepped out.

"It's you, Destiny," he said, as if he was reminding her of her own name. "We are both staying in the same hotel. Did you know that? You do web design, I know, so I wanted to tell you about my cousin who is flying in today. He does web games, so you should meet and talk. I've worked with him. Well, really *for* him. That's the job I'm not really supposed to talk about, so I won't. I did some wireless communications protocols for him, but I shouldn't tell you about that, so forget I said anything. Anyway, he is from Australia and you'd like him because he is very smart, although he is not as good at mathematics as I am, which is why he wanted me to work out the error-correcting codes for this very low bandwidth communication channel he is working on. But I can't talk about any of that. Anyway, Barry gets into Dulles at 2:24 this afternoon on the non-stop from Narita, that's in Japan, the Tokyo airport, but he's from Australia, remember. So, after he checks in, we could all have dinner together." He took a breath and just stared at her.

"I'm sure your cousin is very nice," Des responded, "but I'm busy tonight. Thanks, though." She slipped past him into the elevator. He turned and put his hand against the safety bumper on the edge of the door to stop it from closing.

"That's okay. Barry is here for a week, so we can do it some other night. He'd like you. You're nice to me. Do you know how to phone me? Do you still have my business card? I gave it to you at WebGraph. That was in Boston in 2006, at the Hines Convention Center, right after the seminar on going beyond the Web-safe color palette. Remember?" He looked up at her expectantly.

"Your details are in my contact manager, I'm sure," she lied. "I'll call you if I can get free, but things are very busy for me right now, very busy, so I am not sure it's going to be possible. If you don't hear from me, just figure I couldn't get away."

"Oh, I know how that is. I've got a deadline for all these communication routines I'm writing because this other guy screwed up and didn't deliver his stuff in time, so Barry asked me to do it. Very complicated. Secret stuff, you know, so I can't tell you any more about it." The elevator door started pushing against his hand with more insistence. He pulled his hand back, and the door closed on him just as he was about to say more.

Des laughed to herself as she punched the button for the seventh floor. The poor guy could not stop. And he clearly had some kind of a thing for her. Or maybe he was trying to fix her up with his really smart cousin from Down Under. Or maybe both. It was hard to tell.

She got off the elevator and made the succession of turns to get headed down the right hallway. As she approached her room, she noticed the door ajar. She cautiously pushed it open part way without entering. A heavyset woman dressed in a black-trimmed white housekeeping uniform was bending over her suitcase. "Hello?" Des called, as she opened the door the rest of the way. The woman straightened up quickly and started fussing with the curtains.

"There, I just to finish the clean. All done. There," she said in a heavy but unrecognizable accent. She reached for the upright vacuum cleaner parked to one side and dragged it toward the door. Des was not sure what to make of the woman's behavior, but let her pass. As she did, Des tried to read her employee badge, but was able only to catch the first letter, an S, followed by a string of consonants.

She checked her suitcase, but everything seemed to be in order, so she sat down to read the magazine mockup. The report inside claimed that Blue Leader—apparently the self-nominated head of their team, having been the first to sign onto the current round of The New Game—had stumbled on some information while doing background research for participating. "This is not a game!" it stated repeatedly. "THIS IS FOR REAL!!!" it declared. The story was somewhat discursive and peppered with paranoid musings, but the gist of it was that Life 2.0 founders and full-time denizens Erno and Donna Horvath were not on an extended vacation as their friends believed, but had actually been kidnapped—or worse. Now, some secret cabal of evildoers was plotting a take over of the online empire for unknown nefarious purposes. Instead of playing the game, the team had decided to use their skills and resources to get to the bottom of the real mystery.

"Yeah, right," Des said to herself. "Very clever, but very transparent. Pretend the game is not a game to make it more engaging. Who do you expect to fall for this." At the bottom of the last page was the immediate assignment: find out by any means where the Horvaths were supposed to have gone, verify their actual whereabouts, and report back to the team at their virtual headquarters in Life 2.0. Des thought it might be fun to flex her research muscles a bit, so she started by booting up her laptop and logging into Life 2.0 again, then going to The NewzRoom where updates on the game space and the parent company, Newlands Labs LLC, were posted. Sure enough, two weeks earlier there had been an announcement about Donna and Erno, known to fans and Life 2.0 denizens by their first names only, who would be taking a winter break in the Virgin Islands. While gone, they would be in frequent contact, but the day-to-day running of Life 2.0 would be in the capable hands of their new COO, Truman Siebalt.

Conditioned by years of collaborating on design teams, Des habitually turned to thinking aloud whenever she was working on a new problem. "Okay," she said to her computer, "now we need to find out where they might have been headed in the Virgin Islands." She tried without success to locate some kind of global search mechanism within Life 2.0, so she decided to search the Web instead. Her second query turned up a news item almost two years old about the Horvaths purchasing an estate in St. Thomas. A few more minutes of digging got her a clip mentioning the site with its private beach overlooking Magens Bay. A search for images and quick scans of several pages eventually netted a telephoto snap by some paparazzo showing the main house with its distinctive blue and white tile roof. On a long shot, Des switched to Google Maps, located Magens Bay, and found that she could zoom all the way in to a high resolution satellite view with each house and building along Magens Point clear and distinct. She spotted the bright colored tile of the roof not far from what looked like it might be a resort. A little more digging yielded an address and telephone number for the resort. On impulse, she dialed the number through SkypeOut and got an answer on the second ring.

"Magens Bay Beachfront Resort. How may we be of service?"

"I am really sorry to bother you like this, but I am calling from Washington, DC, trying to get in touch with Donna Horvath on an urgent matter," Des extemporized, "but my cell phone with her telephone numbers in it was stolen this morning. She mentioned she might be stopping by the resort to visit some friends. I know it's a long shot, but I don't suppose you would recognize the Horvaths and perhaps know whether Donna happens to be around there." As she talked, Des clicked on a Skype add-in application to make an MP3 recording of their conversation.

"Of course, we know the Horvaths. The whole island is really like a small town, and the Horvaths are practically neighbors here on the Bay. They frequent our restaurant. Let me put our concierge on the phone. Perhaps she can help you." There was a click and a brief silence.

"This is Miss Calloway, I understand you are looking for the Horvaths. Is that right? Well, I regret to have to tell you that I have not seen them at all recently. They may not be in residence. Are you sure they are on island?"

"That's what I was told. You don't happen to know their number, I suppose."

"Well, I might have it in my Roladex, but I certainly couldn't give it out over the phone. I am sure you understand."

"Of course. I just don't know what to do. My name is Destiny Allen, I'm with Scenaria Corporation, which you can verify by calling them if you wish. We handle security for the Horvaths' company and this concerns a confidential security issue. I am away from my desk, conducting an investigation, but I must reach Mrs. Horvath immediately. She told me to call as soon as I found out anything." She exhaled audibly. "I can't believe that some creep slipped my cell phone from my purse on the train this morning. Is there any way you might help?"

"Well, I really don't know about this. Perhaps I could call and pass on the message for her to call you. What is a number where she can reach you?"

Des spelled out the number of her cell phone. "That's my office direct line," she said, lying. She can leave a message where I can call her back. Thank you, so much. Thank you. I truly appreciate this." She could hear touch-tone dialing in the background.

"It's ringing now, Ms. Allen. Please hold for a moment." Another click and a long silence. "Hello, are you still with us, Ms. Allen? I called the number I have. The member of the household staff who answered said that Mrs. Horvath was not available. When I gave her your number and said it was urgent, she informed me that I was correct in surmising that the Horvaths are not in residence at present. It seems that they left yesterday for the mainland. I am afraid you just missed them. I do have a cell phone number in my record here. You did say it was urgent, did you not? Let me try that number, too." Des could hear the handset being set down and the sound of more touch-tones in the background. "I am sorry," the concierge said. "Apparently, that number cannot be reached at present. Perhaps they are in flight. Is there anything else I can do for you today?"

"No, but I thank you for trying. Have a good day." She disconnected on Skype, stopped the recording, and saved it for documentation to the Blue Team. She was beginning to think that maybe Harry was right about online games. This one, with its mix of the virtual and physical, the real and unreal, was turning out to be a lot more fun that she had expected. She closed her laptop, slipped it back into its case, and left for the conference center.

— —

Dina finally approached the registration tables at half past noon with Karl Lustig in tow. "Hey, there you are," Dina called out. "We've been looking for you."

Des glanced to either side, then said, "Been right here where we agreed I should be for, what, 35 minutes or so."

"That'll teach you to show up early for a rendezvous with me. What have you been up to all morning?"

"You know, the magazine."

"Right. I told Karl here about it and about TNG. So, what did you learn? Karl is actually interested. For the story we are working on. The digital-physical integration is a novel angle." Des filled the two of them in on her detective work, and finished by admitting to feeling self-conscious about Karl's presence.

"Don't be shy about it," he said. "I'm impressed. Good detective work. In fact, you seem to have a knack for espionage. Did you ever think about making *aliyah*, living and working in Israel? I know some people there who might be able to use your talents."

Dina's face lit up. "I knew it. Didn't I say he was involved with the CIA or something? He's talking about the Israeli CIA."

"*HaMossad*, Dina," Des corrected her. "It's called *HaMossad*, the Institute, and he didn't say anything about who he meant who might use my talents, did he?"

"Well, actually," he answered, "I was thinking of *HaMossad*. But it was just a wild idea, nothing serious. Still, maybe moving to Israel would be a good move for you."

"I'm afraid not. I have ties here."

"She means there's a guy," Dina said. "In case you don't know the shorthand code of young American single women." Des gave her a disapproving look.

"So, what's next in your Internet investigations," Karl asked, changing the subject.

"I'm up against a wall. I know where the Horvaths aren't—at least I think I know—but I don't know where they are. I wish I could find out their phone numbers, but there are no listed numbers, no surprise, and a call to the NewLands Labs office got me nowhere."

"Didn't you say you recorded your call on Skype? You can figure out the numbers called from the recording. You just need some decoding software that will read the audio file with the DTMF tones and spit out the digits. I don't know the particular program, but it should be easy enough to track something down on the Web."

"I've got another idea. I think I know somebody who probably already knows the particular program and may even have it installed."

"Great. Look, I really must go and check in with my boss," Karl said. "You two have a nice lunch."

9

THE CONFERENCE PRESS ROOM, one of the smaller meeting rooms temporarily commandeered into service, was crowded, with half a dozen people encircling the white-draped table in the middle of the room and several more chatting by the makeshift bar where coffee, bagels, and soft drinks were spread out. It was a scene all too familiar to Karl. He grabbed the one unoccupied chair and dragged it into a corner where he pulled out his computer and opened it in his lap. This was a role he could play, the dogged technology journalist on deadline, hurrying to upload copy or to complete his next blog entry. It was almost but not quite real. He did not like the deception he was involved in. He was still uncomfortable with the play-acting and misdirection that his assignments demanded, particularly with people he liked. He was finding that he especially liked Dina's friend, Des, although he had no idea why. He found himself wanting to take her in hand and lead her back to Haifa where she would meet a nice Jewish man, settle down, and raise a family while helping to keep

Israeli technology at the forefront. But, there was work to do and no time for indulging in idle fantasy.

He logged into the conference's public wi-fi, which he used to get to a website where he could establish a secure connection. He typed up a short progress note and sent it out in encrypted form to Anat Dorfman in Tel Aviv. Then he switched to his personal account and picked up his email. Along with several sales announcements were emails from Shira, and one from their son, Bini. Bini was already starting his early lobbying for permission to go next year to a summer camp run by an American group that brought Palestinian and Israeli teens together for an intensive wilderness experience in northern Maine. He was also wondering why Karl had changed plans and delayed his return home after the conference in Boston. Reading between the lines, Karl could detect Bini's concern: the last conference in Boston had marked the start of Karl being sucked into the whole mess with the attack on the Temple Mount. At that time, it had all seemed thrilling to Bini, like a home-grown comic-book adventure, but he had matured enough in the year since becoming Bar Mitzvah to look back with the realization of just how perilous it had all been. His email ended with a question about his Uncle Lev. The reference to Lev Novikov, Karl's best friend, a retired spook from *HaMossad*, clinched the real meaning of the message to Karl, who quickly typed a reassuring reply about the prospects for summer camp next year and about the delay being nothing to worry about.

"It's just an extra reporting assignment," Karl wrote in his email, "to cover a conference here in Washington, since my itinerary took me through DC anyway. See you next week, son."

Karl had deliberately omitted mention that the conference was GAME IX, knowing that Bini, a true scion of the digital age, would be insane with envy and would pepper him with special requests. Karl had already accumulated a bag-full of tchotchkes for Bini, including a mini version of the much coveted BallBlast Bluetooth controller and a full-featured, unlocked copy of the PC version of "Saturn: Assault in the Rings" that he had wheedled from Hunted Arts on the basis of his press credentials. It was the only title from their violent catalog that Karl figured Shira might marginally allow, even if not fully approve. It was mostly a high-def update of an old-fashioned space-war shoot-'em-up, at least until the player reached the eighth level and actually was able to board some of the invading interstellar ships, where the targets were decidedly nonhuman aliens. It was not Karl's idea of a nice way to relax on a weekend, but he also knew that if he and Shira tried to ban all such games, the appeal of the forbidden could induce Bini to seek out his own selections and sources. Karl had no doubt that Bini, with his already substantial hacking skills, could easily obtain pirated versions of nearly anything he set his sights on.

The notes from Shira were full of love and trivia that brought a big grin to Karl's face. He was typing an answer, filled with more love and trivia, when his cell phone sang out with the opening vamp from Dave Brubeck's "Take Five." There was no caller ID, but Karl, wondering if it might be from overseas, flipped it open anyway.

"Karl, it's Lev here. How's it going? How's your extra writing assignment going?"

Karl, taken off guard, just said, "Okay, it's going okay. But how...how do you know about my work?"

"Wives, of course," he said. Lev was married to Anat Dorfman, Chief of Technical Services for *HaMossad*, a post that had been Lev's before he retired from the agency. "I don't know what you're working on, of course. Anat is the most tight-lipped, tight-assed adherent to protocol I have ever known. She tells me nothing. But Shira called and spilled the beans about being anxious because, once again, she thought you might be involved with the Institute. Of course, she only knows that you had a sudden change in travel plans and had no clue as to what it might be about. She was hoping to pump me for information, but I told her I would be the last to learn anything. I do wish I were back in the loop. I envy you."

"I'm just a fake journalist being diverted through IAD to cover a story of no consequence."

"Okay, have it your way. Be a tight ass like my dear darling Anat. So, then, how is your novel coming?"

It was a friendly dig. Both men were working on first novels, but Karl's manuscript had been a work in progress—some work but little progress—for nearly ten years. Lev was only a little over a year into retirement and had almost finished the first draft for a big, fat, epic spy thriller inspired indirectly by his years with *HaMossad*. At last count, he was coming up on the six-hundred-page mark of the manuscript.

Karl laughed. "If you are so aware of the extra work on my plate at present, I think you can guess how my novel is progressing—or not. I haven't even opened the file for days, although I did get some writing time on the plane over from Zürich."

"What's the page count now?"

"Oh, you really know how to hurt a guy. It's pretty much right where it's been for the last six months. I had to throw out and rewrite the whole chapter where the computer scientist meets her dead son's pre-programmed avatar in virtual space." Karl's chosen genre was science fiction, which Lev regarded with undisguised contempt.

"Look, Karl, I'm almost finished with writing the first draft of *Unto Your Children's Children*, so, I was wondering whether you might consider reading and commenting on the manuscript. You're the real writer, and I figure you could really help me nail what I was trying to say."

Karl wished he could send a good-natured punch through the phone but also realized he really did want to read his friend's writing. Lev had been very secretive about the whole project. All Karl knew was that it was set largely in the West Bank and featured a Palestinian point-of-view character. Writing from the Palestinian perspective was a daring under-taking for a former Israeli intelligence operative. Karl knew the real reason Lev had taken up the challenge. It was a not entirely subtle homage to his friend and Bini's late father, Migdal, who had been an activist in promoting peace through trade between Israel and the Palestinians.

"Yeah, I'll do it," Karl said. "Just email me the draft, and I will try to read through it on the flight back home next week."

There was a long and unexpected silence from the other end, then the clicking of a keyboard. "I just put two and two together and came up with a dozen. I think I know what you are working on and why. I'm going to send you some URLs to some websites, then you tell me if I'm wrong. Shalom." He disconnected.

— —

In Haifa, Lev's heart was pounding as he read the rest of the news feed that had popped up on his computer. "I can still do this," he said to himself. "I can still connect the dots." It was an exciting feeling, one he had not felt since his retirement send-off. Fiction was no substitute for the reality of the chase, even if it was a chase through cyberspace.

Part Two

10

THE SKY ABOVE THE DESERT, just lightening from charcoal to pale blue, was streaked by high thin cirrus clouds, by a pair of contrails from flights headed into LAX, and by the 30-mile long plume of pollution from the coal-fired power plant ahead. Tricorn Power Station was a small but important employer in the area and a significant contributor to the tax roles of the sparsely-populated county. Warren Mallory, a part-Ute, part-Irish-American in his first real job since graduating from Dixie State in Utah, bounced along in his dirty yellow Jeep, kicking up a trail of red dust as he speeded down the cross-country shortcut that he often took from his home in the trailer park to his job at the plant. Warren, who had put himself through school working as a security guard and part-time ambulance driver, was chronically anxious about his job. He knew that being late for a shift was never recommended practice for recent hires—certainly not in the current economy. His computers and information technology degree had only been good enough to get him a job watching meters and displays, but he was happy to be working at all and was optimistic about his future prospects.

His family had wanted him to follow tradition and go into law enforcement. His grandfather on his mother's side had been with the tribal police, and his father was in the state highway patrol. His oldest brother, pride of the clan, had raised the bar by becoming an FBI agent after returning from Viet Nam. The closest Warren had gotten to law enforcement was his job as a night watchman for a factory outlet complex in St. George. He used much of his time on the job to hit the books and program on the laptop he kept in his locker, then slept through most of his classes at Dixie State. It took him six years to graduate, but he was convinced it was worth it to have the degree. His dream was eventually to convince plant management to let him join the IT team, then ultimately hook up with one of the many small consulting firms beginning to form up in Salt Lake.

He had mixed feelings about working at Tricorn, but rationalized it as a temporary stepping stone. In college he had been active in Students for Ecology and Sustainable Energy, to the embarrassment of his big brother, who kidded him whenever they talked over the phone, calling him a greenie and suggesting that he already had earned himself a fat FBI dossier.

As Warren bounced along in his jeep, a slight rise in the otherwise flat dirt track raised his line of sight just enough for him to notice the dark puff in the pollution plume. It made no sense to him. He slowed and squinted, wondering what could account for such a dramatic change in output, when he noticed another darkening of the outflow directly above the plant. The sunrise at his back glinted off of steel and glass at the station and seemed to turn the tall white stacks into orange pillars of fire. As Warren climbed the embankment and turned onto the paved road heading straight toward the plant, he came to the chilling realization that not all the orange flashes were reflections of the sunrise. The plant was on fire.

Just as he jammed his foot to the floor, a ball of thick black smoke belched from the plant. Part of him wanted to turn tail, but dedication and his first-responder training overrode his instincts, and he raced toward the outer gate of the security perimeter, his long black hair flying in the wind. As he streaked past the guard at the entrance, he held his employee badge as high as the cord around his neck would allow. He was mentally planning his course of action on arrival at the facility when the first bullet struck him in the back. His jeep sashayed for a moment, then hit the ditch at full speed, flipped over, and skidded across the sand and scrub, spinning on its roll bars.

The guard from the booth, gun drawn and held two-handed in front of him, approached the overturned jeep in a running crouch. The sound of alarms rippled across the desert as smoke and steam continued to vomit from the plant.

— —

Out of habit, Marky had taken a taxi from the hotel to the airport, not realizing that the ride from downtown DC to Dulles International would cost him nearly everything in his wallet. He hoped that Barry would not be expecting him to pick up the tab for the return. He still had no idea why his cousin had insisted on being met at the airport, but he was waiting dutifully at the bottom of the escalator near the

United baggage claim, shifting from one foot to the other, when someone came up behind him and said quietly, "Let's go, cuz." He whirled to find Barry grinning at him.

"What are you doing there, er, here? I mean, I was waiting for you to come down the escalator." He looked at his watch. "Your flight just landed."

"No, dweeb, it didn't. Obviously. It landed twenty minutes early and I breezed through Customs and Border Protection. I shipped my bags direct to the hotel, so, this is it." He patted the backpack slung over one shoulder. "My laptop and my Kindle. I'm good to go. Where's your car?"

"I don't have a car here. Actually, I don't have a car. But you know that. You should know that, because I live in Manhattan and I don't need a car there. Nobody does. I took the train down to DC and a cab here to the airport, so I figured we could just go back the same way. Not by train, of course."

Barry Collier-Adams, who preferred to be called Baz, shook his head and looked down at the shorter, nerdier version of himself. They had the same coarse, jet-black hair and obsidian eyes, dark dots that in Marky's pudgier face looked almost cartoonish but in Barry could take on a nearly demonic quality. They resembled their fathers, twin brothers whose genes seemed to have dominated over those of the two very different women they had married, just as the men themselves had dominated over their wives.

Barry and Marky had grown up on opposite sides of the planet after Marky's parents had emigrated to America. The two young men had reconnected in cyberspace out of their mutual preoccupation with playing god, a vocation known to the uninitiated as computer programming. They were creators of worlds, absolute rulers in the digital domains that gave them the perfect and lucrative media in which to express their shared need for control and order. For Marky, programming was something he did without knowing why, an extension of an unconscious inner drive to bring rigor and precision to the world. For Barry, programming was an expression of the self, a projection of his grandiose self image and a means of personal domination. He was in charge, omnipotent in his code, commanding vast armies of processors and ruling over empires of information. His father had lorded it over Barry's mother and three sisters at home but was, in his own and his son's eyes, a failure in the world. Barry was left with contempt for his father, a low opinion of women, whom he saw as weak and unworthy, and a determination to succeed on the grandest of scales. Software was his dominion and scalable solutions were his armada.

"We need to talk, Marky," Barry said emphatically. "A taxi is no place to talk. Did you see the news? Did you see what happened out west? I saw it on the monitor after I landed. One less mega-polluter fouling the nest. Looks like they got what they deserved. And they have no idea who did it or how." Barry grinned again.

"Somebody was killed, I think, a young Native American who they said was attacking the plant. They shot him."

Barry wrinkled his brow. "What an idiot. What the fuck did he think he was doing? Idiot. Don't be an idiot, Marky. Don't be some idiot hero. Just keep writing good code for me. Okay?"

"I always write good code, you know that. I am not an idiot and not an idiot savant, either, like that kid at school always used to call me. Not like that guy on TV. You know the one. He can extract roots of twelve-digit numbers in his head. He could probably break our encryption scheme if he..."

"Look, Marky, just stick a sock in it. I'm tired and hungry and my back hurts from an entire day sitting in that goddamned plane seat wedged between two overweight American tourists. Like damned sumo wrestlers. Americans!" he spat the word. "Get us a cab, and let's just go to the hotel, and do not say anything on the ride. We'll talk when we get to the room, not before. Just shut up." He shoved his backpack at his cousin and started walking toward the terminal exit.

— —

By the time Des and Dina settled into the lobby bar at the hotel and glanced over at the television, the story was already old. Accompanying slightly shaky telephoto footage of an industrial facility shrouded in smoke and wavering in heat distortion, the voice-over narrative was gravelly with fatigue.

"Much of the Southwest was without electricity for hours this morning after an early morning explosion and fire at the Tricorn Power Station, one of the country's biggest coal-fired power plants, disabled generators, sending blackouts rippling through the power grid. Cities as far west as Los Angeles and as far north as Salt Lake City were affected. Las Vegas was without power for several hours, and portions of Los Angeles are still without electricity. Initial reports referred to an unexplained 'industrial accident,' but a later statement from a spokesperson for Wescole Energy Holdings, owner of the plant, said that a terrorist attack had not been ruled out. Still unconfirmed reports from witnesses in the area claim that a suspected terrorist was shot trying to escape the scene. The

FBI is investigating, but Homeland Security has declined to comment pending arrival of their own special investigatory team. Plant employee, Dilman Englander, an overnight supervisory technician who was just finishing his shift when disaster struck, had this to say as he left nearby County General after being treated for lacerations and smoke inhalation."

The scene shifted to an external shot of a hospital emergency entrance and a close-up of a middle-aged man with a small bandage above his right eye and a half dozen microphones waving in his swarthy face. "I was up on the catwalk, about to punch out when number three turbine-generator shook sharply, almost a kind of jerk, maybe four, five times before we heard this loud screeching. As I ran for the control room, smoke started pouring out. We killed the feed to the turbine and pulled the plant off-line as fast as we could, but the overload took out two more generators before the breakers triggered. It's all supposed to be automatic. Should have been faster. We don't know what happened. Maybe sabotage." At this point in the video, the employee was pulled back from the microphones by a non-descript man in a dark gray business suit, just as a young woman in similar attire pushed ahead and leaned toward the waiting microphones.

"No further comment, no further questions, gentleman," she said. "We don't want to fuel rumors. At this time the cause and exact nature of the incident are being investigated by experts from the power company and by the authorities. Whether it was a malfunction or a consequence of some manner of deliberately initiated action simply cannot be determined at this early juncture." She turned away abruptly, her short blond hair bobbing as she hurried back into the hospital.

"That was Anita Paige-Wyler, spokesperson for plant owner Wescole Energy Holdings, a company with electrical plants throughout the U.S. as well as in Brazil and China. Paige-Wyler later acknowledged that damages could run into the hundreds of millions of dollars. The plant, which went online just five years ago after repeated construction delays and a cost overrun estimated at nearly 300 million dollars, has been under scrutiny recently for alleged failure to comply with pollution-control regulations. Wescole company officials have been insistent that all their plants already conform completely and precisely to all relevant state and federal rules and regulations.

"Local hospitals have been treating plant employees and fire fighters for burns and smoke inhalation. In addition to the alleged perpetrator reported to have been shot at the scene, at least one employee is in critical condition after being struck by falling equipment. For more on the story we take you now live to reporter Kevin Lundmore in St. George, Utah."

Just then, Karl Lustig, a glass of Merlot in his hand, approached Dina and Des. "Mind if I join you? I see you're catching up on some of the news we missed while we were all busy watching unending onscreen car chases and learning all the inner secrets of implementing online games using AJAX." He smiled broadly.

"Yeah, we were just catching this story on the cable news. Do you think it really could have been a terrorist attack?"

"I suspect it's possible. It's long been known that the power grid, along with generating plants, are vulnerable, probably even more open to hacking than to direct assault.

You're in the software security field, Des. Is this power company one of your clients?"

"How should I know, there are hundreds of thousands of them, but there's a good chance. Except that from what I've gleaned from our intranet, we are just in the research phase with the kind of specialized security it takes to protect, like, the grid."

"Speak of the devil, Des. Look who's on the cable news." Dina pointed to the screen. Karl turned around just as Richard Talpa was being introduced by a newscaster in the other half of a split screen.

"I'm Nick Desmond, and this is 'Dig.' We have with us in our studios in Washington, DC, computer security expert Dr. Richard Talpa, founder and CEO of Scenaria Systems. Welcome to our program."

"Thank you for having me, Nick."

"Some sources are saying that the incident at Tricorn Power Station could have been caused by terrorist hackers gaining remote control of computer systems at the plant. Is that possible? And is there anything the government can do to stop cyber-warfare by terrorists or rogue nations."

"Well, of course, it's way too early to know just what caused the failure at Tricorn, but yes, an attack through security flaws in the networks that monitor and control electric power generation and distribution is a definite possibility. I would not want to be an alarmist, but the danger has been recognized for years by those of us in software security. We've been pleading for stronger security systems and tighter regulation of networked industrial controls, particularly in the energy sector."

"Is this just hypothetical, Dr. Talpa? What about real examples."

Talpa smiled gravely. "Yes, of course. We all know the story of the Stuxnet worm and the attack—or should I say 'alleged' attack—on an Iranian nuclear plant, but that's still an evolving story, and this goes back much further. For one example, white-hat hackers—computer hackers who try to break into systems in order to identify flaws so that they can be fixed—have demonstrated how a petroleum processing plant could be hacked into and remotely set into a runaway condition that would result in a massive explosion. The chemical industry, of course, counters with claims that redundant automatic safety systems would kick in and shut down the reactor vessels before anything could go out of control, but the hackers are, no surprise, one step ahead. The first thing they would do in any such sabotage scenario would be to program the plant or generator or system into manual override mode, which typically bypasses the regular safety programs."

Nick looked like he was about to interrupt, but Talpa, skillfully controlling the interview, just plunged on. "The bottom line, Nick, is that anything that can be turned on under program control can be turned off; anything that can be controlled remotely can be thrown out of control remotely. That might be called the First Law of Cyber-Terrorism, and it's the dirty little secret that industry and the government does not want the public to know too much about. The specialized systems that monitor and control almost every kind of industrial process or system—they're called SCADA systems—are almost completely unprotected. My company has technology ready to deploy that could secure these systems, but industries will do nothing about it until they are forced to pony up the billions it will cost to do the job right—billions that would actually be an investment in security worth every penny. Only new laws and regulations—or clear and credible threats—are going to bring about a change in the irresponsible behavior."

"That sounds like pretty expensive new regulations, Dr. Talpa?"

"Look, Nick, we already spend billions to guard and protect our borders in order to keep terrorists out of our country, but terrorists don't need to fly here or sneak across the border from Canada or Mexico to wreak havoc. All they need is an Internet connection and some technical knowledge that is relatively easy to come by."

"So, Dr. Talpa, do you think that an incident like this, if it is a first act of cyber-terrorism, might induce congress to enact new legislation or get the power industry to adopt new measures that would better protect the nation's infrastructure?"

"First, let me make clear that this is hardly the first attempted cyber-terrorism. The Pentagon fends off thousands of attempts a day. But the Pentagon uses technology, like the Scenaria software, that keep them secure. The corporate headquarters of energy companies like Wescole Energy Holdings protect their financial and resource management computers with software like ours. But. But the plants themselves, even nuclear plants, are wide open because of vulnerabilities in the networked SCADA systems. It's like locking all your doors with deadbolts but leaving the windows wide open. We have software that locks windows."

"Do you yourself think, then, that the Tricorn incident was an act of cyber-terrorism that could have been prevented by technology like your company produces?"

"It would be irresponsible to speculate at this point about what precisely caused the destruction of Tricorn, but if it was cyber-terrorism, I can say categorically that it could have been prevented by Scenaria technology. It works and is ready to go today."

The view changed to a wide shot of the news anchor in the studio and quickly closed in.

"That was Dr. Richard Talpa, President and CEO of Scenaria in Reston, Virginia, and an expert on software security. In related business news today, Scenaria closed more than 14 dollars up on the NASDAQ. Wescole Energy Holdings closed down sharply in heavy trading on the New York exchange, losing nearly a quarter of its value, while energy stocks in general took a significant hit. Stay tuned for all the financial and business news at half past the hour.

"I'm Nick Desmond, and this is 'Dig.' And now, here's Maggie Bickford with the National Sports Roundup plus the latest update on the controversy surrounding star quarterback, Gil Kalotsky."

Karl turned back to face the table. "Nice plug from your boss, Des. And some good news from bad news, at least for Scenaria. Lucky timing, I'd say, if Scenaria is just getting ready to roll out a comprehensive SCADA security solution."

Dina tapped the table. "I think this could even be Israelis, though I can't come up with a motivation. You know that army intelligence unit—what was it called?—that people said did the number on Iran's nuclear facility. Doesn't this sound similar?"

Karl squinted with one eye. "You're thinking of Unit 8200 of the IDF and the cyber-attack on the nuclear power plant at Bushehr. But, frankly, the Stuxnet worm involved in that caper had more of the hallmarks of the kind of mind games *HaMossad* is known for. Of course, nobody really knows," he added hastily.

"Listen," he said, "unless you lovely ladies really want to hear all about the latest steroid scandal in sports, I was wondering if you both might be interested in dinner? We could use the time to talk about our assignment, Dina, or we could just revert to pleasantries about war in cyberspace. My treat. Our mutual benefactor, InterMetroGroup, covers such expenses when I travel international."

"Lucky you," Dina said. "BNN gives us a per diem that covers about one overpriced muffin in the morning and a burger, no fries, at night. Maybe I am working in the wrong part of the evil empire."

"For me, dinner is out," said Des. "I really need to boogie to keep ahead of my ever-growing to-do list."

Karl turned back to Dina, who shook her head. "I've got a date with LG tonight. He's taking me to this great little Ethiopian restaurant in Adams-Morgan: Meskerem or something like that. I suppose maybe you could come along."

"Hardly, I'd feel like a third wheel on a bicycle. And actually, I probably need to do some work, too. I should do some field research on—you ready for this—Massive Multiplayer Online Games. You know, World of Warcraft and the like. Not sure if virtual worlds like Life 2.0 fall into that category or not, but I think of them as related."

"You should talk with Des, she is really into that stuff. Hey, will you look at the time. I have to run to meet LG in the lobby. But you two, just stay here and talk. Like I said, Des is an expert on this MMOG stuff."

11

IT WAS AN OPENING that Karl knew he should take advantage of, so he suggested that he and Des move out of the noisy bar to a quiet cove just outside the coffee shop. There she opened up her laptop on one of the small round tables.

"Look, I am no expert when it comes to online games," she said. "In fact I just started playing this one game we told you about."

"Well, I'm no expert on anything, just a dilettante who gets paid to dabble and gossip. It's a pretty good gig, except when I have to be away from the family."

"You have kids?"

"Yeah. Here, I'll show you." He pulled a small, leather-bound digital picture frame from his jacket, and opened it. He pushed a button on the side several times and announced, "That's our son, Bini, who already knows more about technology than I will ever learn. He's almost fourteen and in an incredible hurry to grow up so he can serve in the IDF, the army, then join *HaMossad* once he's out. He wants to be a spy. He says it's because he wants to serve the State of Israel, but it's really because he thinks it's a glamorous job. Besides, his father was with *HaMossad*.

"And this," he pushed the button again several times, "is our daughter, Shoshana, better known as Shoshi. She is not quite a year and already yabbers like a talk-show host. She is so smart that I suspect she will be an even bigger handful than her big brother."

"Who was that? The picture you passed by before."

"That," he said, backing up to the picture, "is Shira, my wife. She is a silversmith and also a smart lady who keeps me running to catch up. Not that I'm complaining. At my age it's good to be pushed to stay nimble."

"She's beautiful. And you have beautiful kids. You're lucky."

"For sure."

"Someday. Someday, I hope. I really do want to have kids, to raise a couple of beautiful Jewish kids."

"You will, I'm sure. Your time will come and the right person will come along. You just have to stay open to the possibilities. Fate has this quirky way of working that defies logic and eludes our understanding. You can't let your expectations get in the way. Like those online dating services where people spec out every aspect of a would-be partner, where every dimension and interest has to match? Wrong! I wasn't even looking for anyone when I met Shira, and if I had been, I would not have looked half way around the world nor sought to link up with an artist who already had a son. Some people just look in the wrong places or even for the wrong thing. I have this theory that it's precisely when you're not looking that you find what you were looking for but didn't know you were."

"Do you think there is one special person for each of us, that certain people are fated to be partners?"

"Before I met Shira, I would have said no. Now, I'm not sure. Sometimes I feel like the second string, the lucky bench-warmer who is allowed to play late in the game to take the place of the injured star center. Shira and her first husband were definitely *bashert*, destined to be together. Maybe Shira and I were, too, after his death, but I know far too much about how we were set up, how it was engineered for us to find each other. And I am not talking about God or Fate, just an ordinary but very special human being who wanted his wife and an old friend to find each other and be happy together after he was gone. Marvelous, yes, but not mysterious. A miracle, but not magic."

"I get the impression religion is not a very big part of your life."

"Oh, religion is a big part of my life. You can't live in Israel without it impinging on most everything you do. But, all in all, we are probably more secular than you are here in the States. This country has one of the highest rates of belief in God and religious involvement of any in the world. Also, belief in astrology and flying saucers. And, of course, the new buzzword, spirituality."

Des made a sour face. "Not for me. I'm Jewish but not spiritual and not observant."

Karl laughed, a short pulse of amusement. "And me? I'm spiritual but not Jewish, an observer but not observant."

"What are you, really? What would you call yourself?"

"A rational mystic or a mystical rationalist: take your pick. It's all just me, and I am happy to own up to it. But, enough of this touchy-feely stuff, Des. It makes us geeks all squirmy and uncomfortable. Tell me what you are working on. You've piqued my interest with this detective game or whatever it is."

She waited for her laptop to finish booting up, then logged into the hotel wi-fi and navigated to her webmail account. There was a message from DB waiting at the top of the in-box.

> I decoded the DTMF strings from your MP3 file. The first one checks out as being a St. Thomas number (see below); it's not listed, but a search online turned up a document that pairs it with an address, which is right near the resort you called, which probably means it's the right one. The second one (see below) is a +44 number, in the UK, but the area code, 7924, would make it a mobile number in the Isle of Man, except it probably isn't, because those numbers are often used for international SIM cards, the kind that people who travel from country to country use, which makes sense for the Horvaths, except St. Thomas is part of the U.S. Virgin Islands, so you'd expect them to use a U.S. cell number. Go figure. Good luck.

Des was suddenly aware of Karl reading over her shoulder. "Oh, sorry," he said, and pulled back.

"No, that's all right. It's just a game. What the heck, we could try calling. It's next to nothing on SkypeOut. Want to see what happens when I call the UK number?"

"Sure, go ahead."

She dialed the number but got no answer and no forwarding to voice mail.

"I have an idea," he said. "If you would like to try something else." She nodded. "Okay, these numbers are sometimes sold in blocks to companies or people who buy a bunch of cards at once. What if we dial the next numbers in sequence? As you say, it doesn't cost but pennies on Skype, and what's the worse that can happen? We wake up some guy in London at his mistress's house?"

Des laughed as she dialed the next sequential number. After five rings, the call was answered, and a female voice said, "Yes? Hello?"

Des, caught off guard, hesitated, then said, "I was just looking for Donna."

"Who is this? What do you want? How did you get this number?" The woman sounded as if she had a head cold. In the background a man's deep, accented voice could be heard. "Just hang up, for heaven's sake, dear. That's what to do. Hang up." There was a click and the call was cut off.

"So, who do you think that was? Was that Donna Horvath?" Karl asked.

"How should I know?"

"Well, we should be able to make an educated guess. The Horvaths are pretty famous. Why not try YouTube? Surely they've done interviews. We can compare voices."

One of the first videos they found was a conference presentation with both Horvaths at the podium. "It's them, I think." Des said.

"I agree. Her voice has that same nasal quality, and his accented baritone is unmistakable. He was born in Hungary and never completely lost the accent. Looks like we've found the Horvaths."

"Only we still don't know where they are. We're stuck. It's not like you can trace a cell phone."

"Sure you can. Or at least it can be done. Even when it's not in use, a cell phone lets the nearest cell tower know it's there. In principle, you can locate it approximately regardless of where it is in the world. In practice it's something only an agency like the CIA can do. Or an insider or someone with inside connections in the industry."

"What about your friends at *HaMossad*? Didn't you say you knew people there?"

Karl felt trapped. He didn't want to blow his cover completely, yet he wanted to keep working with Des. "Not really, not exactly. Bini's father worked for *HaMossad*, as I said. And I have talked with some people there." It was a radically understated truth.

"Any chance that any of the people you have talked with would like to play an online game?"

"Oh, they do like to play games, all right, but I imagine they are busy with more important matters, like Israeli security." It was more understated truth. He was beginning to feel more comfortable with playing a role, but had to remind himself not to get too cocky. He knew he had a job to do, and it was not writing an article on game technology.

Des looked at him with her head cocked to one side, as if she didn't quite believe him, as if she could see right through him. She was thinking that there was more to Karl than met the eye.

12

MARKY WATCHED AS HIS COUSIN, still glued to the television, flipped channels, watching anything and everything he could find about the Tricorn disaster. The fact that there were more details and better information on the Web seemed to be of no interest to him; he wanted to see it, live, if possible. Marky remembered vividly a distant day, a day when he was sick and had stayed home from school, a September day spent watching the first footage of the Twin Towers attacks, repulsed and transfixed as the images repeated until finally he was sick and vomited on his green-striped pajamas. He had not really understood the human dimensions of what he watched; it had been like staring into a vortex, pulled in by an infinite spiral of dizzying chaos. He could not then look away, and now he saw how his cousin was also, in the fullest archaic sense of the word, fascinated. His cousin was spellbound, unable to stop looking, hungry and feeding some primitive drive, forever seeking yet another angle on the fumes and flames and the flooded and foam-soaked interiors of the power plant.

Marky, finally tiring of the video loops and text crawls, returned to the small desk on the other side of the hotel room and pored once more through the results of the final tests on the new communication protocols. Nothing had changed, everything checked out. Even with heavy packet losses and outrageously high error rates, the algorithms he had created would deliver a perfect, ungarbled message, a message encoded with his own strong encryption scheme, a code that virtually guaranteed that nobody short of the NSA itself could crack it in a reasonable timeframe. He still didn't understand what his subsystem was being used for, but it had been fun working out an entirely new communication mechanism and a novel encryption scheme tailored to take advantage of the math processing capability of the new generation of high powered graphics chips. Normally relegated to displaying digital images with realistic shadows and intricate surface textures, they were like little supercomputers tucked away inside game consoles, just waiting for some real work that would allow them to truly shine. It was all just number-crunching. Whether it was creating believable highlights for the cleavage of a sexy on-screen bimbo or encrypting and decrypting secret messages, it was just numbers, and numbers made sense to Marky in ways that people, even his dear cousin, did not.

"They're done. That's the last module," he announced, "the fallback scheme for network failure."

"You sure?" Barry asked without turning from the TV screen.

"Yeah. Spot on, as you like to say. I don't know why you say 'spot on.' What is the spot that you are on? But the routines are on it, the spot, right in the middle of it. Oh, right, now I understand. That's what it means, like a bull's-eye. I get it."

"Right. Just upload the damn routines to the distribution dropbox, Marky, so they get deployed."

"Okay," he said with reluctant obedience, "but don't you want to check them out yourself?"

"Naw, I trust you, which makes you a member of a club with two members. You are the only programmer I have ever known who writes code as tight as mine. Just drag and drop it to the engine."

"Barry, what's it for? What does it do? I mean, I know what it does, but why?"

"I told you, call me Baz. Anyway, it's simple. It's a heavy-duty, ultra-reliable messaging system for, well, industrial applications under conditions of high noise and low band-width. You know, where the connection is crap but only absolutely perfect communication can be accepted. The client in this case is very fussy."

Marky nodded but still seemed perplexed.

Baz turned back to the television screen. "I wish I could have seen it jump," he said. "Maybe someday they'll release surveillance videos from inside the plant. I'd like to be able to watch that behemoth spasm and buck as it died."

"Some people died, too, Baz. Now they are saying one of the engineers died in the hospital. And that Indian, well, I mean Native American. He's still in critical condition, the last I heard."

"So? Who knows how many people had their lives cut short by the pollution from that thing, to say nothing of what it and all its fellow monstrosities have been doing to the planet. Bad enough that you Americans use so much more than your share of the planet's resources, but to foul the nest with your shit, your garbage and your greenhouse gases."

"How do you think it happened?"

"Terrorists. Like the man at the hospital said before they cut him off and carted him away. They are hiding something, hiding much. Can't you tell? They know more than they let on, but they don't know enough. It was terrorists. You can count on that." He stabbed at the remote and lucked onto another early shot of the plant while it was still smoldering, another jittery, watery shot taken through a long telephoto lens.

Marky returned to his laptop and finished the process of incorporating his routines into the software system, the relatively small but complicated code that had been built in pieces by several scattered programmers. He had written more than one of the pieces, including the tiny bootstrap loader, the custom-built, single-purpose software that sucked the main body of a larger program off the Internet, installed it, and then ran it locally. It made no sense to him at the time, but he did just as he was asked. He worshiped his cousin, who was taller and smarter and more successful and had never poked fun at him the way so many of the scattered Collier-Adams clan had always done. Baz seemed to understand him, or at least tolerate him, and Marky would do anything for his cousin.

— —

The television in his room was on when Karl returned, the result of some unseen programming or a maid following hotel policy. He grabbed the remote from the nightstand and turned the TV off. The cable news channels were still filled with stories about the power plant, despite the fact that there was nothing new to report. It was a disease of the digital cable age, this need to fill the channels 24-by-7 with something, anything, a profit-driven electronic exaggeration of the gossip-filled village square of ancient times. It had become a self-perpetuating parade of pundits and people from the street passing on the latest opinion or rumor or interpretation. Or nothing.

Karl looked at his watch. It was late, almost late enough to call Israel. He needed to talk with Anat Dorfman, and he wanted to call Shira, but he also knew he should wait another hour or so before trying either of them. He reflexively reached for his cell phone, then slipped it back in its leather holster and fired up his computer instead. If Shira was logged into Skype it would mean she was up early, and it would be okay to call. To his delight, the glyph beside her name in his contact list glowed an inviting green. He was about to click on it when a message popped up:

Hi darling, you're up late.

"You're up early," he typed in reply. "Not that late here. Busy with the conference. Big after-dinner plenary. One of the heroes of the video game world, actor. Flashy keynote with lots of video, demos, no content. Usual."

"Miss you. Couldn't sleep. Bini's home from school, says he has a stomach bug. Has been up late all week. Saves homework until last minute. Always. Deadline driven like you."

"No way. I meet deadlines. Most. More or less. But I miss you. Conference is challenge."

"And other stuff? Institutional stuff?" It was their private code for the occasional work Karl had done for *HaMossad*.

She had never approved, but she tolerated it. Karl wondered how much she knew this time around.

"No. Just journalism," he typed, chewing on his lip over the lie. She knew about his extra assignment, of course, but this was the game he had to play out knowing that she would have to understand and would play along.

"I worry."

"Don't."

"Easy for you to say. You are not sitting here on the home front in Haifa while your darling plays cowboys and Indians in the New World. Who's winning?"

"It's null all at the moment, but your faithful Indian scout is following the trail."

"Be careful of getting caught in a box Kanyon," she wrote. Karl knew that the spelling was not accidental, that it was a thinly veiled reference to the Grand Kanyon, Israel's biggest shopping mall and the site of a terrorist attack when Karl was last involved with *HaMossad*. That told Karl just how worried she was. Time to change the subject.

"How's Shoshi?" he typed. "Can we go voice? Would love to hear you."

"No, she's still sleeping, right here beside me. Also, Bini— on the couch. Don't wake them. You should see Shoshi toddling around by pushing kitchen chairs. Better than a walker. Clever girl. Cute. Misses her Abba. Says 'Abba gone. Abba zoom zoom. Where Abba?' Misses you."

"Bini, too?"

"Yes, but he'd never admit it. Oh, there goes Shoshi, awake and hungry. Gotta go and be Mama." Despite good intentions by both Shira and Karl to keep the languages distinct by using only Hebrew with their daughter and saving the English for each other, Shoshi was already happily using a muddled mixture of languages, even throwing in the occasional Yiddish picked up almost miraculously from the neighbor woman who had been taking care of her some days while Shira put in extra time in her jewelry studio. Karl was Abba, but Shira was Mama. Day was *yom*, night was "nigh-nigh." Karl kept reassuring Shira that the baby would get it straightened out eventually; Shira continued to worry and tried to correct every English word that slipped into Shoshi's swiftly expanding vocabulary. Karl figured it wouldn't matter either way. Modern Hebrew was riddled with English imports, and he was always amazed whenever he was back in America how much Hebrew and Yiddish had entered everyday use. In a hundred years, who knows? Maybe the languages would be all but indistinguishable, just written in different alphabets. He laughed at the thought.

Anat was not in her office, but an encrypted email arrived from someone on her team with news that he had been waiting for. They had made progress on tracking the funding source by way of roundabout transfers of funds through banks in Australia, Japan, and Israel. There was also an attached file and a set of instructions.

13

DES PULLED HER COAT TIGHTER as she crossed the windy street. Karl hurried after and caught up with her just as she reached the revolving doors at the conference center.

"I think I found the Horvaths for you," he said.

"Oh, really? How did you do that?"

"I told you, I know people. I'll fill you in inside." He let her go through the next door swinging by, then caught the following one. He motioned her to the side where they could be out of the traffic flow and continued in a low voice. "They're here," he said. "Well, not exactly, but almost. Baltimore. The phone traced to a cell tower in Baltimore, Maryland, UK card notwithstanding. In St. Thomas they were already within the U.S., so they couldn't be tracked by their passports, but even private aircraft have to file flight plans into major airports. Seems a charter jet flew two passengers from St. Thomas to Baltimore-Washington airport right about the time the Horvaths were said to have left the island. I would guess the first call to their cell phone would have come during the flight, hence no connection. The number you called later and reached them on is no longer active but—ready for this?—the next number in sequence registered through the same network and the same cell tower last night."

"I thought your friends were too busy for Web games. Or weren't interested."

"I found a way to do it myself, a contact at one of the wireless carriers." He was lying, of course, winging it and hoping she wouldn't ask for more details, which he would have to manufacture on the spot. "I have a friend in Toronto who is with one of the national news dailies there. She's working on a Canadian angle." More lies, another plausible cover story. The woman was the *katsa* who should have been on the case from the start. "She thinks the Horvaths may be involved in more games than just online role playing. She would like to talk with you. You know, just informally. Are you willing? She wants to meet with you for an off-the-record interview. Is that okay? Tomorrow?"

"Tomorrow I'll be back at work. I don't think it's such a good idea to meet in Reston. Maybe it's not such a good idea to meet anywhere. It's only a Web game, I mean it's all probably a public relations stunt by the Horvaths. They are not exactly the shy and retiring types, from what I've learned about them. They might just want to boost the media profile of Life 2.0 with some juicy speculation about their whereabouts."

She paused for a moment, wrinkling her nose as she thought. "But now you have me wondering. Aren't you worried that this woman would be stealing your story? I thought you journalists were all about scooping the competition. If there really is a story that ties into the series you are working on with Dina, wouldn't you want to keep it to yourself?"

Karl was saved from having to answer by the arrival of Dina, who came bouncing through the door with a gaudy carry-bag, covered with the logos of half a dozen game publishers, over her shoulder. "Did I just hear my name? Are we talking about the Horvaths again?" she said.

"Yeah, more or less," Des answered half-heartedly.

"Listen, you two," Dina said with a wag of her finger. "I've been doing some research on Life 2.0 and the Horvaths for my articles. Seems things may be less than completely copacetic between them and their second-in-command, Truman Siebalt. It's a strange troika at the helm of Newlands Labs. He's a greeny, an eco-activist working for a company that consumes megawatts per minute keeping their vast server farms of power-hungry computers churning out imaginary life. They are first-generation Hungarian immigrants, hard-working business people out to make a mark and a buck. And there are rumors of financial irregularities, possibly involving Siebalt. Now, word on the street is that, after a series of takeovers and ambitious expansions, the Horvaths may be ready for another round of funding or looking for a buyer and finding the current business climate a little like an ice age."

"You're saying that Newlands might be in financial trouble?" Des put in. "I thought they were growing by leaps and bounds. The home page has that real-time counter reporting the current number of 'denizens' signed up. It ticks over so fast you can't follow it."

"True, but they lack a sustainable revenue model. They set service fees low to suck subscribers away from their competitors in order to build a critical mass of players, but it doesn't cover operating costs, and ad space in virtual space is still a hard sell. Until they bought out that online wholesale buying club, BigBuy, they didn't even have a dependable way of processing fees. And the virtual retailing that they hyped never took off. I hear they may be sucking fumes."

"I think you heard right," Karl interjected. "At least as far as I hear, too." He turned toward Des and shifted his position as if to partially block Dina. "So," he said quietly, "how about a meeting, tomorrow. I'll pick you up just outside the front gate at Scenaria, 18:00."

Dina, craning her neck to look over Karl's shoulder with an inquisitive expression. mouthed some words that Des could not quite figure out.

"Eighteen hundred, huh?" Des said to Karl. "You sound like the big boss. He always uses military time, too."

"It's the European influence on me. Even before I moved to Israel, I spent more time in Germany and Denmark and Spain and France than I did in Boston where I lived. So, you'll do it?"

Dina cleared her throat. "Er, I don't mean to be intruding on anything. Maybe I should buzz off?" she asked provocatively.

Des laughed. "It's business, the game stuff, for his research." She turned back to Karl. "Sure, I'll do it. Ring me on my mobile when you arrive tomorrow. I'll be working late, no doubt, paying penance for three days of conference cavorting."

"Okay!" Karl smiled, nodded, and backed away with a quick hand wave as he merged with the wash of conference goers just arriving. He immediately ducked down a side corridor and used the passcard he had lifted to let himself into the still unopened exhibit hall. As he passed an unattended table, he scooped up a badge with an exhibitor ribbon on it, quickly swapped it for his press badge, and strode purposely past booths being readied for the morning onslaught. He turned toward the Sony exhibit and tried to look busy until there was a moment when everyone at the nearby Aniromoto booth seemed to be occupied with something on one of the demo stations that were arranged in a hexagon around the perimeter. Karl walked over, bent down as if to tie his shoe, and reached around to the back of a server behind the nearest podium. He felt for the telltale rectangle of a USB jack and quickly slipped in a tiny device disguised as an ordinary thumb drive. He counted slowly to thirty while continuing to fuss with his shoe, then reached around to retrieve the device. He stood up to find a young Japanese woman in the black and violet Aniromoto corporate livery approaching him.

"Can I help you? Is there some problem?"

He held up the phony thumb drive. "I dropped my USB stick and couldn't find it. It must have bounced, because I found it hiding behind there." He pointed. "So, no problem. Thanks." He bowed slightly and she responded with a slightly deeper bow.

"Good. No problem," she said. "The exhibits open at ten. Do come back then and I can show you some of the tools that will be coming out later this year." She stood there, smiling, until Karl realized he had to respond, so he bowed and thanked her again, after which she bowed and thanked him, but still stood there, smiling, with hands folded. Karl backed away, doing little bows as if he were praying at the synagogue. Finally he turned and headed for the main entrance where the guard let him out without even a nod.

Karl took his time getting to the Press Room, where he set up his laptop in a quiet corner and logged in at the secure site just as he had before. After several minutes of skim-reading and deleting email, an IM arrived. The Trojan installed by the USB device had pinged the computers back at *HaMossad*, initiating the digital handshaking that would give backdoor access to everything Aniromoto had on its network. Karl's little breaking-and-entering job on the poorly secured conference demo computers had saved the Institute days, maybe even weeks of Internet skullduggery.

Karl smiled, then chastised himself for enjoying the spy games so much. Shira would not smile, but she might, deep down, be envious. Nevertheless, when he finally told her right out that he was still doing errands for Anat, he would get a tongue lashing, envy or not. And he knew he would tell her all about it, not on the phone or by email, but sometime soon over a bottle of California Zinfandel that he would bring back from his trip. He sometimes wondered if there were things she held back from him, but he knew there was nothing he kept from her. Strange, he thought, being married to your best friend. He often found himself the odd man out when men gathered and complained about their wives. It was not that Shira was perfect—she could be a bitch about his obsession for neatness, and she never considered his work to be as real or as important as hers—but to Karl it would have seemed disloyal had he joined in the bitch sessions.

He quickly sent a short, breezy email to her and one to Bini, then switched back to a secure client and typed a note to Anat Dorfman about the successful hack of the Aniromoto computers and about Des Allen agreeing to meet. He started to add a footnote about Des, about hoping that she was not in trouble, then thought better of it and backspaced over what he had written. Later perhaps, he thought, but not now. He closed the laptop, tucked it under his arm, and headed back for the hotel.

He was waiting for the up elevator when the geek who had been pestering Des emerged from another elevator, followed by someone Karl didn't recognize but who looked like he might be the guy's brother. Karl smiled and waved, but the two men hurried away in the opposite direction without responding. Karl, for whom Des's sometime stalker had never been of much interest, made a mental note to follow up with some inquiries about the man. What was the name? Karl thought. Marky, Marky Something-hyphen-Something. It'll come to me.

As he entered the arriving elevator, he suddenly came to the realization that he was getting protective of Des. Watch your step, he told himself, you still have a job to do.

14

HARRY'S CELL PHONE WAS RINGING. Des grabbed it and shoved it under the pillow. "Don't answer it. We have so little time. I haven't seen you in days."

"I'm on call. I have to. The Pentagon boys are trooping in first of next week, and we are still grappling with gremlins. I shouldn't have even come into town today. Plus, I think Dottie might be beginning to suspect something. Maybe we need to cool it. For awhile." He shoved his hand under the pillow and tried to grab the phone. Des jerked it away just as it stopped ringing. He grabbed her wrist and wrenched the phone from her with his other hand, twisting her finger in the process.

"Ouch. Don't pull that stuff on me, mister. I don't like…"

"Shut up. It was from DB. I have to call him back." Harry sat down on the edge of the bed and returned the call.

DB picked up on the first ring. "We found it," he said. "It's a rootkit, very clever little bugger, too. Nothing anybody has seen before. One of the kids in analytics found it. The Remote Services programmers worked out a signature for it, then created a detect-and-repair procedure, but there are still problems."

"Problems? Like what?"

"It keeps coming back. We've dubbed it Cat.9.kernel. We already merged it into the update batch and pushed it out over the Internet to our first-tier customer installations. You ready for this?"

"Don't keep me on hold here. Give me the story on this goddamned Cat.9.kernel rootkit."

"The infection rate is over 80 percent, at least here, but European customers seem to still be clean. Mostly." Silence on the line. "Harry, are you there?"

"Yeah. I 'm here. Any other good news?"

"I saved the best for last. At virtually every customer site that reports in as infected, our software pings back that they are re-infected within hours. It's in the systems and reinstalls itself somehow. Same here. We can't seem to eliminate it. We even took a clean box right from the factory, no connection to the network. Did a scan on it that came out clean. Just to be sure, we did a second, deep scan. The rootkit was there. We don't know what to do next."

Harry stared at his feet. "You say it keeps coming back? Okay. Pull the virus signature from the update batch and push the stripped batch back to every site that got the last update so that the warnings stop. I don't want sys admins around the globe panicking because they keep getting red-flag messages. This could kill us if it gets out. Okay?

"Then, I want you to assemble everyone who has touched this, anyone who knows anything, and I'll get them assigned to me as a special task force; just send me the list. Also, book the Vault and start doing clean room experiments. We need to get on top of this and fast.

"Tell me," Harry said, lowering his voice dramatically. "Does it do anything, this rootkit? Any sign of malicious behavior?"

"Nothing yet. It just sits there and occasionally pings an IP address that seems to be randomly generated, never the same. All that ever comes back is an error code. It's waiting for something."

"Take the damn thing apart. Figure out how it reinstalls itself. Then kill it. Dead."

"Will do. Bye."

Harry slipped the phone into his pocket, clasped both hands behind his head, and stared at the ceiling. Des looked at him with sympathy in her eyes. "It sounds serious. What are you going to do?" she asked.

"Don't know. Back to Virginia, I suppose. Can't decide whether to tell Talpa or not at this point. This is bloody Armageddon. This rootkit is all over the U.S. and half of Europe. It's in our systems. If I tell Talpa, there'll be hell to pay. If I don't, there'll still be hell to pay. Shit! I don't know what to do right now."

She reached out and put a hand on his shoulder. "Is there anything, any way I could help?"

Harry turned to her, one eyebrow raised. "I don't think so. You're not even supposed to know about this problem. And it's not exactly like you're one of our programming geniuses."

Des looked at him, torn between hurt and irritation at being dismissed so readily—and not for the first time—but she couldn't decide what to say. Harry broke the silence. "Okay, babe, here I go, back into the inferno." He finished buttoning his shirt, looked around for his shoes, then grabbed his jacket. "Tell your roommate thanks for scramming for awhile. It was great to be with you again, even just for a few hours. Sorry it ended this way."

Des didn't like the note of finality in his last sentence but decided to say nothing about it. "You know," she said, suddenly inspired and determined to show Harry that she could be helpful, "this rootkit thing, well, I think I know someone who might be able to help you. This guy is apparently some kind of programming genius, a game hacker. So I hear."

"We have our own geniuses. *Time* magazine said we employ the highest percentage of genuine certified geniuses of any technology company in America. We'll figure it out."

"But it sounded like it might be our own code. That could mean the culprits are some of our own geniuses. Can we really trust all the new hires. I hear we even have a kid from Pakistan working with the Systems Technology group. Can we trust him? I mean, really? Doesn't it make sense to get somebody from outside, like this guy I mentioned?"

"Maybe it would be logical, but there is a lot more at stake here. We have to contain this, or we go down. Scenaria will be dead, and we will all be out of a job." He kissed her on the top of her head, then left.

Des, stinging from Harry's brush-off and inspired by her own recent efforts tracking the Horvaths, decided to launch her own attack on the malware. She waited a few minutes to be sure Harry wasn't going to pop back in because he forgot something or had one more thing to say to her before she logged into the Scenaria intranet through her VPN access that gave her the same rights and facilities as if she were at the office. She searched for and eventually found a copy of a newly created detect-and-repair package on the Scenaria servers. She downloaded and ran the software, verifying that her laptop was infected. She selected the "repair" option, then rescanned: clean. Before closing the program, she checked the box labeled "Monitor for re-infection," then went back to answering email.

Suddenly she became aware that her phone was ringing. She looked around the room, trying to follow the sound. It was still in her purse. She dug it out. Too late.

She took it with her back to the desk and checked the call history, which listed the last call only as an unknown number. She assumed it was a wrong number and set the phone down on the desk in case it wasn't and the caller tried again. She was scrolling through her inbox when she noticed the Scenaria logo blinking in the system tray at the bottom of the screen. When she clicked, a red-rimmed message balloon popped up. "Infected with rootkit Cat.9.kernel. Click here to repair."

She smiled as she closed the machine. "Gotcha!" she declared as she picked up her keys and left the room. She took the elevator up three floors, then hesitated at the door opposite. She knew she was taking a game-changing chance and breaking a lot of rules, but it still felt like the move to make. She knocked assertively on the door.

"Yes?" said Marky Collier-Adams, leaning out from behind the door. "Oh, it's you, Destiny. What do you want?"

"Marky, I have a favor to ask of you."

"Oh, gee, I'd love to do something for you. What do you want?"

"It's programming."

"Hey, anything, just name it. I'm real good at programming."

"It looks like my laptop has somehow become infected with a rootkit. I can't seem to get rid of it. It doesn't seem to do much of anything, but it's there. Is this the sort of thing you might know something about? Could you, like, come down to my room and take a look at it? I don't want to go to my own people at the office, because they would blame me, and I could lose my job. I thought maybe you could help."

"Yeah, maybe. Uh, let me grab a disk and tell my cousin that I'm going out. Okay?"

She nodded and waited for him to return. He was slinging a backpack over his shoulder as he pulled the door closed behind him. "My cousin is busy," he said. "So I just left him. Is that okay?"

Des smiled. "Sure. Let's go check my machine."

— —

Marky seemed reluctant to enter her room, but once inside went straight for the laptop sitting on the desk.

"So, I'll boot off this disk and take a look around. It loads it's own little Linux kernel and has all these cool applets that let me look for things and inspect all the stuff on the disk. I can even run your system in a sandbox, so I can try, like, you know, anything. Safe, I mean. I'll show you."

He started typing a string of commands in quick succession, all the time talking about what he was doing, which meant little to Des. Suddenly he stopped and stared at the machine, his mouth working silently.

"What is it?" she asked. "Did you find something?"

"I wrote that," he said, pointing, leaving a fingerprint right in the middle of the laptop screen.

"Are you sure? How can you tell?"

"I have this memory. I remember everything I ever program." He pointed again, running his finger down through lines of code. "That. It's part of a bootstrap loader. It's just a handful of lines that can suck the whole rest of a big program from over the Internet."

"Like what kind of a big program?"

"Well, it could be…well, I am not supposed to talk about any of this. You know, I said I do some secret projects, you know. But it could, like, scan for channels, for indirect connections to special kinds of I/O routines, like. But I shouldn't say any of this, you know."

"It's okay, Marky. Remember, I'm in the security business myself. I'm cleared for top secret stuff. You can tell me what this is about." She smiled and nodded in an attempt to put him at ease.

"I suppose, maybe it's all right, but I would have to check first." Just then his phone rang. He pulled it from the holster at his hip. "Marquee Systems. How can I help you?" He turned to Des and said, "That's my company name, get it? Marky, Marquee." Into the phone he said, "Oh, sure, I just came down here to help a friend. I'll be right back up. Sorry."

He slid the phone back into the holster. "I'm sorry, Des. I'll have to help you later. Right now I need to help my cousin. I'm working on another project for him. I shouldn't have left just now."

"What about the rootkit, the virus?"

"Uh, yeah. I could take it out for you, but it would just come back in because, well, the Bluetooth backdoor. I suppose I could disable that, but, well, I shouldn't have told you about that. Anyway, I'll ask my cousin what I can do. But I have to go now." He hurriedly popped the CD from the drive in her computer, slipped it back into its envelope, and started to return it to his backpack.

"Is there any chance I could borrow that disk from you, Marky? Just for a day or two."

"Well, it's mostly all open-source stuff you can get yourself, free to download, for non-commercial purposes, of course."

"But I wouldn't know where to start. Couldn't I just borrow yours. I'll return it, I promise."

"Okay, I guess. My cousin has a copy, so I could just get his copy and copy that. Sure. Here." He handed her the disk and left without saying anything more, leaving her computer sitting with the cursor still blinking at the bottom of a block of code.

Des reached for her phone again and used the camera to take a picture of her laptop screen. Then she dialed Harry's number but changed her mind and called DB instead. "I've got what you guys are looking for. I even know the source."

DB could be heard typing in the background. "Uh, really? I mean that's great. I think I may have something for you, too, when you're back tomorrow."

"Okay, see you then."

She quickly finished packing up and headed for the lobby. She dropped off her key card at the front desk and turned to leave—Dina would be taking care of the tab when she checked out—but the clerk called her back. "Oh, Ms. Allen, there's a message for you, let me get it." He returned with a hotel envelope with "Destiny Allen" scribbled hastily on the front. Inside there was only a business card from Marquee Systems Services and on the back, a note: "I want to talk. Call me. Marky." She slipped the card into her jacket pocket and started toward the front exit, then changed her mind. She retrieved Marky's business card and was about to call him when she noticed there was a voice mail waiting for her. She listened: "Hi, it's me, Marky. I know what it does. My cousin…oh, wait. I gotta go, can't say why now, but call me." That was the end of the message. She called his number, but only got the Marquee Systems voicemail. She left a message for him with her own cell number, then headed out of the hotel.

She was just about to step out of the revolving door onto the sidewalk, when a man blocked her way, then entered behind her, forcing her to continue back around again with him in the same compartment.

"Don't think you're the only one who can use the fucking Internet. Back off while you still can, bitch!" he said, leaning so close that she could feel a spray of spittle on her ear as he snapped the last word. Then he was out of the door and into the crowd of recent arrivals milling in the lobby. Des struggled to keep her balance as the door continued around again, herding her and her suitcase out onto the street. Heart pounding, she turned to look back into the hotel, but there was no sign of the man. She hadn't even seen his face. He was just a deep voice in her ear. She reached up to wipe her ear with the sleeve of her jacket.

"Des?"

She jumped at the sound of the voice behind her. It was Karl.

"I didn't mean to scare you," he said. "Are you all right? You look petrified." He held out his arms toward her. Des hesitated for a moment but then found herself melting into his arms as if they were old friends.

"There's just too much going on, Karl. Stuff is blowing up at work and now someone just threatened me."

"You want to talk?"

She shook her head, then nodded. "Yes, I do want to talk, but not now. I think I just need to catch my breath. But thanks." She backed away from him and squeezed his hand. "Thanks." She turned and started walking toward the Metro station, leaving Karl staring after her.

She soon realized that she really did want to talk with someone. She fished her cell phone out of her purse without knowing who she wanted to call. She thought of Harry, then rejected the thought. She was just slipping her phone back into her purse when it rang. She didn't recognize the caller ID but answered the call anyway with a curt, "Yes?"

"Look, it's me, Blue Leader. My real name is Liam, Liam Osbourne, and I think we need to meet in person."

"I don't think so. In fact I am having second thoughts about this whole New Game business. It is getting a little too real when some of the other players start threatening me. I think it's time to call the whole thing off."

"You were threatened, they threatened you, too?"

"Well, someone told me to back off while I still could. Only it was said in a less than pleasant manner."

"So you figured it out, too?"

"Figure out what? What's to figure out. I told you, or at least the Blue Team on Life 2.0, everything I know about the

Horvaths returning to the mainland. That's it. What else am I supposed to figure out?"

"It's real. It's not a game."

"Yeah, yeah. I read the ad copy, too. Don't give me that bullshit all over again."

"No, I don't mean that. I mean it's real but not the way they want me... us to think it's real. There's more going on than you think."

"Don't try to scare me or hook me with any more of that 'it's real' stuff. I'm out. And don't keep calling me."

"Look, we have to meet in person. I'll show you what I have and then you decide. But we can't talk over the phone. I'm using a prepaid SIM card, but I still have this feeling like they know everything I do, everything we do. Please, meet me in a half hour at the Caribou Coffee place over on 15th Street Northwest, just a few blocks from the hotel, okay?" The call cut off.

Once again, Des felt like a fool, but she had to admit to herself that she was hooked. In for a penny, in for a pound, her mother always said. Des turned around and headed the other way, past the hotel again. At the coffee shop she ordered a mocha-cinno and waited. After an hour of watching everyone who entered, she felt like a fool and decided to give up and go home.

— —

Richard Talpa was just rolling out of his specially modified, hand-controlled BMW when Harry pulled up in the adjacent parking space.

"Talk about timing," Harry remarked.

"Not accidental," Talpa replied. "Fill me in on what the fuck is going on. Everything. Understand?"

Harry exhaled sharply, then outlined the latest findings. Talpa said nothing. "We'll catch it in the clean-room tests," Harry said, trying to sound confident.

Talpa shook his head vigorously. "Only if you go back to the 2.0 release of the software."

"I don't get it?"

"We had only 27,000 customers then. Who is going to hack into a system with such an inconsequential installed base. Now, with the lion's share of the market, we're a target. Why do you think all the hackers go for Windows and Microsoft Office? Everybody knows that the Mac OS 'Snow Leopard' release is just as peppered with security holes and exploit vulnerabilities, but who wants to work at cracking an eight percent market share when one clever hack can get you into hundreds of millions of machines. We are Microsoft, now. We're the giant all the Jacks are gunning for. What better hack than breaking into the security software itself. It's in Scenaria Shield, Harry. It's in there somewhere. I would look for vulnerabilities in the automatic system updater itself, if you haven't already."

"We're working on it," Harry lied.

"Good. Fix it quick." He swiveled sharply and headed up the ramp to his private entrance, leaving Harry standing in the windy lot.

15

ON HER FIRST DAY BACK in the office, Des had intended to meet with DB right away, but he was nowhere to be found. There was also a note waiting on her desk, a curt message from Sid Hoffman, her boss, to see him ASAP. She was more than a little anxious as she knocked on his office door. It would have been more like Sid to call her, or even to swing by her desk. She couldn't recall ever being "summoned" before. By temperament, she would have preferred to put it off as long as possible, but after a couple of hours of trying and failing to concentrate on the design for the new Human Resources page on the intranet, she had concluded that, if she was going to be fired, it was better to get it over with rather than wait until the very last minute of the day.

Sid had his back turned when she entered, the mottled back of his bald head looking like a satellite shot of Tatooine. He swiveled in his chair and gave her a broad and unexpected smile. "Knew you couldn't stay away for long. How was the conference? Learn anything?"

"More than you want to know."

He squeezed his nose, as he did habitually, as if he were about to sneeze. "Well, maybe you can put all that exciting new stuff to work in your new job."

"New job?" Her anxiety was beginning to border on panic. "You dumping me?"

"You think I would ever do a thing like that? No, this is a good move. You'll still be working for me, but on the customer-facing side. We want you to join the new Customer Experience Group as the Creative Lead. We want you to take charge of the look, the aesthetics of all the new interactive bells and whistles on the public website. We like what you've done with the internal site. Even Talpa has raved." He paused. "You don't look like someone who has just been handed a plum. It's a promotion, Des, and a raise, too. Although I wouldn't go out and buy that new condo just yet."

Des sat with her mouth pursed as if she were about to whistle. "I just wasn't expecting this. I had kinda gotten used to, you know, working on, with, well, the same people." She got up from her chair and started to pace.

Sid gestured at the chair, but didn't say anything. Des, looking chastened and anxious and feeling awkward beyond words, remained standing.

"I think we both know what this is really about," he started to say, "but it's not my place to say anything."

"Sid, you're my friend, too. Just say it." She had met Sid and Helen Hoffman while still in school and had been over to their house many times before applying for a job at Scenaria. She had not expected that she would someday be working for Sid.

"Yes, that, too," he said. "As a friend I'd say the cliché friend things about being careful, about married men, about office protocol, about all that conventional crap." He spoke evenly, dispassionately, but his eyes looked at her with something more than friendship. "As your boss, I will have to tell you that you are flirting with career catastrophe. You are not Harry's direct report, so, strictly speaking, neither of you is in direct violation of corporate rules, but that doesn't mean it couldn't end up costing you dearly once the relationship starts going south, which it will. I just don't want to see you hurt, in either your personal or your professional life. Think, Des, think."

"Look, his marriage is over," Des said, shaking her head as she finally took her seat. "It's already dead. They're just sitting shiva in the house where their marriage once lived. There's nothing between them. They don't even sleep together."

"That's…," he looked at her, searching for words, wrestling with syntax, thinking. He wanted to say: look, my marriage is dead, too, but I'm not having an affair. He wanted to be able to say bluntly that he and Helen didn't even sleep together. Maybe once or twice a year they would indulge in a kind of ceremonial passion, except passion would be too strong a word. Helen was busy with her clubs and her workouts and her day-spa visits and her therapy, her causes and her explanations and excuses, with little time left for her husband. She had lost interest in him and in what he was doing; she was uninterested in listening, only in being listened to. And he was in love with her. He didn't expect Des to understand; Helen certainly didn't, but it was true. After twenty-six years of marriage he was still head-over-heels for the woman he had met as a sophomore English major, a woman who was pulling further away from him with every passing year. Yet, he knew he would never betray her. Betrayal. It was such an old-fashioned word, like commitment, and his was an old-fashioned feeling. Still, there it was: he was married to her and in love with her. He realized that, even if he had been the one, even if the sweet, lovely Des had turned to him, he would have gently, ever, ever so gently, pushed her away.

Aloud, he said, simply, "That's tough." He looked down at the desk blotter as he shook his head, then raised his eyes to meet hers. "I can't tell you what to do. But I can't give my approval either. I just hope it works out for you, whatever."

"Then I guess I'm not being fired."

"Hardly. I just wanted you to know my concern. And to tell you to move your stuff across the hall to the new group."

Des stood as if to go, then leaned over the desk and boldly kissed his forehead. "I'll be okay." She straightened up and turned part way. "He's a bit like you, Sid, a real sweet guy."

Sid smiled and nodded the approval he couldn't speak.

As the door closed behind her, he reached for the phone, punched a speed code, then brought up a browser window and typed as he waited through four rings followed by his own voice on the message from his home answering machine.

"Hi, it's me," he said, after the beep. "I know by the time you get this you will just be back from therapy and the gym, but why don't you freshen up and put on something nice and let me take you out for dinner tonight. I've got us reservations for seven-thirty at a great new place." He switched ears and finished his one finger typing. "It's called Mediteranneo," he read from the screen, "regional ethnic fusion stuff, highly recommended. You'll love it." How could she refuse? he thought.

— —

By mid-afternoon, Des was already at her new desk and agonizing over the design for the proposed portal, searching for a fresh palette of colors and an ensemble of shapes that would let the world know that the all new Scenaria was also the old dependable one. Amidst the whir of computer fans, the wind-up of another soft whine was almost unnoticeable. Looking heavenward for inspiration, Des jumped at the sight of Richard Talpa peering over the top of her cubicle wall. "Don't do that!" she said.

He lowered his iBOT back onto four wheels and spun smartly around the corner.

"I'm sorry," he said. "Didn't want to break the flow if you were really into something."

"No, I'm sorry. I just never get used to the fact that you can, well, 'stand' with that thing."

"To tell the truth, neither can I. After decades of seeing the world from a butt-level point of view, it's nothing short of awesome to be able to look people in the eye. Or look over the top of a cubicle. It's such a damn shame they stopped making these things. How could they ever give up on technology as good as this? But they didn't stop making the Segway. No. Same technology, same inventor. Toys for the able-bodied, two-wheeled transport for lazy mall cops, and whirlwind tours of San Fran for rich Japanese tourists, but nothing for the poor paraplegics or legless vets.

"Sorry about that. I'll get down off my motorized soap-box. Anyway, you're here, and anything you were doing has been duly and irreparably interrupted, so I might as well ask you something."

"You didn't interrupt any flow," she said. "I was sitting stock still in the middle of a dry creek, stranded in a vast design desert. I still can't get used to the fact that aesthetics matter now that I'm working on the customer-facing side of the business."

"Think geek."

"What?"

"Think geek. Remember, our customers are corporate IT security honchos and sys admins. They're all nerds to the core, just like you and me. If it turns you on, it will work for your audience.

"But, back to my question. Any chance you could lend your input to a strategy meeting today? Word has it that you know something about what has been going on with, shall we say, internal security. So meeting, 18:00, my office, you in?"

"Do I have a choice?"

"Do you like it here?" He chuckled. "Of course you have a choice, but I really would like to have you involved. We need to plug all the holes in the dikes, and we need all the help we can get."

Des hesitated for a moment longer than she intended. "Yeah, sure. I'll be there."

"Great." He turned to go. "Remember, green," he added.

"What?"

"Security, safety. The color green makes people feel safe and secure. Just not a tree-hugging green. You know, not eco-chic—none of that crap." He zipped away down the corridor.

Des turned back to her monitor. "Damn," she said to the screen. "Now I have to work green in somehow. Why does everybody and their cousin think they are a designer?" She started tweaking a blue swatch on her screen, edging it gently toward a greener hue.

— —

Des arrived in Talpa's office a few minutes late. She had never seen more than a glimpse of the interior as she walked by on her way to meet with Harry, her only excuse for being in this end of the building. The office was more like a large conference room, with a massive mahogany table, a matching desk the size of Manhattan, a projector suspended from the ceiling facing a hidden screen above the credenza, and ample open space for maneuvering a wheelchair. Still, the room was crowded.

She knew most but not all the people, yet instantly felt that she did not belong. DB was the only other person there who was not from management. But not everyone from top management was present. Harry was there but Sid was not, and Corky Archibald, VP of sales, was also missing. It was a strange mix, and Des was puzzling over the criteria for the guest list when Richard Talpa wheeled out from behind his desk and started talking.

"Okay, I know it's the end of the day, so let's get started. You all know why we are here. You are the ones who have been closest to this shit."

Des scanned the room before raising her hand like a schoolgirl. "I don't know why we are here. I look around, and everyone else is either technical or top management. I'm in Creative, at least since this morning. What gives?"

"Maybe you should tell us," Talpa said. "Word has it that you know something about this mess and may be holding out on us. That true?"

Her heart started pounding but she steadied her voice. "This is about the crisis Harry and DB have been working on, isn't it?"

"Well, except neither of them should have said anything to you or to anyone else not properly cleared or with a need to know."

"They didn't," she said, for some reason deciding to cover for both of them. "I figured it out all on my own. No help from anyone."

"Really? And what exactly did you figure out on your own, Ms. Allen?" He maneuvered his chair around to face her directly. As if on cue, the others in the room, DB excepted, turned to face her. She was surrounded by looks of expectation and accusation. DB was studying his hands.

Des took a deep breath. "I get it, this isn't a strategy meeting, this is an inquisition, and I'm the New Christian." There were puzzled looks around the room, but Des ignored them.

"Talk to us," Talpa said, tapping the arm of his chair for emphasis.

Suddenly emboldened by having her back against the wall, she said simply, "You talk to me." She paused, trying to steady her voice, though she was on the edge of having the shakes. "You talk to me or the next time I talk to you maybe there should be lawyers present." It was a major escalation, she knew, but one she felt was appropriate.

Talpa's expression softened. "Look, we are not accusing you of anything except knowing something. If you can help us, please do. You work for the same company as everyone in this room does."

"You first. I will tell you what I know, but not until you bring me up to speed with the rest of you all. I don't want to be the only one in the room who is not in on the joke."

DB shifted in his chair and started to stand. Talpa looked toward him and suddenly smiled as if he had just gotten an inspiration. "Okay. DB, go ahead. You brief Ms. Allen on what has been going on." Des recognized it as a clever ploy: let the one lowest on the totem pole do the talking, the one least likely to know any of the most damaging inside information. Talpa was good at playing games, and Des began to wonder whether he was always playing, always making moves in a game.

DB, clearly uncomfortable with being put on the spot, hesitated. "I, well, we, I mean," he started to stammer, then just left his mouth open.

Harry stepped in. "Look, DB and I have been working closely together. I can update Des." Now it was Talpa's turn to be uncomfortable. "I'll just speak for DB, if that's okay with the rest of you."

Harry didn't say anything that Des didn't already know or hadn't at least surmised, but the briefing did legitimize the inside knowledge she did already have from Harry's many off-the-record chats with her. When he finished, everyone turned toward her, once more expectantly.

"Well, I do have something new that might be of use." She pulled a disk from her jacket pocket. "This is a system utility disk filled with hacker tools. I was going to pass it on to DB. It confirmed what I had already determined, that my laptop was infected with the Cat.9.kernel rootkit. Supposedly, what's on here can be used to remove the virus completely and permanently. I don't know how to do either, but I suspect your whiz kids in Systems Tech will be able to puzzle it out. And I have a screen shot that shows a piece of the code and maybe the commands that were used to find it. There's a JPEG on this SD card," she said, pulling the tiny card from her phone.

DB reached for the disk and card, but Talpa grabbed them first and handed them off to Vern Jeffers, head of the Systems Technologies group, the innermost circle of Scenaria's many technical circles. "Get your people working on this, stat," he said. Vern got up to leave, but paused at the door. "Don't worry, Vern," Talpa said. "We'll keep you in the loop. We always do."

When the door closed behind Vern, Talpa continued. "There's more, isn't there? Where the hell did you get that disk, and who have you been talking to?"

Des nodded. "Yes, there's more. I think I know who is responsible, or at least I know one of the people who wrote some of the code. But I don't think he knew what he was getting into, and he only had a small piece of the action. He's just some nerdy little guy who did some 'secret' contract work. He's harmless."

"Harmless my bedsore-covered ass," Talpa barked, as he wheeled over in front of Des. "That so-called 'contract work' could be the undoing of this company and quite possibly most of our customers. That's billions of dollars of harm. Who is this creep?" he said, reaching for the iPhone in a holster attached to his chair. "I know people in the FBI who will bring him in on my phone call."

Harry raised his eyebrows. "Do you really think that would be wise at this point? I mean, wouldn't it be better if we used our own corporate security people to get to him first, before the authorities drag him off and the media have a heyday?"

"These are buddies of mine, from Nam. They'll give us first crack. So who is this hacker creep, Ms. Allen."

Des felt trapped. She looked first to DB and then to Harry for a sign. Harry pretended he didn't notice, and DB shrugged his shoulders. "You promise you aren't going to hurt this guy. I mean he really had no idea who he was working for or what he was doing." No one moved or said anything. "Okay, I guess I have to tell now or it will be later in court or something and I'll be an accessory, right?"

"You said it, not me," Talpa said quietly, while drilling her with his dark eyes.

"His name is Marky, Marky something. I don't remember his last name right now. He was at the GAME conference. I asked him to help with my laptop after I found out it was infected."

Harry looked at her with something between pity and contempt. "That's a breach of security. I would have thought you would know better. You let a hacker have at your computer? Your company-issued laptop? Unbelievable."

She looked pleadingly at Harry, but he turned away. She suddenly realized how much better he was at playing games, and she began to wonder how much of their relationship was a game.

DB stood up and waddled over to her. "It was my, my idea," he stammered. "I, I authorized it and told her to try it. I thought it might, might get results. And it did. She didn't break any rules and neither, neither did I. Remember, I was given,...I had free rein on this project. You know that." He looked straight at Harry, who started to rise out of his seat but then sat back down. "I saw this guy when I was over at the conference to, to talk with Des." Des gave him a look that he ignored. "His name is Collier-Adams."

Talpa jerked in his chair. "What's his name again?"

"Collier-Adams. You know him?"

"No, I just misheard what you said. Thanks. Okay, okay. Let's bring the guy in. I'll call my buddies. You all give Vern and his Einsteins all the help you can give. And people, keep this quiet. I am sure that I don't need to belabor how critical it is that none of this goes any further than this room. Not a peep to anyone else, not outside and not even inside the company. Not one word. Now, go get back to work."

The room cleared except for Harry, who hung back after Talpa signaled him. Talpa looked like he was on the edge of exploding. "Regardless of what we get from this little shit, we are going to be hammered. This will eventually come out, and it will hurt us big time."

"Maybe we can spin it right: 'Software security firm secretly saves the world from spreading scourge.' You know, that sort of shit."

Talpa looked skeptical. "Maybe. But first we have to save ourselves from the scourge, the scourge that we ourselves have been spreading. I'm putting you in with Vern's people for the time being. Phil Cummings can honcho the network for awhile."

"But..."

"No buts. I know you don't like Vern, and I know this might feel like a demotion to you, but I need eyes and ears. I need somebody inside that vault who will keep me posted. I would prefer to have you in charge and reporting directly to me, but that way nobody would ever say anything in your presence. If I send you in to assist, you're just one of the gang. I want to know what that gang is up to, minute by minute, what they find and what they speculate about. So, get in there and do what you can."

Talpa dismissed Harry with a wave of his hand, then went over to his desk. From the top drawer he pulled a beat-up old cell phone and a small notebook. He flipped through the book, found a number, then slid open the cell phone and sent off a text message. They would get back to him, in their own time and in their own way. In the meantime, he had his own research to do, and he couldn't do it on the company computers. In any case, Collier-Adams would not be in the company files.

Talpa told his assistant that he was going home early, then headed for the parking lot.

— —

DB caught up with Des as she turned the corner heading for her new cubicle. "I hope, I just wanted to say," he started.

"You don't have to say anything. And I was going to give you the disk and tell you in any case, so it's no biggy. But thanks for covering for me. I appreciate what you did."

"I have something else to say."

"Can it wait, DB? I really need to get out of here. To-morrow. We'll talk tomorrow." She hurried away to her desk, retrieved her purse from the drawer, and left the building.

She was all the way to her apartment before she suddenly remembered she was supposed to have met Karl outside the gate. At six. The meeting with Talpa had erased it from her mind. She checked her phone and found that she had missed two calls from Karl because her cell phone had been in her purse back at her desk. She thought of trying to call him, but it was now almost two hours later. In the morning would be good enough, she thought. He would understand. She dialed Harry's number but hung up before it rang through. Dina would be busy with LG. It was one of those times when she wanted so badly to just talk to someone she could trust.

She scrolled down through her contacts until she got to a number in Glendale. She listened through seven rings and was about to give up when someone finally picked up on the other end.

"Mom? It's me."

16

IT WAS WELL PAST MIDNIGHT when Harry finally pulled into the circular drive in front of his home in Columbia, Maryland. He didn't bother to put the car away because he didn't want to risk awakening the twins, whose bedroom overlooked the triple garage, and because he knew he would be leaving again in a very few hours. The house was what he would uncharitably label as a MacMansion, an oversized theme-and-variation on the neighboring houses in the development. It had a faux brick central façade instead of the composition stone of the one on its left or the stucco on its right; the sidelights on the front door were frosted instead of leaded glass; there was a hexagonal window above the door; and there were three dormers instead of two on the top floor; but it was the same house, nonetheless. He would have preferred a mature neighborhood and a smaller, older house more like the one they had left behind when they moved down from Pennsylvania, but Dottie had insisted on something spacious and more in keeping with what she saw as their rising status.

The house was quiet, but as he headed toward the kitchen for a glass of water, Harry noticed a light still on in the study. When he pushed the door ajar, Dottie, eyes red with fatigue, looked over at him from the computer desk.

"You didn't need to wait up for me, you know," he said.

"And you didn't need to come home so late," she snapped back. "You could have spent the night at the office again. Or wherever you've been sleeping lately."

Harry stiffened. "You know we've got this thing coming up with the Defense people, and I have been coping with crisis and one near disaster after another for days."

"But, still, with plenty of time to slip away to make it downtown for lunch at the Meredith, right? Who is she? Tell me. Nina didn't recognize her, not part of our circle of mutual acquaintances, no definitely not. How old is she? Has she finished college yet?"

Harry opened his mouth, closed it, then adopted a puzzled expression. "Oh, right. Now I know what you're talking about. She's, ah, this woman who works in the Web group at the office. I had to coordinate something with her on this project, and she was tied up at a conference in town, so I swung by to save her a trip out to Reston. We grabbed a bite as she filled me in on the...the specs."

"Right, sure, of course. And then you went up to her room, no doubt to retrieve some documents or something."

"I really don't know..."

"Don't bullshit me, Harry Krebber. Nina's charity get-together ran long. She saw you go up in the elevator and not come back down. A redhead, right? Rather pretty, too, according to Nina. You always did have a weakness for red hair, didn't you. Perhaps I should have started dyeing mine.

Maybe with that slightly streaky look that is so fashionable these days. I mean, among college girls, you know. I could, maybe, put it in a ponytail and take to wearing low-slung jeans that leave my navel exposed. Would that do it for you, Harry? Would it? No, I suppose not. My tits sag too much and the makeup doesn't completely hide the dark circles under my eyes from staying up with sick kids and waiting for my goddamned husband to finish fucking his college girl and come home to his wife and family." She hit the desk with the flat of her hand, knocking over a near-empty glass and sending dark liquid splashing across the scattered papers.

"Oh, shit!" she said, as she wiped ineffectually at it with her bare hands. "Shit, shit, shit."

Harry pulled a wad of tissues from the box on the coffee table and crossed over to help clean up the spill. "You've been drinking," he said.

"Diet Coke. So I don't get too fat. That way I can still compete with some skinny, redheaded teenager. Diet Coke."

"Smells like more than Coke to me."

"Don't pull that superior shit on me, you slime. Rum and Coke, okay? Isn't that what the college kids drink these days? Or, no, that was back in our youth. Nowadays it's hard lemonade or something. It is just so hard to keep up with these young people and their fads. But then, you probably don't find it so difficult. You have your very own personal trainer as a guide to the youth culture. What kind of sex are the young women of today into, Harry Krebber? Tell me, how do they like it with their middle-aged lovers?"

He said nothing.

"Stop with the goddamned cleaning up, Harry. Stop for a minute and answer me. How does she like it? Huh? Any, any fucking way, she's the lucky one, isn't she, because there's nothing left for me, the wife, who sits at home with her twins, one throwing up and the other throwing tantrums, and gets nothing but a late night kiss on the forehead on the rare nights when her husband—her husband, goddamnit—manages to make it all the way home."

Harry tossed the wet wad of tissues in the wastebasket beside the desk and said nothing.

"Not even a word for the wife? Plenty of pillow talk with the exciting young lover, I would bet. Well, you had better start talking, Harry Krebber, while I am still Dottie Krebber, because if I go back to being Dorothy Toby Roth, you are going to learn why our friends back in high school used to joke about the Wrath of Roth. You will pay, Harry, and you will pay dearly and long.

"So, end it. Now! And then start thinking fast of how you are going to start repairing the damage you've done, because there's a lot of damage to repair."

Harry looked around the room, as if scanning for an exit. "It's not that simple, Dottie."

"Oh, it's that simple, trust me. It's over. You fill in the blank. You can pick who, but you don't get to pick when. Either way, you lose, Harry, so don't stand there scheming or thinking you can figure a way to win. This is not some boardroom meeting about marketplace strategy. But pick wisely, Harry, and you don't lose the house and the twins and our friends and our place at the Temple for the High Holy Days—and your wife. Got it?"

"Dottie, please, it's not quite what you think. First of all, Des is not in college, she's twenty-eight, she's..."

"Twenty-fucking-eight! Imagine that! Do you think your forty-something wife gives a shit whether she is twenty-eight or eighteen? I don't want to know anything about your little tart or how it happened or what got into you in the first place."

"Dottie, please, allow me a word or two. You want answers that I can't give now, except to say I don't want to leave you, I don't want a divorce. Neither my father nor my mother ever recovered from theirs. You know the story. She drank herself to death, and he worked himself to death, and it didn't take either of them too many years. I still love you, Dottie. I want to work this out."

She laughed explosively, then started coughing. "I don't believe you, but if you believe it yourself, then get rid of her, because if you don't, I will do it for you. I will find a way, I'll arrange something. I am that hurt and that angry. You think you learned about the Wrath of Roth when you snuck a date with that little shiksa slut in college? Well, you haven't seen anything yet. I should have learned then. It's probably in your genes. Everyone knew that your father slept around, and my mother and her friends cheered when he was finally dumped. What is it with you Krebber men? Or maybe that's the wrong question. What is it with you men? Why can't you understand loyalty or faithfulness or even a simple contract, for God's sake. We signed our *ketubah* with practically everyone we knew as witnesses. I thought Jewish men were supposed to be good at business. You'd think they would understand and be able to honor a simple contract."

"Dottie, sit down for a minute and let's talk."

"Maybe, maybe, after it's over, after it's been over for a good while, we can think about getting into therapy or talking to the Rabbi or doing something to get where we can at least have an authentic conversation again, but right now I don't want to know anything more about you or your mid-life mess or your redhead. I just want her out of your life. Now. Do you hear?"

Harry nodded.

"You can call her right now, then, if you want, for all I care. I'm going to bed. I put sheets and a blanket on the sofa there for you. Make sure you get up early enough and straighten up before the twins come down. That's usually around six, in case you don't remember from the days when you used to come home nights."

She turned out the desk lamp and left Harry standing in semi-darkness. He looked at his watch in the sliver of light from the hallway, shook his head, and started opening out the sleep-sofa. Just before he stretched out, he punched at the sofa arm so hard that a wave of pain shot all the way to his shoulder. "Fuck!" he said, then turned his back to the door and slowed his breathing, concentrating, letting go of the pain in his hand and the hollow in his stomach, distancing himself from himself until there was only the dark and the silence and the troubled sleep of exhaustion.

17

"THANKS FOR MEETING for breakfast," Karl said, putting down his coffee mug and leaning forward to better hear Des across the table. The acoustics in the crowded café were not good, and the room echoed with a cacophony of conversations and commercial tableware clanging on ironstone plates.

"I am sorry about last night," Des said. "I just forgot. Something came up, and I missed your calls."

"That's all right. As it turns out I was just calling you to let you know that the meeting was off. My, uh, colleague got delayed in Canada and couldn't make it anyway, so everything is fine."

"No, everything is not fine, not with me it isn't. I don't even know whether I should be talking with you or not."

"You mean about the Horvaths and the game?"

"No. Yes. That, but also something else completely. There is just too much going on." She hovered on the edge of losing it.

"Go ahead. You can talk with me. You can trust me."

"Can I? Who am I talking with? Who are you, Karl Lustig? And what are you doing here. This whole journalism thing is beginning to sound more and more like a ruse. Supposedly you are working with Dina, but you make a beeline for me and hardly have a moment for her. She feels like she is doing both sides of the work on the series."

Karl almost squirmed with discomfort but tried to just look like he was listening with interest.

A long silence passed before she spoke again. "You're with *HaMossad*, aren't you? You're an agent, right?"

"No, I am not an agent."

"You sound like you mean it, but I would assume they train you to do that, to sound sincere."

"No one trained me to do anything, literally. I have spent my whole life just going ahead and doing things that I was never trained to do. In the final analysis I'm just a guy, like any other guy. Well, except I'm a better listener than most. That is something I was trained for—first as a consultant and then as a sort-of journalist. And, of course, being married to Shira keeps me in training. So go ahead."

Des was still hesitant, but with Karl's nodding encouragement, she reluctantly gave him an outline of the crisis at Scenaria without dwelling on details.

Karl nodded. "So, their software is compromised, and they have been inadvertently spreading a Trojan or virus into all the systems they are supposed to be protecting. That includes us."

"What do you mean us?"

"I mean us, Israel. Scenaria dominates the market in Israel and that includes within the government. They virtually own security there. The whole damned country could be vulnerable."

"Does this have anything to do with the Horvaths and their whereabouts?"

"No, probably not. Who knows." He hesitated, then continued, "In any case, I think the woman from Canada still wants to talk directly with you," he said, trying to make it sound as if he was not involved.

"I don't believe you. You know something that you are not telling me."

"I know a lot of things that I am not telling you, one picks up a lot of things over six decades, but if you mean that I am withholding information about the Horvaths or Scenaria software because I'm a spy or something, well, that's just ridiculous. Look at me. Do I look like a spy to you?"

"Yes, because you don't."

"Now there's logic. I look like a spy because I don't look like a spy."

"You know what I mean."

"Not exactly. But, look, just meet with this woman on the weekend. She's the real thing. Tell her what you know and maybe she can help you. Okay?"

"Okay." She pushed her food away. "I better get going."

"Go ahead. I'll get the check."

After Des left, Karl ordered a refill on his coffee and booted up his laptop. Once he was through the usual detours to get a secure connection, he updated Anat in Tel Aviv. He received an almost instant reply to his email. The *katsa* who was supposed to fly down from Toronto to meet with Des had been detained at the airport by U.S. Customs and Border Protection. Her cover blown, she had managed to slip away and had gone to ground, leaving the Institute trying to improvise another angle. Anat's ambivalence came through clearly in the email. She was worried about Karl and about his abilities, but she still needed to depend on him for a while longer.

Karl replied that he would stay on the job. What he didn't say was that he was now not so much worried for himself as for Des. Switching back to his regular webmail account, he composed a short note to Shira. As he read through it before clicking on "Send," he realized that it said nothing, that the important things were unsaid. He sent it anyway.

— —

Saturday dawned clear and crisp, almost spring-like. Karl had just stepped out of the shower after returning from a morning run up in Rock Creek Park when he found two text messages from Des waiting on his phone. The first read:

mtg w ur canadian 2day 1 hr footbridge in md

The second apologized and named a suburban Maryland park that Karl had never heard of. Whoever Des thought she was meeting with, it was obviously not the agent from Canada. He looked at the time stamp on the messages, then checked his watch and shifted into high gear. He tried to call Des on her cell phone as he hurriedly dressed. No answer. He muttered a curse, tried again without success, then swore out loud. He would have to track her down. His first thought was to search online to figure out where the rendezvous was to be, but he realized that he didn't have enough details or enough time. He threw on his jacket and ran down the four flights of stairs to the lobby. Trying to act the part of a casual tourist confused about where he was supposed to meet up with his hiking companions, he watched as the concierge opened out a big area map and pointed out several places that might fit the somewhat vague description. Ignoring the protests from the young woman, Karl grabbed the map and rushed out of the hotel.

At the bell stand outside, he looked around for an attendant, then boldly reached across and grabbed his keys from the board where they hung. He trotted down the ramp to the parking garage where he located his nondescript rental car by using the button on the key fob to get the lights to flash. Once in the car, he paused long enough to unlock the glove compartment with the key that he had separated from the ignition key before turning his car over to the parking attendant. He removed the Glock from where it was stashed under the owner's manual and unwrapped it, gave it a quick once over, and then tucked it into the back of his pants. The boxy shape pressing against the small of his back was irritating but at the same time strangely comforting.

He had settled on a simple search algorithm: start with the nearest of the three candidate sites, then move to the next farther one until he found Des or ran out of options. The thought of the last sent a shudder through him.

He accidentally squealed the tires as he swung out of the parking garage, then forced himself to slow down in order not to attract attention. Traffic was heavy getting out of DC, and it was almost ten past the hour when Karl located the first parking area with access to the footpath he was looking for. He parked rather sloppily and started at a trot down the path. Early sun cast long shadows across the north-trending trail, and the light strobed in his eyes as he jogged along. He had not gone more than a hundred meters before the trail turned toward the west, giving him a glimpse through the trees of two women ahead both running at top speed: one, a young woman in jeans and a Braves jacket, the other, Des, in the lead by only a few meters. Pushing himself as hard as he could, Karl managed to keep pace well enough not to lose sight of them but was unable to close the gap. Through the trees, he could see a footbridge crossing the stream in the near distance.

Panting, Karl finally rounded the curve onto the footbridge just as the woman caught up with Des. He shouted, "Des!" then pulled the handgun from his waistband. The woman, her back still to Karl, had grabbed Des with one hand and was reaching with the other into her jacket. "Hold it right there, or I'll shoot!" he barked. Just as the woman turned to face Karl, Des hip-checked her against the railing and jerked free the arm being held. Thrown suddenly off balance, the woman struggled to right herself, but only succeeded in shifting her weight farther out over the low wooden railing. She tumbled over and silently dropped into the icy stream far below, making a splash barely audible above the rush of water.

Karl ran to Des and the two of them looked over the side but could see nothing in the dark water below. "Oh, my God, Karl. My God!" She looked at him, pleading.

"Stay here!" he said. He scrambled down the steep bank, gun at the ready. Water sloshed over the rock-strewn stream bed and eddied around small boulders rounded by erosion. At first, he could barely see anything in the shadows at the bottom of the deep gully, then he spotted the bright figurehead on the woman's jacket. She was sprawled partially on the bank, face down, her head oddly twisted, with cloudy water swirling around her short hair. Karl felt for a pulse but found none. He did a hurried search through her jacket and the small bag slung over her shoulder, but there was nothing, no identification, not even a lipstick or tissues. Among the weeds just beyond her outstretched arm, he spotted her pistol. He recognized it as a Beretta, a favorite among his colleagues in *HaMossad*. He hesitated, then decided to pocket it.

"She was a professional—or trying to act like one," he said to Des as he climbed back up to the bridge.

"Is she...?"

"Yeah. Looks like a broken neck."

"Oh, God. I don't even know who she was. I didn't mean to. I just was trying to get away. I thought she was the reporter you said I was supposed to meet, then she grabbed me, but I got away. I think she wanted to kill me. And now..."

"I'm not so sure. If she was a pro and had wanted to kill you, you would have most likely been dead before I arrived. No, I think she wanted something from you or to intimidate you. Anyway, it's all right. Everything is going to be all right," he said as he put his arms around her.

"Shouldn't we call the police or something?"

"No. Not the police. We need to get out of here." He walked quickly back to the bank and surveyed where he had climbed down and back up. It was unlikely they would be able to get a print from the smears in the grass and mud, and it might be days before the body was found—unless someone went looking for it. "Just come on, back to the car," he said. "We need to get out of here." He scraped the traces of mud off his shoes in the sandy path before taking her arm and walking slowly back across the bridge, stopping occasionally to smear a footprint that might be his or Des. The dusty footpath was such a jumble of prints that he assumed it would reveal nothing. As they walked, slowly, arm-in-arm, back to the parking area, Karl was preoccupied with the realization of what the woman's attempt implied. They were compromised. Someone not only knew that they were operating in-country, but knew their next move and could exploit it. Someone had known there was an agent stopped at the border and was able to pretend to be her. There was a leak or a tap or a double agent somewhere in the Institute!

At the parking lot, Karl absent-mindedly opened the passenger-side door of his own car for Des, then slipped in behind the wheel, looked over at her, and drew her close.

Des was still shaking as she rested her head against his chest and let her heartbeat slow to match his. "Who are you, Karl Lustig? Really?"

"What you see is what you get. Well, mostly. As I said, I am a sort of journalist, a nerdy writer. I do live in Haifa and commute a few times a year to Boston. I…"

"That's not what I mean, and you know it. What is going on? Nerdy writers don't carry handguns. What are you doing for *HaMossad*?"

Karl took a deep breath and slowly exhaled. "You have to understand. I want to tell you everything, but that is just not possible."

She pulled herself back from him and looked him in the eyes. "Someone just tried to kill me, and you tell me you can't say what is going on. Fuck it, Karl. If you don't tell me everything, I'll go to the police or the press with what I do have, and then where will you be? Israel may be an ally, but last I heard we have at least one Israeli spy still doing time in a federal prison."

"Israel is the good guys, remember. That's me. You wouldn't do that, not to me. You don't really want to send me to prison. You're not the type to do that."

"Want to bet? Would you wager whether you ever see your family again on that diagnosis? Remember, I just pushed a woman off a bridge. I don't know anymore what I'm capable of, but it's a lot more than I would have thought. Maybe I've already spent too much time in online games."

"You only pushed her because you thought I was going to shoot her, which I was. You thought you were saving me as much as saving yourself. You're not going to do anything to hurt me."

She chewed her lip. "Did you,...did you ever kill anybody?"

Karl took a slow, deep breath, exhaled, and said, "Yes, once." He could still picture the poorly lit basement; he could see his hands in front of him as he took aim and fired; and he could hear the ringing in his ears afterwards as he watched the figure slowly slump to the floor, a dark circle beginning to spread over the front of the man's sweatshirt. And Karl could still see Lev Novikov checking for a pulse and turning toward him with a look of grim finality. "It had been..." Karl took another breath as he struggled for words. "Necessary."

There was a long silence that neither dared to break, although questions and stories hung in the air like a morning fog waiting to be dissolved by the sun. Des looked at Karl with her jaw set. Her chin started to quiver, and then she began to cry. "Oh, Karl. Karl, I..."

"Please don't say anything. Please. I'll tell you. Just listen."

"You don't have to."

"I know. And I shouldn't. It is probably treason, although, shit, I don't know. I just know I want to tell you something about what is going on, what you are mixed up in." He looked around nervously.

"A little over a year ago, the Tokyo police caught a young man who was using a cell phone to buy electronic gear through accounts that weren't his. In Japan, see, there are already lots of places where you can use a cell phone like a swipe-free credit card. Anyway, he was Israeli and gets deported. He contacts *HaMossad*. Back home he tries to work a deal: information for probation. So he starts telling about some of his other programming jobs. He has no compunctions about ratting on his former employer, in part because they dumped him after he failed to deliver some code on schedule. He tells a tale of global conspiracy and vaguely ominous consequences that nobody quite buys, but there is enough small stuff there that checks out, so he walks. Then he disappears."

"Disappears, as in elsewhere, or as in dead?

"No one knows for sure, but we think he's dead because he was already free to go, and then he just vanishes without taking any of his stuff from his apartment. So, my *Mossad* pals get their hands on his computer. Among other things, they find emails referring to Scenaria and software attributed to Aniromoto, plus, he is registered for GAME IX and—are you ready for this?—when they trawl through names in his contact list, they find one that cross matches with both the conference registration and the Scenaria website: that's you. The entry in his contact list was packed with tidbits about you."

"Really? What was this guy's name?"

"Feldersmann, Elliot Feldersmann."

"Wait. I knew an Elliot Feldersmann once, in school, at Phillips Andover: real nerdy guy, kept trying to hit on me."

"Well, maybe he was still trying to hit on you—or trying to meet with you for some reason. He had your work phone, cell phone, home address, a photo pulled off the Web, the works."

"But what's the deal? What is this all about?"

"Well, the techies at the Institute began deconstructing what was on the disk drive, and that's when the turd started hitting the turbine. Not only is there proprietary stuff from several companies in Japan, their copyright claims still embedded in the code, but there is also this stuff that, if it worked, would use any communication channel it happened to be connected to in order to find other communication channels in other forms, looking for and linking up with other versions of itself."

"You said, if it worked."

"Well, yeah, the guy wasn't all that good as a programmer, but he was very meticulous in commenting his code, so it wasn't hard to suss out what he was trying to accomplish, even where he didn't succeed. The comp sci people said it was very sloppy, buggy code. Now, the kicker is that all this linking up was tied into code from Scenaria software. The guess is that this guy was involved in planting a Trojan or backdoor to give access to systems protected by Scenaria software, which includes, among others, the exalted Institute itself. So, they felt they needed to act quickly and find out where you fit in."

"I don't. Except that your pals were right about the Trojan that I mentioned. It's already in the wild, spread through Scenaria anti-virus installations all over. But not much in

Europe, for some strange reason, at least not yet." She told him about the meeting in Talpa's office at Scenaria. "Anyway, the core team at Scenaria knows that this Marky Collier-Adams was somehow involved, and now the software SWAT team at the company is working overtime to disable or remove the Trojan."

"I'll pass on the information about Collier-Adams, although he certainly doesn't impress me as the sort who would be involved in terrorism or extortion."

"I agree," she said, "but you never know. Like, what about you, Karl? I told you before that you don't look the type. I still don't understand how you got mixed up in this. Unless you really are a secret agent. You seem to know an awful lot of privileged information."

Karl looked out the window as if checking to see if anyone was nearby. "If I were the real thing," he said, unconsciously lowering his voice, "I would not be saying any of this to you. I'd be lying through my teeth, using a plausible cover story or making up a serviceable one as I go along. But, I'm just an amateur, so I'll tell you what little I know." He took another deep breath.

"The truth is that I just happened to be over here on business when the pieces fell into place back in Israel. I had all the right excuses to be at the GAME conference and to poke into Scenaria."

"But you are saying it was no accident that we met?"

Karl gave her a thin half-smile. "Not an accident, no. It was not just your name among Feldersmann's contacts. They think there is someone inside Scenaria involved in whatever this plot is. They wanted to use you to get to others at

Scenaria, but they also couldn't cross you off the list on account of the stuff on Feldersmann's disk. I'm sorry."

She stiffened and pulled back from him. "It gives me a weird feeling that all this was manipulated by a bunch of unseen people in a country half way around the globe. I mean, I thought, I thought you liked me. Instead, you were using me."

"I do like you, and I was using you. Look, I don't ask you to fully understand or agree, but much of what happens in life is written by others, manipulated and maneuvered by people and forces beyond our knowledge and control. But not everything. Maybe the best we can hope for is to hold out for one or two special relationships with special people where the manipulation is absent altogether, or at least the smallest and least important part of the story, where we can surrender to each other. It's worth the waiting," Karl said, thinking of Shira and the twists of fate that had led him to her.

"I shouldn't trust you," Des said, holding his gaze, "but I do."

"No, you should. And I will trust you."

They looked at each other in silence. She studied his blue-green eyes, shifting her focus from one to the other, noting the bronze flecks in the left one, then watched as his lips parted slightly, as if he were about to speak. She leaned closer and started to close her eyes.

"We need to go," he said, as he turned the key in the ignition.

"I can't leave my car here."

"Neither can I. Will you be all right driving back alone."

"Yeah, I'll be all right. I'm a big girl," she said, trying to convince herself as much as to persuade Karl.

"Of course. But now you have an extra burden, like Eve in *Gan Eden* after eating the fruit—you have the knowledge of good and evil. You will have to play it really cool at Scenaria. No one must know about me or what we are looking into." His cell phone buzzed in his pocket, two short pulses for an incoming message. He pulled the phone out and looked at the screen. "Oh, shit!" he said and hung his head.

"What? What is it?"

"It's a code word. It means that my *Mossad* contact—the woman coming down from Toronto—has been taken out. I'm on my own again."

— —

Richard Talpa used the stair-climbing mode of his iBOT to maneuver it into the BMW and position it in the open area where the driver's seat would have been. He was so pre-occupied with the task of getting the chair positioned and locked into place that he didn't notice someone approaching. Just as he turned the key in the ignition, the door lock on the passenger side suddenly popped up, the door opened, and a barrel-chested man with straight, jet-black hair slipped into the seat.

"Hello Rich," he said, slipping a small black box into one pocket of his bomber jacket before pulling a pack of Camels out of another.

"Shit! Don't scare me like that, Brian, you son-of-a-bitch. You want to give me a heart attack? Do you want to finish the job that the Viet Cong bungled?"

Brian Mallory reached over with his big, brown, thumb-less hand and patted Talpa's shoulder. "It's good to see you, too, Rich. Nice to see that they didn't take the piss out of you when they took your legs. It's been a long time."

"Yeah, that it has," Talpa said, his thoughts flashing back unbidden to a day in Vietnam, a day late in the war, long after everyone should have been home, a day that ended with the blinding light and the deafening thunderclap of a booby trap that killed two of his best friends, mangled his legs, and left Brian Mallory without a thumb when his M16 was ripped out of his hand by the explosion. "Luck of the Irish," Brian had said at the time. "My father's side. My mother was a Ute, and you know how them Indians always end up losing a lot more than just a thumb."

It had been Mallory who got the two tourniquets in place before Talpa even regained consciousness, and it was Mallory who carried him to the chopper that would take him to the field hospital where Army surgeons completed the work the explosion had started. Talpa knew he owed the man his life and had been expressing his gratitude ever since with countless behind-the-scene favors. It was Talpa's connections in security that had helped Mallory get into the FBI, then helped him set up an independent operation after he left the Bureau. "What took you so long to get back to me, Brian?" Talpa said with a smile.

"I just got back from Utah. My kid brother was shot up pretty bad in that plant explosion. Poor kid is hanging on by a thread."

Talpa paled and swallowed hard. "You mean the guy who was shot was your brother? My god, I had no idea. I'm sorry, really sorry."

"Hey, it's not like you did this. Goddamn security goon mistook my brother for a terrorist, shot him in the back. Like a terrorist would be speeding *toward* the plant *after* it exploded. Duh."

"I am sorry this happened. Really. If there's anything I can do, you know, just ask. I didn't know this was a bad time to be calling you."

"No, it's all right. Nothing I can do for him anyway. The family's there. They'll be there when he opens his eyes. The reason I went out there was to set the goddamn law enforcement people back on the right path. Turns out they know they have the wrong man but are hoping that the real perps will become complacent because they are thinking they got away with it. Meanwhile, the whole of Homeland Security is pushing forward full steam on the cyber-terrorism thread, following…"

"You think they will find anything?" Talpa said, interrupting. "I mean these guys are pretty hard to track, with Internet anonymity, shuffling IP addresses, and layers on layers of indirection and misdirection."

"Oh, they'll get the guys, but it won't be by any of that high-tech wizardry like you pull off around here. It'll be by shoe leather, brains, and sweat, because these types always slip up somewhere and somebody always talks." He turned away, rolled down the window, and spat, then rolled it back up again. "So, what is it that you need, buddy?" he asked.

"I need you to pick up somebody for me. It should be fairly easy. Until yesterday he was staying at the Meredith downtown. He was attending that big video game expo in town."

"His name?"

"Collier-Adams."

Mallory whistled. "You need some more contract work? No, I'll bet something backfired, right? Otherwise you wouldn't need me. So, fill me in."

"Let's just say the guy went above and beyond the call of duty, got carried away with his own programming prowess. I'm betting that he's going to be wanted on federal felony charges any day now, and I want to get to him before your FBI pals do. *Capiche?*"

"*Si, molto bene.* Want me to bring him to your office or...?"

"Not the office. This could be awkward, to say the least. Maybe dangerous. Find a place where we can talk with him without worrying about being polite or bothering the neighbors. You know what I mean."

Mallory punched a thumbless fist into the palm of his left hand. "Got it. We'll pick him up, soften him up, then bring you in." He reached into his pocket, pulled out a cell phone, and dropped it into Talpa's lap. "Use this if you need to talk, but only if it's really important. I'll buzz you when I have something." He opened the door, grabbed the roof, and swung his bulk out of the car. "You take care. And don't worry, we'll get this guy for you." Before Talpa could say anything, Mallory had slipped into the shadows at the edge of the parking lot and was gone.

18

DES LOOKED AT HER WATCH and was startled to realize how late it was. Still shaken up from the weekend incident in the park, she had spent the morning checking the clock, completing her time sheets and expense reports, and looking busy whenever anyone passed by. Then she got her Web mockups back from the marketing focus group and started plowing into dealing with all the feedback. It was the kind of inventive problem solving that she excelled at.

There was a big clock widget always displayed on her screen, but somehow, once she was working, it had become just another blob in the blur of the LCD landscape. Now it was telling her that it was well past quitting time. She had been so absorbed by her design work in Photoshop, that several hours had passed without notice. She was definitely beginning to like the very different challenges of working on the public site. Maybe her father had been right all along; maybe she was an artist at heart.

She quickly gathered her things and started toward the side entrance and the parking lot. DB was still at it in his cubicle, leaning back in his chair enough to almost block the aisle. As she approached, he toggled the screen from Grand Theft Auto to a graph of internal database searches over the past year.

"What's up, DB?"

"Not much. They still haven't figured out that rootkit."

Des frowned at him.

"No, it's okay to talk. Talpa just left, Harry is holed up with the servers, still convinced that if he watches long enough and closely enough he'll actually see something, and you and I are right here. They can't hear anything down in the Vault where Vern's crew are working 24-7. So, it's okay."

"How do you know all this? There's more than one way out of the building. Not everyone passes your desk on their way in or out."

"Yes, but everyone has an RFID badge, and every time you pass a reader, an entry goes into a security log—a database. You understand? A database." Des nodded.

"Do you need anything, Des. I mean software tools, support, technical help. You know? Anything I can do?"

"Thanks DB, but I'm fine. Except for wondering about this rootkit."

"Well, they haven't been able to get rid of it yet, but I found something on the disk Marky gave you."

"You have the disk? I thought Vern and his boys had it."

"A copy. I make it my business to get and keep copies of everything." He paused, as if waiting for either disapproval or an endorsement from Des. She just listened and nodded slightly.

"I found a couple of utilities that were developed here at Scenaria, utilities that the Systems Tech group has never released. The only known copies are—or were—on a clean-room PC in the Vault. Now that's interesting." He again looked expectantly at Des.

"So, what do you make of it?" she asked. "How do you think that software got onto Marky's disk?"

"It had to be through someone on the Systems Tech team or with an A-level clearance, which means from inside the building, with the proper login credentials, and on a machine with the right security chip on the motherboard. Someone inside Scenaria helped out Marky or his pals. Beyond the Systems Tech crew, there are only a half dozen people with A-level access, which includes Talpa, Harry, Vern, and me."

"You? Why would you have A-level privileges?"

"Because my database work touches on everything in the company. Everything depends on and feeds the repositories. So I have to be able to get at everything, go everywhere." It wasn't like DB to brag, but there was a flash of pride in his voice, and the circumstances seemed to fuel his confidence.

"Good for you, DB. So then who is it you're saying is in- volved with the crooks? You?" She winked.

DB looked surprised but missed the joke and seemed genuinely defensive. "No, not me. Not me! I will tell you, it's not anyone in Systems Tech, either. I know them, except for that new guy from India or somewhere. Those guys know only one world, and its inside the Vault. None of them even has a life. They live and breathe malware signatures and code deconstruction. Money means nothing to them. Scenaria gave them the only life they know, and they would give their lives for Scenaria. They are like *jihadi* fighting Internet infidels. No, I would bet the farm that Vern and the guys in the clean room are clean."

Des cracked a smile. "That narrows it down quite a bit: Harry Krebber or Richard Talpa." DB nodded. "And let me guess: you don't think Talpa would hurt his own company, do you." DB shook his head. "Well, DB, you're entitled to your opinion, but I think I know Harry pretty well. He's not the betraying type."

DB opened his mouth as if about to say something but remained silent. Des chewed on her lower lip, shook her head, and walked away.

"Des," he called after her, but she kept walking without turning and without answering. DB shrugged and switched back to his video game.

Des was driving home when she heard the local news on the radio. The body of one Liam Osbourne, victim of an apparent robbery gone sour, had been discovered in a dumpster not two blocks from the coffee shop where she was supposed to have met him. Des's heart started thudding in her chest. People were dying, she had been threatened, and Harry was now suspected of helping in some nefarious scheme involving Scenaria security software.

Des was nearly home when her cell phone rang with the piano ditty that told her it was another caller not in her contact list. There was no place to pull over, so she fished it out of her purse and tried to open the phone while driving one-handed. By the time she answered, the phone had stopped playing Chopsticks. She was about to put it away when it started playing again. The caller ID was VertexGo. "Hello?" she said.

"Des, it's LG. You know, remember me? We met at the game expo, er, with Dina."

"Oh yeah, right. How are you? What's up?"

"Dinner maybe? Like maybe we, I mean we all, we get together at this little place I know downtown. Italian." He pronounced the last word as if the first syllable were "eye."

"When are we talking about, LG?"

"Tomorrow? At seven? Luigi's Little Napoli. You know it?"

"No, but I'm sure I can find it. Okay. See you guys then."

"Right," he said. "Bye."

She still thought LG was a little creepy, but it would be good seeing Dina again and comparing notes on post-conference developments. A flash of annoyance passed through her as she realized that LG's presence would make it hard to talk candidly with Dina. She would have to save the best stuff for when she and Dina were alone.

She checked her mirror before changing lanes to make the turn into her street. The forest-green pickup truck behind slammed into her, the impact snapping her head back and pushing the car into the intersection where it collided head-on with an on-coming van making a left turn. Des found herself in a white, acrid cloud as the airbags deployed. By the time she had sorted out what had just happened, the green pickup was nowhere in sight.

— —

"Harry," she said emphatically, "Don't you understand? I was rear-ended by a hit-and-run driver in a pickup truck not two blocks from my place. What do you mean you can't swing by the hospital and give me a ride home?"

There was a pause of several seconds. "You know, Des, the pressure I'm under. I went home for a few hours last night and Talpa ripped into me this morning for not staying on top of what the boys in the Vault are doing. And, that's not everything I'm dealing with."

"Harry, what about what I'm dealing with here? I wasn't hurt. Not really. But I have no car anymore, no way to get home."

"You can call a taxi, can't you?"

"It'll be a forty-dollar cab ride from here. What's with you Harry? All I am asking for is a ride home."

"I can't, Des. I can't. Not anymore. Dottie knows about us and is threatening me with a messy, nasty divorce. It's over, Des. It was fun for awhile, but it's past tense."

"You are dumping me over the phone?"

"It's not like I'm dumping you. It's just over, time for you to move on and for me to get back to playing the loyal husband and devoted dad."

"You putz!" It was the last straw for Des. In a sudden and uncharacteristic rage, she threw the phone across the room, where it struck the wall and landed beside an empty wheelchair. Embarrassed, she looked around sheepishly, but the others in the room quickly turned away, pretending not to notice. She thought she could still faintly hear Harry's voice, but when she retrieved the phone, it was dead. One corner was crumpled like the nose of a pug, and the LCD screen was a mosaic of thin, glass puzzle pieces.

"Now you've done it, girl. How the hell are you going to call anyone now?" She shook her head slowly side-to-side several times, as if to emphasize the point to herself. She looked around the waiting room again, wondering whom she might borrow a phone from, when Karl walked in. "Karl, you have no idea how glad I am to see you."

He grinned as he approached. "That's good," he said. "You okay?"

"Yeah, shook up some but no broken bones. How did you know I was here?"

"I was three cars behind you when that turkey plowed into you. Afterwards, I just told them I was your husband and asked where they were taking you. Then I got lost trying to find this hospital. Now I'm here." He gestured with both hands outstretched. "Need a ride somewhere? Your car will not be going anywhere for a long while. Oh, here. Here's the chit from the towing company that hauled it away."

"You were behind me? But your hotel is in town. Were you following me?"

Karl pursed his lips, rolled his eyes, and said, "Naw, just watching your back. I guess I wasn't watching close enough— or following close enough, either. That pickup cut off a Camry to get lined up behind you, then backed off before gunning the engine. It was no accident. Somebody has it in for you. The question is who? And why?"

Des took a shaky breath. "Maybe the same people who killed Blue Leader and maybe for the same reasons. Somebody doesn't want anyone poking into the Horvaths' life or sniffing around Life 2.0. Now they're after Blue Point: that's me. Why me? I'm clueless. What do I know?"

"You know where the Horvaths are—more or less. Hang on there, did you say someone from the game was killed, from The New Game? Someone from your pseudo-crime team?"

"Yeah, in fact, he was the only one I know from my team. The rest are all just in-world avatars with cloaked identities. This guy's name was Liam Osbourne. I only know that because he phoned me and asked to meet but never showed. The next morning they found his body. The police said he was robbed and had made the mistake of fighting back. So, now you think someone may be trying to kill me and make it look like an accident? They very nearly succeeded. My car was totaled. I loved that clunker. I..." She started to shake and leaned into Karl. He stroked her hair with one hand and reached for a tissue with the other.

"I don't think this was meant to kill you, more likely to intimidate you. That woman in the park I don't know about. There's been nothing in the news, so maybe she hasn't even been found yet, but that seems unlikely. There were people in the park when we were there. Surely some of them crossed the bridge. No news is not good news. It almost smacks of a cover-up, which would mean..." He handed her the tissue. "Who knows? In any case, we have good reasons not to go to the authorities, starting with that dead woman in the Maryland park. I don't think you should go home at this point. Whoever is after you undoubtedly knows a lot about you. You can stay in my room at the hotel."

"No, I can stay for awhile with my friend Dina. That would really be better. You know what I mean."

"I don't think that would be such a good idea. Right now your friend seems to be on the sidelines, while you and I are already in the ruck of the game. No, we shouldn't risk putting her at risk, too.

"Look, it will be fine at the hotel. Trust me. There are two beds plus a sofa in my room. It will be all prim and proper, I promise."

She leaned back and looked up at him, smiling thinly. "You are a pretty sweet guy, Karl Lustig."

"Just trying to do what's needed."

"Okay, but I need to pick up some things at my place. You can tag along and keep watch. I'll show you how a young American single girl who has just been dumped by her boyfriend and is being stalked by terrorists lives in Greater DC."

"You've been dumped? Hard to believe. Doesn't seem right." He suddenly found himself looking at her differently, not so much with desire as with awareness. For the first time he noticed the hint of freckles across the bridge of her nose and the tiny dimples on either side of her mouth. "We'd better get going," he said, gesturing toward the exit. "Would you believe, they charge in the visitor's lot here. A hospital, already. What is happening to this country?"

— —

Des gasped when she opened the door. The apartment was a shambles, with the contents of her desk strewn across the living room floor, the bookshelf toppled, and pictures torn from the walls. She stepped gingerly around the debris to check whether her personal laptop computer might still be in the desk, but there was nothing there and nothing but papers and supplies on the floor.

"More amateurs," Karl commented. "With pros, you would never have known they had been here. Either that or, once again, somebody is sending you a greeting card."

"Well, then, let's hear it for professionalism," she said, swirling her finger in the air. "They got my computer. Goddamn it. All my personal contacts, everything was in there." She picked up a sofa cushion from the floor and put it back in place, then sat down and stared at the ceiling. She could hear the sound of wheels rolling over the floor from the apartment above. "My neighbor," she said to Karl. "Kid has all these remote toys, plays with them at all hours, endlessly running them around over the bare floors."

Karl held up his hand. "This mess proves you can't stay here. Grab what you can to last a few days, and let's get out of here. We'll take the back stairs. The fewer people who see us the better. Hurry. Three minutes tops. The car is sitting in the lot where anyone could notice that it doesn't belong in your spot. I'll time you: three minutes." He checked his watch.

Des hopped up, headed for the bedroom, and let out a loud groan when she opened the door. She returned minutes later carrying a backpack and towing a suitcase—just before Karl was about to call time. "Wait," she said. "I gotta grab my toothbrush and some things from the bathroom." On their way out of the apartment, Des picked up her dad's rusty sculpture from beside the phone and stuffed it into her purse.

At the back stairs their way was blocked by a young boy in blue jeans and a flannel shirt sitting on the steps, legs stretched across the narrow stairway. By his size, he could have been ten or twelve, but his angular face made him look much older. Karl started to step over him when the boy held up a sheet of paper. Karl took it. It was an inkjet print made from a webcam shot of the stairwell. The boy pointed past them at a tiny camera tucked in the corner where the stairs turned to go up to the next floor. Before either of them could say anything, he ducked between Karl's legs and disappeared up the stairs without a word and without looking back.

The picture was low resolution and of typically poor quality, but both of them could recognize the man standing in the stairwell.

19

LUIGI'S LITTLE NAPOLI was a walk-down on a side street that looked dubious from the outside but had a lavish interior furnished with red leather benches, high-backed chairs, and tables set with white tablecloths, red napkins, and red votive candles that were dwarfed by the enormous wine glasses at each place setting. If the food tasted as good as the décor promised, LG had outdone himself. Des spotted him across the room, facing the door, and waved to him as the maître d' took her coat.

LG stood as she approached. "You look great, Des." He gestured toward the seat opposite him. "Sit down. Here, have some wine." He smiled broadly as he poured from a bottle that looked as if it had already filled a glass or two. "Say, what happened to your head?"

"Just a bad bruise. I was in a fender-bender on my way home last night. Hit myself with my cell phone when the airbag went off. I'm all right, but my car is decidedly not."

"That's too bad. You were distracted, huh? Calling on your phone, right?" It fit completely with her impression of

LG as someone always getting ahead of himself and jumping to conclusions.

"No way. I was rear-ended by a hit-and-run. A pickup. Totaled my car."

"How'd you get here then? You live out somewhere around the airport, don't you? That's quite a hike. Did you take a cab?"

"No, I didn't come from Virginia. I'm staying in town."

"Oh, where?"

"Is this an interrogation of some sort, LG? I'm not one to be happy in the hot seat." LG, looking duly chastened, took a long sip of wine and managed to dribble in the process. Des pretended not to notice. "Say, where's Dina?" she asked. "Late as usual?"

"Not exactly. I think she's tied up or something all evening. A deadline. Maybe for the video games piece. She has been really beavering away at it, you know."

"You're saying she's not coming?"

"Well, yeah, I guess that's what I'm saying. Seemed a shame to waste the reservation and all. Besides, I figured we could, maybe, get to know each other better."

Des narrowed her eyes and gave him a look that could freeze lava but then surprised him by smiling.

"Then it's okay by you?" he said. "I mean, just the two of us?"

"Sure, but it's not just the two of us. A friend is joining us. He should be here any second. He's parking the car. I hope that's okay with you. I mean, just the three of us?" she said, smugly. "You've already met Karl, at the game conference. Remember?"

LG was clearly disappointed by developments. "Ah, you mean the old bearded fart with the white hair. Yeah, I remember. He's from Lebanon or Syria, right?"

"Israel, LG, Israel. You do need to step out of your video game code more often and take a look around at the political landscape."

"That political stuff is for people like you and Dina. That whole part of the world, the Middle East, it's all just 'over there' to me. People killing each other, suicide bombers, rocket-propelled grenades. It's like one of my first-person shooter games, only for real. Israelis, Palestinians, Lebanese—they all look pretty much alike to me, and from what I can tell, they all act pretty much alike."

"You're more or less right, LG," Karl said as he approached the table. "The parties to the Middle East conflict have a lot more in common than they choose to admit, but that does not mean they are identical. The Israelis are the ones who don't make martyrs of their children by strapping plastic explosives and bent nails around their waists."

LG leaned forward. "But aren't they the ones that send their secret agents around the world assassinating people they don't like?"

Karl bent down to give Des an air kiss on the cheek, then spoke to her in a stage whisper. "See, he really knows more than he lets on. Not quite the rube he pretends to be."

"Rube?" LG said, rising slightly and starting to push back his chair.

"No offense, please," Karl said. "Just a little old-fashioned kidding around by a bearded old fart from Haifa." He extended his hand across the table to LG, who was completely taken aback but quickly wiped his hand on his napkin before shaking Karl's.

"Sure, bro, no offense. Sit. It's all good. We don't have to open fire on each other. Hey, and the food's really good here!"

They were interrupted by the waiter who introduced himself as Rafael before rattling off a long list of specials, which LG ignored completely by jumping in first and quickly ordering veal parmigiana from the set menu. Des said that she was still thinking and told Karl to go ahead and order. Karl, who couldn't remember all the specials, but did recall that one of the early ones had sounded intriguing, just said, "I'll take the second one of the specials. What was it again?"

"Herbed bay scallops in a white wine-garlic cream sauce over orecchiette tossed with freshly grated Pecorino Nero. That's served with a side of green and white asparagus topped with shredded prosciutto di Parma and sun-dried tomatoes."

Karl winked at Des. "Very *treyf*. No doubt very good. Yes, I'll take that."

Des grinned. "Me, too," she said. "I'll have the very *treyf* scallops as well."

Both LG and the waiter looked puzzled but said nothing. The waiter left to bring back a requested bottle of San Pellegrino, and Karl, never missing a chance to educate the ignorant, leaned toward LG and explained that *treyf* meant unclean and that shellfish, like pork, was not kosher, the sins being further multiplied by mixing cheese and cream with meat. "See, the only thing worse than a Philly cheese steak is a humble ham-and-cheese sandwich. And putting it on Jewish seeded rye does not mitigate the offense, either. All this is in the eyes of the observant, of course, which clearly describes neither Des nor me."

LG snorted. "Stupid rules. What's wrong with shellfish or ham? I love them. Well, ham anyway."

"Me, too," Karl said, in a conspiratorial voice. "But I prefer shellfish." Des nodded vigorously.

After the food arrived, LG was absorbed by the task of demolishing his veal and the accompanying plate of spaghetti while Des and Karl made small talk. LG finished the rest of the bottle of wine, then asked if he should order more or whether they would prefer dessert and coffee.

"Thanks, LG, but I couldn't do dessert," Des said. "I could go for coffee, though."

"The same for me," Karl added.

LG signaled the waiter, who appeared almost instantly. "We'd like three coffees, please. I'll take a cappuccino." The waiter smiled stiffly as he turned to Dina and Karl.

"Espresso for me," Des said, glancing toward Karl but resisting the impulse to comment on LG's gaff of ordering cappuccino after dinner.

"Make that two," Karl said.

As the waiter discreetly cleared, Karl looked across at LG as if studying his face. "So, LG, I know the first-person-shooter games are your thing, but I was wondering if you ever have anything to do with virtual life or these, what do they call them, MMOGs? What do you know about Life 2.0, for instance."

"Oh, I hang out there some of the time. That's how me and Dina met, you know. For me, it's mostly a clearing house for coding secrets and contract work. A lot of programmers in the game business are there—virtual companies, consortiums, day-labor corners, forums—lots of places to meet and hang out and get work."

"I hear Life 2.0 may be going down. Do you know anything about that?"

"No, they're solid. They have a new big kahuna, Truman Siebalt—what a name, huh—but he is one smart dude. And he pays on delivery."

"You've done work for them?" LG nodded and Karl continued. "Hmm, I wouldn't think that would be up your alley. What sort of stuff?"

"It was low level stuff, for some of the newer games, integration of online with real-world connections, so like you can telephone somebody through Life 2.0, connect to office equipment, stuff like that. I don't even know how they were using it. There was a time when they were subcontracting a lot of stuff through one of the freelance programming pools. A bunch of my buddies did little pieces for them. Good money, and like I said, they paid promptly through PayPal."

The coffee arrived and LG slurped the foam off his cappuccino before taking a sip. "Youch, that's hot." He blew across the top of the cup to cool it, sending a tuft a foam flying toward Des. "Ooops! Did I get you?" Des shook her head.

Karl looked deep in thought as he stirred a packet of sugar into his espresso. "So, you were working directly for Newlands Labs, then."

"No, actually for this Truman dude, mostly. Plus some for charities and stuff."

Des looked surprised. "You do charity work, LG? I wouldn't have guessed."

"Well, non-profits. I still get paid. Like, I'm way too good to give it away no matter who you are. But, yeah, I did some work for Planet Police, you know, the greenies. Dina is really big on that ecology stuff, although she doesn't think too much of the Planet Police."

"I can understand that," Des said.

"Why is that?" Karl asked.

"Because they are a pretty radical group. It started in Australia and New Zealand, but also took off in Japan, where it attracted some serious fanatics. At one point they took credit for blowing up that fishing boat near New Zealand. They claimed the boats were destroying the fishery, pushing the orange roughy toward the brink of extinction. Then, after it came out that there were some deaths on the ship, they reversed themselves and denied being responsible. In any case, it's at the radical fringe and a little mysterious. Their website keeps disappearing, then reappearing at some other hosting service. And you say you worked for them, LG?"

"Well, it was all online, through the Coders' Corner on Life 2.0. It's not like I met any of them over beers, just wrote some utilities for them. Again, low level stuff, input-output drivers for special purpose hardware. They'd give me the protocols, the expected inputs and outputs, tell me what calls the routines were supposed to support, then wait for the working code. Once they verified it was good, they would send money to my account. I'm not even sure what most of it was about, you know. It was all flip this bit, send a pulse through that channel, read this value—fussy, meticulous stuff, a little complicated but not rocket science. Tell me, Karl, are you really interested in this digital diddly or just making conversation?"

"More the latter, except I still have this series to write for my editor, and Life 2.0 is maybe a small piece of the story.

Just looking for angles that might be useful and interesting to readers. Like the fact that Life 2.0 serves as a virtual clearing-house for real programmers doing contract work—that I didn't know. It's interesting."

"You know what's more interesting," LG said, while waving his cup. "About the same time, there were some re-quests for bids on contracts to reverse engineer some code, you know, take apart and figure out what a program does. A guy I know in Life 2.0 got one of the contracts. Turns out it was for code from the Aniromoto game consoles. That's where I draw the line. That's dishonest. I told him, but he did it anyway. Takes all kinds."

"Sure does," Karl said.

Karl insisted on picking up the check, which LG protested only weakly and briefly, then Karl and Des excused themselves. On the way to the car, Des asked him why he hadn't pulled out the picture from the webcam in the stairwell at the apartment.

"Because he gave us useful information. Why tip our hand prematurely when he still might give us more. It's always better to know more about an asset than he knows you know. We know he is stalking you, but we don't know why. We know he was at your apartment probably around the time of the break-in, but we don't know if he was involved or not. We need to string him along for a while."

"And you call yourself an amateur? I have my doubts, Karl Lustig." She gave him a squeeze around the waist.

— —

For the second night in a row, Karl worked late while Des slept soundly on the bed across the room. He was about to call it a day and shut down his laptop when a Skype call came in. It was from Anat. He rejected it and then sent an IM explaining that he didn't want to go to voice and awaken his roommate. Anat responded with a one-word reply:

roommate?

Karl thought about it, then typed:

hard to explain but nothing

The reply popped back:

no need but answer my voice call, too much
   for im

cn I take it on cell in hall?

no, this is better, harder to trace

kk, will call u

Suddenly inspired, Karl fiddled around in his bag for his Bluetooth headset, grabbed his laptop, and went into the bathroom with the door closed. It took him a minute to pair the headset and adjust the microphone. Anat picked up on the first ring.

"We are working on a replacement for the *katsa* we lost in Canada," she began without introduction. "For the time being, though, you are still it. Oh, and there's another whole twist on this business. Shimon's whiz kids have continued to study the contents of the code on Feldersmann's laptop. Some of it was his, and they say that's pretty easy to decipher, but there is also a lot of stuff that was done by others. Some of it is signed by the coders, mostly with handles, like Gaijin or C'coder, rather than actual names. Needless to say we are following up on the names and trying to track the handles as well. I'll send you an encrypted file with the list of what we've pulled, just in case you might recognize any of them.

"The big breakthrough is that one of Shimon's people spotted a section of code that looked familiar from her previous work in automation. She recognized it as a hand-shaking routine for connecting between a PC and a SCADA device. Are you following this, Karl, or do I need to go through what it means. I had to have it explained to me."

"No, I understand," Karl said, talking quietly and practically chewing on the microphone. "Some of the code runs on a regular computer but establishes a connection to a piece of industrial equipment through a Supervisory Control and Data Acquisition interface. And?"

"And there was a table of IP addresses, targeted systems apparently used for testing the software. A string of them trace back to Wescole Holdings." She paused for effect.

"Tricorn!" Karl said.

"Bingo. Now the question is who and why? We're running scenarios and working all the *sayanim* we can who might have clues. Contacts in the power industry would be a bit far afield for you, but we thought you might have some angles to try."

"I do, I do, as a matter of fact. Let me think about it and get back to you." Karl's heart jumped at a light tap on the bathroom door. Thinking quickly, he said, "Love you, honey. Talk soon." He hung up before a confused Anat could say anything.

Karl opened the door and said, "Sorry, I didn't mean to wake you. Just getting in a quick call home."

Des nodded but gave him a skeptical look. "You didn't wake me. I just needed to use the bathroom. That is, if you don't mind taking your laptop elsewhere for a minute." She smiled and Karl smiled back.

20

IT WAS EXTRAVAGANT to fly to California and back in one day, but Celise Greenberg had insisted on meeting in person, and Anat was picking up his expenses. It had been years since Karl had last been in Los Angeles, but on the approach to LAX it still looked to him like the same dirty sprawl smeared from horizon to horizon. It had always been one of his least favorite cities, although not completely devoid of appeal. He liked running barefoot along Santa Monica Beach early enough in the morning so that only dedicated runners and the homeless were around. And he had fond memories of a night hike up Mount Hollywood in Griffith Park with the glittering jewels of city lights fanned out below for as far as the eye could see.

At the airport, Karl rented a car and drove up the 405 freeway toward the UCLA campus where he was to meet Professor Greenberg. He had no trouble finding the recommended parking in the garage at the intersection of Hilgard and Sunset. Realizing he was early, he took his time meandering through the sprawling sculpture garden on his way to Bunche Hall. He spent extra time musing over some of the contrasts in the collection, like the rough aggressiveness of the Rodin "Walking Man" against the almost industrial understatement of the Marcks "Maja." It was, however, a piece by Noguchi—three cast bronze "stones" set in a concrete tablet—that particularly spoke to him, suggesting a simulated reality with a puzzle hidden beneath a placid but impenetrable surface. So little of life seemed real to him at the moment; so much lay obscured beneath deceptively simple surfaces.

Despite lingering over the pieces, he still reached Bunche Hall ten minutes early but then made up for it by getting lost inside, ending up in the history department by mistake, and having to call Professor Greenberg on his cell phone to get directions to her office.

He was met in the hall by a tiny woman, even shorter than her daughter Des, who ushered him into a tiny room crowded with stacks of folders and boxes of books, leaving barely the space for a desk and two chairs. The jutting box of a window behind the desk offered a view across the manicured acres of the sculpture garden he had just explored.

"Thanks for taking the time to see me, Professor Greenberg."

She took his hand with a firm but graceful grip. "Celise, please. I'm only Professor Greenberg to my undergraduate students, except when they are talking among themselves, and then I am 'Professor Greenbitch.' Seems they think I am a tough marker, which I am.

"So, you know my daughter? How is she? When she called the other night, she sounded pretty ragged. I guess you know about the developments at her work."

"Yes, but as I said on the phone, it's something else I want to talk with you about. I want to tap your brain as an expert on energy economics and the power industry."

"Well, I'm an academic, not an industry insider, still, if I can help, I would be glad to. But tell me, first, what this might have to do with your journalistic inquiries into computer games. If I remember right, from what Des told me, you and my daughter met on account of that interest. So how do we get from there to energy economics, Mr. Lustig? It would seem to be an unlikely connection."

Karl had rehearsed a vague but credible answer but by now had gained the impression that Celise Greenberg was unlikely to buy it. "Well, first, just call me Karl, Celise. Second, the connection is through my day job as a muck-raking writer on high-tech developments. It just so happened that the Tricorn disaster hit while I was over here, so, my editor in Israel tells me to do some digging and find out what I can. Some friends of mine seem to think the incident was no accident and, like some in the media, believe it may have involved cybercrime. I'm not taking any position on this speculation as yet, just gathering background. I do find it interesting that no one has come forward to claim credit, which would seem to rule out political activists, maybe even terrorist groups. Those types usually like to brag or give warning. Which brings us to economic motives. I'm trying to figure out who could have benefited from taking out an electric power plant."

"Excellent line of reasoning. So far you're earning a solid B+, Karl. However, I would say it is still not too late for a terrorist group to come forward and claim credit. Plus, maybe it was a test run for something else. But, let's return to possible economic motives. Who do you think might stand to gain from losing the plant?"

"So now I'm one of your grad students? I thought I was here to interview you."

"You didn't say interview, you said talk. And this is the way a professor talks. Ask Destiny. She'll tell you what it was like growing up with me as her mother. Always answer a question with a question: that's the formula."

"So," Karl said, "you want to know what I think? I think it was deliberate sabotage accomplished remotely. That's what I think." He paused, leaving space for a response, but when none came, he continued. "At any rate, the chatter among technically savvy bloggers in this area is that Tricorn might have been a scaled up version of the Project Aurora experiment by Idaho National Labs a few years back when they remotely triggered the self-destruction of a 1-megawatt Jenbacher industrial generator. They didn't even need the Internet. They just hacked into the generator's control programs through signals over the power lines. With every tap on a laptop key, the hacked programs threw the generator out of synch, and that 27-ton monster bucked like an unhappy rodeo bronco. Smoke soon started curling out of it as it shook itself apart. Minutes later, it was toast. A description by that technician of what happened at Tricorn makes it sound suspiciously similar."

"Now that's interesting, Karl, I didn't know about that."

He raised his index finger. "But wait, there's more. This little detail also leaked out. It was even on the news, although I doubt many people had any idea of its significance. Emergency backup power in the plant also failed—or was taken out. That not only meant no control through the regular systems, but it also meant no power to keep the remaining turbine-generator units turning after their emergency shutdown."

She looked a little puzzled. "Why would they have to keep turning?"

"Because they weigh so bloody much that if they ever stop completely, they start to sag and quite quickly go out of balance. So that is why there is no generating capacity at the plant. Only one unit was taken out directly, but all their units will have to be replaced. Tricorn was, at a stroke, effectively destroyed."

"This all implies careful planning and sophisticated, insider knowledge," she said. "It certainly makes the case for deliberate destruction but does not offer much about either the actors in the drama or their motivation. And it is still unclear, to me at least, just how it might have been accomplished. Do you know how this technology works?"

"Yes, mostly. It's about SCADA systems: Supervisory Control and Data Acquisition. These are the distributed systems that implement communication and coordination for industrial equipment and utilities of all kinds: gas, oil, electric, you name it. In theory all these systems are supposed to be independent and separate from the Internet, but the reality is rife with holes. There are cross connections between SCADA systems and office networks so that managers in their executive suites can monitor operations and consolidate data without having to cross the street and put on a hardhat. And some holes in the digital dike are as simple as plugs and jacks on panels in unsecured areas. Somebody could just walk up, plug in the right kind of doctored wireless router, and take over an entire plant through the free wi-fi at the Starbucks down the block. It's a scenario that industry people claim is unlikely, but unlikely is not the same as impossible."

"Okay, go on," she said.

"Well, the SCADA systems are themselves vulnerable to attack. Many companies still trust to 'security through obscurity,' figuring that specialized communication protocols or 'trade secret' proprietary interfaces make them safe from attack, all the while forgetting that everything, including PDF files of all the manuals and protocol specs, can easily be retrieved over the Web. And as for the PCs that host the management software or are otherwise interconnected with SCADA networks, they are a security nightmare. Your daughter knows all about that from her work at Scenaria. Some experts estimate as many as a quarter of all PCs in the world are infected with malware of one form or another; millions of computers have been turned into slaves of the so-called bot nets that spew spam and can be directed at will to launch all manner of Internet attacks."

"So," she said, "you think Tricorn might have been taken out through vulnerabilities in these SCADA systems?" She doodled on the one exposed corner of her desk pad as she waited for his answer.

"I do, but I'm no expert in this area, just a well-informed techie. So, just before I flew out here, I called an old buddy of mine from MIT who is the real thing: an expert. Seems he just returned from a trip. Right after the Tricorn incident he got the call to pack his bags and head west. Homeland Security representatives met him at Las Vegas International. He couldn't say much, of course, but he didn't have to; he's one of the country's top experts on SCADA and network security. That says it all."

"Alright, we have means, now motive? Who stood to gain from the destruction of Tricorn?"

"There you go with the questions again. Who do you think?"

"You first." She winked at him.

"All right. The methods tell us something. This was no open-source hack by a small group of amateurs. This was a well-funded, carefully coordinated, multinational project. So, I would start with those corporate interests that would stand to gain from the new energy security legislation now before Congress."

"And who might that be?" she asked.

"Scenaria would be a major benefactor, if we are to believe the boss man, Richard Talpa. They seem to be out front with a SCADA security solution, or so they claim. If new security measures are mandated, Scenaria gets a big new market in which they already have a head start over the competition."

"A definite possibility, but do you think Scenaria, which already has a commanding lead in software security, would risk a multi-billion dollar business by blowing up a power plant?"

"You tell me, you're the economist."

"Yes, an economist not a financial analyst—or a crime scene analyst, for that matter. We can't rule out Scenaria, but there are other corporate interests that might stand to gain."

"Who? Name one," Karl challenged.

"There are many possibilities: anyone with facilities that are already secure, for instance. There are a few industry leaders, PanPac Electric, for one example, with recently built, state-of-the-art plants that are probably relatively immune to penetration, and they would have already written off the investment. I would suggest digging through industry statistics and perusing annual reports to see if you can spot anything else suspicious."

"You've already done that, haven't you?"

"Of course, and what did I find?"

Karl laughed. "This is becoming just too recursive for me. You are obviously way ahead of me, Professor. I am your humble student; please, enlighten me."

"Consider Wescole as another suspect. Yes, their stock tanked initially, but it later rebounded, and now that the price of electricity is edging inexorably upward they will be among the benefactors. Plus, according to documents filed with the government, the Tricorn plant was insured for full replacement cost. That's coverage that draws a substantial extra premium. Put that beside the allegations that the plant did not meet new pollution or safety regulations, and what are we left with?"

Karl jumped in. "Now, instead of Wescole facing expensive remediation out of its own pockets just to bring Tricorn up to code, the insurers buy them a whole new plant, designed from the beginning to meet the tough standards. But, frankly, it's a big leap from motive to the company destroying its own plant."

"Not so big, maybe. Did you see this little item at the end of a story online?" She shuffled through a pile of paper on her desk and retrieved a sheet. "It claims that the private firm that provides security for the plant had been told at the start of the week to be on high alert because there had been intercepted communications that an attack on the plant might be in the offing, and that the guards, quote, should be prepared to use deadly force if necessary to stop any incursion attempt, unquote. Maybe that Native American was not intended to survive. Although, one has to wonder what possible terrorist scenario could explain his speeding toward the site of the explosion after it happened. Still, dead men tell no tales, although still-unconscious shooting victims might yet get their day in court or week in front of the cameras.

"And now, my apt pupil, I have one last question for you. It will count for two-thirds of your final grade. Do you really expect me to believe that your interest and your presence here in my office is as a journalist writing for iTech Weekly Online? I checked out your blog and feature pieces: industry-insider shop talk and trend analysis, scattered product reviews—and I do mean scattered—and lightweight prognostication about near-term trends. Either you have suddenly morphed into a hard-news reporter in frantic pursuit of a Pulitzer, or you are here in some clandestine role. My question then, is not about what you would expect me to believe, but rather more simply, are you with the Institute or the Company or the lowly Bureau?"

"Are those the three choices?"

"Oh, my good sir, well done. You are a fast learner. But answer the question."

"Do I get one last question of my own?"

"Now it is you who have nested the recursion beyond tracking. Okay. Go ahead. One question, then you must answer mine." She folded her arms in front of her with a triumphant expression lighting up her face..

"And you must answer," he said. "That's the deal! So, my question is: what do you think of J-Street?"

Her face lit up with utter delight as she clapped her hands. "Brilliant, absolutely brilliant. With one probe you sample the whole spectrum of possibilities. Now, I could be flip and say Washington has no J-Street, only I and K. Or I could be pedantic and say that J-Street is a small but growing American Jewish organization trying to present an alternative to the mainstream knee-jerk position that gives unqualified support for Israel and its policies, an entrenched position that regards any questioning or criticism, even reasoned debate or rational reserve, as disloyal or even anti-Semitic. But, my clever student, what you are really asking is precisely where I stand in support of Israel, and I will answer the question that you are really asking.

"I love and believe in Israel. Period. That love and belief does not prevent me from seeing her clearly or calling her on her transgressions, any more than my love and belief in my daughter prevents honest appraisal or inhibits necessary criticism. These would be intrinsic provisions in my job description as a parent. The same applies to my mandate as a Jew in relation to the Jewish homeland. I would love and support the State of Israel less well if I could not challenge or criticize it. There, I have answered. Your turn. Are you *Mossad*?

"No, I am not *Mossad* nor *Shin Bet* nor *Aman*, certainly not the CIA or FBI, but I am certain they all are or would be interested in what you have to say." He held her eyes for several seconds.

"You know," she said, smiling but nodding gravely, "this whole business could make a great case study or discussion question for one of my graduate seminars."

"I don't think so. I don't think that would be a good idea. You would not want to scoop a future Pulitzer prize winner would you? Moreover, it might be upsetting to those people in *HaMossad* or *Shin Bet* or *Aman*, whoever they are these people for whom I do not work. And we would not want to do that, would we, even if we try to be reasoned and balanced in our assessment of what they and their country does."

"You are good, you know," she said, once more nodding seriously. "Maybe you could go for a Pulitzer."

"Well, I don't know about that, but I do have to go. I have to catch the red-eye back to DC."

"The red-eye? That doesn't leave until ten tonight. What are you going to do with yourself? Look," she said, pulling a manila folder from a desk drawer and standing up. "I have a graduate seminar to lead in fifteen minutes. Tag along. We're discussing peak-oil models and economic projection; you'd find it interesting—if you can keep up with the math. Then, I want you to meet my husband. He's a sculptor, but not one whose work you would find in the Murphy collection that you passed through on your way here. We'll take you for dinner. We know a charming little Tex-Mex place not ten minutes from the airport.

"Please, say you will. I promise not to talk about Tricorn or ask any embarrassing questions. That's a promise."

"I see where your daughter gets her persuasive abilities from. Okay, sure, we'll have to meet someplace because I have a rental car, but I'm sure we can figure out the logistics."

"You know, despite my promise, I do have another question. Or two. Or three. Is my daughter all right? Is she safe? And is she safe with you?"

Karl smiled broadly. "Right to the point. Again. Yes, your daughter is all right. I'm watching out for her, and I'm not the only one. And I am happily, deeply happily married. She is safe with me." He felt the need to say it again, but decided not to overdo it.

"Good. Now come along to my seminar."

— —

It was early the next morning when Karl opened the door to the hotel room and tiptoed in as quietly as he could. Des was sitting up in bed, legs crossed, wearing an XXL tee-shirt that served as a nightgown stretched over her knees. Karl tried not to lower his eyes to where her nipples showed through the thin fabric each time she took a breath.

"Where were you?" she began. "I was worried. I was scared. I don't know if I was more worried and scared for you or for me. Where were you?"

"I sent you a text message. I said I had to go to California for the day. You didn't get it?"

"My phone is dead. I killed it at the hospital. Don't you remember?"

"Uh, no, that must have been just before I showed up." He crossed the room and sat on the edge of the bed. "I am sorry." He put his hands on her shoulders, gave her a brief squeeze, and pulled back again. "I didn't mean to make you worry."

"What took you to California?"

"I had an appointment with your mother."

"My mother? What on earth for?"

"She is, after all, one of the world's leading authorities on energy economics, and I thought she might be able to shed some light on Tricorn."

"Are you back on that Tricorn business? Don't we have enough to keep us guessing with the Horvaths and Scenaria?"

"That's a thought. The Horvaths and Scenaria. I should check to see if anything links the two. I wonder if the Horvaths have a stake in Scenaria or if Scenaria services Newlands Labs. That's good, Des. Thanks."

"You don't get off so easy with a deflection like that. So what did you want to ask my mother?"

"The same question I asked you: Who stood to gain from taking out Tricorn?"

"I thought it was pretty plain. It was terrorists. Unless there's some credence to Dina's wild-haired conjecture that it was really some branch of Israeli intelligence."

"Terrorists would be the easy answer, and Israeli intelligence is no answer at all. Your mother suggested harder answers and pointed out a number of corporate interests that had motive. She also gave me homework and promised to keep digging herself and to keep us informed if she finds something."

"You got my mother working for you and *HaMossad?*"

"I'm not with *HaMossad*, remember? So, nothing official, of course, but it was her idea to do some digging."

"She always said that good economics was detective work. Maybe I should have listened more to my mother. Except, of course, my dad was the one who was right about me. I am coming to realize that maybe I am an artist. I really love being on the creative side at work. Someday I want to do real art, not just corporate crap. If I live long enough."

"Don't despair. Our hope, *tikvateinu*, it's what we run on in Israel." He flashed her a close-lipped grin. She pulled away from him to look deep into his eyes. After an uncomfortable silence, Karl moved to stand up. She cupped her hand over his for a moment, then pulled it back. "I need to take a shower," he said as he stood up. "Then I'll run you into work. I can fill you in on the rest of the latest developments on the way."

In the shower, Karl started to turn the knob all the way over to cold, but then chickened out. He had his doubts whether the technique actually worked in any case.

PART THREE

21

THE SUN WAS NOT YET a stain on the horizon when, even earlier than usual, Richard Talpa pulled into his reserve space at Scenaria. Once in his office, he closed the door to the outer office, took a cell phone from the locked drawer of his desk, checked the battery, and dialed a number with an Australian prefix. It rang several times.

A sleepy voice answered with one word, "Yo!"

Talpa considered his own words. "You hacked our software," he said.

"So?"

"Why?"

"Because I could, and because it made it easier to meet the contract. We needed a bot net. Now we have one. It did the job."

"Then move on. The contract is complete. Kill the bots."

"There's more to do."

"No there's not," Talpa said, practically shouting into the phone. "Kill the bots, goddamn it. The job is done." There was no answer; the call was disconnected.

Talpa retrieved yet another cell phone from his pocket, found a single entry in the contact list, and dialed it.

"Goddamned early to be calling, isn't it, Rich?" the voice on the other end answered.

"Brian, you have to get Collier-Adams before he does any more damage."

"We're working on it. He's pulled a vanishing act."

"Brian, I can't say enough about how important this is. Billions may be at stake. We need to know what this sonofabitch knows. Whatever it takes, Brian. I'll make it worthwhile to you."

"We'll find him. I have a couple more buddies from Nam I can pull in on it. Don't worry. I'll be on it as soon as we're off the phone."

"Then we're off," Talpa said as he disconnected. Before he could put the phone away, Harry Krebber appeared in the doorway of the office.

"Your assistant isn't here yet, so I thought it would be okay to just pop in. How many phones do you own, Talpa? Seems like every time I turn around you are talking on a different one."

"Nine, Harry, I own nine cell phones, as if it were any of your business. I make it my business to have one of each major brand—different phones for different purposes, you know. My favorite is the HTC Hero. I don't know why people like the damned iPhone so much. More eye candy than phone. The best of the Android phones are far slicker and easier to use." He gave Harry a look of deep disapproval. "Ask a stupid question, Harry, and you get that kind of an answer. Now, what the hell do you want at this hour? I've got a business to run that's tumbling toward an abyss."

"Well, I've been holed up in the Vault since yesterday morning, so I really have no idea what hour it is, but I have good news and bad news. The good news is the penetration has stabilized at somewhere around 88% here and less than 6% in Europe. It's beginning to look like machines that don't have the rootkit already are not going to get it. We don't know why yet, but we are working on it. In any case, the rootkit does not look like it's going to spread beyond the current infected population."

"And you call nearly 90% good news? I can't wait to hear the bad."

"Well, only 6% in Europe: I'd call that pretty good. The bad news is that we still haven't found out how machines in the wild get re-infected. Some don't, but most do, and we have yet to find the difference in configuration or circumstance that explains it."

"Systems Tech had better find the difference soon, Harry, because we can't keep a lid on this forever, to say nothing of what happens if this bot net ever gets activated. Do you realize how many computers 88% of our domestic installed base is? And we are talking about high end commercial systems with T1 or better connections to the Internet for the majority, not just home PCs with DSL or a crummy cable modem. It is truly terrifying to think what this could be used for." Talpa knew at least one thing it could be used for, but said nothing.

Harry nodded, turned, and started for the door. "I will try to keep Vern on task," he said over his shoulder. "But I think the whole group is exhausted. They've been running on coffee, cola, and chips-and-dip rations for days. I think they're burning out. Maybe it's time we brought in some reinforcements. There are consultants who are good and whose discretion can be trusted. Maybe we should try and work a deal with this Collier-Adams kid."

"We can't work a deal if we can't find him, which we can't at the moment. It seems that he left town after the conference but did not end up back at his New York City apartment.

"No, I don't want to spread this further. If we pull in extra resources, it has got to be internal. I'll let Vern know that he can have his pick of our own best and brightest if he thinks they can help. As long as every reassignment goes through me."

Harry saluted as he backed out of the door. Talpa watched the empty doorway and wondered whether the salute was merely lame humor or nonverbal sarcasm.

— —

Marky awoke abruptly from a dream of drowning, only to discover a huge hand over his mouth and nose.

"Promise not to make a sound, and I will remove my hand. Nod if you promise."

Marky nodded as best he could with the pressure on his face, then gasped for breath as the hand was removed. With the lights out and the heavy hotel curtains drawn, the room was too dark for him to see more than vague shadows, but Marky could just make out three dark shapes arrayed around the bed.

"You will come with us. You will make no sound and do nothing to draw attention. Is that understood?"

"Yes." The blow came hard and swift, exploding bright sparks of blue-white light in Marky's head.

"I said, not a sound, understood? Nod if you understand. If you do not understand or do not remain silent, we will kill you here and now."

Marky nodded vigorously and silently as two of the men grabbed him on either side, pulled something over his head, then lifted him from the bed and dragged him to the door. They shoved him across the hall and into a service elevator, where they bound his wrists with a plastic cable tie as the elevator descended.

When it stopped, he was dragged out, bundled into the back seat of a car, and squeezed between two of the men— men whose breath smelled of anise and whose bulk threatened to crush him. One spoke to the driver in a thick accent that Marky didn't recognize. "What do you wait for? We are ready. Just go." The car lurched forward, zigzagged among parked cars, and bounced as it shot up the garage ramp and out onto the street.

During the long ride, Marky had trouble breathing under the hood but was too terrified to say anything. When the car finally stopped, he was pulled from it and pushed into another elevator. He counted six beeps before the elevator stopped and he was taken out.

"Now you can talk," said the accented voice as he was being tied into a chair with a length of electrical cord. "We want to know all about the bot net. Everything. Exactly how it works and what it does and how to use it. So tell us about it."

"I can't breathe in here. Please take the hood off."

"If we take the hood off, you would see our faces and our 'facilities,' and then we would have to kill you. Now, do you want the hood off?"

"No, I guess not. But see, the carbon dioxide builds up under here and makes it hard to breathe. Too much of this can lead to acidosis, you know, and my asthma…"

The blow to his head came just as suddenly as before and with even more force. "I asked about the software, not about your fuckin' asthma, ass hole. I want to hear about the network code, not some stupid lecture on carbon dioxide. Is that clear?"

"I was just trying…"

This time the punch was in the stomach, knocking the wind out of him. He was just starting to catch his breath again when a rain of blows rocked his head back and forth and left the salty taste of blood in his mouth. "I do not want you just trying anything. I want you to tell me about the code: all about the code, the whole code, and nothing but the code." Somebody in the room laughed. "Now tell me about the program. And anytime you change the subject or I don't like what you are saying, or the way you are saying it, I will do this." A fist struck him in the jaw, breaking two of his teeth and knocking him unconscious. He came to with ice water flooding his face and the feeling that, once again, he was drowning.

The interrogation went on for several hours with frequent blows and occasional pauses. After yet another blow to the side of his head, Marky swooned in the chair, just short of losing consciousness.

"Please," he said, his voice thick and slow. "Could you take off the hood? Just for a minute. Please, I can't breathe."

Another man approached the chair with slow footsteps. "Sure," he said. "We got everything we are going to get from him. We can take off the hood now."

— —

Brian Mallory was already sitting in the BMW when Talpa approached his car. He was annoyed that Brian treated a locked car door so casually, but said nothing about it. "So what have you got, Brian?" Talpa asked as he maneuvered his wheelchair into position.

"We got Collier-Adams. My Nam buddies tell me they found him."

"That's great news. Why so glum?"

"They also tell me he's been taken out."

"Taken out? I was just talking with him on the phone this morning."

"Well, what can I say? He's dead tonight. He didn't survive an interrogation."

"What the fuck? I thought I could trust you. I thought your people were professionals."

"Look, Rich, I can explain. We didn't…"

"I don't want explanations!" Talpa interrupted. "I want solutions. Just get out of my car. You are off the case."

"That's okay by me, Rich, as long as you pay me for services rendered. But I really think you ought to hear me out about what we learned."

"You'll get your fee once I have this damned software nightmare under control, which I need to do right now. So, I am going back into my office to try another angle. I assume that when I return to my car it will be empty." He maneuvered the wheelchair back out of the car and pressed a button on his remote to close the door. As he swiveled to re-enter the building, he noticed Des Allen and a man he didn't recognize headed toward a car in the lot. It was not the beat up Ford that he knew she usually drove. He called out as he whirred in their direction, "I see you are working late again, too, Des."

"Seems everybody is these days. Oh, let me introduce you two. Karl, this is the big boss, Richard Talpa. This is Karl Lustig, a friend from Israel."

Karl shook hands, then pulled out a business card from his pocket and held it out. "So, you're the genius behind Scenaria."

"One of many," Talpa said, looking at the card, "just one of many. Do you have an interest in security software, Mr. Lustig?"

"Call me Karl, please. Well, as you can see, I write for iTech Weekly, so I'm interested in pretty much everything, but right now I'm working on a story about the video games industry. Des and I met at the GAMES IX conference last week."

"Well that is one area about which I know little or nothing."

"Me, too, but I'm learning, which is my job. Say, I don't suppose you'd have time to talk sometime about Internet security. I would love to do an interview for my blog."

Talpa regarded him with a quizzical look, then said, "No time like the present. I forgot something in my office. Why don't you tag along? We're under a lot of pressure at the moment here, but I can give you fifteen minutes once I find my damned cell phone."

"Have you checked your chair?" Karl said in all innocence as he pointed toward the holster attached to the side of the iBOT.

Talpa, looking like a schoolboy caught in a fib, said, "No, my other phone. I try to keep boundaries between business and personal matters. It's a practice I recommend highly to those around me." He glanced toward Des. "The younger generation seems to disdain such separation of concerns. They post in public places on the Web their additions to professional portfolios alongside party pictures and details of indiscretions. It's a brave new world, Karl, as well you know, but few of us thought that big brother would turn out to be not some far away malevolent government but merely our own buddies in the cubicle down the hall reading Facebook entries or following on Twitter.

"But, there I go again, up on my motorized soap box. Come on along and let's do this interview. I have tickets at the Kennedy Center tonight. Fischer is conducting an all Russian program, and I hate to arrive late and have to wait until an intermission to be seated. Alexander Nevsky is a favorite of mine.

"So, come along—you, too, Destiny, if you wish."

Talpa's private entrance swung open as they approached, triggered by a remote or by his RFID badge. He waved them on ahead, then sped past them along the darkened corridor leading directly to his office. There he wheeled up to the big conference table and gestured toward the Aeron chairs lined up opposite him.

"Make yourself comfortable; I am."

Karl opened his leather-bound journal, slipped his LiveScribe digital pen out of its sleeve, and wrote something on the top of a fresh page before resting the pen in the crease of the open journal. Figuring he had nothing to lose and no time to waste, he decided to plunge right in and open with his best shot. "Scenaria stands to gain from the new Industrial Internet Software Security bill currently being debated in the

House after the cyber-attack on the Tricorn installation. How is it that you saw this one coming?"

Talpa smiled. "You're the one who called me a genius, and I'm the one who said I was only one of many. We are a bunch of super smart people on a mission to secure the digital world. But it doesn't take a genius to have seen the writing on the wall about SCADA systems. Many have been calling attention to the dangers for years."

"Still, you announced just over a year ago at a Scenaria Users Group meeting that you were, quote, investigating comprehensive approaches to securing SCADA systems and expected to be rolling out a solution by first quarter this year. Then Tricorn self-destructs right on schedule, as if they were looking at the same milestone chart."

Talpa leaned forward in his chair. "Coincidence. It was all but inevitable that something of this sort would happen. I'm not above taking advantage of random events. Chance favors the prepared. We were prepared with our Industrial Shield product line and our competitors were caught catnapping."

Karl continued to scribble notes in his journal. "Sources among the investigators have claimed that the specific attack would have been, quote, all but impossible without inside knowledge of both of the specific plant and of industry practices in general, unquote. Where would you think the attackers could obtain such knowledge?"

"The same place you or I would: on the Web."

"Are you saying I could learn all about how your SCADA security solution works—this Industrial Shield, as you call it—through the Internet?"

"No, of course not. We are, after all, in the security business ourselves, and we have some of the tightest, most advanced security in the world protecting access to our proprietary technology and information."

"But isn't it true that Wescole Holdings, owner of the Tricorn plant, is among your best customers, a so-called first-tier client? Haven't they been used as a beta site for trials of some of your new software?"

Talpa squirmed visibly, then looked at Des. "Our relationships with customers are not public knowledge. We regard all such information as company confidential and take breaches of confidence very seriously." He continued to look directly at Des.

"I am sure," Karl said, "but this is all a matter of public record and freely available on the Web. Do you want to review my sources? Let's see, there's your remarks at InterSec 2008 in London; a 2009 interview with a Harry Krebber done by Web Watch Weekly; a response from you, personally, to a blogger who goes by the handle InsideCurve; a quote from a Wescole stockholder report—do you want me to go on? Would you like to confirm or deny them individually? I can give you a complete list now." He held out a sheet toward Talpa. "Or, I can email it to you if that would be more convenient."

Talpa's eyes narrowed. "If you are so confident of your sources, there is no need for me to confirm or disconfirm anything, is there? But, of course, one can find almost anything on the Web, including claims that the attack on the Twin Towers was orchestrated by Israel in collaboration with our own CIA. If you believe everything you read on the Web, Mr. Lustig, then I have a bridge in New York to sell you for a song. I'll give you the bank account number where you can wire the money."

"You are so right, Dr. Talpa, the Web is as rife with misinformation and disinformation as it is with the genuine article, which is why I have spoken with experts on SCADA and on energy economics, insiders in the security industry, other journalists, and people in contact with Homeland Security. And now I am speaking with you. Journalists are taught to confirm information by independent means." Karl smiled, proud of how he had, in a single sentence, multiplied his modest inquiries into a virtual army of resources.

Talpa glanced again toward Des. "I hope, Karl, that none of your sources is a current employee of Scenaria. We have a strict policy on breaches of confidence, as I mentioned."

Des started to speak up, but Karl spread his hands as signal to stay out of it. "None of what I have asked you about comes from anyone who works here, and specifically not from Ms. Allen. I was giving her a ride because her car was wrecked. That's it. I don't need to interrogate your employees to get what I can Google from my laptop or easily obtain from third-party sources.

"Oh, but I do have one last question. I met a programmer at GAME IX who claimed to have worked for you. Is the name Collier-Adams familiar?"

Talpa held himself rigid, but his face twitched involuntarily. He looked away as if thinking. "I don't believe so, but we have over 7,000 employees in six countries. A CEO is not going to know all the many thousands who have worked for a company this size."

"But Collier-Adams said he had done work directly for you, not as a Scenaria employee but as a contractor to you."

"Then he was making it up, inflating his credentials, perhaps." Talpa hesitated for a moment, then continued,

"What exactly did this Collier-Adams say he was doing for me?"

"He didn't say, claimed it was confidential, hush-hush."

Talpa, looking noticeably relieved, glanced at his watch. "I am sorry, but I really must go," he said. "Des, I trust you can escort your reporter friend out. You, I'll see tomorrow." He tipped his head toward her.

Des caught the implications of his last words but said nothing. Karl reached out his hand as he stood, but Talpa seemed not to notice as he swiveled toward his desk. Karl thanked him for his time and said goodbye to his back but received only a grunt in return.

As they approached the exit at the other end of the hall, Des spoke up. "You talked with Collier-Adams? He said he had done contract work for Talpa?"

"No, it was a wild guess based on what you said that DB told you. It was a probe, and when I stuck it in, Talpa said ouch. As far as I'm concerned, my guess was confirmed. But I think we'll know for sure in a few minutes. Wait here. I'll be right back."

At Talpa's office, Karl rapped on the open door and walked in without waiting for a response. Talpa was at his desk, staring at a cell phone in his hand.

"Sorry. I forgot my pen," Karl said, scooping the pen from the table and leaving as quickly as he had entered. At the exit, he held the pen up in front of Des. "Remember? It's my digital pen that records everything I write and everything it hears. I would sure hate to lose it; it's a reporter's best friend. Let's go sit in the car for a minute and listen to what transpired after we left."

22

DES WAS ALREADY ASLEEP, and Karl was shivering in his chilly car. After talking with Shira about Bini's summer plans and Shoshi's growing vocabulary, Karl switched to Skype with a recently installed encryption add-on that provided yet another layer of security. He called Anat at her office and brought her up to date. He told her that there had been nothing useful on the pen recording, just the sound of key presses and one word from Richard Talpa: "Shit!" He also told her that he was almost certain that Talpa knew Collier-Adams, had used his services, and was somehow tied into whatever skullduggery was afoot.

Anat thanked him and said, "Here's what we know. Money for Operation Nagasaki, as it appears to have been known to at least some of those involved, was mostly funneled through this virtual world called Life 2.0. Do you know it? Yes, of course, well, there was a clearinghouse of sorts called Coder's Corner where software freelancers could match up with clients in need of short-term programming services. That's where the late Elliot Feldersmann got recruited, picked up his assignments, and through which he got paid. Unfortunately, our attempts to penetrate the shroud that surrounds financial transactions in Life 2.0, particularly those that convert between Newlands Dollars and real currency, have so far been unsuccessful. Our techies have been unable to hack into it, and we have not been able to work our way into the upper echelon of the Newlands organization. We don't know real names or locations for any of the key players except this Collier-Adams, who has dropped out of sight. We're looking, of course. But we need a gateway into Newlands—hardware, software, or wetware—anything that works."

"I think I can help," Karl said. "I'll get on it tomorrow."

"It's already tomorrow here in Tel Aviv. This whole operation looks ready to blow at any minute. If what you say is true, the bot net created by the Scenaria Trojan could bring the developed world to its knees. Can we get somebody inside the inner sanctum at Scenaria so we know what is happening with their containment efforts—or apparent containment efforts? Can we use this Destiny Allen?"

"Maybe, but she's been compromised by association with me and this meeting we had with Talpa. I don't know. I suspect she's going to be watched awfully closely."

"Do what you can while you can. But be careful out there, as they used to say on *Hill Street Blues*."

"I didn't know you were a follower of vintage American TV."

"Are you kidding? I have DVDs of everything Steven Bochco ever did. *Hill Street* and another '80s MTM production, *St. Elsewhere*, were some of the best TV produced anywhere or ever."

"You'll have to lend them to me when I'm back in Haifa."

"Done. So, be careful out there." She disconnected.

— —

After once more confirming the cell tower triangulation on the SIM card, it had been relatively easy locating the right building in Baltimore, but finding the right apartment was a bigger challenge. Fortunately, it was a small, somewhat chi-chi building with large apartments. After bluffing his way past the doorman, Karl took the elevator to the top floor, where he stood in the middle of the hall, called the Isle of Man cell phone number, and listened for a ring before immediately hanging up. He walked down a flight, tried it again, then waited ten minutes before another attempt. He did not want to raise suspicions too much and did not want to risk that the phone would be turned off. The third time was lucky, and just after he heard the ring on his phone, a ringtone could be heard coming from one of the apartments on the floor. This time he let it continue to ring as he walked down the hall. It was loudest outside the door at the end, apartment 3D. He hung up before the phone was answered, then put his ear to the door. The door was too thick to make out words, but he could hear voices.

He walked down another flight, took out his iPod Touch, and selected a Smashing Pumpkins track before pushing the call button for the elevator. He reached in, pressed the button for the lobby, then wedged a toothpick in the button for the top floor. He cranked up the volume on the iPod and slid it onto the elevator just as the doors were closing.

Karl scrambled down the stairs to the first floor, where he waited in the stairwell until the doorman came over to investigate the source of the music. The doorman entered the elevator, looked around, and spotted the iPod at the back just as the doors closed again and the elevator started for the top floor.

Karl trotted to the desk and checked the register before picking up the handset for the intercom and pressing 3D. "Good evening, Mrs. Ventnor. This is the doorman. A courier just arrived with a thick envelope for you. I can't leave the desk right now, but would you like me to send him up? Very good. He'll be right up." Karl ran back across the lobby and reached the stairwell just as the elevator was returning. He took the stairs two at a time as quietly as he could. At the third floor, he had to stop to catch his breath and slow his heart again before pressing the buzzer at apartment 3D.

A short round woman with a salon tan and dyed hair opened the door cautiously, leaving the security chain in place.

Karl smiled as he casually inserted his foot in the door. "Donna Horvath? I'm Karl Lustig with iTech Weekly Online. My editor emailed you and called your office about an interview. I hope this is not a bad time? I have some material that I thought might interest you."

"You have the wrong apartment. My name is Christina Ventnor. I don't know any Horvath."

An accented voice from the next room called out, "Who is it, Donna?"

Karl smiled and spoke softly. "Look, I'm here and I obviously know who you are. What can you lose by inviting me in for a few minutes? Your cover has clearly been blown."

"How did you find us? Who told you where we were? Nobody knows. Who could have told?"

I'll tell you everything, just please open the door."

She looked at him warily as her husband came up behind her. "This man says he is from iTech Weekly. He knows who we are."

"And I know who he is: I recognize him from the headshot on his blog. We can let him in. Why don't you fix us some tea, dear."

The door closed in Karl's face, then reopened wide with Erno Horvath beckoning him to hurry in. He was a tall man who had once been thin but now sported a generous paunch and a jowly face. The hands with which he gestured were large and coarse, and his sleeve slid up to show the edge of a tattoo on his inner arm.

The apartment was roomy and elegant, with coved ceilings, walls the color of buttermilk, and trim the color of merlot. Erno Horvath led Karl through a step-down living room and into a formal dining room, where he gestured toward the tall-backed chair at the head of the table. "Please, you are our guest, Mr. Lustig. Sit down. We can talk over tea."

Karl sat down reluctantly in the large armchair. "Thank you," he said. "There's really no need for anything. I just want to talk."

"I'll get the tea," Erno said, crossing behind Karl and leaving for the kitchen. He returned balancing on his back-turned hand a large tray with a pot of tea, three cups, and a plate of small cookies.

Karl was about to begin with his first question when the door behind him from the kitchen was suddenly kicked open. Karl turned. The man who faced him was built like a cartoon bear, with a small head and jutting nose at the end of a long,

222

thick neck that rose from a pear-like body of outsized proportions.

"Zollie!" Erno shouted. "What the hell?"

Karl started to stand but had only risen partway when he found his arms suddenly pinned behind him. There was a ratcheting sound as a pair of handcuffs were snapped closed just before hands were placed on Karl's shoulders and he was forced back down into the chair. Karl cried out, "Hey!" and tried to rise, but was roughly jammed back into the chair once more.

"Shut up and stay put," the man said, with his face close enough for Karl to be assaulted by garlic and onions on the man's breath.

"What are you doing here, Zollie?" Erno insisted.

"My job. I got the silent alarm from Donna's cell phone. I was in the car across the street. I used my pass key to come in the back way. It's what you pay me for."

Donna Horvath entered the room hesitantly. "I paged him, Darling. I don't trust this man. We can't have anyone know where we are."

"He's a blogger, Donna.

Zollie looked from Donna to Erno. "You know this man?"

Erno shook his head. "Not really, but I know who he is. He just wants to interview us."

"And how do you know who he is and what he wants? I suppose you read it on the Web or you saw his picture and credentials on LinkedIn. You know nothing. You do not even know who I am."

"You are Zoltan Pongrass, my wife's second cousin."

"And by what authority is that known? Did you Google me after we were introduced? Of course, you know who I am, but you know nothing of who this man is or why he has been stalking you."

"He has been stalking us? You knew this and yet you said nothing?"

"I knew no such thing, but how else would he track you here? He and that woman from the security company. They have been trying to find you. He is a spy." He sniffed the air. "I can smell them by their sweat, which stinks of deception. The woman, I don't know. She maybe was just caught up in that hair-brained scheme of Truman's to use The New Game to find you. But this one, this one is a spy. He found us."

"I'm a journalist. We're trained to be resourceful. It was not all that hard finding you. Cell phones leave footprints."

Zoltan regarded him with contempt. "You think I am a dumb bodyguard, a pinhead with a distrustful nature, fast hands, and a short temper. You would be right, mostly, if you thought that, but even the Horvaths don't know that I have a degree in informatics from *Műegyetem*, the University of Technology and Economics in Budapest. So we do not know everything about people, even the people that we know, and I know nothing about you. So, you will talk and I will listen and ask questions."

"Informatics? I did computer science at MIT, so we are both working below our academic qualifications. But I like my work. What about you?"

Zoltan looked confused and annoyed. "I will ask the questions. Am I understood?"

"You are. And it should be fun to be interviewed for a change. So, where are you going to start? What would be the best question to ask me? Would it be about journalism or iTech Weekly? About online games or financial irregularities at Newlands Labs?" Erno Horvath edged forward in his seat. Karl continued, "Would you like to ask me about contract programmers working in virtual space or about in-world organizations, say the Planet Police?"

Donna laughed, a giggle with a tinge of panic. "Don't you see what he is doing?"

Karl smiled. "Of course. I know who you are and what is going on. I did my homework. Obviously you have not been kidnapped nor are you on an extended vacation. You are hiding out. And there are people looking for you, people inside Newlands Labs and people they have duped into assisting."

"See," she said, "he knows about Truman, he knows about the money, he knows about the credit charges."

"Shut up," Erno snarled. "All you do is help to confirm what were only suspicions or mere guesses. Shut up!"

"And what are you doing, my Darling?" she retorted.

"Shut up, both of you," Zoltan barked as he stood and started pacing. "The question is less about what he knows and more about what we are going to do with him."

"You are going to talk with me. You are going to correct me about what I have wrong and help me to understand so that I can carry your story to people who can help you."

"Who can help us?" Zoltan snarled. "Not you, mister blogger. We can take care of ourselves, as we have done quite well so far."

"Right, so well hidden that a random blogger who is not even from this country can find you just like that. Right."

"You are not American? You sound American," Erno said.

"I am from Israel, where your other work, your charitable work, is well known and deeply appreciated."

Erno bowed his head slightly. "I am Hungarian, but after the war and seeing what was becoming of postwar Hungary, I went to Israel, then Canada, and now we hold both Israeli and Canadian passports." He held out his arm toward Karl and pointed to the numbers on his wrist. "I was only a child, already an orphan, when I got this and would have had it only long enough to be gassed with my older brother if we had not been liberated. Israel gave me a new life, and I was prepared to give Israel mine, but I was still too young to join the Palmach and too smart and impatient for the life of the kibbutz, so I married this Canadian girl who came for a year of study and work, and we moved to Vancouver. It was our son who did all the design and programming for Life 2.0, our son who moved to Israel to start his own company, our son who died when a suicide bomber walked into a club where he and his bride-to-be were partying."

Donna gave him a look that only he could interpret. "Why are you telling him all this, Erno?"

"Because he is here and because I want to hear his story, too."

"You are so old-country, Erno. To this day you act as if you were in a *shtetl* talking with a man who just walked toward you leading his donkey loaded with wheat."

"Is that so bad?" He turned to Karl. "Your story, please. And Zollie, take off the handcuffs, please."

"My story," Karl began as the handcuffs were being removed, "is less interesting, perhaps. I went to Israel to escape a plot against my life, to avenge the death of a friend from college, and to marry the woman that I had waited most of my life to meet, but I knew none of this when I first boarded the plane to Tel Aviv. Now I have a son and a daughter, and I am a blogger who wants to know what Truman Siebalt has done and why you fear him."

"And you say that is not an interesting story? As to the story of Truman Siebalt, that is a tale of deceit and betrayal." Erno feigned spitting at the floor. "We trusted him with our business, and he walked all over our trust. He is an embezzler who has siphoned off millions from Newlands. We discovered his treachery only because we were so actively involved in Life 2.0, where he was laundering money by moving it among virtual banks and imaginary enterprises, converting it to hard currency and back and again. When we confronted him, he threatened to bring down Newlands altogether. And then the death threats started."

"Why didn't you go to the police, to the authorities?"

The Horvaths looked at each other before Donna answered. "As you can see, Erno is of the Old World. He is a Hungarian Jew who learned early that the police were not to be trusted and that one must take responsibility for one's own life to survive. So we concocted the story of an extended vacation but then disappeared. We left Truman in charge, but remotely crippled some of the features in Life 2.0 after we dropped out, effectively freezing a large part of his assets. This leaves him with a stake in keeping us alive, since right now, we are the only ones who can unlock the features. Something backfired, though, because we started getting the threats, then we learned that a group within Life 2.0 were trying to track us down and getting too close.

"Zollie tried to scare some of them off. Maybe it worked, maybe not."

Karl looked at the bear-man, sizing him up. "Did you kill that guy from the Game, Liam Osbourne, the one who was called Blue Leader? And what about the threats to Destiny Allen who was on the Blue Team? Was that you?"

Donna looked reproachfully at the big man; he shrugged. "I have killed no one. I tried to scare the woman and that other one on the team to get them off the trail, but I kill no one. As for this one," he gestured with his thumb toward Karl, "I do not know. He knows too much about things at Newlands, and now he knows where you are. What do we do with him?"

"Nothing, you need do nothing with me," Karl said, "except let me go. I am not on deadline. By the time my story comes out, these matters will be settled. In the meantime, I will not publicize where you are or even that you have been located. But you need to go to the authorities. They can move against Siebalt and protect you. Believe me, this is not Hungary during the war or under the Soviets."

Zoltan stood up, towering over them all. "Erno, listen to me. Do not trust this man. He is open, he speaks as a friend, but he is a liar, a trained one. He talks like some of those who trained in Moscow before returning to Budapest to become agents in the ÁVH, the secret police. He answers questions with questions and discloses small tidbits, appetizers to induce us to provide a feast in return."

Karl looked into Zoltan's eyes. "It is true, all of it," he said, as if confessing in court. "I make a living by getting people to tell me things." He paused for impact. "But I am just a technology writer who stumbled onto this stage and now wants to help to write a happy ending for the drama. Here," he took out a business card and quickly scribbled a number on it. "Call my cell phone anytime, for anything. If I can help, I will.

"Now, it is truly late, and I must go." He stood and strode briskly back through the living room before anyone could stop him. From the dining room, Erno Horvath called after him. "Thank you. We will call you."

Karl hurried down the two flights of stairs. He stopped in the lobby, reached across the desk, and picked up his iPod. "Super!" he said to the confused doorman. "I wondered what had happened to it. Thanks for finding it." He turned and walked out before the doorman could say anything.

— —

"I don't like it when you disappear in the night without telling me where you are going or even that you are going." Des was sitting cross-legged on the bed in the same position she had been in when Karl first tried to tiptoe into the room. He had been relieved to find her still dressed in jeans and a hoodie. He had explained what had happened, that he needed to act quickly to get to the Horvaths before they broke bivouac, but she would not let it go. It reminded Karl of times when he was in hot water with Shira.

"I know. I'm sorry." He hung his head, a stance that sometimes worked with Shira.

"Sorry won't cut it. Either we're in this together or we're not. What is it going to be, Karl?"

"If that's the list of options, then we're not." She looked at him with shock on her face. "You're a graphic designer," he continued, "who walked in on a game of high-stakes poker being played by armed card sharks. I'm a journalist with a murky past who knows how to bluff when necessary and is now playing the odds with a tough hand."

Her eyes narrowed, then her face softened. "You know, Lustig, you are not very convincing when you do the hard-bitten professional shtick. You ought to stick to roles that you can pull off."

He smiled reluctantly. "You think so, huh? All right. Then I have a question for you. Is there anyone inside Scenaria you can actually trust? I mean really trust."

"Yeah. DB. I admit he's a little odd, but I trust him. He told me about the Scenaria utilities on the disk from Marky; he didn't tell Talpa or Harry, and certainly not Vern Jeffers, whom he is working under for the nonce. I think he is on our side, whatever side that is. I do wish you could be straight with me, Karl."

"I am being straight with you or we wouldn't be having this conversation. So DB is temporarily an insider with the whiz kids, right? Does he work in the clean room, the Vault, as I think you call it?"

"Sometimes."

"Okay. I want you to get him to get you onto the team and inside that Vault."

"Why would Talpa ever let that happen. He has reason to distrust me now, which is the same reason he distrusts you. And we were together during that interview. I saw the looks on his face. He may not have anything on me, but he has his doubts."

"Fine, then we will exploit his doubts. We'll get DB to suggest that Talpa can keep closer tabs on you if he has you on the Vault team, under Harry's watchful eye. Plus, you have offered important help on the effort, and you are already familiar with the key disk and what's at stake. Finally, they need all the help they can get."

"I'm not sure how much help they think they would get from a graphic designer. The only code I know much about is HTML and CSS, you know, markup languages for websites, which I don't think will go far in what they are working on in the Vault. But we can give it a shot. However, I think it would be better to have DB plant the bug in Harry's ear. I am not sure how much credence Talpa would grant to DB, but I do know Harry has been a close confidant of Talpa's for a long time. Plus, with Harry's distancing himself from me, Talpa is more likely to take the suggestion at face value."

"You think Talpa knows that you and Harry have split?"

"Everybody knows. It seems everybody knew when we were a thing. I think what people most expect about indiscretion is that it be discreet. As long as you don't kiss in the hallway or frighten the horses in the parking lot, people let it go. Make a spectacle of it, and the moralizing chimes out loud and long; otherwise, it's mostly live and let live."

"And you think that's okay?"

"No, probably not. But I don't need to run a bigger guilt trip on myself than I already have." She reached for the light beside the bed and flicked it off. Karl started to flop down on the other bed, then grabbed the pillow and threw it on the sofa across the room.

"Goodnight, Destiny," he whispered as he lay down. But it was Shira's face that swam before his eyes as he stared into the darkness.

23

THE BODY MIGHT NOT have been found for many days had not a jogger taken a different route on her morning run, turning onto the pathway that ran along the far edge of the marshland. The car and its occupants were too far away for her to identify, but she confirmed to police that there were three of them, one dramatically taller than the others. The dead man had been severely beaten before he was killed. The coroner's report confirmed that, in addition to multiple bruises, a broken jaw, and burns on his arms, there was massive trauma from a single blunt blow on the back of the head. Nevertheless, the immediate cause of death had been drowning, since the man had been unconscious but alive when he was dumped face down in the marsh. The victim could not be immediately identified, but police suspected he was connected with organized crime and possibly involved in a double cross.

Barry Collier-Adams gagged when he saw the news report. The battered and swollen face in the photo was almost unrecognizable. "You stupid bastard," he shouted at the screen. "I told you not to do anything stupid. What did you do? What did you do?" There was nothing in the story that told him anything, save for the eyewitness report on the three men who allegedly dumped the body. His anger started to give way to apprehension as he thought about the killers. Who had his cousin told and what had he told them? Who would want him dead? Was somebody onto their system and trying to stop it? Or was someone trying to wipe out a trail? Either way, Barry knew he was in danger and would have to work fast to sort it out. He wondered where to start. He only knew some of the players and even fewer by name. Should he go back to Talpa, or was it Talpa who was trying to cover his own tracks. What about this Mallory kid? Barry could never be certain of his employer's identity, though, but from his reading after the attack, it was his guess that Mallory might have been the one who had initially recruited him and slipped him the detailed specs for Tricorn.

He started thinking about how he might protect himself. He knew nothing about guns and, despite his tendency to sometimes dress like a ninja, was actually a stranger to physical violence with no knowledge of any of the martial arts. His combat skills were entirely cerebral, and his arena was cyberspace. Play your strong suit, his father had always told him, advice that usually followed after the failure of yet another of his father's many ill-conceived schemes.

Barry had already started working on his plan when there was a knock on the door. He tiptoed over and approached from the side, turning out the lights before swinging aside the metal teardrop that covered the peephole. It was the room service waiter arriving with the burger he had ordered. He removed the chain and opened the door.

— —

Talpa finished reading the wire service report from Australia that had been among the first hits in the search results, then checked out the online edition of the Sydney Morning Herald. None of the reports on Collier-Adams said anything about interrogation or mysterious circumstances. Both described it as an apparent suicide, the body having been discovered by the cleaning staff of the serviced apartment in North Sydney where Collier-Adams had been staying. Talpa had to admit that he was impressed by the abilities of Mallory and his people to orchestrate a complete cover up. He had worked his way down to reading some of the more obscure and indirect search engine hits, including an anonymous blogger who eulogized the dead hacker as a genius with unparalleled programming skills, when Jill, his administrative assistant poked her head into the office.

"Your nine o'clock is here."

"I have a nine o'clock?"

"Yes, you yourself entered it directly into the shared calendar. Check it out for yourself: Barry Compote." She snickered.

Talpa toggled over to his view of the calendar. There it was, with his own initials as author and a time stamp yesterday evening. He snorted. "I must be slipping. Send him in." Talpa reached for his coffee as Jill disappeared into the outer office.

When the man entered, Talpa choked and sprayed hot coffee across the green blotter on his desk.

"Surprised to see me?" the visitor said, closing the door behind him.

"What the fuck? I thought you were in Australia. I thought you were dead?"

Barry Collier-Adams snorted. "News websites are among the easiest to hack into. Did you know that? And even police files are just databases. An anonymous phone call that just has to be checked, confirmed by a duty officer from a report he retrieves, an online search that uncovers more details, and presto! A man is found dead in the antipodes, an apparent suicide. Virtual reality trumps reality.

"Appearances can be so deceiving, Talpa, particularly online appearances. You thought I was a dead hacker and I thought you were a legitimate businessman, a trustworthy client with whom I had a simple and satisfactory relationship. I met requirements—and then some—on the work I did for you. You paid on time. That should have been it, until the next job. But now you are trying to get rid of me, you goddamned crippled prick."

Talpa said nothing but followed Collier-Adams with his eyes as the man paced in long-legged strides around the room.

"Nice facilities you have here," Barry said, gesturing. "I bet your house is even nicer. You've done all right for yourself, Dr. Talpa. With my help, of course. But you would be amazed how quickly all of this could be wiped out. I wouldn't even have to say anything, just publish some source code and wait for the open source community to work out what it does and why. Man, I bet the white-hat hackers would have a field day. Or maybe the black-hat gang would figure it out first and devise an exploit. That would be a twisted form of justice. Your competition would relish that, wouldn't they?"

"Are you trying to blackmail me? After what you did? What do you want, anyway?"

"Nothing. I'm not looking for more money. You paid me well enough, and now I have clients who pay me even better. Thanks for the letter of reference, so to speak. No, I just want to make sure you don't do to me what you had done to my poor little cousin."

"Your cousin? What are you talking about? I didn't do anything to anyone."

"No, you wouldn't or couldn't do it yourself. Your kind always has goons to do the dirty work. Besides, you're a goddamned crip in a fucking space-age wheelchair. You're not going to go out in that thing and beat somebody to death, now are you?"

Talpa's heart was pounding, and with his reduced blood volume, he could almost feel his pressure shooting up. "Look, I really don't know what you are talking about. What I do know is that you left a backdoor in our code when you did that job for me, and now you have our software turning our clients' computers into a new and powerful bot net. You could save us some trouble and yourself some grief if you just tell us how to remove it. I'll even pay you as a consultant. Of course, I won't let you anywhere near any of our computers, not ever again, and everything you tell us will get the fine-toothed vetting by our staff of resident geniuses. But you could earn some more money on this, even if it is your own mess you'd be paid to clean up."

Barry struck the desk with such force that Talpa's cell phone and pen bounced. "I do not make messes, Dr. Talpa. You should know that. I make software that is more solid than this fucking desk of yours. No, as I said, I am not looking for more work or more money. I have all I need. I am simply looking to be left alone. So, call off your goons. Now!

Or by next month, you and Scenaria are going down, all the way down, as in down the dunny. I wonder what kind of facilities the Feds have for felons in wheelchairs. Do they have handicap access to the showers?" He chuckled. "Maybe they just throw you behind bars and let you rot on the bunk."

"I don't have any goons, and I still don't know what you think I did. What are you talking about?" Talpa tried to keep his voice from shaking as he rolled out from behind the desk.

"You lying piece of shit, you know goddamned well what I am talking about." He grabbed Talpa by the shirt and tugged. "You killed my cousin, Marky, Marky Collier-Adams. Your hired guns beat him to death and dumped him in a New Jersey swamp. For that, I should finish you and this fucking company off, but I am just not the vengeful type, you know. So I am going to let you off with a warning and a word about a new rider on my insurance policy. So don't fuck with me or it will backfire, and you will take it right in the arse yourself. You hear?"

Talpa looked even more confused. "Insurance policy? I don't get it."

"Maybe not, but you will if you don't cooperate. You really have no idea who you are dealing with or how good I am. If I can take out Tricorn for a client, bringing down Scenaria for myself will be a piece of cake—and a genuine pleasure."

Barry pulled so hard on the shirt bunched in his hand that Talpa started choking as he was lifted up against the seatbelt that kept him harnessed in his chair.

Desperate, Talpa reached for the button that shifted the iBOT into standing mode. The wheels rotated into their vertical configuration and the seat support extended, raising him up until he was eye-to-eye with Barry. "Get out of my office. Now!" he said, squeezing the words out.

Barry's eyes widened. "You pathetic half-man," he said, shoving at Talpa as if to push him over. The computer-controlled iBOT compensated instantly and kept Talpa firmly upright.

Talpa leaned forward, putting his face right in Barry's face. "Get out!" he spat, as he shoved at Barry, throwing him off balance. Barry caught himself against the conference table, then launched himself at Talpa, but even with all his full weight thrown into the lunge, the iBOT only shifted back a few inches as it kept Talpa vertical. Barry was taken completely off guard as Talpa sent the robot chair forward with full force, knocking him to the ground. Barry looked up with a mix of fury and terror at the towering, legless man in the high-powered wheelchair. He struggled to his feet and swung at Talpa, who stopped the swing and locked Barry's wrist in a vice-like grip. Talpa pushed forward against Barry, his powerful arm, toned by years of upper-body workouts and wheelchair races for charity, twisting until Barry's wrist snapped. Barry screamed and went berserk, swinging wildly at Talpa with his good arm, kicking at the base of the iBOT. Talpa fought back, pushing steadily forward until Barry was pinned between the iBOT and the conference table. Barry struggled futilely. Helpless against Talpa's powerful arms and the whining motors of the iBOT, he tried to twist aside. Feedback circuits in the iBOT, in an attempt to compensate, spun Talpa to one side, throwing Barry off balance and tumbling him to the floor. One wheel of the iBOT started to roll over Barry's neck, tilting Talpa precariously to the side. Talpa's instinctive shift forced the iBOT to roll further forward before reversing and getting back on the level again. Talpa looked down from his high-tech tower. Barry, his larynx crushed, didn't move.

Talpa looked up to see Jill and Harry staring at him in horror.

"What happened?" Harry shouted.

"Are you all right?" Jill asked, shaking her head and running toward him.

Talpa struggled to get his breathing under control. "He tried to kill me," he said, as calmly as he could manage. "We better call the police."

— —

Harry stood in the doorway of Vern's office, which Talpa was taking over temporarily while the police finished their work in the executive suite. "They took their time taking your statement and all, didn't they. What did you tell them?"

"That he was some hacker, an extortionist who threatened to wreck our systems if we didn't pay him. When I refused and moved to leave to get help, he tried to stop me. In the struggle, he ended up under a wheel of the iBOT."

"And they bought it?"

"It's true, basically. And what cop is going to doubt the word of a double amputee up against an able-bodied maniac? They'll check his record, confirm that he was a consummate computer hacker with a criminal record and a trail of shady dealings. Accidental death, self-defense. Case closed. When it hits the papers, our PR people will no doubt spin it as 'brave CEO fends off crazed computer criminal.'"

Harry hesitated at the door. "Did he ever work for us? He told Jill while he was waiting that he had worked for you. I checked with human resources, and they had nothing on him."

Talpa looked at Harry, trying to take the measure of him, trying to guess about the finer points of his personal priorities and loyalties. "Close the door, Harry, and have a seat."

24

DES WAS THINKING that she was in over her head. She had called in sick before catching the early flight to O'Hare. She had used the flight out and the cab ride from the airport to get her story straight and to convince herself that it was just an interview with a businessman. In the end, she knew she had failed to delude herself. When the taxi pulled over to the curb at the ugly, green-glass-and-Corten trapezoid that was the Newlands high-rise corporate headquarters, she fumbled nervously with the change from the cab fare before giving up and simply thrusting everything back at the driver, over-tipping him as a result and forgetting to ask for a receipt in the process. At the fifteenth floor, she handed a business card to the receptionist seated in front of a gargantuan rendering of the Newlands corporate logo.

"And what can I do for you, Ms. Gustafson?"

"I'm here to see Truman Siebalt," Des said, reminding herself that she was Dina and to stay in role and play the reporter.

"Do you have an appointment?"

"No, but just tell him I have a message from Donna and Erno. I'm quite sure he'll want to see me."

"Let me call his assistant and find out. You can have a seat over there."

"I don't want to have a seat over there, and I don't want you to call and tell his assistant anything. I want you to tell Truman Siebalt that I am from the Business News Network and that I have a message for him from Donna and Erno Horvath. Is there any part of that you would like to have me explain again?"

"Miss, I hope I do not have to call security. In any case, there is nothing I can do now. Mr. Siebalt is not here. He rarely comes into the office this early."

"Fine, then I will wait. I'll just take a seat over there, as you suggested. Thanks."

It was more than an hour of flipping through magazines and full-color corporate brochures before she spotted Siebalt stepping off the elevator amidst a small knot of men in nearly identical business suits. Siebalt, a full head taller than any of his entourage, was dressed in a safari jacket and dark blue slacks. As Des stood and walked toward him, two of the men took a few steps to position themselves between her and Siebalt.

"I have a message from Donna and Erno Horvath," she said, leaning to one side in an attempt to talk past the two men running interference for Siebalt.

"Oh, you saw them in St. Thomas?" he said, forcing a smile, a sliver of white teeth slicing across his broad, sun-leathered face. "I do hope they are enjoying their holidays there. I envy them. But I am afraid I have no time to chat. I have a board meeting to prepare for. Give my regards to the

Horvaths when next you see them, thanks. Cheers." He signaled his companions to follow.

"They are not in the Virgin Islands," Des said, "and we both know it. So did Liam Osbourne of the Blue Team. I think we should talk, don't you?"

One of the men took a step toward Dina, but Siebalt put out a hand to stop him. "Of course," he said. "How rude of me. I can take a few minutes out for a friend of Donna and Erno. Please, come on into my office." He turned toward the receptionist. "Harriet, would you please hold my calls and ask Randall to be a love and bring us coffee." He glanced briefly toward the knot of men standing stiffly waiting, then led the way alone through the double doors to the side of the reception area.

Siebalt's corner office, with floor-to-ceiling views over downtown Chicago and the waterfront, was larger than Des's entire apartment. The scale was exaggerated by the spare décor: a desk and matching conference table topped with thick green glass, four custom-designed pedestal chairs around the conference table, and a massive throne of a chair in green leather behind the desk. The wall to the right of the door through which they had entered was a single massive projection display filled with windows showing real-time stock quotes, in-world activity in Life 2.0, and news feeds.

Siebalt gestured toward one of the chairs at the conference table, then walked behind the desk and seated himself in his green leather chair just as his assistant showed up with a tray of coffee. "Thanks, Randall," he said, "Don't bother to pour." Randall, a slim, long-haired youngster in an Italian-tailored charcoal suit, nodded and placed the tray on the corner of the desk before retreating. Siebalt, ignoring the coffee, leaned forward, elbows on the desk, and confidently tapped the spread fingers of both hands against each other.

"So, Ms. Gustafson," he began, "where is it that you think the Horvaths might be, if they are not at their place in St. Thomas? I must say, it is not like them to change plans without telling anyone or to take off on a whim. I do hope there is nothing untoward going on. Did you actually talk with them?"

"Not actually," she said, opening her notebook and placing the digital pen on the table beside it. "One of my colleagues at BNN did. As you know, I am sure, Business News Network is a large news organization with a special focus on technology companies. We file stories and share information. I am just following up on some of the findings in my colleague's notes that have already been passed on up. I am trying to fill in some of the blanks to complete the picture. And I wanted to get your side of the story."

"I don't know that there is a picture to complete, Ms. Gustafson. Nor do I think there is any particular story for which you might need my side."

"You don't think your own story is interesting?"

"My story? I'm just an Aussie tall poppy who grew too big for the outback. I herded techo start-ups in Singapore and Tokyo through to IPOs, helped build value on the share markets, jumped ship, then swam over to come aboard Newlands two-and-a-half years ago as CTO, moved up to become COO, and now am acting CEO in the Horvath's temporary absence. Once they return—from St. Thomas—I will be back to my regular position running the day-to-day operations of their virtual empire. There is not much of a story in that."

"Perhaps, but you did have a rather radical past, did you not? After completing your studies at Sydney University, you were a greenie associated with various so-called direct-action environmental causes. This," she said gesturing around the office, "is rather far removed from that. The only thing 'green' about this venue would seem to be the chair you are sitting in, assuming that it's not real leather."

"We all do things in our youth that in our maturity take on a different tenor. I am a businessman. My conservation efforts are nowadays focused on conserving capital and on building value for our shareholders."

"The Horvaths expressed concern about declining value, about assets that were being diverted. They implied to my colleague that you might know something about that. Just what can you tell me about the financial state of Newlands Labs?"

Siebalt held her eyes and smiled another sliver of a smile. "I thought we were here to talk about the Horvaths and some unsupported assertions that they are not where all of us knew them to be. Just where is it that your colleague thinks he has seen them? I am quite certain that it must have been a case of mistaken identity, unless he saw them at their private estate in St. Thomas, which is where I understand they are enjoying a much-needed respite from the pressures of the business. I have no such fortune, of course, which is why we will need to keep this interview brief. There are many matters to which I must attend."

"I am sure. Might one of those matters concern a malfunction in the InterBanc network within Life 2.0 such that it no longer processes transaction overrides and special transfer orders?"

Siebalt continued to lock eyes with her, but his smile wavered slightly. "Life 2.0 is an extremely complex hardware and software system, in all comprising something like three-and-a-half million lines of code, not counting the operating system itself. In anything that massive there will always be little operational glitches. We are forever finding and fixing bugs. That's life in Life 2.0. Whatever problems you may have encountered with banking functions, I am sure our technical support people can assist and put things right again."

"I'm not the one with problems, Mr. Siebalt. I was thinking of the problems you might be having with online finances."

His eyes narrowed but he never turned away. "I don't believe I have had any problems, but I could check with Customer Support to see if there have been any customer complaints needing attention." He reached for the phone on his desk.

"That won't be necessary. But perhaps you can shed some light on the fate of Liam Osbourne, one of the players on the Blue Team in The New Game."

Siebalt stared at her without blinking. "I believe you mentioned the name before, in the lobby, but I have nothing to do with any of the in-world games. Frankly, I am much too busy for games. I fear now that I must return to pressing matters, Ms. Gustafson. I'll have my assistant see you out."

He must have pressed a silent signal because Randall appeared at the door almost immediately.

"Randall, would you please escort Ms. Gustafson out. Her interview is finished. Make sure she gets a taxi to wherever she needs. And thank you, Ms. Gustafson, for your interest in

Newlands. I am so sorry I could not have been more helpful to you."

"Oh, you have been most helpful," she said, picking up her notebook and walking quickly past Randall without a backward glance.

In the lobby, Randall asked her if she needed a taxi, and she told him that she was headed for the airport. He turned to the receptionist and, in a voice dripping with treacle, said, "Harriet, please arrange for a limo to the airport, prepaid at our expense, of course." At the door to the outer office, he paused halfway through and said, "Ms. Bourbon will let you know when your limo arrives. Have a safe trip." He turned abruptly and shut the door behind him.

It was less than ten minutes before the receptionist announced, "Your limo is waiting outside the East entrance, Ms. Gustafson."

"Oh bother," Des said, checking her purse. "I forgot something. Tell the driver to hold a minute." She strode past the receptionist and then Randall's desk in the outer office and pushed through the doors to Siebalt's inner office without knocking. Siebalt was standing behind his desk with his council of lieutenants arrayed before him."

"I beg your pardon, Ms. Gustafson, but I thought you had left."

"I did. Or I am. I just forgot my pen. She scooped it up quickly from the conference table and slipped it into her purse. "Sorry to interrupt. Carry on gentlemen."

She spun around and exited as abruptly as she had entered.

— —

It was not until Des was airborne on her way back to DC that she plugged the earbuds into the jack in the LiveScribe and tapped on the legend in her notebook to replay the end of the meeting with Siebalt. The acoustics of the glass-walled office had been less than ideal, but the voices could still be understood, and Sielbalt's Australian accent was easily distinguished from the flat, Midwestern drone of the others.

"You have no idea how helpful you have been, Truman Siebalt," she muttered to herself. "And thanks for the warning that I would be followed, although I'm not terribly surprised. We shall see how long it takes before your detective squad figures out they are following the wrong woman. I just hope I haven't gotten Dina into trouble by pretending to be her, but it just made so much more sense to be a journalist."

— —

Karl was packing when Des got back to the hotel room. "Where have you been all day? I was worried," he said, annoyance and impatience staining his voice as he stuffed a book in amidst the clothes in his open suitcase. "I tried to call, but your cell phone was always unavailable. What were you up to?"

"Oh, I see, it's all right for you to take off cross-country without warning, but not for me?"

"No, that's not it at all. I was just concerned. Say, by any chance have you seen my LiveScribe pen and notebook? I seemed to have mislaid them."

"Ah, well, sorry. I borrowed them today. I needed them for some research. But it's my turn to ask what you are up to now. You're not leaving in the midst of all this mess, are you? Or is everything settled?"

"Things are far from settled. I'm just moving to another hotel. This arrangement is just not working. If I check out, it might also draw anyone who might have me in their sights away from you. And don't worry, InterMetroGroup will keep on picking up the tab for this room as long as you need it. As soon as I'm settled in my new digs, I'll call, but I really should go."

"Not until you hear this," she said, pulling the LiveScribe out of her purse. "And you have to show me how to download a recording from this thing." She turned on the pen, dug out the notebook, and started the playback. Tinny voices, her own and Siebalt's, came from the tiny built-in speaker.

"I recognize your voice, but who are you talking with?"

"Truman Siebalt. I spoke with him at Newlands headquarters in Chicago."

"You what? You should have checked with me first."

"Why? Do you check with me before talking with my mother?" They locked eyes in challenge, but Karl couldn't hold his gaze.

The playback continued. "Wait a minute, he just said 'Ms. Gustafson.' Was Dina there, too?"

"No, just me playing the role of BNN reporter. But shush, here comes the good part."

There was a long silence in the recording interrupted by several voices speaking at once. Siebalt silenced them with a barked command, then started giving orders. Gustafson was to be tracked, someone named Figuerra was supposed to make sure there was no trail from Osbourne, and someone addressed only as "you," was told to "find the fuckin' Horvaths." An argument started up before Siebalt could be heard again calling for silence by shouting, "Just fix it! Just fix the goddamned software. Find the problem and fix it. How hard can that be? If you can't do it yourselves, call in one of those genius hacker freaks that hang around in-world. They don't have to know what it's all about." The recording ended just after Des had entered to retrieve the pen.

Karl grinned at Des. "You are a fast student," he said. "And more successful than I was when I tried to pull the same trick with your boss. But you were taking too many chances going directly to Siebalt. Now they know that we know about the Horvaths and Siebalt's financial fudging, as well as linking Osbourne's death back to them. So you know way too much for them to leave it alone. And you may have put your friend Dina in the line of fire. We are going to have to get under cover quickly."

"I'll be back at Scenaria in the morning, working in the Vault. What could be safer?"

"You haven't heard, then."

"Heard what?"

"It's all over the news. Your boss killed an intruder, supposedly by accident and in self-defense, some cyber-criminal who, allegedly, was trying to shake down the company. His name was Collier-Adams."

"Marky? Talpa killed Marky Collier-Adams?"

"No, the other one, the one from Australia. But Marky is dead, too. They finally confirmed his identity from dental records. They found his body yesterday in a swamp up in New Jersey. It looked like a drug-related gangland hit, according to the papers, but what do you want to bet the two killings are related. And Talpa is looking dirtier by the minute."

"Then what about Siebalt and his geek-squad goons? What's the connection?"

"Don't know yet, but we had better sort it out before we are the ones being scrambled." He took a deep breath and exhaled sharply. "Look, change of plans. I'm going to put the room into your name, but you are going to be gone. I want you to leave right now, through the shopping level of the hotel complex. Take your time there, go in and out of shops, and try to make sure no one is following you without being too obvious about making sure. Take the Metro to Clarendon." He handed her a battered business card and a credit card. "In Clarendon, catch a cab to this motel and use this credit card to check in. For the time being, you're Elana Weingarten, okay? The motel is run by a *sayan*. They won't ask questions once they see the card. I'll try to get you some more documentation, just in case. Leave all your stuff here; I want it to look to anyone who peeks in like you are still around. You can use that credit card to buy whatever you need. Now go, now! Take the stairs. I know how to reach you through the motel. And here's a cell phone to use in dire emergencies."

"Do I go to work?"

"Did you call in sick today?"

"Yeah."

"Okay, stay out and stay quiet for a few days while we work things out. I'll contact you. Now go!"

Des went to the door, then turned back and walked over to Karl. She said, "Thanks!" and kissed him lightly on the lips before turning to leave. As the door closed behind her, Karl could still feel the brush of her lips on his, still smell the musty sweetness of her breath as she had spoken, one word, a word still hanging heavy in the air, fraught with other meanings, like some *Mossad* code word.

Shaking, Karl sat down on the bed, retrieved his Glock and attached the suppressor that he had bought, an under-the-table purchase in a DC pawn shop. He waited, watching the door, not knowing who he was waiting for or how long it would be.

25

LIKE A SHADOW all but invisible on a moonless night, the sound of a keycard sliding in and out was almost too quiet to be heard, yet Karl was instantly awake. As the handle of the door turned slowly, he tiptoed across the room and stood behind the door. Karl waited until it opened a few inches and a hand and foot were just visible before he slammed his body against it with all the force he could muster. He pulled it open, grabbed the arm, jerked the disoriented man into the room, and placed his Glock to the man's temple while using his foot to push the door closed again behind him.

"Move and you're dead," Karl said with all the menace he could muster. "Who sent you?"

Silence. Karl was wondering what to do next, when the man decided to speak. "We just want the bot net. Your midget coder told us everything we need to know, but apparently he didn't know the pass phrases to unlock the network. Either that or he died for nothing, which is what you will do if you don't give us what we want. So just give us the damn key disk. The guy said he gave it to the girl." His Slavic accent was evident, but Karl was not sure of the exact nationality.

"My partner" the man said through his teeth, "will be here in a minute to help persuade you. Gregori, he can be very persuasive, and killing me would only motivate him to be all the more so. We are cousins, you know. It is a family business, soon to be much expanded."

Karl said nothing, but patted the man down and extracted a Beretta from his coat pocket, which he tossed onto the bed, then retrieved the man's wallet. It had several hundred dollars plus a few bills in Euros but no credit cards or identification. "Put your hands behind you," he ordered. The man grunted as Karl maneuvered a cable tie into position and pulled it tight around his wrists.

Karl shoved him across the room and onto the sofa across from the door. "While you're waiting for your friend to show up—if there is a friend to show up—you can tell me who you are and who sent you."

"I told you, turd, Gregori is my cousin. We work for no one, except when we are contract programming. But now we work for ourselves, and then we will work no more, ever!"

There was a tap at the door and a loud half-whisper: "Stefan? Stefan?"

Karl leveled the gun at Stefan's head and held his fingers to his lips. In the hall, the man incautiously tried the handle before calling out again, "Stefan?"

Karl backed toward the door, opened it, and stuck his foot out, tripping the man, who ended up sprawled on the carpet, one arm under him and the other, holding another Beretta, extending into the bathroom. Karl straddled the man, kicked the gun under the sink, then stepped forcefully on the back of the man's head. "You must be cousin Gregori. Please put your hands behind your back, cousin, or I will happily put a bullet in the back of your head." Gregori lay still, arms splayed, until Karl ground his heel into the man's neck. Letting out a deep groan, Gregori put one hand behind his back, then struggled to bring the other around. Somewhat awkwardly, with the Glock still in one hand, Karl slipped another cable tie around the man's wrists and cinched it tight. "Get up! Sit! Over there."

With both men seated on the sofa, Karl paced back and forth in front of them, trying to figure out how to make his threats believable. "I need to know who sent you and why you are here. What do you want?"

Gregori spat air. "We tell you nothing. You tell us where the girl is so we can get the key disk."

"That's not how it works." Suddenly inspired, Karl picked up the telephone on the nightstand, yanked the cord from the wall, and struck Gregori in the face with the base. It was straight out of the movies, but seemed to be effective.

Gregori spat, bloody spittle landing on the carpet just short of Karl's feet. "I tell you. I already say who we are and what we want. But we are not alone. Bogdan waits in the car, and we have connections. When we deliver the bot net to the Ukrainians, they will pay us and we will be rich. If we do not, they will send others after us, who will kill us and you. It is simple. Give us access codes from key disk, we try them, and then we are gone. We do not care anything about you, because once we have control of the bot net, nothing stops us. Nothing!"

Karl decided to go for broke. "What about Talpa? What about Siebalt?"

The men looked puzzled. "Who?" they said, almost in unison.

"You are the ones who killed Marky Collier-Adams?"

"You want confession?" Stefan laughed. "Then I kill no one. Did you kill anyone, Gregori?"

"No, I kill no one, too. We just talk, ask questions. We kill not anyone. Stefan and me, we are genius programmers from Sofia. Not like Bogdan, who is dumb-ass farmer." Both men laughed heartily.

Karl shook his head. "Programmers, perhaps, but geniuses, hardly. From where I sit, it looks like the only two men who knew anything about the passwords you want are both dead. Now you will have to go home to the bosses in Sofia with nothing." He picked up the wallet he had tossed on the bed. "It does not look like there is enough here to get you back home. Maybe I can help arrange transportation."

He picked up the two matching Berettas, emptied them, wiped them with a corner of the bed sheet, and slipped them back into the men's jackets, then returned the wallet. "All right, gentlemen, let's go for a ride," he said, waving his Glock toward the door just as his cell phone started playing Dave Brubeck.

He glowered at the men as he flipped open his phone. "What's up?" he said. When he heard the voice on the other end, he switched to Hebrew and said, quietly, "Listen, this is not really a good time for us to talk. I'm busy with something. Better to send me email. Okay?" He closed the phone and took a deep breath before steering the two men toward the door.

He led them to the elevator at the bend in the hall, and when it arrived, shoved them in, pushing them to the floor.

He used his foot to keep the door from closing while he placed a call with his cell phone.

"It's me," he said into the phone. "I'm at the Meredith. Call the DC police right away and pass on a tip: some illegals on a watch list, at the Meredith, a couple of burley Bulgarians in cheap business suits. The cops will figure out which ones these two are. And have them be on the lookout for a third man parked in the neighborhood. They're all carrying, so tell the police to consider them armed and dangerous and to hurry before someone gets hurt."

He pressed the elevator button marked "Lobby" as he continued to hold the door, which started buzzing and pushing insistently against his foot. He looked at his watch and watched the seconds crawl by. After a full two minutes, with the elevator alarm starting to ring, he said, "Have a nice trip!" and removed his foot from the door. It slid shut as the bell and buzzer stopped.

Karl sprinted for the room, gathered up all of his stuff, swept the 9mm rounds he had emptied onto the bed into his pocket, and checked the bathroom for anything forgotten. He ran to the far end of the hall, where he took the stairs all the way down to the parking garage.

By the time the Bulgarians reached the lobby, they had managed to shove themselves against the back wall and slide erect. They were still struggling to get out of the cable ties when the elevator doors slid open. Two of DC's finest were waiting with guns drawn.

— —

Zoltan Pongrass watched from his green pickup truck as the black Continental suddenly pulled from the curb into the heavy downtown traffic. It turned immediately down an alleyway just as a police cruiser, siren wailing, turned into the street behind the Hotel Meredith. Zollie waited until the cruiser turned the next corner before pulling out and following after the Lincoln.

"He is secret police that one," he said, as he accelerated to catch up. "I can smell it by the stink of death that follows him, that contaminates his clothes and his car and everything he touches.

"Of course, none of them are with the government anymore; there are not enough jobs now. So, they work for themselves; they are the new mafias. This one looks like Bulgarian scum. I will get you, Bulgarian scum. Here I come."

26

IT WAS MID-MORNING in Haifa. Bini Markham, standing at the ready, whipped opened the door to the apartment at the first tap, startling Lev Novikov, whose hand jerked instinctively toward his brown leather jacket and a handgun that was not there and had not been there for years.

Bini suppressed a laugh. "A bit jumpy, Uncle Lev?" He motioned him in. "I don't want anyone to know you're here, especially Ima. She's down in her workshop trying to finish this big jewelry order. She left me in charge of Shoshi, who has finally decided to nap as she was supposed to an hour ago. Thanks for coming right away."

Bini, with none of the wiry awkwardness so common among thirteen-year-old boys, marched into the kitchen and sat down straddling one of the chairs, waiting for his uncle to follow. Bini was quick, strong, and compact like his late father had been, with his mother's kinky hair, dark eyes, and inventive intellect. His cherubic face said little of the intelligence churning behind it. Among his circle of online friends, he had built a reputation as a top-gun programmer and imaginative problem solver. He and his small network had even once cracked the code of a terrorist group by cobbling together a vast network of personal computers commandeered into a bot net by way of their own custom-coded Trojan.

Lev helped himself to a glass of water before sitting down across from Bini. "What's this about, Nephew?" he said. "Your IM was very emphatic but not very informative."

"But you came."

"Well, I am your Uncle Lev. So what's up?"

"I think Abba is in trouble. Ima won't say anything, but I know he's working with Anat again, and there is just something in his emails that doesn't compute. When I called him today, he wouldn't talk, said he was busy, but there was something wrong. I could hear it in his voice."

"Yes, you're right. I should not say this, but I can and will because I figured it out on my own. He is doing something for the Institute. Not that my wife will say anything to confirm or deny it, but, yes, he is. Still, remember, Karl is clever and very resourceful when he needs to be. He can take care of himself. I am sure he is fine."

"Do you have any idea what he is working on?"

"I shouldn't say anything, as I said, but here we are, a retired spook and a teenage Web surfer, and you have some suspicions and I have some guesses: just things that link up and point in a particular direction. I...."

Bini interrupted. "No, Uncle Lev, let me guess. It's connected with Animoroto and Scenaria and that power plant that blew up in the US."

Lev raised his eyebrows. "And just how do you figure that?"

"Duh. It's pretty obvious. Suddenly Abba just has to go to a video game conference where Animoroto is making a big splash with their new system. Then this power plant is hacked into…"

"That's speculation, Bini, we don't know that."

"Yes, we do. It may not be in the news, but it's all over the 'Net. And, conveniently, Scenaria comes along as the white knight with new security software that it claims could have stopped the attack."

"But how do you think this ties in with Animoroto?"

"Just wait. See, Scenaria deployed a new set of virus definitions and a special fix-it kit that started setting off alarms like crazy. Then, only hours later, they pulled it back without notice, and not a word about it since. That is suspicious."

"How in blazes do you know something like that?"

"My friend Nancy Silva in Boston works part time for a company that uses Scenaria security software. She thought that all that bait-and-switch updating was pretty interesting, so she recovered an image of the virus signature and the repair routine in the version before Scenaria secretly recalled them. It turns out that there's this rootkit still in all the computers at her company, despite the fact that the Scenaria software now says they are all clean. Now that's gi-normous suspicious, so she got our group working on reverse engineering this rootkit."

"Is that TechNahal?" Lev asked, referring to the group of technology-obsessed teenage campaigners Bini had started a couple of years earlier.

"Well, we don't call it that anymore, and we've lost a few members. Boner, that's Bono McClaren, well, he's graduated and got a job doing embedded systems programming for this robotics company in, well, someplace in the States, Washington or something. And, well, there's a few of us still working together. We have an idea for a new kind of anti-virus software that tracks changes in code, and…"

"Bini, just stick to the subject."

"Yeah, right. So the rootkit has pieces of code that are also in the operating software of the new Animoroto game console. And, get this, Nancy's Animoroto console recently updated itself. She checked the deltas—that's the differences between versions—and the new code was something she recognized. See, she's still in school but has done some PLC programming—that's industrial automation stuff—and computerized numerical control, like. Remember? Nancy?"

Lev recognized the name. She was the group member who, under the handle of NancyPants, had figured out some PLC programming in robot bombs that had been targeted for Jerusalem.

"I remember, Bini, but what about Animoroto?"

"Oh, yeah. Well, she finds a handshaking routine for establishing connections with some SCADA boxes used—get this—to manage generators."

"This is in the game consoles?"

"Not exactly. Most of it is in software in some of the PCs that the consoles can link up with after they are updated with the new revisions. It gets those through its Bluetooth or radio link from other consoles or from PCs that have the Bluetooth lash-up."

"This sounds pretty tenuous and indirect."

"Don't you get it, Uncle Lev? The rootkit is a Trojan that talks to the game consoles and shares software with the Animoroto ConNEXTivity network. The rootkit is actually in the Scenaria software distribution, the update that went out almost two years ago, Nancy says. Any computer using that version of Scenaria software or a later one is infected and connected with this game box network, which can talk with SCADA boxes." He spread his arms in a dramatic gesture.

Lev closed his eyes and stroked his nearly white goatee. "I wonder if Anat and her people have figured this out yet. I should give her a call. Do you mind? Can I use your 'private office?'"

Bini smiled and pointed toward his bedroom. "Sure, go ahead."

Lev walked slowly to the bedroom, thumbing a number on his cell phone as he went. He closed the door behind him. When he came out several minutes later, he was chewing his lip.

"They knew most of it already, but hadn't connected every last dot yet. And, remember that I did not say that to you, Bini. We are not having this conversation. And not a word to your friends, either—not one word. There is some serious shit going down and a leak could be disastrous. You understand?"

Bini nodded. "You know you can trust me. So what kind of shit? Is Abba in trouble?"

Lev sat down at the table, folded his hands, and leaned on his arms, saying nothing for long seconds. "I don't know if I can trust you, Bini. You have a history of playing spy games and not knowing when to quit the game, even when you are told."

"I was just a kid then, Uncle Lev," he said, referring to a time that was only shortly before his recent bar mitzvah. "I know enough now to keep my mouth shut. So tell me, what shit?"

"At least two of the hacker programmers they think were working on the project have been killed. I really don't believe your dad is in any danger, but I really don't want you poking around anymore. *HaMossad* will take care of things from here on out. Understand?"

Bini looked across at his uncle, staring without blinking. He stood before speaking. "Sure," he said without conviction. "Maybe you had better go before Ima comes up."

Lev nodded. "I'll take the back stairs."

— —

At the ground floor of the building, Lev slipped out into an alleyway, then walked around to the front and peeked in the window of Shira's studio. He could see her at the back, her blackened goggles reflecting the flame of a small torch. He tapped on the window, but she did not appear to hear. He wondered if he should tell her what Anat had told him, that they had lost contact with Karl, that he seemed to have dropped off the map. Perhaps it was better not to say anything to Shira. Not yet, he thought, as he turned into the wind and started down the street.

— —

Karl did not know where he was. It was suffocatingly hot, his head hurt, and his arms, tied behind his back, were beginning to go numb. As he exhaled, his breath showered heat back over his face, and he realized there was a bag over his head. He tried to stand, but discovered his feet were also tied. Bare walls echoed the hollow wooden sound of his efforts. Suddenly, the floor beneath him rocked and bounced. He was in some kind of a vehicle and it had started to move.

He remembered getting a call from the phone he had given to Des for emergencies. She had said only that he should meet her, then disconnected. He had taken a cab to the motel where he had sent her earlier. Knocking on the door to her room was the last thing he remembered.

Now, he twisted his head inside the bag and called out, "Des! Are you there? Are you all right?" There was no answer. "Des?" He started inching his way across the floor as it bounced and wobbled. He collided with something soft. When he leaned to that side, he could smell Des's perfume, even through the hood on his head. "Des! Des!" he said in a loud whisper as he gently nudged her with his shoulder. She groaned in response. "Des, wake up. It's Karl."

She groaned again, then said in a strained voice, "I'm sorry."

"Don't be sorry. Waste of time. What happened? Are you okay?"

"I think so. Mostly. I can't feel anything in my arms, but...They made me call you. I didn't want to, but they kept hitting me. They said if you came they wouldn't hurt us. They just wanted information, then they would let us go. They kept hitting me. I finally called you and tried to warn you, but they hung up before I could say more. That's the last thing I remember. I'm sorry. I should have been stronger."

"No, you did fine. We'll get out of here. Look, can you turn over on your side and use your hands to try and help me get this hood off so I can see where we are?"

He squirmed around until his head was aligned with her hips. She rolled to one side and bumped against his head. She was able to grab and hold onto the hood as he wiggled out of it.

"We're in a small moving van, like a U-Haul. Here, I'll help you get your hood off, then we'll figure out what to do next." He inched his way around to where he could grab the hood from behind. "Now, wriggle your way out of it."

"Whew, I can breathe again. So, any bright ideas?"

"No, but I have a Swiss army knife in my right pants pocket. Never without it. Whoever these guys are, they are mere amateurs or they would have emptied my pockets. See if you can reach in with your fingers and pull it out." It took several minutes of maneuvering to coax the knife out of his pocket. Karl took it from her and fussed with it, finally getting a blade open. His fingers cramped painfully as he rotated the knife and tried to position the blade against the tape binding his wrists. "Ah, shit!" he cursed quietly between clenched teeth.

"What happened?"

"Cut myself."

"Here, let me take the knife."

"No, it's not bad. I can do this."

"Men! You are all alike. You always have to do everything for yourself."

"Look, the blade is really sharp, and this is not easy to do with your hands behind your back."

"Then let me do it with my hands in front."

Karl looked over his shoulder. She was holding her arms out in front of her. "How'd you do that?"

"Just slipped them over my legs. Can't you do that old man?"

He smiled, shook his head, and turned so she could take the knife from him. She expertly made a half-inch slice

266

between his wrists in the top edge of the tape. "Now just pull them apart. The idiots used duct tape; it'll tear."

Karl strained against the tape until it started to tear where it had been nicked. He twisted his arms and pulled until the tape finally gave way enough that he could grab it between his wrists and peel it from one arm. He switched hands and quickly ripped it off the other arm, taking a crop of hair with it. "Youch! Now I know why I would never go for a wax job. Here, let me get you free." Karl steadied himself with one hand while he sawed away at the tape on her arms, but the tape had bunched up when she had brought her legs through, and it did not want to start tearing. He ended up having to cut all the way through before he could help her peel it off. They quickly cut the tape around their legs and stood up, holding onto cleats embedded in the walls, steadying themselves as the van lurched.

"Now what?" she asked.

"We get off," he answered, edging toward the tailgate.

"How fast do you think we are going?"

"Too fast, probably, but they will have to slow down for curves. We wait for the best moment, then jump and roll." He found the inside safety release for the sliding door and pulled on it. Through the widening gap he could see a dirt road rushing by. "From the looks of the road, I think we may be getting close to where we are headed, so we better go now." He slid the door up slowly so as not to make too much noise and attract attention. "Wait. My knife." The truck started into a turn, and Karl dived for the pocketknife as it skidded across the floor, managing to take another slice out of a finger as he grabbed it, closed it, and tried to jam it into his pants pocket.

"Now!" he snapped, as he nudged her toward the lip of the truck bed. Des, remembering her gymnastics lessons in childhood, backed up and took a diagonal run at the opening, expertly launching herself toward the weed-choked ditch at the side of the road and falling into a perfect tuck-and-roll.

Karl smiled and grabbed the edge of the sidewall to follow after her. The truck suddenly swerved, as if to avoid something in the road, and Karl was knocked off his feet. He grabbed instinctively for the edge, but ended up swinging out over empty space before losing his grip and dropping to the road. He landed on his side, shoulder first, and tumbled out of control.

Des yelled, "Karl!" and ran toward him as the truck careened around the curve and disappeared down the road. When she reached him, he was not moving and his head was tucked awkwardly under him. She was almost sick to her stomach as she remembered the woman on the bridge and her broken neck. She felt for a pulse as she leaned over and spoke into his ear, "Karl, Karl please! Please be okay."

His eyes fluttered open. "Okay," he said. "I'll be okay. Just can't move."

"Are you paralyzed?"

"Don't think so. I can wiggle things, at least it seems like I can. Am I wiggling my foot?"

"Yes."

"But everything hurts like hell. Help me up. We have to get off the road."

She reached under him and tried to get a grip as he struggled to sit up. Suddenly he grunted in pain. "I think I broke something. Collarbone, maybe. Hurts like it. Shoulder, too, maybe. Come around to the other side and see if we can do this together." She came around to his right, and practically lifted him on her own. "You are one tough, lady," he said between grunts. "You know that?"

"I just do what's needed," she said, looking into his face as she helped him toward the ditch. His face was twisted in pain, but he didn't complain as they made their way down the short embankment and up the other side, heading toward the woods a few meters away. Just as they reached the tree line, a dirty tan car passed, kicking up a cloud of dust. Both of them were covered with burrs, and Des paused to remove as many as she could while Karl propped himself against a tree and pretended that he was all right.

"I don't suppose you still have a cell phone on you," he said. She shook her head. At the sound of an approaching car, she pulled Karl behind the tree and threw herself to the ground. It was the tan car again, this time coming in reverse at an alarmingly high speed from the direction the truck had gone minutes before.

"Somebody is looking for us," she whispered, as the car slowed to a stop not far from where they had bailed out of the truck. A stout, forty-something woman wearing a blue and white bandana got out and started studying the road. She bent over to pick something up before swiveling slowly until she was looking straight in their direction. She cupped her hands at her mouth and shouted, "Tagline!"

"What the hell?" Des whispered.

"Quick, get me to the road. That's help."

"What are you talking about? We don't know who that is?"

"No, but whoever it is, they are on our side. Tagline is my *Mossad* code name. Quick, help me to the car."

As soon as they started struggling toward the road, the woman came running to help.

"I'm Velma, from the motel. Let's get you two out of here before that truck discovers they lost their cargo."

Karl grimaced in pain as the two women helped him into the car. Velma gunned the car in reverse down the road until it widened slightly, where she whipped the steering wheel to the stop as she backed to the brink of the ditch, whirled it the other way as she pulled forward, and spun the tires as they headed back down the road trailing a hurricane of dust.

"I was a stunt driver when I was young," she explained. "Pretty good, too. But I lost Shmuel while filming a chase scene in a B-movie James Bond copycat and just had to get out."

"You're obviously still good, Velma. But can anyone tell me what's going on?" Des asked impatiently.

"Velma here is a *sayan*, a sympathizer who lends a hand now and then to *HaMossad*."

"That's right. I heard the ruckus at the motel, saw the moving truck squeal out of the parking lot, and decided to tail it. I was turning onto the dirt road and missed when you two jumped, but when I caught up to the truck, I saw that the door was open and the back was empty. I decided to hightail it out of there before they saw me in their mirrors or stopped and discovered their loss."

"How did you know where to find us?"

"You left a lot of tracks, including this." She held up a black Swiss army knife. "I found it in the road and figured it might be yours, Tagline."

Karl thanked her and reached for the knife, but his injuries stopped him. "Oh, God, that hurts," he said.

Des took the knife from Velma and to Karl said, "I'll keep it for you for now."

Velma felt around on the seat beside her to retrieve her cell phone, then drove one handed as she dialed a number. Without putting the phone to her ear, she said, "The tagline is written." She winked at Karl as she thumbed the phone off and put it back on the seat beside her. "We'll have to get you both some new quarters. These guys are mean. But we'll get them. I passed on the plate number to our people, they'll track the rental to a credit card or somebody. Our boys will get them or sic the FBI on them."

Des was not sure she believed the woman, and Karl had passed out in the back seat.

27

HARRY SAT AT HIS DESK and stared into space. His world was crumbling before his eyes, a slow-motion implosion that made him dizzy. His wife had found out about his affair and was holding the threat of divorce over his head. His lover was not only no longer his lover, she wasn't even showing up for work. His boss had killed a man, an apparent extortionist who had hacked into the Scenaria software. And, to top it all off, Talpa had taken Harry into his confidence. Now Harry knew things that he wished he didn't know, things that put him in an almost impossible bind. If he did and said nothing, he was an accessory after the fact to a major commercial crime. If he revealed what he knew, he would not only lose his job and be branded for life as a disloyal whistle-blower, but he would bring down the entire company and send its CEO to jail.

"It's not really a crime, Harry, just dirty tricks," Talpa had said. "Everybody does stuff like this: corporate espionage, industrial spying. Call it competitive analysis, unconventional market research. It's how the game is played, how business is done in the world today. We just did it better, smarter. We used the technology to our advantage before someone else thought of it and did it to us."

Harry did not find the rationalization at all reassuring. Shaking his head in sad disbelief, he said, "Let me get this straight. You hired this freelancer to hack into our own software so we could spy on our customers?"

"Not our customers so much as our competitors. We knew companies like SimonTech and MacAlbee ran copies of our software to evaluate it and see what they could learn from it. So I got Collier-Adams to create a Trojan that could be embedded in our software and that would give us backdoor access to any computer that it was installed on. The beauty of it was that it could get past the anti-virus software because it was *in* the anti-virus software. It was only intended to be in one release, then would be wiped out by the next version update. But I got hooked. I found the business intelligence that it gave access to was really valuable, so I never killed it. It allowed me to sift through corporate data and email archives to know what the competition was planning and how they were doing. We had the best technology, we all knew our anti-virus techniques were way ahead; this just gave us the extra edge we needed to build on that lead."

It sounded like rationalizing bullshit to Harry, but he said nothing.

"But that fucker, that hacker fucker," Talpa droned on. "He fucked us over. He hacked our software completely, even planted a backdoor into our production facilities, even gained access to the Vault. He stole tools from us and used them against us, turning every computer with Scenaria software installed, including our own computers, into a slave in a vast bot net. Our anti-virus scanners couldn't detect the breach because they had been hacked, too, and the malware was built into the very heart of our own software."

Harry looked puzzled. "Wouldn't some of our Systems Tech people have found it eventually? Wouldn't some programmer notice code that didn't belong, that didn't make sense?"

"Sure, in principle, eventually, but don't forget how complex our systems are, how many millions of lines of code there are. Things that are stable don't get touched, and old code that is stable is left completely alone, for fear that it's fragile, that any change might break it."

"And Collier-Adams? Do you think he has used this bot net?"

"Maybe not. It's a sleeper network, a kind of slow virus that lies dormant until it's awakened by special codes. Collier-Adams seemed to be more interested in the elegance and perfection of the programs and the sense of power and accomplishment they gave him than in exploiting them. He was a geek, not a goon. Although, he did seem to have used it on one occasion on behalf of a client. He bragged about it when he came here."

"And?" Harry tried to sound nonchalant.

"Apparently he was behind the hacking into Tricorn. For a client, I suppose, but he didn't say who it was or why. All he cared about was the intellectual challenge and the chance to use his army of bots. He was very good and was paid well by his anonymous clients, including me."

"Was he really trying to shake you down for more money, is that what happened here?"

"That's the story, and the only story that anyone needs to know now. Once we get his hack completely figured out, we'll find a way to kill it, either quietly or publicly with the right spin. Simple. End of story."

Talpa had then ushered Harry out of his office without saying anything more. But as Harry sat alone in his cluttered office, he knew it wasn't going to be simple, and the story was far from ended. Too many people were working on the narrative, trying to solve the mystery. Tricorn had been so blatant that the feds would eventually connect it back to the hacked code and the hacker who created it. They were not going to let go of it until they knew what had happened, who did it, and why. And once the bot net was uncovered, the trail would lead right back to Scenaria and Talpa.

The other spanner in the works was Des and her new friend from Israel. Harry was beginning to wonder just how far their friendship extended. Talpa had said that dealing with Des was up to Harry, but Harry had no idea what to do, aside from keeping an eye on her by pulling her into the team working in the Vault. That might be one way to buy time while he concocted a strategy, but for the present, he couldn't even find her. He had called her apartment and her cell phone repeatedly but never even reached her voice mail.

And what exactly did Talpa expect of him? What was implied by 'dealing with Des'? How far would Talpa go to save himself and the company, and how far would Harry go on his own behalf? Harry shuddered and tried not to think about what he might be asked to do and what he might be capable of.

If he thought about it, Harry knew that his cell phone would be useless in the heavily shielded Vault where he was headed, but he picked it up from the desk reflexively and slipped it into his pocket before leaving his office. He took the elevator to the sub-basement, where a hired security guard checked his ID and waved him in through the outer door. At the inner door, Harry held his RFID pass key in front of the reader as he entered his 10-digit pin on the keypad beside it. The lock released with a loud metallic clunk, and Harry pushed the heavy, metal-lined door open.

The Vault was an eight-meter square outfitted with long workbenches arrayed with an assortment of computers. It looked much like any of the programming clusters at Scenaria, except there were no windows, no Ethernet outlets, and only one telephone—an old-fashioned wired box prominently positioned on one wall. The seamless walls and ceiling looked ordinary enough, giving no hint of the metal shielding beneath the surface. The room was a Faraday cage, a metal grid that stopped radio signals of any kind from passing in or out.

Harry knew that security, even for an isolated facility like the Vault, was only relative. Absolute isolation was an elusive illusion. If people could cross the threshold of a room, the room was not truly isolated, not truly secure.

Eight people from the Systems Tech group were scattered around the Vault, hunched over terminals, and at the moment, the loudest sound was the steady rattle of keys at half-a-dozen keyboards. Vern Jeffers was leaning over the shoulder of one of Scenaria's youngest programming geniuses, a Pakistani Vern had recently pulled onto the team on Talpa's authority. The Pakistani was working on an H1-B visa for now but was fast-tracked for a green card and eventual citizenship. Scenaria had a reputation for getting and keeping the very best young talent from around the globe. Harry had no idea how the system worked, but he figured it was another product of Talpa's connections in the government, particularly in the intelligence community and Homeland Security.

Vern looked up from the screen he was studying and gestured for Harry to come over. "Take a look at this. We finally managed to fully clean a dirty box."

As Harry approached, the Pakistani programmer suddenly exclaimed and pointed at a blinking blue light on the panel of the laptop on which he was working. "That," he said in heavily accented English, "Should not be." He quickly typed a series of commands, and Harry watched as a window popped up with a score or more lines of machine code in tiny text. Another popped up with the same text and a flashing message at the top: "100% match, code signature E400-6A11, bridge." Both Windows continued to show slowly growing listings of identical text.

Harry turned to Vern. "That's part of the cat.9.kernal Trojan?" he asked.

Vern nodded. "Did you bring a Bluetooth device in here?" he said with an accusing edge to his voice.

Harry reached into his pocket and sheepishly pulled out his cell phone. "Forgot," he said, as he pushed the on-off button and held it down. The code windows on the laptop stopped scrolling, with the text cursor blinking in the middle of a line.

Vern grabbed at the phone. "What kind of a phone is that?"

"An HTC, one of their smartphones, why?"

"HTC? That uses the Android OS, right?"

"No, this one is Windows-based."

"Turn it back on. I want to try something."

Harry thumbed it on again; after a few seconds, the Bluetooth pairing indicator on the laptop started blinking again, and, after another short pause, the code windows scrolled a few more lines of code before they stopped and the blue indicator winked out.

"I'll be damned. They have a mobile phone virus that talks by Bluetooth with the Trojan or some piece that it leaves lying around. I thought that this laptop was supposed to be clean, Salim."

"Yes, it was clean. I checked. But now it has some of the code restored. That block, E400-6A11, is a network bridge enabler that can make links between different channels: IEEE 1394, Ethernet, whatever. Such code is built into network interfaces and operating systems, but this block works down at the device level and does some funky stuff we haven't deciphered completely yet because we were focusing more on other parts of the Trojan. Plus, we weren't absolutely sure whether this was part of it or just some oddball code fragment that got left behind from software that had been uninstalled somewhere along the line."

Vern shook his head in disbelief. "Harry, do you see what we have here? It's a complete malware system, a distributed computing complex with pieces in infected phones that can re-infect a PC by Bluetooth even after it appears to be clean, because something is left behind that can accept the code through the Bluetooth connection, or at least there's enough to kick start the whole thing again. That's why it kept coming back. My guess is that all it takes is any box anywhere on the network with Bluetooth and all the previously infected machines get infected all over again because some little Bluetooth bootstrap loader is still hiding somewhere."

"That's what I told you, Harry." It was DB, who had just entered the Vault. "I said the supposedly isolated boxes were getting re-infected through thin air."

"I thought you were joking. And I thought we had it nailed once we knew that the vector for the virus was our own software."

"That's only part of the story," DB said, smiling broadly. "Like Vern said, this is not just a Trojan, it is a complete multiplatform system. I would not be surprised to learn that different parts of the system reside on different devices that need to cooperate for the whole thing to work. Sort of like what Animoroto does with distributed computing on their ad hoc game-console network."

"DB, you have one of their new boxes, don't you? Is it here at work? Can you run and get it and bring it down here?"

DB shrugged, turned, and sauntered out of the Vault without a word.

Harry tapped Vern on the shoulder. "Can you give me a hand with something for a few minutes, Vern? In my office." He nodded toward the door.

"Yeah, I suppose. I'll be back in five, guys," he said to the group.

In the elevator, Harry pushed the stop button between floors. "I don't think it makes sense to be using an Arab on this, much less having him inside the vault."

"Salim is not an Arab, he's a Pakistani. And he's been thoroughly checked and rechecked. Talpa's FBI pals assured us he is absolutely clean."

"That's what you said about the laptop that just re-infected itself. I don't care what the FBI says. It's an unnecessary risk, and it doesn't look good. I want him off, reassigned."

"Who's calling the shots here, Harry. Salim is my man, not yours, and I'm head of Systems Tech, not you. Unless you and Talpa have done some re-org that I haven't heard about. It seems like every time you are someplace else, someplace else turns out to be Richard Talpa's office. You two have become real buddy-buddy lately."

"Not sure what you are getting at, Vern, or what your sources might be, but I'm just a network manager working with you on a mission-critical project. We can't afford to have leaks or sabotage or a double agent of some kind."

Harry restarted the elevator, which opened at the ground floor. "We all do what we have to do, Vern," he said stepping out. "You need to get back to the Vault, and you need to get rid of Salim." As the elevator doors closed on Vern Jeffers, Harry was thinking about what he had to do, that he had to do something about Destiny Allen.

28

DES LABORIOUSLY PROGRAMMED the address from the sticky-note into the GPS system on the rental car. She wished she still had her old Ford, but at least she had wheels for the weekend, courtesy of Harry. It was against her better judgment to accept the invitation, but Harry had been very insistent, calling her over and over again, leaving messages that always said the same thing: that they needed some time to talk, just to be together. She had not said anything to Karl, knowing how he would see it. After all that she had been through of late, she felt deserved some down time, and maybe one last weekend with Harry would be good. She knew she might be playing the sucker, but somehow couldn't stop herself.

She scanned the parking lot of the motel for signs of anyone or anything that didn't look right. Karl had been teaching her, teaching about surveillance awareness and about the difference between alert caution and paranoia. For days she had felt that someone was following her but had never quite spotted anyone actually on her tail. Karl had been driving her back and forth between Scenaria and the new motel, every day or two switching cars, all of them provided by *sayanim*. He was always looking out for her, checking her room before she entered, tracking phone calls, and tracing unexpected email. It was sweet and made her feel safer, but she also chafed at the attention and resisted the feeling of dependence that it left her with.

With no one in sight at the moment and the street clear, Des pulled out of the parking lot and started to follow the mellow female voice of the text-to-speech system delivering its turn-by-turn directions. Intent on the directions rather than her surroundings, and lost in thought about the phone messages from Harry, it was some time before she became aware that the programmed route did not match her innate sense of direction. She couldn't shake the feeling that she was heading the wrong way. She had never been to Richard Talpa's cabin, but she knew it was somewhere near Spring Falls. She was also becoming aware that the map displayed on the GPS did not precisely match her surroundings. It would sometimes show a cross street where there was none or an upcoming right-angle turn that would turn out to be a hairpin. She tried to make sense of the anomalies but gave up, figuring that rental car companies probably did not always update the maps in their GPS systems too frequently.

Her cell phone rang. She fumbled for it in her purse, slid it open, and thumbed on the speakerphone. It was Harry. "Des, I'm sorry. I've been delayed a couple of hours," he said in slightly jerky, static-filled telegraph speech. "I'll catch up and explain later." Click. She thought it was strange but concluded that she might as well just stick with the plan.

As she kept driving, secondary roads turned into unpaved country roads, and hazy sun gave way to twilight. There did not seem to be a map in the car, and, other than by the GPS, she really had no idea where she was. At least she could always use the GPS to get her back home. Unless it was defective, of course. She started to think of the implications of being somewhere in the middle of nowhere with a defective— or deceptive—navigation system.

The thought was interrupted by the turn-by-turn guidance announcing that she had reached her destination. She looked around. There didn't seem to be anything but trees in all directions, but then she noticed a narrow gravel driveway nestled between thick stands of pine. She turned in. The drive ended in a circle in front of a rustic but spacious cabin perched on the slope of the mountain. In the fading light, the cabin certainly looked like it could be the legendary Talpa retreat that Harry had raved about to her.

The cabin was dark when she arrived. She quickly found the key under the mat where Harry's email had said it would be. She let herself in and flicked the light switch beside the door. A chandelier in the shape of a wagon wheel blinked on, revealing a room furnished with simple but expensive furniture. She put her suitcase down beside a rustic chair, thickly padded, with hewn wooden arms thicker than her thighs. Outside she heard a car pulling up. She was excited to think that maybe Harry had gotten away in time after all. She peeked through the octagonal window in the front door and was startled to realize that it was not Harry's convertible but a minivan. Suddenly she felt like an intruder. It was too late to turn out the lights, so she decided to hide. She still did not know who had been after her or why, but she was suddenly scared. Who would even know if something happened to her out here in the middle of nowhere. Now she wished she had said something to Karl, but, knowing he wouldn't approve, she had foolishly snuck away at the last minute without a word.

She quietly hurried upstairs and slipped into the first bedroom just to the right at the top of the stairs, stepping around to the hinge side of the door and waiting as she slowed her breathing.

She heard the front door creak open and cursed herself for not thinking to lock it again. The sound of heavy footsteps across the floor below was followed by silence, as if whoever had entered had stopped to look at something. Suddenly, she remembered her bag sitting right where she had left it next to the chair. There were more footsteps, then the sound of heavy breathing as the steps advanced slowly up the stairs. She held her own breath and waited. The door opened and the floor creaked loudly as someone stepped into the room.

In the wedge of light from the hall, she could clearly see her visitor's feet. Red sneakers. It was DB. He was the stalker; she had been wrong to trust him. She had been tricked into coming to the cabin. Maybe Harry was involved, maybe not, but DB was definitely in on whatever was going on.

She pressed back against the wall, making herself as skinny as she could, but as the door opened fully, it bumped against her jacket, rattling the car keys in the pocket. DB jumped, then she jumped. She kicked the door away from her, but DB was already in the clear. He clicked on an LED flashlight, which cast it's cold, diffuse glow into the gloom of the bedroom. He started to turn it in her direction just as she landed a high kick on the underside of his wrist, sending the flashlight flying onto the bed and his arm flying up into his own face.

"Ow!" he shouted.

Des heaved herself at him with all her strength. He was tougher than she had expected, but she succeeded in knocking him back against the edge of the bed where his knees buckled. As he floundered trying to catch himself, she was out the door and scrambling down the steps. At the bottom she circled around, jerked open what looked to be the door to the basement, and quickly felt her way down a flight of steps, already cursing herself for not simply heading out the front door.

At first, everything was just a black fog, but as her eyes adjusted, she realized that faint moonlight was filtering in through a wall of glass sliders on the down-slope side of the room. She ran toward them but struck something hard in the middle of the room, barking her shin, and pitching herself forward. She caught the edge of the coffee table with her hip as she went down. She started to cry out in pain, but suppressed it to no more than a high-pitched grunt. She stood slowly, painfully, and shuffled cautiously toward the light coming from outside. The sliders were locked. She tried to puzzle out how to open them, but heard footsteps coming down the upper flight of stairs. She ducked back into the shadows, keeping her eyes on the doorway at the top of the stairs. DB's rotund silhouette appeared. As she shifted her body to pull back further into the dark corner, the pain in her hip made her catch her breath.

"Is that you, Des? Des? It's DB. There's nothing to be afraid of. It's just me."

She looked around for something that might serve as a weapon. The coffee table, which she could now see clearly, was too large and ungainly. It was flanked on either side by short sofas. No chance there either. Opposite her was a stonework fireplace. Her eyes fell on a wrought-iron poker nestled in a stand beside it. Counting on DB's eyes being not yet adapted to the dark, she darted as fast as she could across the open space between her and the sofa. Her hip was now a bright fire that flared and ebbed, grabbing for her attention. As she gritted her teeth and started crawling slowly along behind the sofa, she was hoping she hadn't broken anything. Just short of the fireplace, she reached out across the gap to try and quietly lift the poker out of the stand. As it came free, the rest of the fireplace tools clattered noisily onto the hearth.

"What the hey! Who's there?" A note of fear had entered into his voice. He lumbered cautiously down the stairs and slowly crossed the room. Naïvely, he approached where the fireplace tools lay like pickup sticks in a pile and stared at them highlighted in a pool of light from his flashlight. Des jumped up from behind the sofa and swung with the poker. She caught him full in the stomach. The poker seemed to bury itself in his flesh, and DB dropped with a sound like air escaping from a balloon. Des stepped around his body and started running toward the stairs.

"Can't...can't...I..." He struggled to speak. "Can't breathe."

She was halfway up the stairs before deciding she could risk going back to check on him. She returned, bent down beside him, and struggled to push him over onto his back. He stared up at her, eyes and mouth wide in a pleading look. She was about to try mouth-to-mouth, when he suddenly gasped and wheezed.

He lay panting for some moments before trying to talk again. Des reached again for the poker that now lay sticking out from under the sofa.

"No, please!" He shook his head violently. "I just wanted to warn you. I've been trying to look after you, keeping track of where you were and what you were up to. He's after you. He's on his way. I think he is going to kill you."

Had she been wrong about DB, or was this a lame attempt to trick her? "I know he's on his way," she said. "That's why I'm here. He called me, left a message. I know it's over, but it's hard to accept that he'd want to kill me."

DB looked up at her, puzzled. He was about to explain what he meant when Des put her hand over his mouth. "Shhh! I hear something upstairs," she whispered close to his ear. "Stay here. Keep quiet." She pressed down on his chest as she rose.

The pain lanced through her hip as she started to tiptoe up the stairs. She gritted her teeth again and kept going. As she reached the open doorway, she saw movement out of the corner of her eye. She turned and froze. A man in an all-black outfit and carrying what looked to be some kind of automatic weapon was walking, crouched, away from her. As he swung to one side, she could see the long snout of night-vision goggles projecting obscenely from between his eyes.

As she started to back down the stairs, her foot slipped, causing her to fall against the door, which slammed into the wall. The dark figure whirled toward her and fired, but Des was already around the corner. Ignoring the pain in her hip, she flung herself over the handrail and dropped awkwardly to the floor beside the stairs, choking off a cry as her hip took the shock. The man was right behind her, scanning from side-to-side as he took the first step through the door. He spotted DB by the fireplace just as DB turned his flashlight on and shown it toward the stairs. The intense light overwhelmed the man's night-vision system, and he fired off a wild, one-handed burst in the general direction of the light as he flipped up the goggles with his free hand. While he was still blinded, Des leapt and grabbed for his leg through the railing. She missed, then launched herself again with such force that she hit her head on the railing. At the same instant, she caught his ankle and held tight, pulling his leg out from under him as she fell back, sending him tumbling down the stairs into a heap at the bottom. Des hobbled over to where the assault rifle had skittered across the floor. She swung it like a baseball bat at the prone figure, battering him again and again. The man didn't move.

"DB, are you all right?" She shuffled across the room, wincing in pain as she went.

"Yeah, I think so."

"How? He was shooting right at you."

"Well, at least he was shooting right at my flashlight, but I was down here and it was up there." He stretched as high as he could reach with the light and flicked it on, then immediately off again. "I hear voices upstairs. Two, maybe three men. Give me the gun. And quick, go check the body for extra ammo for this thing."

She returned with two clips, then both of them ducked down between the end of the sofa and the fireplace. Before they could even think of a plan, the glass slider shattered. Two men crashed through from outside just as two more appeared at the top of the stairs. DB kneeled and got off two short bursts toward the stairs, swiveled, fired at the first man to make it through the splintered slider, turned, fired again, and then back for a longer burst at the top of the stairs just as another intruder entered. Flashes from the muzzle of the man's weapon sprayed toward the ceiling as he fell back through the doorway.

Silence. They waited. Nothing.

Des located the flashlight and panned it around the room. In addition to the battered body in a heap at the bottom of the stairs, there were now five more bodies. DB had gotten off five bursts, perhaps a dozen or so bullets in all, and had hit five targets before any of them could return fire.

"Where the hell did you ever learn to shoot like that?"

"Halo. Counterstrike. Doom 3. Games. I've had a lot of years of practice."

"But this is no video game, DB. This is the real thing."

"It's all the same. Aim, shoot, aim, shoot. It's all the same. I was well trained for this." He shuddered. "It's not real, Des. You think stuff like this happens in real life? I couldn't handle this if I let myself think it was real. It's one of those things you just do without thinking about it, just like in the games."

He laughed, a staccato laugh without humor, a laugh to cover feelings that he could not face. "Of course, it's a damn good thing the safety was off on this mother," he said, waving the assault weapon, "because I wouldn't have had the faintest idea where it was or how to switch it. Now that I think of it, I was also probably smart or lucky to fire in really short bursts because this thing climbs like crazy when you shoot. There's no recoil with a video-game weapon."

He surveyed the room and shook his head. "What a mess. I suppose we better call the cops or something." DB reached for his cell phone in its holster at his belt. "Aw darn! Must have fallen on it." It was smashed. "You have yours?"

"It's in my purse. In the car." DB was staring at her. "What?" she said.

"Why do women do that? Why don't they ever keep a phone handy? Why a purse? Look, you got pockets in your jeans just like I do. You should use them."

"DB, this is no time to start your sex education. Men and women are different, see. Anyway, let's go get the phone and call for some help, but not the police."

There was a groan from across the room. Des jumped, but DB strolled over and casually pointed the gun at one of the men sprawled on the carpet of glass splinters. "Don't even try it," he said with faked bravado while stepping on the man's arm.

The man struggled to turn his head. To DB he looked vaguely Asian, Japanese maybe. "You won't stop us, you know," he said between coughs. "No one will. It's for the sake of the planet. To preserve and protect."

DB gave the man a kick in the side of the head.

"Stop it, DB!" Des said, grabbing at his arm.

"No need to call the police anyway, Des. You heard what he said. He is the police: the Planet Police. Those damned neo-Luddites have this wacko agenda to stop progress by using technology against itself. They are worse than Earth First ever was."

"Not stop progress, idiot," the man said between shallow pants. He struggled to get his arm free from beneath him. His hand peeked out holding a walky-talky, which he strained to lift. "Preserve and protect the planet. There's no progress if the planet is dying, raped and ripped apart, choked by her own children. Tricorn was just a beta test."

"What are you talking about?" Des asked. "Tricorn? You're talking about the coal-fired plant in the Southwest that blew up last month. What can you tell us?"

The man coughed, closed his eyes, and was still.

A brief flash of light played across the trees outside. "We got company again," DB said. "Let's not wait here." He grabbed Des's hand and pulled her out through the slider, gingerly avoiding the sharp shards of broken glass. Outside, he led her up the slope and around the corner of the cabin. Two cars, lights on and engines running, were pulled up behind Des's car and DB's van in the circular drive. Several young men were milling around, while two others stood in the headlights talking.

"I know that guy," DB said in a lowered voice. "I met him at a conference in Vancouver. He's with Whiteforce. They're the good guys. At least I thought so," he added.

"I don't know a lot about the Planet Police, but I know absolutely zip about Whiteforce."

"Well, you should know them. Whiteforce are white-hat hackers, you know, cowboy coders who sometimes help us with so-called zero-day exploits, like where a vulnerability in software is discovered and exploited by the hackers even before the software companies know about it."

"I know what a zero-day threat is, DB. I work for the same company as you do. I just never heard of Whiteforce."

"Well, that's the way they like it. And, frankly, nobody knows much about them or the Planet Police, either, partly because they have deliberately kept a very low profile. But both groups are hackers with a mission, especially Planet Police. They consider other hackers who show off their programming prowess with highly visible malware to be amateurs. Their one-page manifesto, which keeps appearing and disappearing on the Web, says they are out to save the planet by radically reducing energy consumption and cutting carbon emissions through direct action. They don't say how they intend to do it. It's rhetoric, empty threats, conviction without commitment. I always thought they were a bunch of hot heads full of hot air."

"DB, if we believe our dead friend back there, they are the ones who took the Tricorn plant out of commission. Pretty impressive hot air, I'd say, to say nothing of the level of desperation shown by this attack. I still don't know why they would want to kill me."

"Maybe it's not you. Maybe it's The Mole. Isn't this his place? They wouldn't necessarily know that you and Harry were going to be using it at this time. Maybe Scenaria's security systems are getting in their way. It will be even worse if the new Industry Shield SCADA security software gets deployed. Or maybe it's because of something you know."

"But what do I know?"

"You know a lot of things. We just don't know what of these things matter or how they fit together. You know about The New Game on Life 2.0 and where the Horvaths are. Outside of Vern and his Vault crowd, there are still only four people in the company who know about the Trojan: you, me, Harry, and Richard Talpa. You were not supposed to know, except Harry blabs to you. I probably should not have known as much as I did, but Harry tends to trust me. Three of the four of us would have been here, except Harry didn't show.

Convenient? Coincidence? And Talpa, he would have a lot at stake if anyone found out Scenaria had a virulent Trojan in its system and was spreading it through its security software. How far would he go to keep it quiet? He killed that Australian hacker, supposedly in self-defense, but nobody saw what happened or actually heard what they were meeting about.

"But Whiteforce?" he said. "That has me stumped. What are they doing here? Let's go find out."

One of the young men separated from the group and crossed over to DB and Des as they emerged from the bushes at the edge of the slope. "Hey, DB, what's shaking?" he said, casually. "I thought that might be your car." He pointed at the bumper sticker that read "Fifth Normal Form or Nothing," a database insider's slogan.

"MicMac, what the hell? How the hell did you find this place? *Why* did you find this place?" MicMac, who took his nickname from his passion for the Apple operating system and his First Nations heritage in Nova Scotia, where he was born, was shorter than DB and looked like he might weigh half again as much. He nodded shyly toward Des before facing DB again. Except for the color of his hair and the long braid in which he wore it, he looked like he might be DB's kid brother or nephew.

"Oh, we know people." He gestured toward a skinny young man wearing textured blue jeans, an untucked white dress shirt, and a plaid tie loosened halfway to his waist. Behind his rimless glasses, his eyes smiled. "Meet Bono McClaren, he's got connections in Israel, in Haifa. Bono, this is DB, the database whiz at Scenaria that I told you about. And this is Destiny Allen, our target."

Bono stepped forward and extended a hand to DB, then to Des. "You don't look so good. You all right?"

DB answered for her. "We're okay. Des has a limp and I have a welt across my gut, but we are better off than the other guys. We just finished a round of arcade shooting, only with live ammo. There are…" He chewed on his lip. "There are six dead Asian gorillas in there. I doubt if anyone heard anything way out here in the mountains, but I also suspect that when these guys fail to report back, somebody is going to come sniffing around."

"Then let's exit stage right," MicMac said, signaling his companions back into the cars. "You can ride with us or DB, Miss, but I wouldn't recommend driving your rental car back. It's broadcasting a homing signal, and we would not be surprised if the onboard computers had been hacked."

"I thought there was something funky about the navigation system on the way out here."

"That may not be all that's funky about that car," he said with a wink.

Des opted to ride with DB. The caravan had just reached the road, when the abandoned rental car shook from an explosion and a ball of fire erupted behind them.

DB whistled. "Now, that will get somebody's attention. Good thing you decided to ride with me. I'm not sure how they detonated the car, but that was no accident or coincidence." As they sped down the road, the burning car set fire to the cabin, and the night sky was soon alive with flying sparks. "The forestry service will be first on the scene, most likely. By the time the local sheriff gets here, it is going to be mighty hard to decipher what went down."

DB looked over at Des. "You should stretch out and try to catch some winks on the way back. I'm going to take the long way home. Do you like West Virginia this time of year?"

Des closed her eyes for a moment, then reopened them. "You're an interesting guy, DB. Complicated. Not exactly WYSIWYG."

He grunted but said nothing.

"Can I ask you something?" she said.

"Sure. I suppose."

"Is there somebody? Is there somebody in your life?"

"Somebody?"

"You know. Is there a girl? What about that picture on your desk, the dark-haired girl?"

DB laughed nervously. "Mariana, you mean? She's the foster child I sponsored for years. In Columbia. All grown up now, already married. Still writes." He laughed again.

Des nodded and smiled at him. "That's cool. I never would have guessed. Like I said, you are not exactly WYSIWYG."

29

TRUMAN SIEBALT PACED back and forth between his desk and the conference table, the bright blue LED of a Bluetooth headset winking in his ear. His thin lips worked in and out, back and forth, as he stared out over the Chicago lake front and listened with impatient concentration. The connection was good, and the voice on the phone was speaking English, but Truman Siebalt could barely understand what was being said. "Damn it, Ken. Say that again. I can't understand you."

In thick, slow syllables, the caller repeated, "I said we need the money. You made promise of more money. There have been expenses. We have lost people. Many. We still do not have all the control protocols. We have to pay our researchers. Every installation is different. We have coders on the payroll trying to work around the lockouts in the Life 2.0 InterBanc subsystem. They all want to be paid. We don't want them to get unhappy and complain to somebody."

Truman shook his head and wondered why the Australian government had ever decided to let such people in. He considered the days of the "White Australia" policy with nostalgia, days when, as he would put it, they kept the black fellas in their place and left the Japanese and the Filipinos and the Taiwanese in their own countries where they were free to garble English to each other and scratch out a living writing hilariously indecipherable product manuals for imported electronics.

"Listen you dumb chink, I can't get the money until we unlock the funds. I can't unlock the funds without a work-around for the goddamn Horvath tinkering. You managed to kill all the people who might have helped. You and your yellow comrades in arms."

"We kill nobody, not anybody. Someone else is in the game and playing for high stakes."

"*HaMossad* is not someone else: they are God's own avenging angels, and they hate everyone who is not Jewish. So you need to get your ninjas to split those two Sheilas from their Israeli protector and get them to lead us to Donna and Erno so you can pay your mercenaries and I can get the programming I need, because we absolutely need that last block of code. That bastard hacker left the damn system with some sort of missing part. It's like a bloody shotgun without a barrel."

"Have you tried the launch codes."

"Of course, we tried the bloody launch codes, you Taiwanese twit. All we get is a message about some bloody missing DLL. There's a whole dynamic link library absent from the base software. I paid that Aussie asshole, and he leaves the job unfinished."

"I am not Taiwanese. I study in Taiwan, but I am from Japan. We will get the codes and the software. To preserve and protect."

"Yeah, yeah, preserve and protect. But I don't care where you are from. You nips and chinks are all alike. None of you can speak the Queen's English so that a reasonable person can understand. We are starting to slip schedule for Operation Nagasaki."

There was silence on the other end, then the sound of voices speaking in Japanese. Siebalt, assuming they were doing it to annoy him, pressed the button at his ear to disconnect. An instant later, he heard the ringtone in the headset. He tugged it from his ear and tossed it onto his desk.

"Solve the problem yourself, you Jap bastards," he shouted at the headset. "If you are such a damn smart race, then solve the problem and leave me alone." He knew they couldn't hear him, but he continued to rail at the blinking headset until Randall came up behind him and started rubbing his shoulders.

"I won't ask," Randall said. "But I assume that the word from the coast is not good."

"We lost the entire strike team in Virginia and still no key disk. Our people don't even know what happened and can't get near the place because the FBI is all over it like ants at an outback picnic. All we know is the ruse to lure that Jewish Sheila out there worked, at least according to the tracking feed, but shortly afterwards there was an explosion and fire. It wiped out a safe house and 30 or 40 acres of forest around it. I suppose we can be grateful for the fire and hope it destroyed any evidence that could trace back to us. We don't know if the Sheila was killed or not. The bottom line is, we are still stuck in a deep billabong with a bloody salty grinning at us."

Randall hugged Siebalt from behind, but Siebalt shrugged him off. "We're at the office, ya bloody poofta. And we are not lovers anymore, even when we are away from the office. You may be a prancing poofta, but I'm bi and have other options. So get out, leave me alone, and come back with some coffee—a short black, the real stuff, not that weak American piss you usually try to pass off. And find out whether that Mallory brat is still hanging on. Jesus H. Christ, there are just too many bloody untied lines. Nobody does the job they're paid for anymore."

— —

DB was working late as always, alone at his cubicle, cranking hip-hop through his Bose headphones as he squinted at the screen and tried to find the bug in a block of code that was returning the wrong record on certain queries. Talpa, had left about 10:20, Des and Harry soon after, and Vern and Salim were the only ones still down in the Vault. A light in the system tray on his display winked to signal an opening exterior door. DB, who had doctored access to all the building's security systems, toggled over to a view of the security camera feed and scanned the slowly panning monochrome images painted across his screen in four rows of five. The image in the upper left corner showed an empty front lobby, and DB guessed the night watchman must be on rounds. The second thumbnail in the third row was black. That was a feed from an infra-red camera covering the parking lot from a mount just above Talpa's private entrance. DB double-clicked on the image to the left of the black square, a shot of the empty corridor leading from the entrance. It went black instead of expanding to full screen. He was about to flip to the RFID tracking log to see a list of recently detected badges, when the rest of the camera images started blinking to black in rapid succession.

He picked up the handset of his desk phone and punched the button for the Vault. "Vern, it's DB. Better lock down. We may have something going on up here." He swiveled his chair and scootered across the aisle to grab a cordless phone off the desk there. He slid the clip over his belt next to his cell phone hanging in its holster, extracted a keychain from his pocket, and quietly opened the locked bottom drawer of the green metal four-drawer filing cabinet beside his desk. From behind the hanging folders he fished out a pistol and stuffed it into the back of his pants. As he cinched his belt and hitched up his pants, the drawer slid shut on its own. In the silence of the empty building, the metallic clack of the latch echoed like a gunshot. DB tensed and listened. There was a sound like the soft scurrying of kittens across a bare floor. DB whirled.

Two figures in running shoes, coveralls, and black ski masks leapt toward him. He fumbled for the pistol at his back and got it up just as the first of the two reached him. DB fired directly into the man's face just as the second man came around to the side and kicked the gun from his hand. The man he had hit screamed and whipped off his mask. His face was decorated by three bright blue blotches, and he spat as he used the mask to wipe his eyes and mouth.

"A fucking paint gun. You think you can hold us off with a fucking paint gun?" he said, as he pushed DB back down into his chair. "You Scenaria geniuses are not nearly as ingenious as you think.

"Did you see that, Mort, he shot me with a paint pistol. Argh, that smarts." He kicked wildly at DB as he rubbed his left eye. "You stupid shit, you got paint in my eyes." He tugged at his shirt sleeve, pulling it down over his arm, and rubbed at his eye again.

"You cry baby," Mort sneered, "got some paint in your eye, did you? Big wup. Listen, we got a job to do." Mort turned to DB and punched him in the face. "Just give us the CD and we'll leave you. Otherwise, it's going to be a very long and painful night. And nobody's going to come and help you. Your guard is, shall we say, indisposed." He took two steps back before kicking DB in the side of the head with a practiced kick-boxing jab. DB reeled and slumped sideways. Blue Face grabbed him and sat him back upright.

DB, slipping in and out of consciousness, tried to say something. Blue Face grabbed him by the hair and tipped his head back. "What, genius? What did you say? I couldn't hear you."

"I got a lot of CDs. Which one you talking about?"

"The fucking CD with the tools on it that the kid gave you," he shouted, punctuating his words with punches to DB's stomach.

DB struggled to breathe. "Don't...have...it."

"Oh, you better have it, shit for brains, or we are going to spread your brains from here to the end of the hallway." He drew back his fist. DB turned to the side to avoid the blow, taking it just below his left ear. He tried to open and close his mouth, but his jaw wouldn't work right. Through slack lips he tried to tell them there was a copy, but they kept punching him, taking turns until he fell unconscious and slipped off his chair, striking his head on the edge of his desk as he went down.

"I think the dweeb was trying to say there was a copy. Maybe it's in with these CDs on his desk." The men rifled through the two CD files stacked beside DB's monitor screen, then started dumping out the contents of the filing cabinet. The bottom drawer wouldn't open.

"Let me try it, you wimp." Mort slipped up his ski mask and kicked at the drawer before straining to pull it open. "Did anyone ever tell you these ski masks are too damn hot to wear indoors?" He kicked and tugged again.

"Here, let me try."

Mort stepped aside and said, "Okay, Mister Hulk Hogan, do your stuff."

Blue Face pulled a .40 caliber Smith and Wesson M&P from his pants and fired at the lock, then walked over and casually pulled open the mangled drawer. "Brains over brawn," he said.

"Fuck you!"

"We better just find that disk before we are both fucked."

"If you didn't blow a hole in it with your macho stunt. Wait, here it is. Looks okay. We are good to go," Mort declared, holding up a CD-RW in a green slimline case. "This guy is real organized. It's that Marky dude's software tools disk."

"How do you know."

"See," he shoved the disk in front of his partner's face. "It's labeled: date, source, everything."

"Okay, let's get out of here before someone shows up."

"You're the one who had to start shooting, you stupid shit. My ears are still ringing. Let's go!"

"What about the geek."

"Leave him. We got what we needed. Now it's payday."

They started at a trot down the corridor toward the private entrance. Just as they reached for the big square button to open the automatic door, they heard a shout.

"Hey you, stop right there!" Vern Jeffers was just stepping off the elevator.

Blue Face whipped around and fired two shots before slipping through the widening gap as the door swung slowly open. The two men ran down the ramp toward their van parked at the far end of the lot.

They scrambled in, and Blue Face was about to turn the key in the ignition when both front doors of their van whipped open.

— —

DB swooned as he struggled to his knees. The top three drawers of his filing cabinet rested upside down in the aisle, their contents scattered. The bottom drawer was open, too, with a bullet hole in place of a lock. DB figured there was no need to check it's contents. The disk had been at the front and would have been hard to miss. He put his hand to his face and winced when he felt his jaw; it was probably broken. His first thought was to check on Vern. He tugged the cordless handset from his belt and dialed the Vault. Salim answered.

"You all right down there," DB mumbled, trying to speak without moving his mouth.

"Vern went topside fifteen minutes ago. He hasn't called in as he said he would. You okay?"

"I'll live, I think. Let me look around for Vern." He disconnected, returned the handset to his belt, and started to stand. It proved a lot harder than he expected, and he ended up waddling out into the corridor, stopping every few feet to hold onto something and catch his breath. As he rounded the corner, he spotted Vern Jeffers by the elevator, lying in a pool of blood.

— —

Talpa's face was blanched, his voice wobbly. "I got here as fast as I could. What the hell happened?" he asked DB. "I arrived just as the LifeFlite chopper was taking off from the parking lot. The trooper at the door said they were taking Vern Jeffers to the hospital. And you, you look like you just went three rounds with Hulk Hogan."

"I did, I did," he said through clenched teeth, his jaw held shut by bandages. "They got my copy of the tools disk."

"Your copy? Are you talking about the disk from that hacker kid? You made a copy of the disk?"

"It's my job. Keep copies of everything. That's what I was told; that's what I did."

"But that? That was top secret. There was stuff on there that only the boys in the Vault should be looking at." DB blinked but said nothing. Talpa continued, "Okay, get yourself stitched up, but be here in the morning. We have a lot to straighten out. God, I can't believe we have police all over the building for the second time in a week. I don't know how we are going to survive the publicity."

"Yeah, and then there's your cabin, too."

"My cabin? What are you talking about?"

"I'm talking about the fire."

"What fire? Nothing's happened to my cabin. I just talked this morning with the caretaker who was there, trimming the shrubs and checking the place out. What do you mean about it?"

DB would have bitten his tongue if he could have. "I,…I'm a little punch-drunk. Don't know what I mean." He put his hand to his head. "They want to take me to the hospital, then the police want a statement. I better get going."

"Right. You tell the police everything they need to know," Talpa said, emphasizing the word "need."

DB nodded. He trundled over to a medical technician, who took his arm and gently helped him onto an ambulance stretcher.

Talpa watched as two EMTs wheeled DB out to an ambulance, then waited until he heard the first burp from a siren. He turned toward his office, figuring that he might as well check email as long as he was already in the building. There was the usual stack of low priority messages in his in-box, but one flagged with a smiling emoticon in the subject line got his attention. It was from Salim, with a time stamp less than an hour earlier, and only two words in the body: "Found something!" He was about to head for the elevator to the Vault, when their was a ratatat on the doorjamb of his office.

Talpa tried to sound casual. "Come in, Officer. It's Detective Jenkins, right? I thought I recognized you from that mess last week. What can I do for you?"

"You might want to know that we already found your intruders."

"That's good news."

"Well, not exactly. We found them in a van parked at the far end of you parking lot. They were both dead. There wasn't any sign of the computer disk that your employee said had been stolen."

"What happened?"

"I am afraid I can't say any more. I need to ask you some questions. You're going to have to come to the station with me. I've ordered a wheelchair-accessible van that should be here in a few minutes."

"Can I talk with one of my engineers here before we go?"

"I'm afraid not. We'll be taking statements from everyone in the building at the time. I'm sure you can understand that we can't have you talking with each other first."

"Of course, but this is a security matter that needs my attention. It will only take a minute.

"Sorry, you'll have to come with me now."

"All right," Talpa said as he put his computer into standby mode, turning the screen black.

Part Four

30

WHEN TRUMAN SIEBALT STEPPED off the elevator from the parking garage, his receptionist raised a finger to signal him, then held out a telephone handset toward him. "It's Kenichi Takasawa on the private line for you, Dr. Siebalt. He wouldn't say what it was about."

"I'll take it in the office," he said as he hurried through the double doors and closed them behind him. He picked up the phone that he called his hotline and said, "Ken, any news? Talk to me. What's happening?" Static filled the line. "Are you there?"

"Yes, I am here. We have the disk."

"That's brilliant. Get on a plane and bring it here. There's nothing more leaving tonight, but I think United has a six o'clock flight out of DCA in the morning. Come straight to the data center; I'll meet you there."

"I don't think so."

"What did you say? It sounded like 'I don't think so.'"

"That's exactly what I said. We have the disk, but it's not going to be used for Operation Nagasaki."

"What are you talking about? We have to show that Tricorn was not a fluke, that we can do it again whenever we want, even if somebody jumped the gun on us the first time around. It's just like Truman, the president. He had to show the Japs in Nagasaki after Hiroshima." He could almost hear Takasawa grinding his teeth on the other end of the line. Takasawa had relatives who had died of cancer decades after the bombings, supposedly the result of exposure to radiation. "We have to do whatever it takes to convince them. This time we hit the East Coast and show that we can penetrate even a nuclear facility. We'll cripple the Seabrook reactor in New Hampshire. We won't take it out, just make it very difficult to restart. That will show them we are not just crude amateurs. Then we will lay out the demands, and they will have to comply."

"No."

"Did you say no?"

"I said no. It makes no sense to threaten. They won't deliver. The United States does not deliver on its promises. They signed but never ratified the Kyoto Protocol. They will promise the moon and deliver only a pollution-darkened sky. They will agree to the energy savings and then will make excuses while they track you down or find a way to protect their precious power plants. No, the time for negotiations was passed after Kyoto, and the time for threats is also now in the past, now that we have the technology simply to stop them."

"What are you proposing, Ken?"

"We are not proposing. We will not ask them to make drastic cuts in energy use, we will make the cuts for them. We already have the protocols we need for fossil-fuel plants representing nearly a third of the generating capacity of the country. When we are satisfied that we can breach half of them, we will take them out, just like the ATF at Waco, just like the Israelis at Entebbe. Direct action to preserve and protect. That is what the organization is about. We don't wait for them to act; we act, a preemptive strike. It is the art of war, and we are at war to save the planet."

"Did I understand you correctly? You want to wipe out, at a stroke, half of the U.S. electrical generating capacity? Do you realize what that will do?"

"I realize. Of course, I realize. Electricity from fossil fuels accounts for 40% of this country's greenhouse gas emissions. In an instant, we stop most of that merely by taking out most of the coal-fired plants that represent some 45% of generating capacity."

"If I wanted a goddamn lecture on electric power generation stats and climate change, I could have tuned into NPR. Don't preach to me, damn it. Don't forget, I wrote the goddamn bible on eco-terrorism."

"I am not preaching, Truman-san," he said with mock politeness. "I am merely informing you about what we are doing."

"You are not doing any such thing." Truman thumbed the mute button on the handset with one hand while pressing the buzzer for Randall with the other.

Randall stuck his head in and struck an inquiring pose.

"Find out where Kenichi and his ninjas are hiding out. The secure phone he is using can be tracked. Put another team from the DC area on it, and let me know as soon as you have anything." He lifted the phone back to his ear. Takasawa was still droning on about direct action and their mandate to protect the planet. "Look," Siebalt said, interrupting, "this is a matter for the Executive Council. You cannot take such an action without approval from the top."

There was a laugh on the other end of the line, a laugh bordering on a giggle. "The Executive Council? You are the Executive Council. Who are you kidding? No, we have discussed this, and everyone here agrees. This is the way to go forward. It's the new military policy for the Planet Police: Don't ask, just tell."

There was a click and the phone went silent. Siebalt threw it at the door and yelled, "Randall!"

— —

Truman's silent pacing was beginning to irritate Randall, but he said nothing. Then, suddenly, Truman stopped directly in front of him and spoke.

"There must be a way we can lock them out of the system, prevent access to the attack sequences. If the Horvaths can lock us out of the in-world banking system, why can't we do that with the Nagasaki software?"

"Because it's crabapples and orange trees. The beauty of the network architecture Gaijin created for us is that it is a distributed intelligence, a redundant, self-extending, self-replicating network. If one channel is blocked, traffic takes another; if one component fails, another assumes its function. The system doesn't care where it gets its instructions from as long as the codes are correct and the orders can be authenticated. Any place with Internet access can be the control center. In fact, a game console could, in principle, launch an attack, it just might take longer initially for the order to propagate through the system and reach it's target, but it could be done."

Truman frowned, pursing his lips out of nervous habit. "But the network can be updated on the fly, right? We can reprogram it so that it won't do what Takasawa and his psychotic eco-ninjas are threatening."

"In theory, yes, we could do that. But there are two big things you are forgetting. First, we don't have Gaijin right now. He hasn't checked in at the Coders' Corner, and he hasn't responded to any direct message. He was our point of contact for the project team that he himself assembled. We really don't know exactly who he had working for us except for that Collier-Adams guy. Takasawa's team learned that he had a key disk, which at some point got passed on to people at Scenaria by way of that Allen girl, and a copy of which Takasawa's squad have now somehow obtained. But Collier-Adams was killed in New Jersey, and none of our own people know as much as Gaijin did. I am not even sure anyone left standing knows how to reprogram the system. It's not like we have a user manual. Second, it is an enormous, amorphous peer-to-peer network spread all over the world. Major changes take time to propagate, and it is all but impossible to guarantee that all nodes have been reached, although Gaijin claimed to have a way to query all nodes about their status. Our people don't know how it's done."

"Get to the point, Randall."

"The point is that it could take days to be reasonably sure that a change has permeated the network. Do we have days? What if Kenichi broadcasts his own update to stop us from stopping him.?"

"I don't know, Randall, I don't know, but we have to try. Do you realize what happens if Takasawa succeeds. Half the country's electric power wiped out at a stroke. It will cripple us, it will cripple the economy, it will be economic chaos. Newlands will go down right along with everybody else. Critical networks and services will have backup power, but how long will that last? How long will our own diesel generators keep us up and running? The Internet will be a shambles, telecommunications will be overloaded and fall apart. This country, the world, runs on electricity. And what stops Takasawa from carrying his direct action around the world? What about China, one of the worst polluters? There will be riots around the globe. This is more than just a matter of reducing energy consumption and cutting greenhouse gas emissions. Takasawa is preparing to launch war on civilization itself. This isn't about green politics or even direct action for the sake of the environment anymore. This is simple terrorism. Terrorism by another name, which smells just as bad."

"We can go public, Truman. Planet Police can issue a warning so the targeted plants can be protected."

"Protected? Getting around so-called protection is the whole point of the Nagasaki Network. The only way the power plants can be fully protected in the short term is if they are taken completely off-line—off the Internet and off the grid, meaning not operating. Same result: the lights go out. In the longer term, yes, they might be protected; this Talpa chap at Scenaria thinks he has a solution to SCADA vulnerability, but how long to deploy it? Months, in the best, crisis-driven scenario, maybe a lot more. We may have only days or hours. No, if we go public, the only thing we buy is a shortcut to jail for what Takasawa will have done anyway."

Truman slumped down in his enormous desk chair. "God, I wish we weren't in this position. I don't know who took out

Tricorn, but if I ever catch the trigger-happy bastard, I'll carve him up and serve him to the salties. We weren't ready. We just weren't fucking ready."

31

KENICHI TAKASAWA WAS NO programmer. He was a fifty-three-year-old terrorist who understood computers mostly as a user. He had been trained as a biochemist, but, after studying in Taiwan and teaching in Australia, he had moved to the United States and spent most of his working life as a manager running research labs for the likes of Monsanto and Archer-Daniels-Midland. It was his New Zealand-born wife, Pamela, who had drawn him into the Planet Police and launched him into his second and invisible career. Their first operation together had been the duly infamous sinking of a New Zealand fishing boat. The crew on board were supposed to be picked up by Greenpeace zodiacs circling nearby, but not everyone had made it off the ship before it heeled over and went straight to the bottom with the captain and his son still on board. That had been his first experience with the human price of direct action, and Kenichi took it hard. By the time Pamela was killed in a failed raid on an oil-drilling platform, he had become a hardened revolutionary who expected that casualties were part of the cost of preserving and protecting the planet. He had not even cried when he heard that the recent raid on the cabin in the woods had failed, and the entire team, led by his son, were presumed dead. Each loss only stiffened his resolve.

His years of leading research teams to pull off break-throughs on difficult deadlines had taught him a tactic that had served him well on several operations, including Nagasaki: buy what you need to finish the job and always hire professionals. When his own people in the Planet Police couldn't do something or deliver in a reasonable time, he had dipped into the pool of freelance talent, always hiring the best from the digital demimonde of hackers and contract programmers. The Nagasaki project had been particularly expensive. Reestablishing contact with Truman Siebalt had been the stroke of luck and genius that had made the whole operation feasible. Despite appearances, Siebalt had never completely abandoned his eco-action ideals as he rose into the upper echelons of the Internet business world. His activities would not have earned him brownie points with the greenies, but he did feel guilty, and that guilt could be exploited. It had started with providing on-line resources and secure commu-nications embedded in Life 2.0 and from there had built to a steady stream of financing for the Planet Police.

Kenichi didn't even care that Siebalt was also siphoning off funds into his own offshore accounts, as long as the funding for Operation Nagasaki continued. It was an ambitious and complicated, high-stakes undertaking that required spreading a lot of cash quite widely. There was a real risk that the money thrown at so many programming paladins would attract attention, but Kenichi had been careful. The man known to Kenichi by his on-line handle, Gaijin, was the only person who knew the whole picture, and the two of them had never discussed the real purpose of the project, although he surmised that Gaijin was smart enough to have figured it out. It had been Gaijin who had hired people—and fired people—and parceled out the work in pieces small enough not to reveal too much. It was Gaijin who reassembled the scattered shards and tiles of software into a mosaic, a cohesive whole: the amoeboid megalith of the Nagasaki Network.

Now Gaijin was gone, and Kenichi's money had run out. He had drained his own account to outfit the strike team and hire the mercenaries needed to complete the roster for his son on the mountain raid, the failed raid on the safe house. Besides his son, two of the dead were Planet Police regulars and had been good friends with Kenichi. The second team sent directly to Scenaria had finally succeeded in recovering a copy of the missing key disk—more by blind luck than by planning or skillful execution. They had heard gunfire as they pulled into the parking lot and were greeted by two men running out of the building waving a computer disk in the air. It took no advanced mathematics to put two and two together and decide to relieve the apparent amateurs of their small burden.

Kenichi still didn't know anything about the original thieves; they had been identified by name in news stories, but that told nothing about their interest in the disk. The published story was that they had died in a shootout with police while trying to escape; the real story, reported to Kenichi by his hired guns, was that the two men had been taken out when they refused to turn over the disk. It was unfortunate that no one thought to first ask who the thieves worked for or why they wanted the key disk, but at least it had been recovered. The fact that the Virginia police were releasing a phony story implied that they were onto something about the assassination and in pursuit of the mercenaries, but Kenichi was confident his men would elude the authorities as they had on many prior occasions.

Unfortunately, the recovery of the key disk was an empty accomplishment without money to complete the project. With Siebalt's financial flim-flam exposed and disabled by the Horvaths and the Horvaths nowhere to be found, Siebalt was unable to replenish the working funds right at a time when the payoff was at hand.

The temporary U.S. headquarters of the global operation of Planet Police was a concrete block self-storage rental unit not far off the Baltimore-Washington Parkway. The garage-style door had been fitted with a blackout skirt and padded with sound insulation. Electricity had been surreptitiously tapped from a light pole and Internet connection was provided courtesy of an unsuspecting neighbor down the road whose house had been burgled and whose router had been modified to talk to a repeater that beamed the wi-fi signal to the storage complex. The room was furnished with folding chairs, card tables, two camp cots, and a portable electric heater. The skimpy overhead fluorescent strip was augmented with task lights next to each of the four laptop computers in the room. A water cooler and chemical toilet in the corner completed the setup.

Kenichi brushed his coarse black hair from his eyes and, grim-faced, reread the message that had just arrived from a hacker who went by the handle Digitalis. Digitalis had proved to be smarter and more resourceful than his resumé had conveyed. He not only had managed to acquire the SCADA protocols and programming sequences he had been assigned, but had figured out what was really going on. Having decoded the game plan and then filled in the blanks for the rest of the SCADA systems connected to coal-fired plants across the country, he was demanding more money—lots more. And he was smart enough to insist on being paid upfront before he would deliver the files to Kenichi.

"We are screwed!" Kenichi declared out loud as he closed his MacBook.

David Suzuki, a Japanese-American programmer with bleached and spiked hair, looked up from the Lenovo laptop he was working on at the other folding table. "What's wrong?" he asked. David, who Kenichi had recruited to the Planet Police from a student protest group at UC Berkeley, was a good engineer but only a passable programmer. He was currently working on a scheme for permanently disabling a Chinese pressurized water reactor at Tianwan without triggering a full meltdown. In the end, the Planet Police hated nuclear power as much as fossil-fuel plants, though with a different rationale.

Kenichi explained to David how they were being extorted and David smiled. "Then screw him," he said. "I know the drop-box he uses to stash his stuff online. I can hack into it and grab his files."

"You can do that?"

"Sure. It may take a little time to crack his encryption password, but it's doable on that system—if I can get some real computing power. Maybe we could run it on the Newlands servers?"

"Not anymore, we can't. That bridge has already been burned. You get started on setting things up to break the encryption and let me think about where we can get some number-crunching power without having to pay for it. If I were still back in Sydney, at the university, I could just submit a job, even without an allocation. Security was a joke there. You know, they had this fancy keypad system controlling access to the buildings, but I once dropped in for a visit years after I had left the university and discovered that my PIN code still opened the doors; it had never been deleted from the database.

"That gives me an idea." He flipped open his MacBook again, plugged an Ethernet cable into the jack on the side, and started working his way down through directories. "When I got this thing with the supersize hard drive, I moved all my old files and programs into a compressed archive. Maybe, just maybe, I still have it. Yes, there it is, the document with instructions for remote access to the university's computer system and my old assigned ID and password. Can you make sense of this and see if it might still work?"

He pivoted the laptop toward David, who quickly scanned through the document and said, "Piece of cake." Ten minutes later David announced, "We're in. Seems that your old IT department never purged the faculty database. The computing system has been completely updated some number of times over the years, and details of the login procedure have changed, but as far as the university IT facilities are concerned, you are still on the faculty and still have faculty access and full privileges. You were right: their security still sucks. Do you want me to start a job to crack the encryption?"

"Yes, do it!"

— —

Randall strode into the office without knocking, crossed to Truman's desk, and sat down. Truman, emerging from the private ensuite bathroom, gave him a disapproving look.

"You'll never guess what I just found in Life 2.0?" Randall said, rocking back in the chair.

"Don't play around, Randall, just tell me."

"There was a posting by a programmer calling himself Digitalis asking if there was anyone interested in SCADA access protocols. No details. I retrieved his account details and messaged him offline. Seems he has a set of protocols for most of the coal-fired plants in the United States and is willing to sell to the highest bidder, starting with a reserve of $12 million."

"This is good news and bad. It's good news because it means Takasawa doesn't have what he needs yet, and he certainly can't get that kind of money. He's tapped out. It's bad news, because we can't buy this guy off either"

"What about your own funds? Aren't you worth that much?"

"I'm worth that much and more—on paper. But it's mostly in Newlands shares and tied up in real estate, which is only minutely more liquid. I couldn't come up with 12 mil in cash even if I wanted to. And in the end, why should I bankrupt myself to save civilization? If the country really does go under, I'll move back to Australia and a station in the outback, off the grid and self-sufficient. No, we have to come up with a better way to deal with this bloodsucker. He's absolutely balmy."

"How about we go to his house?"

"You have an address for him? How?"

"This guy is just a smart programmer, not an amateur intelligence operative like that elusive Gaijin character that we were never able to track down. All this guy's real details were in his Newlands account, which I retrieved."

"How do you know they are not phony, like Gaijin's?"

"Because I already checked phone records and tax rolls. This guy is just some twenty-six-year-old living alone in an apartment in Cambridge. Let's get some people to pay him a visit. And I'm not talking about the Welcome Wagon."

"Okay, do it. And take down the posting in Life 2.0 before somebody else notices and starts poking around or, worse, actually buys what this creep is selling. With Takasawa stalled, we'll have the time to find him and end his little rogue operation. Then we can go ahead with Nagasaki as originally planned."

— —

Karl finished his IM and Anat's reply came almost instantly: "Yes, we saw it."

Karl quickly typed: "I know Cambridge. Do you want me to bop up there and have a chat with this guy?"

"No, the stakes are too high now, and there isn't time for you to go winging up there. We are handing this one over to the Americans, the FBI. A SWAT team is on their way as we speak."

— —

Within bowshot of Tech Square and MIT, Edgar Jordan sat in his Harvard Street apartment and congratulated himself. He had spent the morning putting the finishing touches on the project: his magnum opus, his ticket to Tahiti and beyond.

The grunt work was complete, now he only had to wait for all the work to pay off. It was an auction, just like on eBay only with more digits, and he simply had to wait for the bids to roll in. Sitting in his bathrobe at his computer desk, surfing the nether regions of the Web, he jumped when the heavy banging on his door started.

"FBI, open up. FBI!"

In a panic, Edgar reached down and punched the power-off button on his computer, then released it quickly as he changed his mind. It would not stop anybody; it would be better if he got rid of some files first. He canceled out of the shut-down dialog, then right-clicked on a folder labeled SCADAdocs, and selected "Shred" from the context menu. He cursed as a confirmation message box popped up and asked him if he really wanted to make the contents of the folder named SCADAdocs and all of its subfolders permanently and completely unrecoverable.

"Yes, you stupid software!" he said, clicking on the "OK" button.

The apartment door flew open amidst splinters of wood, and three men in black Kevlar vests and carrying assault rifles burst into the room. FBI, in large, white sans-serif capitals, emblazoned the fronts and backs of their vests. The man in front gestured with his gun as he shouted, "Hands in the air. Do not touch anything. Slowly step away from the computer and place your hands on the top of your head.

"Brian, you take care of the computer."

Brian rushed over to the computer, saw what was happening, and reached around to jerk the power cord out of the wall socket. A beeping signal started, but the dialog on the screen kept flashing and the disk kept churning. "It's got a built in battery backup; I'll try a hard reset." He found the on-off button on the front of the case and held it down. After a few seconds, the screen went blank, the cooling fan stopped whirring, and the falling pitch of the disk drive winding down broke the silence in the suddenly quiet room.

"We'll have to see how much can be recovered from the hard drive on this thing," he said, as he slid the computer out from under the desk. "Let's cuff him, grab what we can, and get back to the van."

Edgar, terrified and confused, wondered why they hadn't read him his Miranda rights.

32

ANAT PUT DOWN the secure phone and turned to Rahel. "So much for doing favors for other services. We give them the go ahead and the FBI stiffs us. Not only did they not inform us of the raid going ahead, they did not tell us the outcome. It was better in the last administration."

"And worse before and better prior to that, Anat. These ties fray and knit, fray and knit. In the end the Institute and Israel are on their own. You know that."

"We should have gone in ourselves and paid the consequences later. What a mess."

"So, what happened?"

"Our insider at the Bureau said they were too late. By the time the SWAT team got to the apartment, there was no sign of the hacker or his computers. At first, the FBI thought he had somehow been tipped off and had fled, but then—get this—a neighbor asked why the FBI team had come back a second time. That sent the Bureau in hot pursuit of a group impersonating federal officers. Meanwhile, the local police show up at the apartment, only to catch three men leaving the building in a big hurry. There was a typical American-style high-speed chase, which ended in typical American style with a car wrapped around a tree, only in this case it happened to be the vehicle the FBI was driving. It seems that as they were chasing the imposters, the three fugitives from the apartment were chasing them, who were, like some absurd Keystone cop classic, in turn being chased by the Cambridge police. In the melee that followed, one FBI agent was killed, apparently by friendly fire from the police, two of the Cambridge police were wounded, and a state trooper arriving late on the scene was injured when he fell as he exited his vehicle. The car in the middle took the brunt of the battle—to no one's surprise—and only one of the men, an Eastern European with false papers, survived. He is in critical condition, and now there is a jurisdictional dispute over who he belongs to. We have a man at Mass General who will keep us informed of developments. We even have the ICU at the hospital bugged."

"Really? How?"

"There's so much high-tech gear in those rooms, you could plant a satellite upload with an audio-video mixer and a dish antenna and nobody would notice. Anyway, it looks like a lot of people are interested in what that young man was trying to auction off. He and his computer are in the hands of the phony FBI contingent, whoever they are. They vanished somewhere in the wilds of Boston's western suburbs after abandoning their vehicle less than a kilometer from the site of what our informant referred to as the 'Great Arlington Heights Shootout.' Just wait until the media get hold of this one."

— —

Kenichi jumped at the faint sound of a car pulling up outside the storage unit. "Send the code!" he said in a half-whispered shout.

"But we don't have all the take-down sequences, not even a third," David answered.

"A third is a lot of CO_2; it will be enough to make a difference and to teach a lesson." Kenichi walked over to the garage door and cocked his head trying to listen despite the thick sound insulation.

David was just finishing typing the parameters on the command line when the door exploded, instantly killing Kenichi. David pressed the 'Enter' key just as the first of the bullets hit him.

"Hold your fire! Hold your fire!" the team leader said, raising his hand as he stepped through the jagged opening in the metal door and advanced toward the dying young man. He looked at the laptop. The image on the cracked LCD screen was distorted by rainbow-like pools of color but was readable. A simple text message in the middle of the screen said, "Attack codes confirmed. Attack sequences validated: 202 targets. Attack sequences sent: 18:03:34. Awaiting field responses."

"Son-of-a-fucking-bitch!" he shouted as he shot another round into the body on the floor. "Get Siebalt on the phone. We were too goddamn late. The stupid bastards launched the attack."

— —

Lev looked at Bini pleadingly. "It's after midnight, Bini. If your parents knew I was letting you stay up doing this, they would not be happy."

"But we have to, Uncle Lev. I've got everything here. Bono duplicated the disk from that DB guy's other copy from Scenaria. There has got to be something we can use."

"Bini, what makes you think you and Nancy and Bono can do what the Institute and the FBI can't."

"Because we can think different. We're hackers, Gaijin was a hacker. We can think like he did. We've been over this code. These tools are amazing, Uncle Lev. Gaijin was beast, Uncle Lev, I mean beast, trained by the best, absolutely OCD, a real perfectionist. Everything he wrote reads like a field manual for hacker special forces."

"I don't see what good that does us. If he was obsessive-compulsive that just means it is likely to be all the harder to hack his code. Or am I wrong?"

"You don't understand. If this guy was as obsessive and thorough as we think he was, he would have followed good, standard practices. For instance, he probably would have built a backdoor into the code so that he could get quick access with a simple password if he needed to in a hurry."

"So now we have to guess a genius hacker's spare password. Sounds time-consuming. What else would the perfect gentleman hacker have done? What did you do when you were creating viruses and hacking into the FaceFolder.org site? Wait a second, if I remember, you had a way to kill your multi-platform Trojan, a kind of software suicide pill."

"You're right. He almost certainly would have had a kill-switch. There would have to be a way to stop the thing." As he talked, Bini scrolled through directories in his image of the tools disk. He had looked through one called Services and one labeled Special Apps and was scanning the contents of one named Utilities when he shouted, "Ba-bam!" and pumped his fist in the air. "There it is, right there: killnet.exe. What do you think? Should we do it?"

"No."

"No? Why not?"

"Let me call Anat. We shouldn't do this on our own. Stay here, Bini, and don't do anything. I want to talk with her in private." He headed for Bini's bedroom office.

— —

The damaged laptop sat on the bench, its screen cracked and a corner of its case melted but still stubbornly refusing to die. Unsure what to do next, the team leader reached for his radio.

"Siebalt. Perkins here. We located them right at the co-ordinates you sent. It was one of those self-storage parks northeast of the city. We had to blast our way in. Takasawa is dead, but his little punk programmer launched the attack before we could stop him. He's dead, too. His laptop is a little worse for wear, but it's sitting here with a message that says it is waiting for responses from the field. What next?"

"Let me put Randall on. He's my go-to guy for all matters technological."

There was a brief pause before Randall shouted, "Don't turn it off! Don't let its batteries run out. Get it plugged into a converter or portable generator before you move it. The field responses are coded messages that confirm that the target SCADAs have been located and linked and the system is ready to start the destruct sequences for the various generating plants. Unless there was a time of execution specified, it will still take another confirmation from that computer after all field responses have been received. They go back to whatever computer sent the original messages. If we lose that computer, we lose track of what is happening. Is there any other message?"

"Yeah, it now says '3 of 202 connections confirmed.' Does that mean what I think it does?"

"I'm afraid so."

"Listen, I hear sirens. We have to get out of here. We are just going to have to unplug the laptop and hope its battery holds until we get back to my place. We'll call you again when we get there or if anything new comes up."

"Right. And call me if the lights start going out."

Perkins held his breath as he disconnected the power and gingerly picked up the laptop. The screen flickered, then brightened again. He carefully carried it out to the Grand Cherokee and gently set it down in the front passenger seat. He looked around, suddenly aware that the rest of his team were not there. The sound of the siren was getting closer. "Josh? Caleb? Let's hit the road." He got in behind the wheel and pulled his seatbelt on. He was wondering whether he should try belting the laptop in somehow when he felt something cold at his neck and a voice said, "Drive."

— —

Zoltan Pongrass took the back way up to the apartment. He gently set the computer down atop the butcher-block table and was just plugging in the charred brick to power it when Erno entered the kitchen. "What the hell is that piece of junk? And what is it doing here?" he demanded.

"That, Erno, is what your renegade CEO has been up to. In recent days he has been getting sloppy, and I have been able to track more of what he has been doing. Our Australian activist was diverting funds not only into his own pockets but also to those eco-terrorists, the Planet Police. They have been scheming to knock out most of America's electric power, sending the whole country back into a low-energy dark ages. I took this thing from one of the eco-terrorists who had just wrested it from some others. Seems there has been an internal struggle between rival factions. I have no idea what doctrinal differences they are arguing over. The guy I have tied up down in the basement storage area was not terribly talkative nor were his companions I subdued earlier. But I did learn that this laptop was used to trigger an attack and only it can be used to stop it. Look," he pointed to the distorted display. "It's trying to access your wi-fi. What is the password?"

"Is that a good idea, to connect this."

"It's a good idea. It's the only idea at the moment. What's the password?"

"Budapest99."

"How clever," he said, entering it twice in the connection dialog, thankful that the A and S keys still worked despite their broken keycaps. After a short delay, the message box in the middle of the screen updated: "31 of 202 connections confirmed."

"What is that all about?"

"I'm guessing that they are trying to take out 202 power plants and about 15% of the connections needed to do that have been made."

"If you are right, we have to do something."

"Like what?"

"Call somebody. The police. I don't know. No, wait, I do know. We need to call that guy, the blogger who found us."

— —

Karl rested the phone on the bed and shook his head as Des entered the room. "I just don't know what to do, Des. We don't know enough. Talpa doesn't know enough. Siebalt doesn't know enough. The Horvaths know even less, except they have the computer. Nobody has the whole picture. Only the mysterious Gaijin could see the complete canvas because he was the one who had painted it. Right now nobody knows enough to stop it."

"But maybe we do," she said, drawing out the word "we."

He looked at her and nodded. "Right, three cheers for teamwork: corporate America's answer to everything. But what—exactly—do you have in mind?"

"I'll fill in the details for you on the way to Reston. Scenaria has a videoconference facility, and I am pretty confident that Newlands has one, too. You tell the Horvaths to bring the computer and meet us at Scenaria. I'll impersonate Dina again and use a little persuasive threat to convince Siebalt to take a call."

"It will take too long for the Horvaths to get there and it will mean moving the laptop, which seems to be rather fragile at the moment. I'll get them to be ready with Skype on another system or something. You talk to DB, give him the Horvaths' number, and have him ready to patch everyone in together. Let's go, I'll drive."

"You? With one arm in a sling? You think I'm going to let you drive? You call DB, I'll drive."

— —

DB had done his usual fast and thorough job. On the wall of the videoconference room, one large screen displayed a high resolution image of the Newlands facility in Chicago. Truman

Siebalt and Randall Bakewell, with their heads together, were talking quietly. The other screen showed a somewhat pixilated image of the Horvath's kitchen in Maryland. Erno was staring into the camera and Donna sat to the side, half in and half out of the picture and looking uncomfortable.

"Talpa's on his way," Karl announced, "He should be here in ten minutes. I thought Vern Jeffers ought to be in on this as an expert on the cat.9.kernal virus and the Scenaria Shield software, but he is still recovering in the hospital. He suggested Salim here, who was already working down in the Vault. Is there anyone else?"

Karl turned to Des and nodded toward the door. Once they were in the hallway and around behind the door, he said quietly, "I'd like to bring the Institute in, but I am not sure under the circumstances, with all these civilians, whether it would be a candid and full collaboration. Plus, I would only be digging myself in deeper for breaches of confidentiality. Under the circumstances, I suppose that's not too important, but…"

Just then, DB poked his head out of the conference room. Through clenched teeth, he said, "Someone is trying to reach you by Skype on your machine, Karl. I thought you might want to take it."

Karl shook his head when he saw the ID. It was Bini. "Not now, Bini," he typed.

"Now, Abba," he got back, the little scribbling pencil animation telling him that Bini was typing more. Bini's next message finally popped up: "Ima is at some jewelry show and Lev is staying here with Shoshi and me. Lev and me think we found a utility to kill the network. Lev is talking to Anat right now, trying to get a decision whether to try it."

Karl typed with one finger: "R u you on ur laptop? Call back in 1 on vid." He looked up from his laptop. "DB, can you project a Skype video call from my laptop and patch in the audio, too."

"Sure, split screen on the right. It will all be lashed up as a four-way conference call. Consider it done. Just don't ask me to talk too much." He held a hammy hand to his wired-shut jaw.

Bini called back just as DB finished connecting the VGA and audio cables to Karl's laptop. He and Lev could be seen huddled together in the kitchen of Karl's apartment in Haifa.

The door to the conference room swung open and Richard Talpa wheeled in. He scanned the room, glanced at the video displays, and barked, "Okay, goddamn it, somebody tell me what the hell is going on here."

Karl stood up and gestured toward a gap in the chairs around the table. "Pull up and listen. I was just about to brief everyone."

"You listen, this is my company and my facilities, and I don't know who all these people are or why DB had to get me out of bed and down here at this hour."

"If you want to have a company and facilities tomorrow, you had better listen now," Karl said. He quickly outlined for everyone what he knew of the situation and then urged anyone who had anything to add to throw it in.

Talpa and Siebalt stared at each others' images, their lips taut in expressions of disapproval. Talpa spoke first, but not to Siebalt. "Douglas Botteneau and Destiny Allen, you are both fired as of this instant. You will leave the premises immediately. I am calling security to have you escorted out now, and I will be bringing charges in the morning."

"Hold it, hold it right there. You are going to do none of the above," Karl said, putting his hand on Talpa's arm. Talpa jerked it away and glared at Karl. "At the moment," Karl continued, "we have a crisis to resolve, and both DB and Des could be useful. From where I sit, you are in no position to be bringing charges against anyone. As I said in my summary, both you and Siebalt are in similar positions. You can try and squirm out or point fingers later, but right now is no time to be thinking about covering your asses. We have a country at stake. Now, anyone have any ideas? What do we do? My son thinks he has a routine that can disable the network that is targeting the power plants. Shall we use it?"

Almost at once, everyone said, "Use it."

Lev's image on the screen lagged noticeably behind his voice as he spoke. "We don't really know what this little program does. And we don't have, what should I say, authorization. Karl, you know what I am talking about. She won't or can't take responsibility. She said she'd talk to somebody else. That could take more time than we have. We're on our own."

Karl nodded gravely. "Looks like it. The farm team is at bat. No, we are not even the farm team, we are just the amateur leaguers, every damn one of us. Bini, do you have any idea how this routine works, what it does? Have you looked at it?"

"Abba, it's an executable. It's—let's see—some 400K. I can decompile it in a couple of minutes, but I can't say how many days it would take to suss it out."

"Siebalt, you hired these guys through the Coders' Corner on Life 2.0. What do you have?"

"Randall here is my techo. Randall?"

Randall shook his head. "The guy who went by the handle of Gaijin was the big kahuna for the development. He designed everything and honchoed all the programmers. I just told him what to do and paid the bills when he did it. He's the one who created the code. I don't even know his real name or what his code runs on, just that it's out there, everywhere."

Karl spoke up. "It runs on Aniromoto game consoles and Scenaria Shield anti-virus software."

Talpa leaned forward in his chair. "Then, I think I know Gaijin's name: Barry Collier-Adams."

Des opened her mouth, but DB spoke, "The guy you killed?" Talpa nodded.

Siebalt leapt to his feet, putting his head out of frame on the monitor. "You killed Gaijin? That was real smart. Why the hell did you do that?"

"It was an accident."

Karl raised his hand for silence. "Look, we need to figure out what to do right now. Anybody else have anything else possibly of use?

"Bluetooth smartphones," Salim interjected, "It runs on smartphones, at least those running Windows Mobile. They are part of the peer-to-peer network, maybe others. We don't know. It's a multiplatform distributed system."

"Zoltan, are you there?" Karl asked. Zollie's head poked into the view from Baltimore. "Give us an update. What's happening?"

"It says 43 connections are confirmed. At this rate, we may have a few hours, maybe much less."

"Okay. Bini, I want you to launch that utility program. We don't really know what it is, but I think that's our only option at the moment."

Talpa raised up his chair and looked down at Karl. "Who put you in charge?"

"No one. But I'm in charge. In this case because Bini is my son. Do it, Bini."

Bini brought up a C: prompt, typed the name of the routine, and tapped the Enter key. "Shit!" he said.

"What happened?"

"An error code. It threw an exception."

Siebalt said, "What does that mean?"

DB answered, "It means there's a bug in the routine. It doesn't work."

Siebalt sneered, "Okay, brilliant man in charge, any more bright ideas?"

Zollie's face reappeared. "Yeah, I've got an idea. The laptop here was the one being used for the attack. It might have a more up-to-date version of the routine. Maybe I should check."

"No, don't fiddle with the laptop directly," DB snapped. "It's on your local network, right? Good. Listen, use your own laptop to see if the thing is visible on your network. If it is, do a global search for killnet.exe."

There was a long tense silence as everyone waited for Zoltan to respond. "It's slow doing the search over wi-fi, and this thing had a big mother of a hard drive." More silence as people around the room leaned forward in anticipation. "Yes, there it is!" he pointed.

"What's the creation date on it? Bini, what about your copy?" Bini's version was several months older. "Okay, Zollie, suck the file over to your computer and let's try again."

They waited until Zollie said, "It executed, but just says: 'Incorrect parameter.' Let me try a question mark. Maybe there's help. Nope. I'll try 'help.' Nope, same thing: 'Incorrect parameter' again. What next?"

Des said, "Try a-l-l."

DB frowned at her and Talpa said, "That's silly."

Karl smiled at Des and said, "Go ahead, try it, Zollie."

"It worked! It launched and gave me a message: 'Disable all Nagasaki nodes and cancel all pending commands? Y/N.' What's Nagasaki?"

"It's the code name for the operation and the network. That's it, we got it. Hit that Enter key, Zollie."

"Nothing. Okay, I'll type Y. There, now the disk is churning. And another message: 'Kill flag set. Waiting for confirmation from nodes.' Then there's a blinking cursor."

"I think he's got it, people!" Karl said triumphantly. "Let's wait and see what happens."

They waited several minutes, during which people in the room started chit-chatting and the screen showing the Newlands link went black.

Suddenly, a loud voice barked a few words in Hungarian before switching to English. "I have a message back. It says, quote, MAC address does not match queued commands, kill command aborted."

"What does that mean?" Des asked.

"It means exactly what we suspected, that to override any commands you have to use the same machine that sent them. We can only kill the network from the broken laptop." Karl sighed wearily.

"Do we dare try that?" Zollie asked. "You told me not to fiddle with that machine."

"I don't think we need to," DB interrupted. "We can fake it."

"Right," Karl said. "Zollie, do you know how to fake a MAC address, can you retrieve the network adapter address from the fried laptop over the network?"

"Of course, remember, I have degree in informatics. I can do it." There was a clacking of keys, a pause, more keystrokes, and pauses, and finally, "There. All set up. There, sending the command again, and once again waiting." Everyone held their breath. "Bingo. We have confirmation, command accepted, first node disabled, and...nothing. Blinking cursor."

"It's looking for other nodes, worming it's way through the network. It could take awhile," Karl explained.

DB did not look happy. "There are most likely by now many hundreds of thousands of nodes. If it is going to take this long for each node, we are looking at days to take down the network. And, let me think. Toward the end, as the distribution becomes increasingly sparse, it could take longer and longer to reach all the remaining nodes."

"What can we do?"

"We have to propagate the wave front faster," suggested DB.

Des frowned. "Say that in a way that a Web wonk can understand, DB."

"We have to use broadcast instead of relying on the grapevine. We need some way of getting the command out all over the place at the same time. Maybe Siebalt knows something we can use to speed up the process. Are you there? Newlands?"

There was no response.

Karl reached over to his laptop and awkwardly typed an IM to Bini's computer:

> Looks like Australian and friend may have
> departed. Lev, cn u pass the word 2 Anat?
> See if somebody might intercept before
> they reach antipodes.

"Can do," Lev said aloud, as he slipped out of view of the webcam.

DB looked deep in thought. "I think we can do it from here using the product update push system of Scenaria Shield. What do you think, Salim?"

"Yes, I am thinking you are right. If we send an update to all our customers, yes, we could do it. We would need some special code to spoof the MAC address and maybe the IP address, too. We would want the kill command to come out in a blast, then everything resets, so the confirmations end up routed back to the same computer in Maryland."

Bini chimed in, "I have been working on a script that can do most of that. I'm sending the file."

Salim started for the door. "Let me grab my laptop."

Talpa wheeled over to the door and blocked his way. "Nobody is going to use Scenaria Shield to hack our own customer's systems."

Karl laughed. "It's a little too late for the moral protest, I would say. Compromising your own software is how we got into this mess in the first place. You're the one who hired Collier-Adams to create a Trojan."

Talpa, chastened, backed out of the way and returned to the table.

Bini could be seen typing away, his mouth twisted in concentration. "Zollie," he said. "Send me a copy of the updated version of the killnet routine and an IM with the MAC and IP addresses I need. I am going to try and reactivate the bot net that my friends and I used to use for hacking and see if I can get it to help broadcast the kill command. We have a lot of bots scattered around Europe and the Middle East. That could help spread it faster."

"Good idea. It's worth a try," Zollie responded.

It took nearly an hour for DB and Salim to ready everything to push the new code out over the Scenaria installed base.

DB pounded Salim on the back. "You are good." He looked around the table as he patted Salim. "This guy is good," he said. "Okay, Karl, we are good to go. How about you, Bini?"

"Not quite, you go ahead. I am having a little trouble waking up our bot net. It looks like some of our code has been spotted and blocked by some people's anti-virus software. It's what happens when you don't stay on top of things. I'm paging Nancy and Bono to see if they can help."

Karl nodded toward DB and Salim who were huddled over Salim's laptop. "Okay, let's try it." Talpa looked pained but gave a nod before swiveling his wheelchair around to face the screen. "Zollie, keep us updated on what you see on your machine. Salim, fire when ready."

"Photon torpedoes away!" Salim said gleefully.

It was only minutes before Zoltan shouted again in Hungarian. "Holy shit!" he said in English. "They are coming in so fast that I can't follow the scrolling. Dead, dead, and dead. The counter in the corner is turning over too fast to read, except now it's into five digits. Make that six. It's starting to slow down a bit. Now it's taken off again, spinning like a slot machine. I don't know what happened."

Bini could be seen pumping his fist on the other view. "We got the bot net back up. We just blasted out the codes through another thousand machines."

"Way to go, Bini!" Karl called out. He put his arm around Des. "You were right. We could do it."

"We don't know yet. We don't know for sure. All we have is messages on some computer screens from software we really don't understand. I wish we had some way of knowing for sure, or at least alerting the targeted plants."

33

THE GROUP STAYED LINKED and Zollie regularly updated everyone as the confirmation messages continued arriving and finally slowed to a crawl. Salim at one point announced that he had done a curve fit and could assert that by this point they had knocked out 99 percent of the network at a 99 percent confidence level. Karl pointed out that this meant there could be several thousand nodes not yet reached, potentially more than enough to complete the operation set in motion by the Planet Police, depending on how the network was configured to deal with failed nodes or flawed channels of communication. "We simply do not know what the behavior of the system is when degraded," he said.

"Hell, Mister Lustig," Talpa said, "You don't even know what the behavior of the system is when it's fully operational, either. What if it is self-healing? What if disabled nodes can be re-enabled?"

Salim paled. "We know it is true that infected PCs can be re-infected over Bluetooth through a hidden network bridge and bootstrap loader. And we don't really understand, do we, just how the game consoles figure in. They, too, perhaps, can be another vector for re-enabling nodes."

The stunned silence and the depressed looks around the room were interrupted by the telephone on the conference table ringing. Karl reached for it with his good arm, but Talpa picked it up first. He recognized the voice of the security guard who said, "This is the front desk. There's a man here who wants to see you. Says his name is Brian Mallory."

"Escort him to my office. I'll be there in a minute." To the group he said, "A business matter has come up. I'll be back."

"A business matter? At this hour?" Karl asked. He looked around the room. DB and Salim were hunched over the laptop, working on something. "Des will go with you," he said.

Talpa turned at the door. "Des will not go with me."

"Then I will," Karl said. "Take your pick." Talpa nodded toward Des, who fell in behind him as he wheeled out of the room.

When they arrived at Talpa's office, Mallory was waiting, sitting at the conference table and trying to spin a CD-ROM case on it's corner. "I have something for you," he said, tossing the case to Talpa, who caught it one handed.

"And what is it, exactly?"

"A confession of sorts, proof of innocence, you name it. These are files me and my men recovered from the computer of a rather incautious coder in Cambridge, a hacker in the hire of the Planet Police. It includes a folder containing scripts for targeting electric power plants across the country by way of their SCADA interfaces. I assume that all makes sense to you. To me, it's just another damn terrorist plot. But I thought you might think of some use for a copy. The originals are now in the hands of some people I know in Homeland Security. My brother has been exonerated. He's still a paraplegic, but he's no longer a suspected felon."

Talpa's expression was unreadable. "Why are you here, Brian?" he said.

"Because I wanted to finish my sentence, damn it. You interrupted me at the end of our last meeting; you never let me finish. You need to know that my men did not kill Marky Collier-Adams. You didn't let me tell you that before you fired me and told me to get lost. You may be smart, old buddy, but you have always had a short fuse and still could use some lessons in listening.

"The guy who killed Collier-Adams, or at least one of the bunch who did, is in an ICU at Mass General up in Boston." He turned to Des. "Tell your *Mossad* pal that the Bulgarians and the Ukrainian mafiosi have been dogging his footsteps and know everything he and his crew have been up to."

"How do you," Des said, then restarted. "I mean what makes you think he has anything to do with Israeli intelligence. He's just a journalist."

"Very good, lady, very good. You could have a future in this business," he smiled broadly. "It's my business to know things and to find out whatever I don't know. I'm good at it. Here's my card. Give me a call if you ever are looking for help—or a job." He winked broadly at her and walked to the door. Des started to follow him, then turned and grabbed the CD off the table before Talpa could protest. She pushed past Mallory to run down the hall. He followed her, strolling, in no evident hurry.

— —

Des burst into the conference room out of breath. "I've got a list of targets, here," she said, waving the disk. "Would that do any good?"

"Maybe. Let's take a look at it." Karl took the case, removed the CD, and handed it to DB who slipped it into the drive on Salim's computer. The two of them squinted at the screen as Salim tapped away at the keyboard.

"There's a folder in here full of files with names that are nothing but strings of numbers," Salim said, pointing. "There are 202 files in the folder. What do you want to bet they are instructions for destruction?"

"So," Karl said, "there's one for each targeted power plant, but we don't know which plants they are. Let's open one of the files in a text editor and see if there's anything useful."

DB studied the screen. "Nope. Some kind of scripting language, maybe PLC code or CNC, hard to tell, but nothing really readable."

"Can we try to find out what the numbers are? Maybe they're codes for facilities. Try Google."

DB sighed and shook his head. "This isn't going to work. Searching online for numbers will get us nowhere. We would have to get the right database."

Des pulled her cell phone from her purse beside the chair and thumbed a number. "Hi, Mom, it's Destiny. And, yes, I know what time it is. Look, I have some numbers here that have something to do with electric power plants. Can I read some of them off to you and see if they mean anything?" She read several numbers into the phone.

Her mother's sleepy voice came over the phone. "Des, honey," she said, yawning, "of course I recognize those.

They're trade association numbers. The first three digits before the dash identify the member company, and the rest identify a site."

"Mom, if I emailed you a list of some 200 of these numbers, how quickly could you tie them to particular plants by name and location?"

"I don't know, Des, it's all in a database at the University. I use it for research purposes."

"Mom, I'm going to hand the phone to a friend. His name is DB. I want you to tell him the name of the database file, how to find it, and how to get access to your account at the University. And this is an emergency, so don't argue or ask any questions." She handed the phone to DB without waiting for a response. As she did, she notice Brian Mallory standing in the doorway with his arms folded.

"That's good," he said, "really good. When you have the list, I know some people in Homeland Security who will know what to do with it and who will not waste a lot of time with checking stuff out or getting the right authorization."

DB looked up from where he was typing away at Salim's computer. "Give me an email address where I can send the query results," he said to Brian. "Or do you want them on a disk?"

34

THE TEAM AT SCENARIA spent the night firing off three more volleys of photon torpedoes each time the responses to the kill command began to taper off. After each new wave, a spike of returns confirmed additional kills, but each spike was markedly smaller than the one before. At some point, Lev and Bini had apologized and signed off. At daybreak, Des watched the morning news streaming off the Web as DB scoured the hacker networks and Salim surfed the Web looking for references to the night's events.

A bulletin on the morning news reported that a small coal-fired plant in West Virginia had been disabled by an attack that resembled the earlier one on the Tricorn facility, but the report made no mention of the Nagasaki network, the coordinated attack attempt, or even the Homeland Security interventions. By noon, the group was convinced that it was over. Between their efforts and the quick action by Brian Mallory's contacts at Homeland Security, only one electric power plant had ended up crippled by the SCADA attack, and the lights had stayed on.

Before Des left the office for some much needed sleep, she checked her email and found, to her surprise, a message from Brian Mallory with a subject line of "Box score: 1 in 200 ain't bad." In the end, each of the power companies had dealt with the threat differently. Some heightened their security and warned operating personnel to be ready to act quickly. Some called in professional help, consultants who may or may not have made any difference but who undoubtedly billed extravagantly for their services. A few plants, including all of those belonging to Wescole Energy Holdings, opted to take no chances and actually took the targeted plants completely offline, isolating them from the grid and from the Internet. The result was some frantic shuffling of load and redirecting of output on the nation's power grid, with suppliers in Canada making up the needed difference. All in all, it had been an expensive exercise but not the disaster it might have been.

Karl finished out the day with DB and Salim, mostly just keeping them company and occasionally running out for coffee. In a gesture that surprised and puzzled Karl, Talpa had intercepted Harry when he had arrived in the morning and escorted him into his office. Karl saw no more of either of them again until the police arrived late in the afternoon just as Karl was returning from the men's room. A squad in riot gear escorted Talpa out without a word.

"What was that all about," he asked DB in the conference room.

"Oh, you must have missed the piece in the online edition of *Wired*. They tried several times to take it down, but it kept reappearing. Now it's all over the news. Here, take a look." He swiveled Salim's laptop so it was easier for Karl to read. "Note the byline."

Karl skimmed it. It was a long article, full of names, dates, and details, allegedly written by Barry Collier-Adams. There was no mention of the Planet Police or Nagasaki or Tricorn, but the accounting of Talpa's misdeeds and Collier-Adams's role seemed rather extensive. "He wasn't killed by Talpa?"

"No, he was, but before he died—the first time, that is, when he faked reports of his suicide in Sydney—he created a little time-release hack, a program that would post a story through a bogus columnist's account on *Wired* if the countdown wasn't reset manually by Barry within a time limit. It was his insurance policy. The alarm went off today, and Talpa is toast." DB fluttered his fingers as if shaking crumbs off of them.

"What do you think is going to happen with Scenaria, DB?"

"Things will be tough, but Harry just sent out an all-personnel email saying that he was in charge, not to worry, and announcements of new organization and direction would be forthcoming. Harry is no Richard Talpa, but he is a dogged detail man and just might get us through this."

Karl was skeptical but forced a smile. "I'll be rooting for you, DB. Thanks for all you've done." He shook DB's fleshy hand and left.

— —

Karl waited until he was back at the motel to check in with Anat.

"So, you did it, Karl!" she said dramatically, her voice, hoarse with fatigue, rasping from his laptop speakers.

"I didn't. It was a group effort. Your husband and my son even played a part in it."

"A part that neither of them should have played, mind you. And I dare say you rather overstepped your authority, a violation of protocol and policy that I will have to condemn in public, though I am grateful to you for it—but only in private. God, I don't know what to do with you two. You and Lev are going to be the death of me yet. I am getting too old for this level of chaos and crisis. I thought Technical Services was going to be a relatively tame posting, but you kept me up all night, and then I spent the entire day mending fences and patching cracks."

"It's a young man's game, all right," Karl said with a smirk. Anat growled into the phone.

"One thing is bothering me, though," he continued. "This ex-FBI free agent, Brian Mallory, said that the Bulgarians or the Ukrainians or both knew our every move, at least my every move. How? Is there an Eastern European mole inside *HaMossad*? How did they know what was going down? You wouldn't happen to know anything about that, would you?"

"Indeed I do. It pays to have sources listening inside major hospitals. You were bugged, Karl. You were the leak."

"I was bugged?"

"Yes, through one of your shiny new high-tech toys: your digital pen."

"My pen was a bug? It was planted on me? How? Why?"

"You already know how. Remember where you retrieved your raffle prize, at one of the game booths on the first day of the conference? The Ukrainian game company, U-Crane Games, was a sponsor of the raffle. They just arranged for your name to be announced as winner, and you complied by gladly accepting their heavily customized pen. After that, they knew everything you did as soon as you docked the pen to a

USB port and were connected to the Internet. The extra shadow memory they added could record for days before maxing out."

"But I don't see how they knew to plant it on me in the first place."

"They were already watching Aniromoto and tracking some of the Operation Nagasaki programmers who had been less than perfectly circumspect. They knew about Elliot Feldersmann. Plus your name was already tagged on their radar screens by way of the Bulgarians, some of whom had supplied material for the assault on the Dome of the Rock. We could only do so much to keep your name out of the press. At home, here in Israel, yes, but abroad, there was little we could do beyond distraction with other stories from the incident."

"I guess I better dump this thing," he said, wistfully turning the fat silver-grey pen over and over in his hand. "Pity, I was beginning to really depend on it. It's a journalist's dream."

"No, bring it back with you so our engineers can study it. I'll buy you a new one. Deal?"

"Deal. Oh, wait, one more thing: *Hill Street Blues*. I get to borrow the complete set for a month."

"Deal." Click.

Karl paused for a moment, staring at the phone. Without warning and without knowing why, he started to cry. He wiped his eyes and quickly placed another call. The voice that answered in Hebrew was like the taste of honey and apples at Rosh Hashanah.

"It's me, darling," he said, trying not to choke up again. "I'm coming home."

35

KARL AND DES STOOD outside the weathered door to his room at the cheap strip motel in Northern Virginia, saying nothing for what seemed like several minutes but was more likely only achingly long seconds.

"I can drive you to the airport tomorrow," Des said, hesitantly breaking the silence.

"There's no need. I can take a cab."

"It's no problem, really. I'd like to."

"Farewells are no easier at the airport, you know."

"No, but they happen later, at the last minute, and you are protected by time limits and by the presence of strangers and Homeland Security from doing and saying too many stupid things that will only make it all worse."

Karl studied her, his eyes flicking from her hair to the faint freckles on the bridge of her nose to her lips. He leaned slowly forward, tipping his chin as he approached and kissing her lightly on the forehead before taking her hand and holding it.

"Karl, I feel so stupid," she said, her voice starting to quiver. "I am always making the wrong choices. First Harry and now you. My whole life feels like one mistake after another."

"Destiny Allen, you are anything but stupid," he said, holding her at arms length as he reproached her. "Harry wasn't a mistake; he was part of your life, part of you becoming you. Everyone we have ever loved becomes a part of us, sculpting and texturing us and making other things possible. Everyone."

"You, too?" she asked, wiping tears from her eyes with the back of her hand. "Am I a part of you, Karl."

Karl looked away from her and then toward the cloudy winter sky, not seeing it, but squinting as he tried to remember. To the clouds, he started to recite:

> If but there were more time
>> And lives to lead
>> And lines to follow leading up,
> Then I could love you, too.
> But here we stand,
>> Our footprints traced across the wetted sand
>> Already fading in a rising tide.
> And life afar, with her, so deeply etched inside,
>> Reaches out across the gulf within.
> The shore's chaotic and unsteady wind
>> Now lifts unspoken whispers
>> And sweeps them from the scene,
> Leaving only sand and silence
>> In the salt-strewn space that lies between.
> If but for this—
>> and all the world—
> Then I could love you, too.

"I don't recall the poet's name," he said after a long pause. "Some obscure radical from the 60s. I never was very good at remembering those things."

"But you remembered the poem."

"Well, I memorized it. Those were the days of my youth when there was time for that sort of thing. Something in the bittersweet melody of it spoke to me, but I had little idea of what it really meant, not in the deepest sense, not until now."

He took a breath before continuing. "Don't drive me to the airport. I am already on my way, partway to Haifa. Just wish me Godspeed now. And promise you will visit us someday in Israel."

"I will. Godspeed, Karl Lustig." She slowly let her hand slip from his and stepped back a few steps, stumbling at the curb. Karl smiled and Des grinned awkwardly, spilling rivulets of tears down her cheeks.

She turned and ran to her car parked three rows away, turned again and shouted, "I love you, Karl Lustig. Damn you."

"Damn me," he said, but not loud enough for her to hear as she started the car. He stood without moving, watching as she drove out of the lot, down the hill, and turned onto the highway, watching until the car was no more than a speck lost among many.

His cell phone rang as he was fishing for his room key.

"Hello, it's me darling," Shira said. "I was just heading for bed and thinking of you. I love you."

"I love you, too. I was just thinking of you, as well. You realize I'll be home Friday, in time for Shabbat."

"I know. It seems like you've been away so long, like so much has happened. I think that not knowing when you would get back made it seem all the longer. When I can count down the days to a date, they seem to go faster, like Counting the Omer between Passover and Shavuot."

"It has hardly been 49 days, my love."

"No, but it felt like it. I missed you so—we missed you. You won't even recognize Shoshi. Babies grow so fast; blink and you miss something."

"Kids grow so fast. Blink and they're off to school, blink again and they are leaving home, blink…"

"Stop it! Stop it. I'm not ready for that. I just want you all around the table Friday night—and every Friday night. Forever."

"You got it, Darling. Forever it is."

"Are you all right? You sound tired or a little down or something."

"A lot has happened; I've learned a lot on this trip."

"Me, too."

"Really? And what have you learned?" Karl asked, thankful for not being pressed to elaborate on his comments. That would come later, when they were in the same room.

"I have learned that I can't trust you. That you don't keep your promises," she said with a laugh, but with an edge in her voice.

Karl's heart started to accelerate as he asked, "What? What are you talking about? This is Karl Doggedly-faithful-and-true Lustig you are talking about. I keep my promises."

"You promised you would not do any more work for the Institute, then I hear you have been shot at, kidnapped, beaten up, pushed out of a moving van, and…"

"Disinformation, all of it, spread by espionage agents to throw the enemies of Israel off guard. I was in a luxury hotel and hanging out at a video games conference, an all-expenses-paid vacation. I even picked up some great wine out in California. But that's another story. I'll fill you in on the details over a bottle of the Zinfandel I am bringing back with me."

"You do that, Karl Lustig. You just do that. And you better keep your story straight because, remember, I have other sources." The smile had returned to her voice.

"I will. I will fill you in on all the places I have been and the people I have met. You know that."

"I do know that. I just miss sharing the stories with you. I keep turning to say something to you and then realizing you are not there."

"Me, too, my beloved, my *bashert*."

There was silence on the line. "You've never called me that before," she said at last.

"I never knew it before. I told you, I've been learning. I'll see you on Friday afternoon."

"I'll be waiting. I love you."

"And I love you, too." There was a click and static on the phone, but Karl kept it to his ear as if he were still listening to what was happening in Haifa, as if the sounds of his life there were already growing louder and clearer.

36

DINA TOOK ANOTHER SIP from her coffee. It had been several weeks since Karl had left and weeks since she and Des had found any time to talk. Des had finally agreed to meet at the Meredith for lunch. They had talked their way through Cobb salads and foccacia, touching lightly on work and Dina's ups and downs with LG.

"There is still a lot I don't get," Dina said between bites. "What is going to happen to Richard Talpa? Is he going to jail?"

"Not from what I hear. He is too valuable to be sent off to some federal farm for executive miscreants. The scuttlebutt around the office is that at least two branches of our own intelligence community are trying to arrange a deal to get him to work for them, and everyone is terrified about what might happen if he opted to go over to another party. It seems that Brian Mallory, the old army buddy that he had been helping over the years, has some useful connections of his own among the clandestine services. So, Talpa will be just fine following the time-honored path of malicious Internet hackers. They almost all end up becoming security consultants. Most likely, he will just keep on doing the same sort of thing only in enforced anonymity and with a budget paid for by congress but without any oversight."

"Scum." Dina wrinkled her nose. "These guys always seem to get away with murder and come out smelling good."

"I don't know. Talpa doesn't strike me as all bad. Maybe he was too driven to succeed at any price, and his ethics were rather flexible, but I just don't see him as Mephistopheles. You know what he did? He donated one of those iBOTs, the high-tech wheelchair he parades around in, to that Indian kid, Mallory, who was shot in the Tricorn incident. And he set up a foundation to service it for the rest of the kid's life."

"That's cool. I didn't know. What about that Truman Siebalt, CEO of Newlands? You know, I can't believe you impersonated me to interview him. I told you that his henchmen came after me, didn't I? I wet my undies when these guys came pounding on my apartment door, but they took one look at me, apologized, and turned tail. So, what is with Siebalt?"

"He made it as far as Australia, stepped off the plane in Melbourne, and was promptly shown into a cell where he currently awaits extradition. Donna and Erno Horvath are back in the driver seats at Newlands—I guess you knew that—trying to hold together a hemorrhaging business. Personally, I think they'll make it."

"I don't know, virtual life is becoming sort of yesterday. Industry trends are holding, but the growth rate in users is slackening off and profits are way down. At least that is what it says in the article I just handed in to my editor." She grinned at Des.

"Thank you for the market report, Dina. You are clearly up on all the latest."

"Maybe. But this whole Tricorn business is still a bit of a mystery to me, and I don't fully trust what has appeared in the press. Your boss didn't blow the thing up, did he? No. So it was the terrorists, the Planet Police, right? No? Who?"

"None of the above. This story isn't out yet, so you have to keep your mouth shut, strictly off the record and not for publication."

"You're going all serious on me, Des. Is this for real? You know something that's not public yet?" Des nodded gravely. "Then I want an exclusive. Or a first interview. Or something. You have to promise me. I need it. My boss was not happy with what came out of that game industry assignment. And, I was not helped by your so-called journalist friend, who pretty much dropped out of sight the moment he got back to Israel, leaving me to write nearly everything myself. You have to promise that I get to tell the story when it's ready."

"I'll have to ask my mother."

"Your mother? You still need to ask your mother's permission? Grow up, Des. Cut the cord," she teased.

"It's my mother's story," Des said. "I think I can persuade her to give you an interview as soon as she finishes her research." She leaned across the table and lowered her voice. "My mother was studying power industry records and found something suspicious. She dug deeper and has now confirmed that it was Wescole that arranged for the sabotage of its own plant. Thanks to none other than your ex-boyfriend, LG, she was able to obtain copies of messages that went back and forth in Life 2.0 between somebody at Wescole and this hacker who went by the name of Gaijin. Wescole execs hired him anonymously through the Coders' Corner. He jumped at the opportunity to get paid twice for what he was already programming for the Planet Police, so he sold out to Wescole and effectively jumped the gun on his other client's plans. Wescole stood to be ahead by millions when their insurance paid for a brand new plant that was more efficient and met all the latest environmental regulations. So, what he was asking for sounded like a bargain to them. He already had the system in place for the Planet Police, all he had to do was send the right coded message over the Nagasaki Network, and bang, no more Tricorn Power Station."

"Wow, if this is for real, I can start working on my Pulitzer acceptance speech."

"It's for real, all right. I'll talk to my mother about your request; she'll probably say yes. She sends her regards, by the way, and says to tell you that you were right to ditch LG. As if it were not enough that he was hanging around and trying to hit on me, after he turned over the message copies that my mother had asked for, he tried to get more money out of her."

Dina looked deep in thought. "What about Karl?" she asked abruptly.

"What about him? He's okay. He's back in Haifa with his wife and kids. I got an email from him saying that he had arrived okay and they were off for a weekend away."

"You make it sound so casual."

"It is, Dina, nothing happened. We're friends. That's it. End of subject."

"Okay, okay. Changing the subject to something completely unrelated, did you ever find out what was with your renegade Roomba? Did you tame it?"

"Yes and no. Turns out another hacker had hacked into my hacked Roomba through the wi-fi that DB had installed. No security, it seems, so this teenager in the apartment above taps into it and starts playing around with the code. We catch him because he tries to download a new program to it just when DB happens to be at my place doing diagnostics on it. Seems the kid was trying to gain access to the camera that DB had installed to allow it to recognize objects. The kid was apparently hoping to catch glimpses of yours truly traipsing around the apartment in the altogether. Anyway, before I can stop him, DB is up the stairs and banging on the apartment door. That guy may be chubby, but he can move when he wants to.

"Anyway, the kid's parents go bananas, but DB convinces them to make the boy do penance by working with him to refurbish the Roomba. DB is actually pretty good with kids, maybe because he still is one himself. Anyway, in the process of working on the Roomba makeover, DB concocts a clever new security scheme for these low-end systems like Roombas and robot lawnmowers, which he is patenting, now that he is no longer under the Scenaria thumb. And my Roomba is behaving itself. It knows when I am home and when I am not, and can spot a fuzzle from across the room even with the lights out, owing to its brand new IR webcam and infra-red LEDs. Cool, huh?"

"Yeah. So back to you. How's your love life, now that the creep, hairless Harry, is out of the picture?"

"He's not a creep. Remember, there were two of us in the relationship, both of us adults. Anyway, he's running things at Scenaria, now that Richard Talpa is gone, and he's back trying to patch things up with his wife. I think he's sincere about making it all work—both his marriage and the business. As for me, I have given up on men, Dina. Completely. I'm not even looking. I'm more interested in friendship than romance now."

"You'd like me to believe that, wouldn't you. You'd like to believe that yourself. But I've known you far too long to fall for that."

"Well," Des said, stretching out the word. "Maybe there are some possibilities. I ran into Jimmy Goldberg, a guy I knew from Phillips Andover, but nothing ever happened. I think I told you about him once. He was younger than me. Even more than I knew, because he had skipped a grade before coming to prep school. Anyway, turns out he went into EE, graduated from Cal Tech, and then got involved in alternative energy. Now he works for this Israeli solar outfit but is back and forth on joint projects with American firms. He looked me up on the Web after seeing my name mentioned in a Washington Post piece about Scenaria. He's back in Israel now, but we have had some email back and forth and a couple of really nice times together before he left the States. He promised to call next time he's in town and asked me to look him up if I make it to Israel."

"Did you, uh,…?" Dina grinned and raised her eyebrows into a high arch.

Des kept her face as straight and unrevealing as she could manage.

"You did! You did. I can tell. And you didn't let on about this new love to me? You don't tell your own sister when you fall in love?"

"Did I say anything about love? Dina, when I fall in love, you will be among the first to know. Jimmy and I, we're becoming friends. No hurry. Full stop."

"Speaking of friends and men and an earlier topic, what really is the story with Karl. I never got a chance to say good-bye."

"I did. When I saw Karl off at the airport—which I wasn't supposed to do, but I went anyway—I told him that I was getting out of the security business. I said that all I really want to do is to make beautiful things. I tell you, the man almost cried when I said that. Seems I was quoting his wife. I also said I wanted to meet her, and he told me that I would. So I'm taking a sabbatical and heading for Israel. Who knows, I might connect up with somebody there. Karl said not to get my hopes up too much when it comes to Israeli men. Men are just men, he says."

"And you, what do you say?"

"Well, I told Karl that I disagreed. There are men like Richard Talpa and men like DB, men like Barry Collier-Adams and men like Karl Lustig. Just between you and me, I'd take a Karl, if I could find one."

"Me, too, but I hear it's best not to be looking for them or they don't show up. Wait a minute! You said you're going to Israel. Didn't you say this new guy, this Goldberg guy, was returning to Israel? Coincidence?"

Des smiled warmly and took another sip of her coffee.

— —

Also by Lior Samson: *Bashert* and *The Dome*
www.liorsamson.com

Afterword

Does it count as life imitating art if the art is unpublished? My first notes and sketches for *Web Games* date from early 2003, but life, work, and another novel kept me from returning to the story in earnest until May of 2008, and the manuscript was not completed until August of 2010. From my consulting background working with groups involved in industrial automation and power generation and distribution, I was long familiar with PLC programming and SCADA systems and their many vulnerabilities. I was confident that the scenario envisioned in *Web Games* was entirely feasible even if still safely fenced off in the realm of fantasy.

But safety is so often illusory and fences can prove to be so permeable. I certainly did not expect my plot to be trumped by headline news. The world caught up with me and the border with fantasy was breached when the Stuxnet worm was created and unleashed. Stuxnet, first reported in June 2010 by a Belarus security firm and the subject of wide press coverage in September 2010, is a new order of malware that established a number of breakthroughs. It combined several technological firsts to enable it to infect precisely the sort of industrial control systems targeted in *Web Games*. The Stuxnet worm was, in effect, an unexpected real-world proof of concept of the kind of cyber-warfare attack envisioned in *Web Games*.

The fictional cat.9.kernal Trojan that I invented back in 2003 and the real Stuxnet worm have a lot in common. After initial infection through one medium (USB flash drives for Stuxnet, anti-virus software for cat.9.kernal) the worm can then exploit other connections to spread throughout a network. Like cat.9.kernal, Stuxnet involves a rootkit and after deployment can be upgraded via peer-to-peer communication. It employs several previously unexploited vulnerabilities in PLC and SCADA systems and the PC software that connects with them, allowing the worm ultimately to generate hidden modifications to PLC programs that could disable or degrade the performance of industrial equipment. Ominously, Stuxnet also resembles cat.9.kernal in that it, too, appears to be able to re-infect systems that have been seemingly scrubbed clean.

In the case of Stuxnet, the apparent target was the Iranian nuclear power infrastructure, although it also infected systems in a number of other countries, including the United States, albeit on a much smaller scale. It remains at this writing uncertain who was behind the attack, but speculation has focused on the sophistication and complexity of the code, which would seem to require the kind of advanced programming resources available only to a nation state. Not surprisingly, the United States and Israel have led the list of usual suspects, with many more fingers pointing toward Israel and its aggressive intelligence community. On the other hand, so much of the technical detail needed to construct such an attack is publically available that a concerted and coordinated well funded effort by an ad hoc team of skilled hackers is far from ruled out.

Terrorists come in many stripes, and extremism in pursuit of political and social agendas is not the exclusive province of the Right or the Left, the East or the West, nation states or underground radicals. The tools of technology know nothing of the hands that wield them. In the hands of peacemakers they can become engines of progress and reconciliation, in the hands of fanatics, implements of chaos and destruction.

Lior Samson
Munich, Germany, October 2010

Also by Lior Samson: *Bashert* and *The Dome*
www.liorsamson.com